Praise for *New York Times*

"Wild rides and pages that si
—J. R. War

"The future belongs to Knight."
—Emma Holly, *USA Today* bestselling author

"Powerful romantic suspense . . . Hot enough to burn."
—*Romance Reviews Today*

USA Today bestselling author Jennifer Ashley

"Danger, desire, and sizzling hot action!"
—Alyssa Day, *New York Times* bestselling author

"Exciting, sexy, and magical!"
—Yasmine Galenorn, *New York Times* bestselling author

"[A] sexually charged and imaginative tale." —*Publishers Weekly*

National bestselling author Jean Johnson

"Jean Johnson's writing is fabulously fresh, thoroughly romantic, and wildly entertaining. Terrific—fast, sexy, charming, and utterly engaging. I loved it!"
—Jayne Ann Krentz, *New York Times* bestselling author

UNBOUND

Angela Knight
Jennifer Ashley
Jean Johnson
Hanna Martine

BERKLEY SENSATION, NEW YORK

THE BERKLEY PUBLISHING GROUP
Published by the Penguin Group
Penguin Group (USA) Inc.
375 Hudson Street, New York, New York 10014, USA

USA / Canada / UK / Ireland / Australia / New Zealand / India / South Africa / China

Penguin Books Ltd., Registered Offices: 80 Strand, London WC2R 0RL, England
For more information about the Penguin Group, visit penguin.com.

This book is an original publication of The Berkley Publishing Group.

Berkley Sensation Books are published by The Berkley Publishing Group.
BERKLEY® SENSATION is a trademark of Penguin Group (USA) Inc.
The "B" design is a trademark of Penguin Group (USA) Inc.

Berkley trade paperback ISBN: 978-0-425-25779-1

An application to register this book for cataloging has been submitted to the Library of Congress.

PUBLISHING HISTORY
Berkley Sensation trade paperback edition / March 2013

PRINTED IN THE UNITED STATES OF AMERICA

10   9   8   7   6   5   4   3   2   1

Cover art by Don Sipley.
Cover design by George Long.
Interior text design by Laura K. Corless.

ALWAYS LEARNING   PEARSON

TABLE OF CONTENTS

ENFORCER

Angela Knight

ACKNOWLEDGMENTS

"Enforcer" is dedicated to my son, Anthony, who proved his courage and determination to achieve good health when he had gastric bypass surgery on November 5, 2012. I want to thank his surgeon, Dr. Paul Ross, and the nurses and medical professionals of Spartanburg Regional Healthcare System's Surgical Weight Loss Unit. Their kindness, dedication, and professionalism made a procedure that could have been agonizing and dangerous much less painful and far safer. As Anthony's neurotic mother, I can't thank them enough.

I would also like to thank Cindy Hwang, my editor, for her understanding and unfailing support. She and my agent, Jessica Faust, have been both helpful and patient as I dealt with a number of health issues while writing this book. (Even when Hurricane Sandy plunged Jessica into darkness and closed the Penguin offices.)

I want to congratulate Leis Pederson, Cindy's assistant, on her promotion to editor. Leis has held my hand and saved my bacon on many occasions, so I was delighted to learn of her new job. It's well deserved.

Then there's my talented team of beta readers, all fabulous authors themselves: Shelby Morgen, Kate Douglas, Diane Whiteside, Camille Anthony, Eileen Gormley, and Marteeka Karland. The only one of the group who isn't a writer is Virginia Ettel, my dear Bookdragon, who never hesitates to kick my butt when needed. (I'm afraid butt-kicking is often warranted—yet it's always greatly appreciated.)

Most of all I want to thank my own personal romance hero, my husband of twenty-eight years, Michael Woodcock. It's a huge comfort to know that a six-foot, three-inch cop always has my back. Alerio has nothin' on you, babe.

And thanks to *you*, my reader. I deeply appreciate those who have patiently waited for the climax of the Time Hunters series. If you're not familiar with my work, I have attempted to write "Enforcer" in such a way that new readers won't be lost. Either way, thank you for buying *Unbound*. I hope you enjoy the story of Alerio and Dona as much as I loved writing it.

CHAPTER ONE

The dark, narrow stairway stank of murder. The reek seemed to coat her tongue with rot and terror, turning each breath into a bloody assault. Dona Astryr ignored the nauseating taste. She was too busy listening for the killers who'd butchered everyone in the house.

In the crowded town square beyond the house's neat white shutters, a crier read the American Declaration of Independence in a rolling baritone. The Philadelphia crowd hooted and stomped for the more inflammatory lines, bellowing support for the Continental Congress. If there were any Tories among them, they had the good sense to keep their snarls to themselves.

A fist-sized evidence bot zipped past Dona, riding the blue glow of an anti-grav cushion as it searched for murder victims. She snatched the bot out of the air in a blur of cyborg speed. If there was a killer on the second floor, she didn't want the device giving her away. The bot lit up, about to beep a protest, but Dona thumbed a button to mute it. Bot in one hand, shard pistol in the other, she cocked her head and scanned with every sensor implant she had.

Just below the roar of the crowd, a female voice whimpered pitifully in despair and pain.

Somebody's still alive. Dona thumbed off the shard pistol's safety.
And they're damned well going to stay that way.

Had to be Lolai Hardin. According to her dossier, the temporal
guide owned this house, using it as a hostel for the time-traveling
tourists who hired her to show them life at the time the Declaration was signed. The United States was considered the direct
ancestor of the Galactic Union, and its historic milestones were
major tourist attractions.

Hardin's latest tour group had gotten a hell of a lot more than
they bargained for. A vicious attack by forces unknown had left
thirteen people dead or injured. Hardin's two twenty-third-century
employees were among them. Only Lolai herself was unaccounted
for—a bit surprising, since she'd been the one to send the courier
bot that had alerted the Enforcers that her tour group was under
attack. She'd suffered at least one minor wound before she sent the
bot; a bloody thumbprint had marred its smooth, white surface.
Hardin's fingerprint.

*Damn, I wish we could have gotten here before the bastards
attacked.* Unfortunately, nobody had ever managed to prevent this
kind of massacre—and plenty of people had tried. You just couldn't
change history no matter what you did.

Of course, Lolai could have been working with the attackers.
Could have been bought off or intimidated into cooperating. She
could have been the killer. But that whimper suggested otherwise.

Maybe Dona could save her. *Victim's condition?* Dona started
up the stairs in a padding rush, soundless as a ghost.

Extremely serious, replied the computer implanted in her brain.
*Sensors detect multiple stab wounds and extensive blood loss. She
must have medical attention in the next 3.2 minutes, or she will die.*

Which wouldn't necessarily end the poor woman's life. If Dona
could get Lolai into regen at the Outpost infirmary within seven
minutes of the time her heart stopped beating, she could be

brought back. After that, brain death would be too extensive for regeneration, and she really would be dead.

Victim's location? Reaching the top step, Dona paused for another scan.

First bedroom on the left.

Any sign of the attackers?

No.

That meant nothing. The killer or killers could be sensor-shielded, invisible to both Dona's eyes and implants.

The evidence bot jerked in her hand, trying to escape. She stuffed it into one of the pouches on her armored belt and padded silently toward the bedroom door. *Damn, I wish I had backup.*

Unfortunately, every other Enforcer on the ten-agent team was either busy searching the house's first floor or dealing with the two critically injured victims.

So I go in hard and pray I won't find some bastard waiting to play "Let's Kill the Time Cop." Dona braced herself a meter from the bedroom's locked entrance, lifted her shard pistol, and slammed an armored boot against the thick oak door. Propelled by cyborg muscle, the door crashed open and banged against the wall. "Temporal Enforcer!" She shot through the opening, crouched low, weapon ready.

Oh, fuck.

An arc of bright scarlet splatter marked the wall on her right. A small round rug squelched under her boots, bleeding streams of red across the polished wooden floor.

To her left, a naked woman lay spread eagle on a canopied bed, wrists and ankles bound to its tall cherry posts. Dozens of wounds marked her breasts, belly, and thighs, drooling blood like witless red mouths. Her attacker had been particularly vicious with her face, cutting off her nose, slashing her cheeks and lips. It would take a DNA scan to identify her with any certainty, but Dona was willing to bet it was Hardin. Weight and height were right, anyway.

Send a message to Dr. Chogan, Dona told her implant as she padded toward the bed. Her feet left bloody footprints across the polished pine. *We've got another survivor confirmed, condition critical.*

One of Lolai's eyes opened, rolling with terror until it fixed on Dona. The other appeared glued shut by dried blood. A tear spilled as her crusted lips moved soundlessly.

"I'm Temporal Enforcement agent Dona Astryr," Dona told her, giving the room another quick, wary scan. Bed, armoire, washstand with china bowl and pitcher wreathed in painted roses. No attacker—or at least none visible. "I'm going to get you into regen." Bad as her injuries were, a few hours of regeneration would heal everything but Lolai's memories.

The woman's lips moved again, but the only sound she made was a low wheeze.

Where the fuck is Dr. Chogan? Dona wondered as her eyes flicked over the room again. *Maybe I should just pick her up and Jump back to the Outpost. Comp, would she survive a temporal warp in her current condition?*

Negative, the neurocomp replied. *Given her wounds, an unprotected Jump would probably cause systemic organ failure and brain death. It would be better to wait for Dr. Chogan to bring a regeneration tube.*

Frowning, Dona watched the woman's bloody lips move. Her single open eye looked desperate. Leaning closer, Dona told her comp to amplify audio. "What did you say?"

The words emerged in a painful, wheezing hiss of superhuman effort. "He's . . . still . . . here!"

Dona spun, bringing her shard pistol up as a figure in red and black temporal armor melted into view like a ghost. *I knew it.*

Botfucker was *hiding behind a sensor shield.* She fired before he finished his big reveal.

A spray of needle-sharp tritium shards hissed across the room to hit the killer's chest. Instead of carving him into hash, the metal fléchettes bounced off the suit's armored scales in a chorus of musical pings.

She knew that red and black armor. *A Xeran. Figures.* Jolting aside, Dona barely avoided the spray he fired back at her. *The bastards did a major upgrade of their tech a month ago. Their armor's probably better than ours.* Ducking, she listened to another round of fléchettes hiss overhead.

It was a diversion. The Xeran charged in a blur of red and black and muscle. The impact of his powerful body knocked her breathless as they reeled backward, hit the bed, and tumbled across the victim's bound and helpless body. Lolai wheezed in pain. Crashing to the floor, the two cyborgs rolled, each fighting to aim a shard pistol somewhere vital.

"Bastard!" Dona snarled into the Xeran's black faceplate as she managed to jam the muzzle of her weapon against the underside of his jaw. The armor's scales were thinnest there to avoid interfering with turning the head. He grabbed her gun hand and twisted, trying to break her wrist.

Fuckit, I'll go for a head shot. Ignoring the fragile fingers threatening to snap in his crushing grip, she twisted her wrist until the weapon scraped over his faceplate. *Backup!* Dona snapped to her neurocomp. *Dammit, get me some backup!*

Requesting backup . . . Chief Dyami says the agents downstairs are also under attack. He will have to fight his way free before he can assist.

The comp was right. Shard fire hissed and whined downstairs, along with the thump of colliding armored bodies. A familiar Vardonese war cry rang out over the shouts, followed by a deafening crash. The Xerans responded with a chorus of curses. They sounded pained.

Chief Dyami really didn't *like* people who murdered unarmed tourists.

That's why you don't piss off time cops. Dona peeled her lips off her teeth in something that definitely wasn't a smile. *Especially me.* Despite the Xeran's attempts to force the weapon away, she braced the shard pistol's muzzle against his visor.

But before she could pull the trigger, her foe's polarized plastium faceplate went transparent, revealing a twisted smirk she knew all too well. "Hello, baby. Miss me?"

Ivar Terje.

Dona stared at him for one suspended instant of disbelief that promptly dissolved into howling rage. "You bot-buggering *traitor!*" She slammed her left fist into his throat, aiming for the larynx, meaning to crush it right through his armor. Ivan merely gagged, but she felt his savage grip loosen. Just a fraction, but that was all she needed.

Dona wrenched free to slam the pistol into his faceplate. She wanted to beat his head in, but breaking his visor made a fine intermediate step. "You almost killed me, you son of a bitch. You ruined my life, my reputation, my career. They thought I was a traitor because of you!" Another furious swing sent more cracks radiating across the reinforced plastium, but the visor still protected her hated enemy's face.

The third blow had every last superhuman erg of Dona's cyborg strength behind it. Her ex-lover's faceplate finally shattered into jagged, glittering fragments. "I can't believe I was ever stupid enough to *love* you!" She aimed the pistol between his eyes, her finger tightening on the trigger . . .

Ivar slapped the muzzle away from his face. The blow looked casual, but it sent her heavy pistol sailing across the room as her arm went numb from hand to shoulder. Now *there* was a data point she could have done without. *Oh, seven hells, he's been playing with me. He's easily three, four times as strong as I am. Maybe more.*

That must have been some tech upgrade.

"You're worse than a traitor. You're a fucking *fool*." Thrusting one booted foot against her belly, Ivar kicked her airborne. She sailed over the bed and crashed down into the midst of the washstand, pottery exploding, wood splintering into tinder from the impact of her armored body. Her helmeted head hit hard enough to dent the wooden floor. She tasted blood.

The battleborg rolled to his feet with a grace that was astonishing in a man so massive. "Every lie I told you, you believed. Love you? Why in all the hells would I love *you*?" The contemptuous jerk of his head made light flash off something inside the dark confines of his shattered helmet.

She squinted. A pair of objects glinted bright and sharp among the disordered, sweat-darkened tufts of his red hair. Something that looked almost like . . .

. . . A priest's horns.

Xeran religious orders marked rank by the size, number, and length of their surgical horn implants. *He's a Xeran priest now? They accepted* him *into their priesthood? A traitor?* Dona rose from the wreckage of the washstand, though her back howled in bruised protest. Sinking into a crouch, she drew a knife from her boot. The blade chimed, a pure, high note that somehow sounded menacing. *Well, not for long, you treasonous son of a bot.*

Temporal Enforcement's techs had improved the quantum weapons they'd invented six months before. The originals had been battle axes even Dona could barely swing, but the new blades were far lighter. And just as capable of cutting through heavy combat armor.

Another deep male roar sounded downstairs. For a split second, Dona felt comforted. *Somewhere the chief's kicking ass. Just like I'm about to. Tech or no tech.*

Her quantum dagger hummed a higher note as she circled Ivar, boots crunching through broken crockery. "You've had this coming for a long, long time, you son of a bitch."

"No, *you're* the one who's about to get a taste of what you've had coming." He bared his teeth. They flashed at her from the darkness of his broken helmet. "So, are you still fucking Dyami?" Misinterpreting her shocked expression for surprise, he curled a lip. "Did you really think I didn't know you were betraying me with that sanctimonious Warlord prick?"

"I never . . ." she began, before she realized she didn't owe him explanations anymore.

"Don't waste the oxygen." Ivar lunged, crossing the distance between them in a blur of battleborg speed. "I always knew you rutted with him, you little bitch-whore." His fist flew at her face.

Dona twisted, avoiding the blow by millimeters as she drove the quantum blade at his armored belly. He knocked her wrist away, and she went with it, spinning aside before his backhanded blow could hit her head. "I never betrayed you, Ivar," she gritted, knowing she was wasting her breath. "You were the one who spat on everything you ever claimed to believe in. Me. Chief Dyami. Your Enforcer's oath."

"My *oath*? Only an idiot would buy that beefershit." He curled a lip and paced to his right, circling. Looking for an opening. "Unlike you, I'm not that stupid."

He's so busy sneering, he forgot to keep his guard up. Dona's eyes narrowed, focusing on the left hand he'd dropped out of a proper defensive position. The only chance she had was to hit him hard and hit him fast.

Even before the Xerans upgraded his nanotech, Ivar was a combat-class battleborg, easily a foot taller and fifty kilos heavier than Dona, every gram genetically engineered and nanofiber-reinforced.

But she was faster. Dona drove the quantum dagger at her foe's massive chest in a blur of merciless strength.

He hit her so fast, she didn't even see the blow coming. The stiletto cartwheeled from her hand as Ivar slammed a punch into the side of her head, knocking her off her feet and sending her skidding into a corner.

If not for her helmet, the blow would have shattered her skull.

The battleborg was on her before she could scramble up and away. Dona threw up a forearm block, but his fist still hit her right in the center of her visor. It cracked as her head bounced against the floor. Flat on her back, she counterpunched anyway, a diversion for the kick she planted right between his legs. He only snarled and started pounding her as she tried to twist aside and rise. Punch after punch thudded into her head and torso, smashing her back against the floor.

Starbursts of pain thundered through Dona's skull, but she ignored them as she fought to scramble to her feet. She managed it somehow, reeling upright, slamming punches and kicks into Ivar's big body. He didn't react to the blows at all. *Seven hells, it's as though he doesn't even feel them.*

And it was possible he didn't, if his implant had blocked the pain. *Yeah, I'm fucked.*

A blur of red hit her face so hard, her skull felt like it would detonate. The world seemed to blink.

Lifting her head, she realized she was flat on her back in the middle of the room. And she had no idea how she'd gotten there.

Ivar stepped into view and loomed over her, a savage grin on his face.

Oh, fuck. Frantic, desperate, Dona drove both feet into his gut in an effort to kick him the hell away from her. He didn't even try to block the double kick. Barely even rocked on his heels.

"You're dead, bitch." His eyes glittered with a rage that was not entirely sane.

He's going to kill me. He'd already made far too much progress toward that goal. The room revolved around her, and her head throbbed with a relentless kettledrum pounding.

Warning! her neurocomp blared. *You have sustained a severe concussion. You cannot continue to take blows to the head without suffering traumatic brain injury.*

And what the hell do you suggest I do about it? Terror spiced her rage like sawpeppers, tongue-searing and bitter. A punch she never even saw exploded against her faceplate, snapping her head back as the plastium shattered. Shards peppered her face, but she barely felt the sting as she staggered. Even with the helmet's protection, Ivar was bouncing her brain around inside her skull like a grav-ball.

The comp's right. He's beating me to death.

Ivar rammed her into the wall with such force, white flakes rained around her shoulders as the plaster cracked like dried mud. Stunned, disoriented, she hung in his grip as he reached up and did something to the underside of her jaw. Her helmet lost its grip on her skull. He pulled it off her head and tossed it aside to hit the floor in a series of rolling thumps.

Oh, fuck. Blearily, she peered at him, hanging limp in his hold, barely able to focus on his face as the world swung around her.

Grinning like a skyshark, Ivar drew back one huge fist for the blow that would likely shatter her skull.

Red alert! her comp squealed. *Take defensive action immediately or . . .*

Gods curse him, I am not going to let this bastard butcher me. I will fight him to my last breath.

Drawing on the last dregs of her strength, she swung a clumsy fist toward that hated smirk. He merely swatted the blow aside.

"Is that the best you can do, cunt?" Ivar laughed, eyes glittering hot with knife-edged pleasure. "Then I guess you'll die." He cocked his fist back for one final blow . . .

And vanished.

Deprived of his support, Dona fell, tried to catch herself. Hit the ground anyway in a heap of knees and elbows. Dazed, barely conscious, she lifted her aching head.

A couple of meters away, Alerio Dyami hammered punches into Ivar, relentless as a metronome. The traitor reeled as he fought to protect himself, arms jerking in a futile effort to ward off crunching blows. He'd lost his helmet, and his face was almost as bloody and bruised as Dona's. Each blow tore a grunt of pain from his lips. Battleborg tech notwithstanding, Ivar was no Vardonese Warlord.

Alerio *was* a Warlord, however, and he was *pissed*.

Safe, Dona thought in dazed relief. *I'm safe. The chief won't let him kill me.*

Darkness rolled over her in a black flood. She didn't feel her head hit the floor.

Chief Alerio Dyami stalked Ivar Terje around the scene of the fucker's latest crime, the instinct to murder growling in his heart.

The bastard *needed* killing. Deserved it. Alerio fully intended to give him those just deserts.

A nude woman lay bound to the bed, blood smearing her body from multiple stab wounds. Alerio's sensors told him the slick gleam on her spread legs was Ivar's sperm.

But even as that crime filled him with a cold, righteous fury, what really drove Alerio insane was the sight of Dona Astryr lying in a bloody heap. If he hadn't been forced to fight his way through all those Xeran priests downstairs, he could have spared her the savage beating Ivar had so obviously dished out.

The minute his neurocomp received Dona's call for help, Alerio ordered the implant to send him into *riaat*. The stew of biochemicals the computer pumped into his bloodstream had instantly thrown him into the berserker state that made Warlords so feared.

Ivar certainly should fear him, because *riaat* increased Alerio's already considerable strength by a factor of ten, while making him almost impervious to pain. All of which made it easy to beat the blood out of a traitor who richly deserved it.

One of Ivar's eyes was already swollen shut, but the other glittered feverishly at him. "You're such a fucking hero, aren't you?" The battleborg's bloody lip curled in a sneer. "But you didn't save the bitch on the bed, did you? Or the ones downstairs. Even the kid. We butchered them all, and there's not a fucking thing you can do about it. You can't change history. No matter what you do, no matter when you Jump, they'll die because we killed them. You failed, Chief." He laughed. "Big hero. Big, noble Warlord. Utter fucking failure."

Alerio ground his teeth against the need to kill. *Get control, dammit. He wants me blind stupid with rage. He wants me to make mistakes.* "You're right." He forced himself to retreat one step. Then another. Getting room to fight like the calculating warrior he was instead of a berserk killer. "I *didn't* save the fourteen people you raped and murdered."

But despite his battle for control, his murderous fury must have shown. Ivar's gaze flickered, and for an instant, Alerio saw fear flash through his enemy's eyes.

And that was the opening he needed. *Oh, botfucker, you'd better be scared.* Alerio whipped into a spinning kick.

Ivar ducked, throwing up a forearm in an attempted block. Neither effort kept the chief's boot from slamming into his jaw. The battleborg bounced off the wall behind him, almost went

down. Alerio, still balancing effortlessly on one leg, reversed the
kick and snapped the toe of his armored boot into Ivar's jaw.

The battleborg crashed backward, shattering the wall's plaster
but somehow managing to keep his feet.

Alerio took a gliding step forward and punched him squarely
in the face with a left-right combination that rocked Ivar's head
on his shoulders. "You're finished," the chief growled. "You'll spend
the rest of your life in a penal colony, thinking of all the women
you'll never fuck."

Ivar steadied himself, one corner of his bleeding mouth lifting
in a smirk. "It's not going to be that easy, Chief." A punch blurred
out of nowhere, bloodying Alerio's mouth and making his skull
ring.

Huh, Alerio eyed his opponent's vicious grin. *Guess he's got a
little more left than I thought. He's definitely stronger and faster
than he was the last time we fought.*

"The Xerans gave me an upgrade," Ivar told him smugly.

Alerio curled a lip. "It's not going to save you, asshole."

"Yeah, well, yours definitely won't save you, Chief. You, or any
of those fucking tourists you're so determined to protect. We've got
T-suits, motherfucker." He grinned, smug confidence in the bloody
curve of his split lip. "The whole temporal plane is our little play-
ground. We can screw and kill every tourist who falls into our
hands. And we will." His glinting eyes narrowed and went cool.
Almost sane. "Unless you turn yourself in to the Victor's . . . justice.
You. Your little whore Dona. Those abominations, Nick Wyatt, his
Warfem bitch Riane. Jessica and Galar Arvid. All of them." Now
those eyes went damned icy. "And most of all, we want the T'Lir.
So be a hero, Chief. Or watch me kill everything that moves."
Energy began to swirl around him, preparing to coil into a tem-
poral warp that would shoot him across time and space.

Fuck, he's getting ready to Jump. Alerio lunged toward his foe.

Too late. A deafening sonic boom and a flash of light blinded him as Ivar's T-suit armor warped space and time, catapulting the traitor far from the Warlord's reaching hands.

When Alerio could see again, Ivar Terje was gone.

Jumped. Goddess knows where. He glared at the empty space where Ivar had been. Yeah, run now, cocksucker. Sooner or later, I'll hunt you down.

In the meantime, Alerio had more important things to worry about. Starting with Dona Astryr. One long pace took him to his agent's sprawled, unconscious body.

But before he could begin a sensor scan to determine the extent of her injuries, a sonic boom thundered from the floor below. Another sounded, then another, and another, until Alerio felt the whole house sway in the grip of temporal forces like a tree in a storm. The priests were following Ivar's lead and Jumping for home.

And there wasn't a damn thing Alerio or his agents could do about it.

"Chief," commed Galar Arvid, his second-in-command, *"the Xerans have all Jumped, presumably for Xer. Do you want us to pursue or . . . ?"*

"What, chase them all the way back to the Crystal Fortress, where ten thousand just like them wait to kick your ass? Fuck no. Start getting the wounded to the Outpost and the dead into stasis. We'll figure out what to do about the hornheads later."

"Understood, Chief."

Wearily, Alerio sank to his knees by Dona's side. She looked like he felt. The Enforcer's pretty face was battered, both eyes blackened, her lips cut and swollen. Bruises distorted the clean lines of her high cheekbones and delicate jaw. He was almost afraid to scan for internal injuries. He was pretty sure he didn't want to know. He scanned anyway. And swore.

Com Dr. Chogan, Alerio told his neurocomp.

The doctor answered a heartbeat later. Evidently someone had already fetched her from the Outpost. Good. *"What is it, Chief? I've got my hands full with Riane. She took a gut wound."*

"Astryr got the worst of it in a fight with Terje," Alerio said shortly. *"She has a pretty serious concussion. My sensors say her brain is swelling."*

"Let me get Riane into regen, and I'll head up there."

Dona moaned, a breathy sound of pain that made the muscles in Alerio's chest clench. It was more than the ache he'd normally feel over an injured agent. Her remarkable violet eyes opened to slits in her swollen lids. Registered him. Tried to widen. "Terje," she gasped, apparently trying to warn him. "The traitor's . . ."

"Already Jumped for home," Alerio told her roughly. "Along with the rest of the Victor's priests."

"What about . . . woman . . . temporal guide . . . owns . . . house. She's . . ." Dona lifted a wavering hand, gesturing weakly toward the bed and its bloody occupant. "Alive when I . . . came in. Is she . . . ?"

He frowned at the still form. *"That's* Lolai Hardin?" he said, only to ask himself an instant later, *Well, who the hell else could it be?* According to the Temporal Jump plan Hardin had logged with the Outpost, she was the only one unaccounted for. It had not even occurred to him that the woman on the bed could still be alive, considering the extent of her injuries. *Scan her,* he told his comp.

No cellular activity, the implant reported. *Based on decay, she has been dead too long for successful revival. At least ten minutes.*

Alerio cursed himself and Ivar with equal venom. "She's gone," he told Dona's swollen violet eyes.

"Dammit." A tear slipped down a bruised cheek. "I was hoping I could save her." Her delicate jaw worked as if she ground her teeth. "Fucking . . . Ivar . . . wouldn't let me Jump her . . . out." She stopped to pant. "They all died . . . didn't they? Ivar and the priests . . . killed everybody."

He had no idea, so he commed Galar to ask about the two survivors. When the answer came, Alerio ground his teeth. *Devils drag Ivar right to the seven hells.* "Chogan did her best, but . . . no. Couldn't even save Hardin's coachman, much less the boy. Both died in regen." Which said everything that needed to be said about the savagery of the attack on them, since regen could heal damn near anything.

Alerio leaned over to give her his most determined stare. "The Xerans are going to pay for what they did to these people." Lifting one delicate, chilly hand, he wrapped his big fingers around it. "We'll make sure of that."

"I know. You always get justice for the . . . victims." Her bruised eyes slipped closed.

"Dona!" Stiffening in alarm, Alerio ordered another scan.

She has a concussion, his neurocomp reported. *There is swelling in a bruised area of her cerebral cortex that must be addressed before it becomes serious. Fortunately, her neural computer is compensating, and her other injuries are not life-threatening. She will heal quickly once in regeneration.*

Alerio sighed in relief and sat back on his heels, studying Astryr's battered face. Like most Enforcers—and the Warlord himself—she was a cyborg. A network of biocrystal grew through her brain like a second nervous system, feeding her brain sensor data even as it gave her control of most bodily functions. A lacy sensor network lay beneath her skin, designed to detect everything from the DNA of a murder victim to the temporal warp fields produced by T-suits during a Jump.

The tech didn't stop there. Nanotech filaments reinforced her bones and strengthened her muscles, making her far stronger than any ordinary human, male or female. Yet even given all that, Dona was no match for a battleborg like Ivar Terje. His implants were even more extensive, and his muscles were reinforced with nanofibers three times as thick as hers, giving him far greater strength. She'd known that, yet she'd still gone after Terje, determined to save a dying woman even if it meant her own life.

"Chogan!" he bellowed.

"Gods, Alerio, I'm *here* already." Dr. Sakari Chogan stalked into the room, trailed by a seven-foot regeneration tube that wafted like a leaf on a streaming blue anti-grav field. The doctor looked pale and grim despite her ethereal good looks, and she'd gathered her iridescent green hair into an untidy topknot that looked as if she'd been dragging her hands through it. As usual during temporal missions, she wore a bright red T-suit marked with a prominent white *M* for "Medical." To most opposing forces, no matter how brutal, that would have made her a noncombatant.

The Xerans had proven time and again that they didn't give a damn whether medical personnel were off-limits or not. If they'd gotten their hands on the doctor, they'd have shown her no more mercy than they had Lolai Hardin. Yet that hadn't stopped Chogan from doing her best to save the injured and obtain justice for the dead.

"How's Riane?" Alerio rose to help the doctor with the regenerator.

"Better. Going to be in regen awhile, though."

When they had it positioned to her satisfaction, the doctor flicked her fingers over a series of controls. The device obediently lowered to engulf the injured Enforcer. Seconds later, a pink healing mist flooded the tube, obscuring Dona's unconscious face.

Chogan leaned over the huge device, her hands sweeping through its control field in graceful arcs that triggered a series of medical scans. Within seconds, the results flashed into view, scrolling over the three-dimensional schematic of Dona's body. Heart rate, blood pressure, oxygen levels, cerebral activity, others Dyami didn't recognize. Some readings appeared in shades of healthy green, but others pulsed a warning crimson.

"Looks like the botfucker banged her brain around pretty

hard," Chogan told Alerio, a frown forming between her swooping green brows as she studied the readouts. "I never did like that bastard. There was just something so bloody *mean* about him. He hurt people and enjoyed it. Including Dona, lover or not."

"Yeah, he's a bastard." Brooding, Alerio gazed through the tube's transparent lid, studying Dona's unconscious face. Her battered features were already healing, bruises fading, cuts vanishing under a tide of pink, healthy skin.

Alerio felt knotted muscles begin to relax between his shoulders. "Terje needs a fatal ass-kicking," he told the doctor absently as he braced his palms on the regenerator's lid and stared into Dona's sleeping face. Her closed eyelashes looked incredibly thick and dark as they fanned over her cheeks. "Too bad he got away before I could give it to him."

Chogan sighed. "At least now we know what lies under that slick smile. That's preferable to being blindsided."

None of them had known Terje was a hornhead double agent until the Enforcer had damn near strangled Jessica Kelly to death. The pretty redhead's only crime had been her choice of roommate, a woman named Charlotte Holt, who turned out to be Xeran herself. Charlotte had managed to piss off the Xerans' so-called "god," the Victor, by trying to protect an alien race he wanted dead. The Victor had apparently decided to have her killed, along with anyone she might have talked to. Including Jessica.

So what the hell did Holt know that the Victor wanted squashed?

Then there were Holt's alien friends, the Sela. Big-eyed, six-legged, cuddly little creatures—with one fuck of a lot of power. The Victor considered them abominations, and he intended to exterminate every damned one of them. Now the Xeran "god" had apparently decided to expand his hit list to include every temporal tourist he could get his hands on, along with Alerio and his Enforcers.

Question is, how the hell do I stop him?

Minutes later, Dr. Chogan, Lolai Hardin's body tube, and the regenerator containing Dona made the Jump back to the Outpost infirmary in the usual showy explosion of light and sound. With them safely away, Alerio rolled his knotted shoulders and headed back downstairs to check on the rest of his team.

He found the nine of them hard at work bustling around the bloody murder scene. To his relief, no one else had been as badly injured as Riane Wyatt, who was already in the infirmary.

We got lucky.

When he was satisfied they'd gathered all the evidence they'd need if this mess ever went to trial, Alerio gave the order to begin the Jump for home. His eight remaining agents began warping out from the wrecked parlor in teams of two, accompanied by evidence bots and body tubes loaded with the tourists they'd failed to save.

As was his habit, Alerio was the last to leave in order to cover his team's retreat. Which, as usual, left him half-blind and completely deafened from the flash and boom of temporal warps. Luckily the T-suits' dampening field kept anyone more than ten meters away from sensing the effects. No Philadelphia natives would wonder why there was a thunderstorm raging *inside* the house next door.

By the time it was his turn to Jump, the chief's ears were ringing so loudly, it was all he could hear. Until the androgynous mental voice of his neurocomp began reciting the familiar string of coordinates that was the Outpost's space-time address. *Outpost coordinates confirmed,* he told the implant. *Engage temporal warp.*

Engaging temporal warp in three . . . two . . . one . . .

It felt like being hit by lightning, a teeth-rattling electrical assault that shook his body until his consciousness blinked out . . .

. . . And . . . he was back again.

Temporal warp to the Outpost successful, the neurocomp announced.

Alerio made no answer, blind, deaf, stomach knotting in violent rebellion, muscles jerking from the electrical assault that was a side effect of the Jump. Bracing his knees, he stayed upright by will alone and waited for his implant to compensate. *My team?*

All members of the investigation team present and accounted for.

The chief breathed a silent prayer of thanks to whatever Vardonese goddess happened to be listening.

He'd lost a Jumper once. Riane Arvid's sabotaged T-suit had bounced her back and forth across Terran temporal space before finally dumping her in the twentieth century. Her suit was dead as a stone by then, unable to generate even the weakest warp field.

To make a bad situation truly gods-awful, a team of Xeran assassins appeared minutes later. They'd have butchered her with their usual viciousness if not for a timely rescue by Nick Wyatt, half-breed Xeran and superhuman guardian of an alien race called the Sela.

The two had bonded as they struggled to elude the Victor's assassins. By the time Nick helped Riane return to the Outpost, the couple was desperately in love.

Still, almost losing an Enforcer was an experience Alerio had no desire to repeat. Especially considering Ivar's threats. *We can screw and kill every tourist who falls into our hands. And we will. Unless you turn yourself in to the Victor's . . . justice.*

Like hell, 'botfucker.

Blinking the lingering Jump spots from his eyes, Alerio glanced around the cavernous room called Mission Staging. Heavily shielded to control the raging forces of temporal warp, it was lined floor to ceiling with evidence and equipment lockers, as well as regeneration tubes for the injured. Most temporal missions began and ended here, especially those featuring a large Jump team.

Though the chief longed to head for the infirmary to check on Dona, he controlled the impulse. If his Enforcers managed to bring the Xerans to justice, he was damned if the killers would go free because somebody broke the chain of evidence.

"All right, let's get the physical evidence stowed," Alerio said in a command bark that had every Enforcer jumping.

Apparently inured to his growls, Chogan's medical techs strode out, accompanied by a pitiful parade of body tubes. He ignored them as he rapped out instructions. "The evidence bots are to be logged in and their contents transferred into evi-stasis. And make damned sure they're all *our* bots. Last thing we need is to give the Xerans another shot at sabotaging our central computer."

The last time a spy had attempted such sabotage, the virus he unleashed almost killed every senior agent on the Outpost—including Alerio himself. The horrendous delusions the virus created had almost fragged his consciousness and stopped his heart. Not an experience he wanted to repeat.

Especially with the Xerans playing for keeps.

CHAPTER TWO

One thing Alerio had to say for his Enforcers: they were efficient. Within minutes, the agents were scanning and decanting each bot, then sealing the biological evidence in stasis tubes. That finished, they logged in data on each hair, fiber, and blood cell with the Outpost's main computer.

Skillful hands slid the tubes into wall slots that fired them into the evidence safe deep in the facility's core. If the Enforcers—or the Galactic Union's Temporal Court—decided they needed so much as a single hair, it would be instantly available.

The procedure was one his people had done hundreds of times before. They didn't need Alerio hovering over them like a Soji Dragon with one egg. Especially since he was only putting off a job even more onerous than the one they were doing.

Alerio folded his arms and rocked back on one heel, frowning. Somehow he was going to have to persuade Colonel Elana Ceres to order a moratorium on temporal tourist visas. At least until Ivar was captured . . . or Alerio twisted the traitor's head off his shoulders.

That action would not be legal under Galactic Union law, his neurocomp informed him primly.

I do not give a stinking pile of Soji shit. Especially if he even thinks about going after my team.

Particularly Dona, who'd become Alerio's obsession over the past two years. As Ivar knew all too well. The battleborg had been violently jealous of her even back when he was still pretending to be a loyal Enforcer.

Watching Ivar abuse Dona with those little needling digs of his had driven Alerio into a frigid fury. There'd been times the Warlord had ached to kick his subordinate's ass from one end of the Outpost to the other.

Unfortunately, being Ivar's commanding officer made that impulse impossible to carry out. Especially since Dona never reported her lover for his conduct. Alerio wasn't sure whether she just didn't notice—which strained belief, Dona being pretty damned observant—or whether she just had a very thick skin.

Even though it looked so incredibly soft . . .

Within the hour, all evidence was logged in and preserved in stasis tubes. The evidence bots were safely slotted into their charging stations, beeping quietly to themselves as they waited for the next round of collections.

Housekeeping chores complete, the Enforcers streamed out of Mission Staging and into the corridor beyond. Alerio knew they'd either head to their quarters on the Residence Deck or make for the Outpost Mess for a meal. Normally the agents joked and laughed after a mission, but tonight's bloodbath had left them all in a grim, silent mood.

Alerio felt pretty damned grim himself.

He stalked toward his office through the murmuring human stream of agents and administration staff. Normally Enforcers would stop him along the way for greetings or questions. Tonight, though, his expression was apparently so pissed that anyone who started toward him quickly veered away.

The Chief Enforcer's office was located on the administrative level, sandwiched between the residential deck and the infirmary. As Alerio put the finishing touches on his report, he dropped into the command chair behind his massive black desk. Its gleaming surface instantly lit, scrolling a color-coded list of the tourists, historians, and documentary crews presently passing through the Outpost on their way to various temporal destinations. Like Britain and the ancient world, the Americas were popular with time travelers.

Alerio grimaced, knowing every one of those tourists had just become an unwitting target. They had to be warned, but he knew damned well he'd better get permission first. He was on thin ice as it was, after the disaster with Ivar and Chief Investigator Alex Coridon.

Coridon, though supposedly investigating Ivar's crimes for TE Headquarters, was actually a spy and saboteur for the Xerans. He was the one who'd infected every computer on the Outpost with a really ugly virus—including the Enforcers' nuerocomps. And in the process, he'd plunged them all into hell as the virus made them experience their worst nightmares . . .

By the time the chief found the fourth mutilated body, he was running. He didn't even break step. If there was anyone left alive, it was his job to save whoever it was.

Too late for the rest.

He needed his weapons. His armor, his knives, a shard rifle at the very least.

Had to be Xerans. Had to find the sons of bitches. And kill them. He'd grieve once his enemies had paid for what they'd done.

Alerio charged into the armory, fury, grief, and guilt boiling inside him like a toxic stew.

Just inside the door, he slid to a stop as shock rolled over him like an ice-water bath.

Ivar Terje looked up at him from Dona Astryr's butchered body. The traitor was covered in blood. "I told you I'd kill her."

Alerio's scream of anguish rang in his own ears, tore at his throat . . .

Alerio jerked himself out of the flashback. *It didn't happen. It never happened anywhere but my nightmares. I haven't lost my people. I haven't lost Dona.* "Courier, prepare for Jump."

A door in the wall behind his head slid open, and a courier bot floated out with an inquiring beep.

The North American Outpost was actually situated in the sixteenth century, deep inside what would later be known as Georgia's Blue Ridge Mountains. It was a good site, being situated on a central node in space-time that made it easier to generate temporal warps. As a result, Jumps required less energy, which made temporal warps cheaper to create. That was particularly crucial for large tour groups; a Jump was enormously expensive. First there was the energy cost in generating warps there and back, then the price of buying the group food and clothing appropriate to the period. And finally, you had to hire enough experienced personnel to make sure none of the tourists did anything fatally stupid.

There were a great many ways to get dead in centuries not your own.

If it was hard to finance a trip back in time, living there was a real pain in the ass. Luckily for the Enforcers, all the activity around the Outpost helped convince the area's native population that the mountains were haunted. They avoided the area, making life much easier for the agents who would otherwise have had to deal with them.

Which meant the Enforcers could do as they damned well pleased.

The one drawback to the location was that any communication with Temporal Enforcement's twenty-fourth-century headquarters had to be sent by courier bot. Com messages couldn't travel through temporal warps. Not that it mattered. You couldn't change history. As much as Alerio would have liked to travel back to the moment the Xerans attacked and stop them, it just wasn't possible. His team would have ended up dead, or they'd have jumped to the wrong location, or all their suits would have failed at the same time. *Something* would have stopped them, just as something had stopped all the other teams who'd tried to prevent crimes before they happened.

Every one of those attempts had failed.

Every single time.

Eventually, temporal physicists had finally worked out the equations that explained why history could not be changed. Alerio even understood the math. He didn't like it, but he understood it.

So when he'd received the bot with Lolai's hysterical plea for help that morning, he'd summoned his team and Jumped to the moment after the courier had left. Not before. Never before.

"Ready to record," the bot said in a smooth, androgynous voice.

Jolted back to the moment, Alerio told his neurocomp to send the report to the courier. The implant obediently transmitted both the report and its assorted attachments: trid recordings of the crime scenes, a few gigs' worth of data on the blood, sperm, and fiber evidence, his comp's recording of Ivar making his threats.

"Message received and logged," the bot said. "Recipient?"

"Colonel Elana Ceres."

The bot acknowledged his command and vanished with a deafening crack and retina-searing flash. Alerio grunted and sat back to await the colonel's response. It wouldn't be long. Ceres could take her sweet time considering all the angles and still program the courier to arrive within five minutes of the time it left. Time travel could be either damned convenient or a huge aching pain in the ass.

While Alerio waited, he started wrestling with the problem of how to protect the scheduled temporal tours with the personnel he had available. *Ivar is damned well not going to claim any more victims on my watch.*

He'd barely settled down for some serious plotting when the courier made its thunderous reappearance. "I have the colonel's response," it announced in its prissy Galactic Capital accent.

"Proceed." Alerio braced one elbow on his desk and waited to see what beefershit his superior would bury him in. He'd commanded the Outpost for five years now under the direction of three different TE colonels. They'd all been career politicians who viewed Alerio and his agents as stepping-stones to some more significant post.

Elana Ceres was the worst of the lot.

What's more, she'd just decided to run for the Terran Regional Governor's office. A victory would make her the leader of five planets, fifteen moons, and a couple of asteroid belts, besides giving her a seat on the Galactic Union Council of Governors.

All of which was a long step up from Temporal Enforcement. Luckily for Ceres, she was a member of a politically well-connected family, backed by all the money that came with that kind of power. She was generally considered the odds-on favorite in the governor's race.

Unfortunately, the mess Alerio had just dumped in her lap could complicate that easy jog to victory. *She won't like that one bit.* He braced himself for an icy chewing-out delivered in Ceres's silken drawl.

The courier beeped, and projected the colonel's trid just above his desk surface. As always, there was no expression on the woman's beautiful face, as if she feared creating creases in her flawless skin. Hair the color of champagne tumbled in shimmering curls around the dark blue shoulders of her Temporal Enforcement dress uniform. Huge eyes stared from a screen of thick, dark lashes, their irises a brilliant shimmering green streaked with amber. Every bone of her delicate face looked as if it had been mathematically plotted for perfection.

Alerio had known combat droids with more personality.

Fortunately for Ceres, she could fake character well enough if a trid camera was aimed her way. But today there was no larger audience than Alerio, so she didn't bother to fake humanity, much less civility. Not for a mere Vardonese Warlord.

"I have discussed your report with my fellow Temporal Enforcement regional commanders," Ceres announced. "We're all of the opinion that informing the public of this . . . terrorist's threats would do more harm than good."

Alerio snorted. "Especially when it comes to your gubernatorial campaign." He wasn't recording a response—she'd be shocked to receive one—so he could say whatever the hell he wanted. Not that he'd ever hesitated to tell Ceres what he thought, though he usually tried to do it with some pretense of diplomacy.

"Making the public aware of Terje's attempted blackmail could have a negative impact on temporal tourism," she continued with the cold objectivity of a combat droid. "Considering the licensing fees involved and current Galactic Union budgeting constraints, we simply can't afford to start a panic. However, if the situation becomes more fluid . . ."

"In other words, if more people end up dead," he muttered, grinding his teeth so hard they creaked as if on the verge of cracking.

"We will certainly reevaluate our decision. In the meantime, you're ordered to do everything possible to apprehend these killers while preventing further collateral damage."

" 'So don't let anyone else get dead.' " He clenched his jaw again. It was starting to ache from the pressure. "Believe it or not, I didn't need that last bit spelled out."

"Please know we take this situation very seriously, Chief

Dyami. However, I have faith in your ability to prevent further losses and apprehend those involved."

Ceres paused. The corners of her lips lifted slightly. By her standards, it was the equivalent of a sadistic grin. "However, you should be aware that a number of my fellow commanders have raised concerns. Some still think you should be reassigned, especially in light of Terje's treason."

Yeah, he'd figured the bastards would want to strip him of his command. He supposed he was lucky they hadn't fired him already. Fortunately—or not, depending on your point of view—he'd make a highly convenient scapegoat if the public should somehow learn of the scandal.

"I, however, argued that given the . . . volatility on the Xeran home world, it was best to leave you in place."

So you can toss my bleeding corpse to the media wolves and run like hell if anything goes wrong.

Ceres's lovely eyes narrowed to blazing green slits. "Don't make me regret that clemency, Chief Dyami." Her image vanished, revealing the courier floating serenely on a blue cushion of anti-grav energy. "Is there a response?"

"Such as, 'You're a gutless political hack, and you're going to find yourself in a media shit-storm if this gets out?'" Alerio rubbed his aching forehead. He knew from past experience that nothing he could say would move Ceres one millimeter once she'd made up her mind. He looked up at the bot. "No, courier, there is no further message. Return to your charging station."

As the bot disappeared back into the wall, Alerio stared sightlessly at his desktop. Within the desk's gleaming dark surface, lists of temporal tour groups rolled like the credits of some ancient movie in glowing greens and blues. Men, women, and children, all targets for Ivar and his vicious ilk.

Alerio's main priority now was the same as it always had been: the safety of those people. Making sure they all made it home.

According to the Outpost's main comp, there were a dozen tours scheduled for the next week. Each would require the protection of between three to six agents. Which left him with a serious manpower problem.

To make matters worse, a number of his Enforcers were on leave back home in the twenty-fourth century. He could recall them, of course, but some of those agents really needed the break. Temporal Enforcement tended to extract a heavy toll, particularly on good people who cared about solving cases and protecting the public. Because sometimes you found yourself fighting history's infinite inertia.

Then you were just fucked.

Which brought him right back to the original problem. How was he supposed to protect all those tourists with the agents he had? *Hell with it,* Alerio finally decided in disgust. *I'm heading to the infirmary. It's time for Dona to get out of regen.*

He wanted to see her, whether it was a wise thing to do or not.

The Outpost occupied the core of Spirit Mountain, a huge high-tech cylinder cut into five levels that were in turn divided into offices, science labs, and sleeping quarters. Then there was the Concourse, a sprawling complex dedicated to serving temporal tourists with hotels, restaurants, bars, and stores selling everything from period clothing to kitschy souvenirs.

Chogan's infirmary took up the Outpost's fourth level, its circular central ward surrounded by a ring of medical offices and lab facilities. Normally the ward would be crowded with as many as ten hemispherical sterile fields, each of them sheltering a patient's bed. At the moment the only patients were Dona and Riane Arvid, both of them still occupying regeneration tubes.

Alerio scanned the med-sensor data that floated, glowing, above the massive cylinders. He saw with relief that both agents were recovering nicely, though neither was conscious yet.

Dammit, he wanted to see Dona. Needed to see her. *Professionally,* Alerio reminded himself. *Just professionally.* It couldn't be anything more than that.

"I wondered when you'd be by." Dr. Sakari Chogan leaned a hip against a counter by the far wall, sipping one of her habitual cups of stimchai. Soft music played in the gently lit ward, though if it was intended to soothe, it wasn't doing its job.

At least, not on Alerio. *Then again, maybe I'm just wound a little too tight.* He gave the doctor a tired smile. "How are your patients, Sakari?"

She grimaced. "Better than the fourteen people whose autopsies I'm currently putting off." She held up a hand as if to deflect criticism—not that he intended to offer any. "I'll get to 'em. I just . . . need a little break."

Alerio gave her a sympathetic smile, knowing the doctor's work ethic would drive her to start work on the first of them by the time she finished her stimchai. "The crime scene was pretty ugly." One of the worst he'd ever seen in twenty years as a time cop, in fact.

The bastards had tortured a *child.*

"Yeah, it was definitely ugly." Her expression brooding, Chogan took another sip. "I'm just glad we didn't lose any of the Enforcers. We came damned close, what with the bloody great chunk that priest took out of Riane's intestines. Thank all seven gods for regen."

"When are you going to spring her from that tube?"

Chogan shrugged and sipped her stimchai. "Hour or so."

"What about Astryr?" He glanced at Dona's tube again and frowned at the floating readout. He didn't like the looks of that cerebral pressure reading.

"Sorry, I don't dare release her tonight," Chogan said, confirming his suspicions. "Neural tissue just doesn't regenerate as fast as the rest of the body. Her brain needs a little more time to heal from the battering Ivar gave her." Her voice dropped to a mutter. "The botfucker."

Alerio curled his upper lip in agreement. "There's one I'd love to put in a tube. And I'm not talking about a regenerator."

"And I'd love to watch you put him there." She gave him a dark smile over the rim of her cup. "You'll get your chance, Chief. I've got confidence in you."

He snorted. "I'm certainly going to give it my best shot."

Hearing claws click on the infirmary deck, Alerio looked around just as a pony-sized black wolf trotted into the ward. Beside him strode a tall, dark-haired man. Though handsome, the human's angular, sculpted features were a bit too broad and starkly cut to be the product of genetic engineering.

And they weren't; Nick Wyatt had been born in 1977.

"How's Riane, Dr. Chogan?" he asked, green eyes worried as he dropped one hand to the wolf's head. "Frieka tells me one of the Xerans tried to gut her."

"Until I ripped out his throat," the wolf rumbled, the blue lights of his vocalizer flashing among the thick fur around his throat. Frieka's toothy wolf muzzle wasn't structured to produce Galactic Standard, though his powerful neurocomp and genetic engineering made him more than intelligent enough to speak. The vocalizer solved that problem by giving voice to his often snarky thoughts.

"When will I be able to speak to her?" Wyatt demanded. As if reacting to his obvious anxiety, the huge green gem inset in his silver armband flashed with a dull glow.

Chogan moved to give the Guardian's brawny forearm a pat. "Patience, Nick. Give her another hour in regen and I'll discharge her."

"Told you Riane's going to be fine," the pretty red-haired woman said, strolling into the ward on the arm of a tall, massively

built blond man. She was delicately pretty, particularly compared
to her companion.

Like Alerio, Galar was a Warlord, though he was a product of
House Arvid, the corporation which had gene-gineered and raised
him. Unlike Alerio, Galar had refused to wear the traditional
facial tattoo of his House. He'd never really explained why, though
Alerio suspected his ugly childhood had something to do with it.

But if his childhood had been unhappy, he was making up for
it now. He and Jessica had been married for almost seven months,
but they were still surrounded by a happy newlywed glow.

The Master Enforcer was also Alerio's most trusted officer, a
skilled and deadly agent he'd trust with his life. There was no
chance whatsoever Alerio would keep Galar in the dark about the
danger they were in. Or any of his people, for that matter. "I'm
afraid I have some news you're not going to like," Alerio told them.
"At all."

Nick straightened. Frieka's ears flattened, and Galar's hand
went to his hip, as if to draw a weapon he wasn't wearing. His wife
glanced up into his hard face, visibly worried.

In short, stark sentences, Alerio recounted Ivar's ultimatum
and Colonel Ceres's reaction to it. When he finished, an appalled
silence fell.

"Well," Frieka observed, "that sucks."

Jessica gave the wolf an amused snort. "Fuzzy, has anyone ever
told you that you've got a talent for understatement?"

"Just a couple thousand times." The wolf paused, as if recal-
culating. "Well, more like 3,452. Give or take."

"Why not just set a trap for Ivar?" Chogan gestured at Nick's
gemstone. "You could bait it with the T'Lir. That *is* what that god
of his wants, right?"

Nick shook his head. "The T'Lir's still pretty drained from my
last fight with the Victor. If something went wrong, it could end
up completely dead. Just like all the Sela souls it shelters."

"Sela souls?" Chogan lifted a skeptical eyebrow. She picked up a carafe and refilled her cup, then held it up in question.

As Jessica moved gratefully to accept a cup, her husband explained, "The T'Lir shelters the spirits of all the dead from one particular Sela colony . . ."

"In this case, the one Nick serves as guardian," Frieka added.

"Their souls are the source of the gem's power," Wyatt continued. "If I drained it, none of those spirits would be reincarnated in the next generation."

"And since Nick's mother is one of them, she'd be among the lost," Frieka put in. "That would suck."

"Oh. Yeah, I can see why that's not a good idea." Chogan drained the cup in one long gulp and tossed it into the recycling unit that popped out to catch it.

Alerio gave her a slight smile. "It's not a bad plan. It just has some seriously ugly consequences."

The group discussed several more ideas over the next hour, only to reject them all. Finally Chogan called a halt to the discussion in order to release Riane from her tube.

The moment the cylinder's lid opened, Nick bent and scooped the pretty young Enforcer into his arms. Riane moaned something that might have been a greeting before pulling his head down for a kiss. The raw passion in that kiss blazed with such intensity, Alerio had to look away. Absently, he rubbed a palm over his aching chest.

"Pheromones!" Frieka gasped, pretending to stagger. "Choking . . . clouds of lust!" Straightening, he gave the couple a stern look. "Go find yourselves a bunk before you reek up the whole Outpost."

Nick pulled his mouth away from Riane's long enough to smile down at the big cyborg beast. "You're just jealous."

"And you're still not married," Frieka retorted. "Get it together, would you? I want another cub to spoil."

Riane laughed and reached down to ruffle his thick fur. "We're working on it, Fuzzy."

"That's the Goddess's own sweet truth." Frieka rolled his vivid blue eyes. "Sharing quarters with you two is like being trapped in a porn trid."

Jessica held up both hands. "Okay, that's it. I don't need to know any more."

Alerio headed for the infirmary door. "And on that note, I'll leave you all alone."

"Oh, gods, please don't," Chogan muttered.

The next morning, Dr. Chogan helped Dona climb out of the tube. The help was appreciated, considering her trembling knees. She glanced around the ward, trying to ignore the usual post-regen spins.

The chief wasn't there.

The disappointment Dona felt was completely irrational. So was the sudden flash of pique. "Any problem with me going to the gym and sparring with a combat bot? I feel the need for some exercise."

"You mean you feel the need to beat up a dead ringer for a certain traitor." Chogan handed her a tablet to sign. Paperwork might not be printed on actual paper anymore, but that didn't mean it wasn't as obnoxious as ever. "After all that time in regen, you're as healthy as you were before Ivar bloodied his knuckles on your face."

"Good. I really need to hit something."

It took Dona the better part of an hour to work out her frustrations on the combot. It put up a lively enough fight that she was nursing bruises by the time she decided she was ready to cool down.

At least I'll be able to sleep tonight. Without, if the gods are merciful, dreaming about the chief.

She was halfway through a second set of repetitions with a grav-bar when Alerio stalked through the gym's double doors in a pair of black snugs and a very bad mood. Spotting her, he gave her a wary look.

Despite his dark, lowered brows, Alerio's half-naked body made Dona's own body purr in hungry approval. He looked nothing short of massive with all that genetically engineered muscle on display, rippling beneath tanned skin and a dusting of black body hair. His waist appeared even more ridiculously narrow compared to his powerful shoulders, and his abdominals rolled with every step above the waistband of his thin black snugs.

And his ass was a true thing of beauty.

"I see Chogan let you out of regen," he said, his voice a delicious velvet rumble.

"Yeah, thank the gods. Those things make me claustrophobic." She tried to concentrate on raising her grav-bar and controlling her breathing. "Too much like a coffin."

Alerio's gaze flicked up and down her body. He could see a lot more of it than usual, since she wore only a narrow breast band and snug shorts, both in vivid blue.

Something hungry stirred in his dark eyes, making her acutely aware she was slick with sweat and probably smelling like a goat-buck. She certainly didn't feel sexy, not with her aching, exhausted body and the bruise forming on one cheek where she'd missed a block.

"You've been sparring." The erotic hunger in his eyes vanished behind a wall of disapproval. "You sure that's a good idea, considering the concussion Ivar gave you yesterday?"

Dona shrugged. "Chogan said she had no problem with it."

"Oh." He looked away. "As long as you got her approval."

Was it her imagination or did he look embarrassed, as if he'd expressed inappropriate concern? But Alerio was her commander; of course he was entitled to question her about anything affecting her fitness for duty. Unless it was more than that.

Feeling heat flood her cheeks, Dona pretended to adjust the grav-bar while watching him out of the corner of one eye. Alerio had drawn his shoulder-length hair back in a tight, severe club. It only emphasized the masculine elegance of his Warlord's angular bone structure and square chin. The gym's stark lighting shadowed the deep hollows beneath his cheekbones and the wolfish line of his nose. The intricate green and gold lines of his facial tattoo only emphasized those stark good looks.

Dona had once researched Vardonese tats, so she knew the chief's denoted his rank during his service with the Vardonese military, his combat history, and his status as a product of House Dyami.

And I'm staring. He's going to notice. Trying to distract herself, she looked down at the grav-bar she held braced, half-forgotten, in both hands. The quarterstaff-length rod was equipped with a grav-field unit that amplified its weight according to the settings the user chose. Dona had set the bar at two hundred kilograms, a weight her cyborg muscles could handle with ease.

If I had any brains at all, she thought, ordering her implant to increase the bar's setting by another fifty kilos, *I'd head for the showers and leave the chief to his workout.*

Which she fully intended to do—after she'd watched him bloody "Ivar's" simulated face.

Dona had missed Alerio's actual fight with the battleborg, since she'd been unconscious at the time. She was going to enjoy watching the traitor get his ass kicked—even if "Ivar" was only a combot in disguise.

As Alerio entered the combat circle, a door opened in the bulkhead. The combot stepped out, its big body as gray and featureless as a kiosk mannequin's. Obeying some silent command, a wave of color washed over the android's translucent surface as its trid imagizer projected the face and form of Ivar Terje across its bland surface.

The pseudo-Ivar was dressed in the same crimson Xeran T-suit the real traitor had worn the day before. Only the helmet was missing, leaving the bot's head bare, red hair bristling in a novice priest's cut, silver horn implants jutting from his temples. He was blandly handsome in the way of the genetically engineered, with a narrow, ruler-straight nose and a wide mouth that looked far more sensuous than it actually was. All in all, the bot looked exactly like Ivar, which made the sneer he aimed at Alerio all the more chilling.

"Begin hand-to-hand practice match," the main Outpost comp intoned from its hidden speakers. "Full contact rules."

Which essentially meant there *were* no rules. Combots were designed to let Enforcers go full-out, to practice the moves they'd use in the field against opponents intent on killing them.

The chief didn't say a word. He simply lunged at the combot, exploding into a whirl of punches, blocks, and kicks that forced the big android to retreat across the combat circle. Its big arms blurred as it tried to block Alerio's attacks.

After that first flurry of blows, the two spun apart to stalk each other.

Dona absently pumped out another set of repetitions with the grav-bar, barely aware of its weight in her preoccupation with Alerio.

He dropped into a combat crouch, knees flexed, his hands raised loose and open. Muscle rippled up and down his powerful torso, biceps, triceps, and deltoids rolling under his smooth, tanned skin. A pattern of black hair formed a cloud across his broad chest, narrowing into a thin trail that dove into the waistband of his snugs.

Dona ached to touch that tempting trail. Burned to follow it, find out where it led . . .

Idiot. He locked you in a cell just a few months ago, remember? He thought you were a traitor. He believed the frame fucking Alex Coridon constructed. Just because you were dumb enough to fall in love with Ivar.

Or at least, she'd thought she was in love with Ivar. In retrospect, Dona realized she'd only used the traitor to distract herself from her inappropriate infatuation with their commander. Which was why the condemnation in the chief's black eyes had flayed Dona to the very soul.

So why couldn't she drag her eyes away from him now?

CHAPTER THREE

Dona tried, but she couldn't seem to stop watching Alerio battle the combot. She'd rarely seen the Warlord go full-out. He fought with a kind of cold, focused concentration, his intent black gaze missing nothing. Weaving to avoid the combot's deadly fists, he threw brutally powerful punches with the full strength of his Warlord body behind them. Even the combot had a hard time blocking those merciless punches.

The bot re-created Ivar's fighting style perfectly, in all its ruthless strength and agility. Alerio must have recorded their battles as a template, because the android precisely duplicated Ivar's speed, strength, and reach. Right down to the way he dropped his left hand, leaving a weakness in his guard. She'd been too busy fighting the thing off to notice that before.

Dona opened her mouth, but before she could point out the weakness, Alerio went on the attack, hammering the bot with blows that rocked its head on its shoulders. The android snarled one of Ivar's favorite curses and spun into a kick. The Warlord leaped over its scything leg and, still in midair, kicked the bot in the face.

As the combot staggered and nearly fell, Alerio landed, light as a dancer. Any impression of delicacy vanished as he moved in hard, hammering its face and body with punch after punch. The bot roared and hit him hard, actually knocking him flat on his ass.

Where he promptly kicked the bot's legs out from under it.

The android hit the ground hard as Alerio surged to his feet and pounced. Right into a kick in the gut hard enough to make Dona wince. The Warlord reeled backward, fighting to suck in a breath.

She froze with the grav-bar half-raised, watching, just as breathless as he was. *Idiot.* Shaking off her hypnotized fascination, Dona belatedly felt the grav-bar's weight and started pumping out reps again.

Alerio shook off the blow and surged toward his opponent again as the combot leaped to its feet. It closed with the chief yet again, slamming a brutal punch past his guard into his hawkish nose. Blood spurted.

Dona winced. And caught her breath as rage blazed in the chief's eyes. *Uh-oh.*

The bot threw another punch, but Alerio ducked and counterattacked, ramming his bladed hand into the bot's throat. A blow like that would have laid a human out with a crushed larynx, but it only made the bot cough and shake its Ivar-like head.

The chief didn't give it any more time to recover. Snapping into a savage spinning kick, he drove his heel into the bot's ribs. It reeled backward to slam into the rear bulkhead with a crash, barely catching itself before it fell on its face.

One arm curled protectively around its side, it wheezed as if nursing broken ribs. The bot didn't actually have ribs to break, of course, but it was programmed to react to blows of sufficient force as if it did. It backed away, watching the chief warily.

Sweat streamed down Alerio's broad back, but his steps didn't hesitate as he circled his enemy. His hooded eyes glowed with red sparks that suggested he was deep in *riaat*, the Warlord berserker state. Otherwise his face was as expressionless as an executioner's.

Despite herself, Dona felt a deep, familiar heat gathering in her belly as she watched sweat trace gleaming trails down the chief's sculpted chest and long legs.

Lost gods, I want him.

Too bad Dona knew better. She was damned if she'd get caught in *that* trap again. *Not after what happened with the colonel . . .*

"Dyami!" Bellowing the war cry of his House loud enough to make her jump, Alerio lunged at the bot yet again. He bulled right past its defective guard to shoot a pair of vicious punches into its "broken ribs."

Obeying its programming, the combot went down to one knee.

Alerio fell on the bot like a starving wolf on a stag. One hand clamped around the droid's throat as he cocked a fist.

Coldly, deliberately, Alerio hit "Ivar" once, twice, then a third time, the blows landing with punishing force. Dona would have winced if the android hadn't been wearing the traitor's face. Instead she felt only a dark satisfaction as the chief methodically beat the shit out of "Ivar." Especially when the bot slumped into faux unconsciousness, simulated blood spilling from its nose and mouth.

Alerio's mouth twitched into a grim smile distorted by bruises as he rose and backed away from his beaten foe.

"Match complete," the main computer intoned. "Chief Alerio Dyami is the victor."

The Ivar projection vanished, and the bot rose slowly to its feet. "I am damaged," it announced in a voice that had developed a definite wheeze. "I will not be available for further sparring until I have been repaired." With that, it limped back to its charging bay, presumably to undergo servicing for whatever damage it had suffered.

"You broke the combot." Dona returned the grav-bar back to its rack and walked over to join Alerio.

"Or it broke me." With a groan, the big Warlord fell back against the bulkhead, breathing in pumping pants.

Which was no surprise. Practice bots were notoriously tough. But then, they had to be. Most Enforcers were combat-rated cyborgs who did not pull their punches even in practice matches. Alerio certainly hadn't.

"Don't be too impressed." Grimacing, he grabbed a towel from a nearby shelf and wiped his sweating face. When he started rubbing slow circles over his broad, slick chest, Dona's eyes helplessly tracked the towel with more interest than was good for her.

"I doubt I'll be able to walk tomorrow," the chief continued, apparently oblivious to her fascination. "That bot can hit almost as hard as Ivar." With a wince of pain, he dug long fingers into the thick trapezius muscle that bulged between his neck and left shoulder as if trying to massage a knot that had coiled there. "But then, I did recalibrate its strength to match Ivar's. I think the Xerans upgraded his tech again."

"I thought so, too." They'd done so at least once before, at least if you believed Ivar's boasts. "When we fought six months ago, Ivar was a hell of a lot stronger than he'd ever been before. And he's even more powerful now." Frowning, she absently rubbed her face, where Ivar's big fist had left so many bruises. "He certainly kicked *my* ass."

"What do you expect? He's half a meter taller than you are— *and* fifty kilos heavier," Alerio told her bluntly. "Add in the genetically engineered bones and the triple-thick nanofiber reinforced muscles, and you've got a battleborg monster. That's not even counting whatever the hell the Xerans did to upgrade his tech."

She shuddered. "I noticed."

"You'd better. Just look at what he did to Lolai Hardin . . ."

"Okay, okay, I get it. He's a psychopath." Dona folded her arms and avoided his sharp gaze. "I don't know whether he's always been twisted, or if the Xerans did something to him . . ."

"Either way, he's a vicious son of a whore. You'd do well to keep the hell away from him." The chief pulled a thick cloth towel from a wall dispenser and scrubbed it over his sweating face and torso before shooting it into a recycler. "Don't worry—I'll bring the fucker to justice. He's going to pay for every last crime he ever committed." His dark eyes seemed to add, *Especially against you.* "If you're ever in the position of having to fight that bastard, run," he continued. "Consider that a direct order. You can probably outrun him, but you can't outfight him. Don't even try."

Stung out of her hypnotized fascination with his feral masculinity, Dona straightened. "I'm not exactly a wimp, Chief. I'm combat rated. Hell, I went in for a level six upgrade just last year. I could wipe up the floor with ten humans Ivar's size."

Alerio shook his head. "Impressive as that is, it doesn't mean shit when it comes to Ivar."

She gave him a tight smile. "Never underestimate the power of pissed."

The chief sighed. "Dona, you're one of my best agents. You're smart, strong, and hell on wheels in a fight." His gaze met hers with rough honesty. "But *Ivar is. Not. Human.* If he ever manages to get you alone, run like hell. I don't want you ending up like Lolai Hardin, and you came too damned close."

"Hardin's life was at stake." Dona raised her chin and met his intent stare with her own. "I couldn't leave her, not as long as she was still alive."

Alerio folded his massive arms and rocked back on his heels. And loomed. "Which would have done her no good at all if Ivar had killed you."

Remembering the wounds that spoke of the torture, Dona looked away. "You're assuming I deserve any better."

"Oh, for the sweet sake of the Goddess . . . !"

"You can't deny if I'd been more suspicious of Ivar's crap, less willing to believe whatever shit he fed me, maybe I would have realized he was a traitor *before* his fist hit my face. Maybe I could have prevented what happened to Jess, or Corydon's virus attack, or . . ."

"Stop," Alerio snapped. "Just cut it out, Dona. I'm tired of watching you torment yourself." One long pace brought him so close she could feel the heat radiating from his body. He stared down at her with eyes that burned in the shadows of his thick brows. "You are *not* responsible for Ivar's crimes."

All she had to do was reach out and touch that bare, sweating chest. She could feel the heat, the vital male power, radiating across the inches between them. So seductive . . .

"You aren't the commander of this station, Astryr," he continued, apparently oblivious to her hungry gaze. "It's not your job to protect your people from greedy, treasonous assholes. That was my ball to drop."

"I'm still Temporal Enforcement. And it *is* my job to know when I'm being lied to." She curled her hands into fists so tight, her nails dug into her palms hard enough to draw blood. Trying to hold onto some vestige of control. "But when it came to Ivar, I completely missed all the signs."

"So? All that proves is that you're human," he growled roughly.

"And so are you." Dona gazed up into his roughly handsome, angular face, the genuinely sensual mouth, the deep hollows and fierce eyes that burned even in the well-lit room. A Warlord's eyes shone red like that in *riaat*—or moments of passion.

Rage or desire? Dona thought. *Which made those black eyes burn?*

She opened a stinging hand and reached out, scarcely aware of what she did. The tips of her fingers brushed the hot skin of his chest, still heaving from his fight with the combot.

A bead of sweat rolled slowly down his right pectoral, sliding around the taught, brown peak of one male nipple.

Dona had never felt as starkly aware of a man as a being of raw sex, raw aggression. Raw need. She could feel his heart pounding under her fingers as the crimson sparks brightened, as if the emotion he felt was intensifying. Growing as hot as his eyes.

They stared at one another, unspeaking. Suspended in a moment of mutual awareness. Her lips parted, and her heartbeat began to pound in her ears. Each lush minute crept by on velvet paws, stropping over her skin like a cat.

"Dona," Alerio said, voice hoarse, eyes hot. "Aren't you tired of regret?" He lowered his head until his breath puffed warm against her lips. Almost a kiss. Almost. The sensation teased and maddened her. "Don't you want to feel something more than guilt?"

Hypnotized, she stared into the scarlet sparks deep in those night-dark eyes. "Yes. Gods, yes."

He groaned. His mouth touched hers. Just a soft brush of lip on lip at first, not demanding. Requesting. "Are you sure?" he breathed.

"Help me feel something else," she murmured back. "Anything else. I'm so sick of regret. And guilt tastes like coals and ash."

He made a low, fierce sound, dragging her against his chest with powerful arms and hands that trembled. Parting her lips with a sound as much moan as sigh, Dona let him in. His tongue slipped deep in a slow, erotic stroke. The heat of that delicate probe raced right to the base of her belly.

And set her aflame.

Heat raced through her, a blaze of red need stronger than anything she'd ever felt for any other man. Even—*especially*—Ivar. So she whispered the stark truth she'd always fought to hide against those velvet lips. "I want you. I shouldn't. Gods, I know I shouldn't. It's not smart."

"No, it's not smart at all," he agreed in a rough whisper. "And I don't give a pile of Soji shit."

"Neither do I." Dona leaned in, letting him gather her in until his big, hard body pressed the length of hers.

He rumbled a purr against her mouth and deepened the kiss even more. She opened recklessly, letting herself float in the pure, creamy pleasure of his warm lips, his exploring tongue. His cock pressed against her stomach, a thick, hot ridge that tempted her to roll her hips against it. A thought flashed through her mind: *I won't have the guts to do this again. I've got to make the most of it.*

Hooking a long leg over his hip, Dona ground into him with shameless hips. Sliding her hands down his chest, she savored the rolling muscle and smooth, warm skin against her palms. "The door," Dona murmured, "hadn't we better do something about the door?"

Alerio drew a bare inch from her mouth and rumbled, "Outpost main computer, Chief Alerio Dyami."

"Your orders, Chief Dyami?" the computer asked in its androgynous purr.

"Lock door of gymnasium three. Mark as fully occupied." His mouth covered hers again, then lifted. "And dim the lighting to thirty percent."

"Yes, Chief Dyami."

The door chimed a signal as its lock clicked home. Alerio kissed her slowly, hungrily, as the room's stark illumination dimmed to the creamy gold of candlelight. Finally he drew back, a question in his gaze. One hand slid the length of her torso. She covered it with her own and guided it to the closure of her top. His fingers found the slight indentation that marked the seal and slid along its length. The top's seal obediently parted, baring the skin from waist to high collar to the pink buds of her nipples. He pulled the top from her shoulders and tossed it aside.

Dona grabbed the waistband of her shorts and dragged them

down the length of her legs until she could kick them away. Straightening, she stood shamelessly naked. Her bare breasts gleamed softly in the dim light, the smooth muscle of her torso sweeping down to the triangle of soft hair between her legs. Her nipples puckered into tight points, both from the gym's cool air and the hot arousal storming through her blood.

Dona's breath caught as he froze, his eyes locked on those pink tips.

Then he sank to his knees.

Goddess, she's beautiful, Alerio thought. Her breasts were as perfect as her flawless face, sweet curves that called to his hands. He wanted to feel their smooth skin, their warm round weight.

Alerio drew in a breath as his fingers closed gently over taut, candy-pink peaks. He looked up to find violet eyes watching him, hooded with heat above flushed, parted lips. Stroking her nipples, Alerio watched as those lovely, luminous eyes slowly closed. White teeth sank into her lower lip as he stroked, tugged, and pinched. Dona shivered, her expression dreamy, lost in sensation.

Leaning in, Alerio closed his mouth over a jutting tip. She caught her breath, a sound almost as erotic as the taste of her tight flesh. He increased the pull of his suckling into a hard draw that made her gasp, eyes widening in obvious delight.

She feels so damned good in my arms. Soft here, firm there, as lush with sensation as a rose in bloom.

Sliding a hand down her hip, he discovered the soft hair of her sex. Carefully, he slipped a finger between her lips to find her so incredibly slick, so swollen tight, his cock jerked in lust.

Dona's arms curved around his head, fingers tunneling through his hair, gently directing his mouth down to her neglected right breast. As he drew on her in deep, hard pulls, she braced her legs apart. Her soft sigh sent a shudder of lust down his spine.

Straight to his cock. The long shaft jerked against the seam of his snugs as if demanding its freedom. With a growl, Alerio began nibbling his way lower, down the smooth, toned length of her torso, pausing to explore the firm muscle of her abdomen before continuing to the sable hair curling over her sex. He paused, studying the delicious sight of her vaginal lips pouting between strong thighs.

And slid his tongue between plump lips, groaning at the taste of slick, tight flesh. She moaned encouragement, the breathless sound of pleasure rushing right to his straining cock.

Alerio reached for it, stroking a hand over the seam of his snugs. Dona's brilliant violet eyes widened as his shaft tumbled free, its heavy length provoking her into a feline purr of pleasure and anticipation.

Dona stared down at Alerio's cock, entranced. She'd fantasized about how he'd look naked for two furtive, guilty years. Granted, his T-suit armor hugged every powerful centimeter of that big body, but it also protected—and concealed—his genitals.

Yet now he knelt before her, gorgeously naked and lushly erect.

And so damned beautiful. Sometime during their play, she'd pulled his hair free of its club to tumble in wild strands around his wide shoulders, leading her gaze down his powerful chest and tight abdomen to the beefy length of his cock.

It was delightfully long, flushed dark and rosy with blood until it jutted like a lance above the soft, furred sac of heavy balls.

Dona dropped to her knees and reached for that impossibly tempting cock. Wrapping her fingers around the smooth, thick shaft, she stroked it from balls to tip, entranced by its elegant erotic promise.

Glancing up, she found his eyes now blazed like a pair of torches, not one fleck of black to be seen. Entranced, she stared until one corner of his lip curled up. Catching her shoulders, he turned her, still kneeling, to face a waist-high gravity bench. Knowing what he wanted, she rose to drape herself over it, spreading her legs wide and bracing her feet apart.

Ready for whatever he cared to do.

As Alerio's fingers parted her vaginal lips, the wall in front of her shimmered, its surface shifting from matte to mirror. Probably at some silent order from Alerio's neurocomp. Dizzy, her lips dry, Dona stared into her own eyes as lust rolled through her blood in waves hot enough to singe.

Then he licked her.

One long, wet stroke that wiped every thought from her brain. Dona shuddered at the feral delight. In the mirror, her reflection's eyes widened, as he began to lick her like a melting icecone, slowly, as if savoring the taste.

Gods and goddesses, the pleasure felt thick, creamy, as his hands cupped her ass, his tongue alternating long licks and short, hot flicks. Bent as she was, Dona couldn't see what he was doing, but she could see her own expression as delight curled her hands into claws on the padded bench. Pleasure jolted her again and again in sizzling electric pulses that soon had the muscles of her thighs twitching.

The orgasm hit her like a wave of heated honey. Her legs lost all strength, and she damn near tumbled right off the bench with a yowl of delight. Shameless as a cat.

When Dona finally opened her eyes again, Alerio had risen to his feet behind her. His burning eyes met hers in the mirror, drinking in the dazed pleasure in her eyes. He stepped against her, his gaze dropping to her ass as he caught his cock in one hand. The smooth mushroom crown brushed her vaginal lips as he leaned in. Dona inhaled sharply. His entry—feeling so thick, so hot, so damned good—made her entire nervous system thrum like a plucked harp string.

Despite the torchlight lust in his eyes, Alerio took it slow. Slow, patient, spacing his thrusts far enough apart to give her heat time to grow. Hotter, higher, until she swore she could feel it leaping in her own eyes.

Alerio drove deep in a long thick thrust that tore a strangled scream from her lips as she shook in the grip of blazing sensation. He watched her reaction with absorbed eyes, his irises solid sheets of flame. His satyr's lips curled into a smile that was half snarl, and he began to thrust with lazily rolling hips. Deeper, faster, until he lanced that big cock in and out and *in* and *out*, circling his hips to screw her in luscious digs.

Dona screamed, helpless and overwhelmed in the grip of an orgasm that flashed through her like a firestorm.

Alerio leaned closer, one hand sliding between their grinding hips until he could strum his thumb over her clit. Gasping, she arched her spine, pushing back onto his probing cock. His free hand glided up her torso, found one breast, and pinched its tight, flushed nipple.

A third orgasm spilled over her. Dona screamed, so lost in delight, she was barely aware of Alerio shoving to the balls, roaring in animal delight as he came, pulsing heat spurting into her depths.

Floating in a kind of sweet, dreamy contentment, Dona savored the sensation of Alerio's strong arms wrapped around her, his body warm and sweat-damp against her back.

She'd had fantasies like this, secret midnight dreams with one hand busy between her thighs. Yet she'd never thought she'd actually make love to Alerio Dyami, Warlord and Chief Enforcer of the North American Outpost. She'd never expected to feel his hands gripping her ass as he suckled each nipple in turn and his cock drove into her slick core, fucking her with impossibly deep, greedy strokes.

I never thought I'd be this stupid, a mental voice whispered, acrid as bitterfruit. *To make such a mistake once, that's understandable. Twice, even. But three times? After Ivar? Hell, after the colonel?*

Shut up. Dammit, not now. She didn't need that vicious inner voice ruining this moment. All she wanted was to savor this sweet, fragile peace before something snatched it away.

Something always did.

Unfortunately, her inner bitch had no intentions of leaving her in peace. *He put you in the brig, Dona. Locked you away. Didn't even listen when you tried to explain. He believed you were the kind of woman willing to spit on her honor and her friends for tainted Xeran galactors.*

Dammit, shut up.

He betrayed you, just like the other two.

He's not the colonel. And he's sure as hell not Ivar.

He's wanted a taste of your hot little ass since you arrived on this station. Now he's had it. And you know what that means.

He's a Warlord. They're not like . . .

He won't love you. The whisper was damn near a shout now, pounding away at her like Ivar's fists. *Why would he? They never do. Take what you've got and get out with what's left of your pride before it gets sticky.*

Shut up.

You've got a good thing here. Better than you deserve. Don't fuck it up the way you did on Arania.

Suddenly Alerio's weight seemed crushing, as if someone had turned up the Outpost's gravity. Dona fought the growing claustrophobia, but it grew worse by the second.

"Dona, what's wrong?" Concern colored Alerio's voice as his arms suddenly tightened, drawing her tighter—and intensifying the sensation of being slowly smothered.

He's already feeling sorry for you. He's going to start noticing the cracks in what passes for your soul. Get the fuck out while you can.

"I can't breathe," she wheezed. "Get off. Please, just get off!"

"Yes, of course." Alerio rolled off her before her voice could quite spiral into a scream. His concerned gaze searched her face as he helped her to her feet. The crimson had vanished from his irises, leaving them a deep, velvety brown verging on black. "Are you all right?"

Means nothing, the voice whispered as she fought the panic attack. Her heartbeat filled her ears, and she gasped helplessly. Yet somehow she could still hear that fucking whisper. *Ivar could fake it, too.*

"Dona, what's wrong?" She could almost feel the sweep of his sensors, registering her galloping heartbeat, her labored breathing, the sick nausea churning her stomach.

Don't let me toss, she ordered her computer.

Anti-nausea procedures activated.

Spotting her top on the floor, she pounced on it and started shrugging it over her head as if it were combat armor and she were under fire. Once she was a little less naked, her panic began to ease.

Before she could start the search for her shorts, Alerio held them out to her. "Look, what's going on? Did I . . . ?"

"You didn't do anything." *Yet.* "I just need to go." She considered adding a lie, but knew his Warlord sensors would spot it like a signal flare. "I . . . just don't feel well."

His frown deepened. Her sensors detected his worry intensifying as his confusion deepened. With it came anger—and more than a little hurt. Hurt? Why would he feel hurt?

They like to be the one to end it when they want it ended, the frigid whisper reminded her. *They don't like it when you take control.*

She started for the door, wanting only to get away from him before she humiliated herself any further.

"Dona, wait . . ." Alerio sealed his own snugs, stepped into one low gymboot, and glanced around for the other. "I think I should walk you back to your quarters."

"Dammit, stop scanning me!" Dona snapped, the words bursting from her twisted lips like a shard pistol's fléchettes. "Give me a little fucking privacy, would you?"

He rocked back on his heels, his brows shooting for his hairline. There it was again—hurt flashing across his face.

Ah, seven hells. To make matters worse, she sounded like a bitch. And a crazy bitch at that. Just the impression she wanted to give her CO.

That's what he is, she reminded herself. *My CO. That's all.*

Alerio stiffened. "It's my job to be concerned for those under my command," he pointed out in a cool, level voice. Obviously fighting to control his temper. "And that includes you."

"I know, I know. I'm sorry, I just . . ." Throwing up her hands, Dona spun toward the door, ignoring his growled Vardonese curse. "Look, I've got to go . . ." She told her comp to order the door open.

It didn't budge, sending a quick spurt of panic into her bloodstream.

"Let Enforcer Astryr out," Alerio growled, and the door slid open with a sigh.

Oh, right, the chief had ordered it locked. Naturally it wouldn't respond to her counter-command.

Not when you're nothing more than a mere Enforcer. Unimportant to the Outpost—and to Alerio Dyami.

Dona fled from the gym, driven by the stinging, acid whispers that somehow managed to drown out the delicious memory of Alerio's passion.

Almost.

Frustrated, confused, Alerio watched her escape through the gym doors as if something with a lot of teeth was chasing her. What the flaming hells? He'd thought he was finally making progress . . .

Hell, he *had* been making progress. According to his sensors, she'd been enjoying the same post-coital bliss he'd felt. At least, until a wave of self-loathing had triggered some sort of panic attack, though Alerio had no idea what had brought either of them on.

Oh, fuck. Ivar. Of course.

This was probably the first time she'd made love to anyone since the romance with the traitor ended six months ago—when Ivar had beaten her half to death.

Instinct demanded he go after her, somehow pull her out of the emotional death spiral she'd obviously been caught in. And if he'd been nothing more than a Vardonese Warlord, Alerio would have obeyed that impulse.

Unfortunately, he was also her commanding officer.

Temporal Enforcement didn't forbid sexual liaisons between a superior and a subordinate—as a rule. However, the agency took a very dim view of sexual coercion. The regs were clear: a superior could not pursue a subordinate who had walked away.

Alerio's own sense of ethics agreed. He didn't want Dona to feel he was pushing her into a relationship she didn't want. Especially since he wanted everything she was willing to give him. *Her heart. Her soul . . .*

He needed to think this through.

Twenty minutes later, Alerio had showered and dressed in his dark blue duty uniform. The heels of his low boots clicked sharply on the deck as he stalked back to his quarters, his mood spectacularly foul.

"Hey, Chief!" A familiar gruff rumble made him break step and look around just as Frieka trotted up. The wolf gapped his jaws in his signature fang-filled grin. "Up for a drink?"

Alerio hesitated a beat before surrendering. "Why not?" Frieka made a good sounding board, wise old beast that he was. *And I need all the help with Dona I can get.*

CHAPTER FOUR

Knowing his audience, Alerio gave the wolf a grin. "I've got one last bottle of Vardonese ale stashed in my quarters."

Frieka's blue eyes lit until they damn near glowed. "Gods, I haven't had Vardonese ale since the last time the kid took leave."

"Where is Riane, anyway?" Alerio asked as they turned down the corridor and headed for his quarters. "You two are usually attached at the hip."

The wolf snorted in lupine disgust. "Where she always is every minute we're not on duty. In our quarters, mating with Wyatt."

Alerio almost choked on his tongue. "Ah."

"I can't sleep for all the yowling," the cyborg beast continued gloomily. "I need my own place, Chief. They're driving me buggier than a flea festival."

Somehow Alerio managed not to laugh. "I'm sure that won't be a problem."

The doors to his quarters slid open at their approach, and he paused to let the wolf enter first. "I think there's a couple of vacant rooms near the main lift. Make a formal request and I'll sign off on it."

The wolf sighed in relief as he trotted inside. "You may have just saved my sanity."

"Such as it is."

"Ha. Ha." Frieka watched with obvious impatience—and more than a hint of greed—as Alerio walked over to one of the gleaming black cabinets that lined his quarters. He reached into one and extracted a glass and a shallow bowl, then turned to gesture the wolf toward the leather love seat. Alerio collapsed into the grip of the matching well-upholstered couch. Both faced the room's single window; Alerio never tired of those glorious Outpost views. Today the Blue Ridge Mountains rolled in mist-shrouded violet waves to a brilliant blue horizon, the sun riding above it in cloudless splendor.

Leaning forward to brace his elbows on his knees, the chief sent a mental order to the long, low cocktail table that sat in front of the couches. A drawer slid open in the smooth, black lacquer surface, revealing a single bottle. As he lifted it out, sunlight danced over the expensive cut glass and shimmered in the golden depths of its contents.

"Ohhhh," Frieka breathed in admiration, catching sight of the bottle's label. "You buy the *good* stuff."

"No point in settling for less." As Alerio poured each of them a generous portion of the potent liquor, the wolf jumped up on the love seat. The short couch creaked and writhed as it sought to accommodate his lupine haunches. Finally arriving at a comfortable grip, the seat quieted.

Alerio slid the bowl down the length of the table. Frieka stuck out a paw to catch it, then leaned down to lap noisily.

Smiling at his guest's enthusiasm, the chief took a warily careful sip from his own glass. Even a Warlord had to treat Vardonese ale with respect.

The liquor tasted sweet and fruity for about a tenth of a second before it detonated like ancient napalm and seared its way down his throat. Tense muscles promptly began to relax in the ale's heat. Alerio sank into the couch's grip and sighed in appreciation.

"So." Frieka glanced up from his bowl. "You and Dona finally mated. Took you long enough."

Alerio, in the midst of a second sip, damn near spewed ale across the table. "By the Goddess's sweet tits, Frieka! Did anybody *ever* teach you tact?"

"They tried." The wolf flicked a disdainful ear. "Didn't take."

"You might have tried."

"Why? So I could tell pretty lies like you humans? You'd be better off hearing the truth." Frieka grunted in ripe disgust. "Humans. You'd rather pretend you don't smell the Soji shit instead of grabbing a shovel and taking care of the problem. Annoys the hell out of me."

Alerio considered the point before risking another sip. "Okay, you may be right."

"Of course I'm right." With a regal sniff, the cyborg returned his attention to his bowl.

"How did you know? About Dona and me."

Frieka rolled blue eyes up at him. "Same way I know the kid is banging Wyatt like a kettledrum. There's this smell . . ."

Alerio threw up a warding hand. "Enough. I don't want to know any more."

"So don't ask, Warlord."

"Oh, I won't. Ever again. And if I ever forget, I'm sure the psychic scars will remind me."

Silence fell, broken only by the sound of Frieka's enthusiastic tongue sucking up ale. Until there was enough of the liquor in Alerio's bloodstream to let him voice a few uncomfortable truths. "I've wanted Dona for the past two years. Damned if I know why. Yeah, she is lovely . . ."

"Genetically engineered," Frieka pointed out. "Those girls don't come in 'ugly.' "

"Well, no." Alerio swallowed another mouthful of fire and meditated on its potent blaze. "But it's not her looks. There's something about Dona that . . . Well, it fits me. And the longer I know her, the more convinced I am that's true." Cradling the glass between his palms, he began to roll it back and forth, staring down into the shining amber liquid. "My sensors tell me she feels the same attraction . . ."

The wolf snorted. "No shit. Chief, I don't know if you've noticed, but there's this pheromone fog bank that surrounds you two whenever you're together."

Ignoring the wolf's habitual sarcasm, Alerio continued, "But the thing is, she's never said anything about how she feels . . ."

"Like, oh, 'Fuck me hard, big boy'?"

Alerio snorted in lieu of a laugh. "Smart-ass."

"See, this is exactly what I was talking about." Frieka tilted his muzzle to the left. "Here we have a big pile of Soji shit." He turned his head right. "Here we have a shovel. The problem's so simple, a cat could solve it. First you kick Ivar's cyborg ass, then you tell the girl how you feel. *Voila*: your basic happily ever after. All you need now is a fairy godmother and a magic glass dildo."

Alerio's swallow of ale slid down his windpipe. Once he stopped coughing, he wheezed, "Glass *slipper*, not glass dildo."

"You've got your version, I've got mine."

The chief swallowed and blinked the tears out of his eyes. "And I *definitely* do not want to know your version."

"Pussy."

"Seriously, about Dona . . ."

"I thought we *were* being serious."

"I'm her superior officer. If I make a move before she does, it's an abuse of my rank."

"And she's your *subordinate*," Frieka retorted, the humor disappearing from his eyes. "What, you want her to suggest an affair to somebody who outranks her by as much as you do? What if you said no? Never mind that we both know you wouldn't—*Dona* doesn't know that. But she does know that if your romance goes sideways, she's just blown her career out the air lock."

The chief stared down at him, struck by the insight. "You know, you understand the finer points of human relationships a hell of a lot better than you pretend to."

"I hate to break this to you, but it's not exactly astronavigation." Frieka dipped his head for a few more laps, his vocalizer flashing as he drank. "You people like to think you're soooo complicated, but take away the tech, and you're just bare-assed apes."

"It truly pains me to say this, but you've got a point."

"A whole mouthful of them. See?" Frieka raised his muzzle to display the teeth in question. "The difference between us is that I know I'm an animal. Your problem is those opposable thumbs give you delusions of grandeur. Speaking of which, use 'em on that bottle, would you? My bowl is distressingly dry."

"That's all I need—a hundred kilos of drunken timber wolf." But Alerio refilled Frieka's bowl anyway before topping off his own glass. Settling back into the couch's heated grip, he took a deep swallow, barely feeling the burn anymore. *Which is probably a bad sign.* "Then there's Ivar. Tits of the Goddess, I'd like to take a blade to that bastard. Or my fists. Or hell, my boot." He gestured with his glass, ignoring the ale that sloshed over the rim. "Right up his ass."

"Yeah, I've been waiting for you to tube that botfucker. Baran would have slit Ivar's throat years ago for some of the shit he's pulled on Dona." Riane's father, Baran Arvid, had been Frieka's first partner. The Warlord was something of a legend in Temporal Enforcement; he'd been the first to figure out you couldn't change history.

Alerio nodded boozily. "I knew there was a reason I liked Baran."

"Well, he's a likable guy when he's not gutting people that piss him off." The wolf added earnestly, "Mostly just the assholes. It's a public service, really."

"I've always thought so." Alerio picked up the ale bottle before reluctantly setting it aside again. "I have wondered if my jealousy made Ivar seem worse than he was."

"Nope, he was pretty damn fucking bad," Frieka opined. "And then he got worse. I do *not* understand why Dona didn't slam his 'borg ass right through the nearest bulkhead. It was almost as if she believed whatever Ivar told her."

Alerio nodded, ignoring the way the room spun. "I had the same impression."

"He'd say the most vicious shit in this really concerned voice, like honey poured over rotten meat." Frieka growled softly, ears flattening. "I was tempted to bite the fucker, oh, half a dozen times, but Riane said you'd throw me in the brig for attacking another agent."

"She was probably right. Though I'd have secretly cheered while you chewed." A new question occurred to him. "Frieka?"

"Yeah?"

"Why would the Xerans allow a human traitor to wear the horns of a priest? Especially considering how seriously they take that lunatic religion of theirs."

"Do I look like the source of all fuzzy wisdom?"

"I'm serious."

"And *drunk*."

"True, but beside the point. Look, when Terje first defected, I assumed they'd pay him a pittance and send him off into one of their flesh slums to drug himself to death. Instead they've got him leading missions. How the hell did *that* happen?"

"A complete lack of common sense and simple primate decency?"

"We're talking Xerans, so yeah, that's a given." Alerio frowned as his instincts clamored at him through the ale haze. "But something tells me we'd better figure out just what the hell Ivar Terje has on the Victor."

You idiot bastard, Ivar thought viciously. *You and your stupid ideas. "I'm bored—I'll become a Xeran spy." And look where I ended up: the puppet of a psychopath with delusions of godhood.*

He floated in a mental fog that numbed his every sensation and left him as helpless as an infant. If he concentrated, Ivar could see out of his hijacked eyes, hear what the Victor heard, detect the thoughts running through his own stolen brain.

But he couldn't do a damn thing about any of it.

The Victor had seized Ivar's cyborg body in the aftermath of his battle with Nick Wyatt. Six months later, he still showed no sign of releasing control. The fucker was convinced his own priests were plotting against him.

And though the Victor was unquestionably paranoid and borderline batshit, he was also absolutely right. His priests *had* turned against him. The rebels meant to destroy him and seize control of the Xeran theocracy.

It was all Nick Wyatt's fault. *He* was the one who had exposed the Victor's lethal weakness and blown him into ooze. Though the half-breed hadn't quite succeeded in finishing the Victor off, Wyatt *had* destroyed Ivar, who was, for once, nothing more than an innocent bystander.

Bastard, Ivar thought, not even sure if the thought was his own or the Victor's. *I'm going to kill that half-breed abomination if it's the last thing I do.*

Actually, that particular thought sounded more like the Victor's than his own. It was sometimes hard to tell his mind from that of his hijacker/rapist.

Another thing he could thank Wyatt for.

A memory emerged from the mental fog: Wyatt, half-breed guardian of the alien Sela, his human body wrapped in the glowing energy form of one of their ancient warriors. The creature had looked something like one of the Earth's extinct tigers—if the tiger in question was the size of a grizzly, with six powerful legs tipped in claws like daggers.

Wyatt had used that deadly Sela construct to rip into the Victor like a grizzly with a honeycomb. Despite the Xeran god's nine-foot golden body and massive two-handed sword, Wyatt had beaten him right into the ground. Then he'd blasted the Victor into a black, oily rain. Too bad it hadn't stuck.

Turns out the Victor's original cyborg body had been dead for more than a century. All that remained were the microscopic nano-bots that had once enhanced his strength and intelligence.

His priests had frantically raced around, trying to collect the Victor's scattered nanobots. Some of the ooze had crept up armored legs, silently pleading for rescue and protection. Gods, the memory of those frantic moments scalded his pride. Wyatt needed to die for that humiliation alone.

Even as they struggled to collect the Victor's components, his priests had been horrified to realize the truth about their golden god: he was nothing more than a bot colony that hadn't been human in a century.

True, the nanobots retained the memories of the original cyborg warrior who'd once declared himself the god of the Xer. Yet the colony itself was neither god nor man. In fact, it had no real idea *what* it was.

By sheer bad luck, a particularly large glob of the nanobot ooze had found Ivar and promptly crawled up his boot, slimy and deter-mined. It was like being attacked by an enormous hunk of sentient snot.

He'd been revolted, of course. After all, Ivar was no priest. Besides, the thing reminded him entirely too much of a *nilik*.

Back on his home world, that particular predator had the habit of disguising itself as a puddle across some well-trafficked forest path. Whenever an unsuspecting victim fell into the *nilik*, he'd be horrified to discover the "puddle" was actually five meters deep—and it had started digesting him alive. It usually took the poor fucker an hour to stop screaming. A day later, there'd be nothing left but bones.

Which was exactly what happened to Ivar.

The Victor's bots had quickly seeped through his skin and into his bloodstream, then climbed his brain stem until they'd found the nanobot filaments which led to his neurocomp. Since the Xerans had already installed a series of nanotech upgrades to his various systems, the comp had no way to keep them out. And once the bots controlled the neurocomp, they controlled Ivar. Within hours, he found himself nothing more than a puppet.

No. A slave.

Wearing Ivar like a cheap suit, the Victor had ordered his priests to surrender whatever bits of ooze they'd collected. He'd then absorbed it all, regaining his power and memories with every drop he reclaimed.

Using Ivar's body and brain as templates, the colony could rebuild the Victor with greater solidity than he'd had in decades; he'd been growing more and more unstable since the death of his human host.

But just when the Victor thought he had everything under control, a group of renegade priests refused to surrender the nanobots they'd collected. The rebels coolly informed their incredulous leader that they were tired of licking the boots of some bot with delusions of godhood. And who could blame them?

Well, the Victor, for one.

The god had used Ivar's stolen body to lead his loyal priests in battle against the rebels. The resulting religious war had claimed thousands of lives and left the Xeran home world in blasted ruins, all in the space of six months. Only the Victor's iron control over the planet's media had kept the Galactic Union from finding out what was going on.

In the end, the god colony managed to recover the last of its missing nanobots. It then ordered the execution of the captured rebel priests. Once they were all safely dead, the colony warily left the shelter of Ivar's hijacked body and reformed into the familiar towering persona of the Victor.

Even so, the nanobots refused to release their grip on Ivar, maintaining tight control of their battleborg slave. Just in case.

Though Ivar hated the Victor's guts with a spitting hysterical fury, he knew he'd have done the same thing. No matter how the surviving priests sought to demonstrate their extravagant submission—wrapping their genitals in spiked silver wire was one popular gesture—the Victor knew the truth.

The seeds of rebellion still lurked in his priests' traitorous hearts.

He needed to make some really spectacular gesture that would scare the fuck out of everybody. Something even bigger than the bonfire of burning priests he'd lit in the capital square.

Something like, say, executing Nick Wyatt and exterminating every last one of the alien Sela like the abominations they were. Gods, how the little creatures revolted him. There was something intensely disturbing about their huge, glistening eyes, six furry limbs, and pacifistic ways.

Creepy fucks.

Then he'd kill every Temporal Enforcer who'd ever stymied his plans, beginning with Galar Arvid and his Sela-infected abomination of a wife. Next he'd do Riane and her flea-bitten, unnatural wolf. Of course, by then the little bitch would probably find her execution a relief, what with Wyatt so spectacularly dead.

He'd save Alerio Dyami and his whore, Dona, for the bloody climax, when they'd suffer his most viciously inspired butchery. Something medieval perhaps. Like the executions ancient human kings once used to send a message to their rebellious subjects.

Perhaps drawing and quartering. Ivar had seen a human killed

like that during a mission once; he'd been fascinated by the shrieking agony of the victim, not to mention the truly impressive blood
splatter.

So he'd start by disemboweling Alerio the same way. Slowly,
while Dona watched. He'd do it in the Crystal Arena with the
capital's entire population in the stands and Xer's trid services
broadcasting the whole thing to the rest of the planet.

After he'd personally gutted the Warlord, he'd cable Dyami's
arms and legs to a quartet of combat skimmers, which he'd send
jetting in four different directions. The chief would be ripped into
four bloody chunks while his whore shrieked and the people
cheered.

As for Dona, Ivar would order her raped to death by his priests.

He was God, dammit. He'd kill any motherfucker who thought
otherwise. He . . .

No, wait. That was the Victor. *He* was Ivar Terje. Who was . . .
Nobody. Not anymore.

But somehow, some way, I'm going to change that, Ivar thought
in the one hidden nook of his brain he could call his own. *I'll get
back in the driver's seat, and everybody who ever fucked with me
will pay in blood. Wyatt, Riane, Frieka, Dona, Dyami . . .*

And the Victor.

Especially the Victor.

Dona was still cursing herself the next morning when her comp
told her Alerio had called an assembly in the Main Briefing Hall.

He'd probably come up with a battle plan for dealing with Ivar
and his threats. Knowing Alerio, he'd been up all night working
on it, considering all the tactical angles and running computer
simulations to check his conclusions. The chief was the most thorough commander she'd ever had, being both a brilliant investigator and a damn fine tactician.

What's more, he was genuinely concerned for the people under his command. If you had a problem, odds were good Alerio would show up at your quarters with a bottle of Vardonese ale. Before you knew what hit you, you'd be spilling your guts.

In retrospect, it was surprising the chief had kept his nose out of the situation between her and Ivar as long as he had. Gods knew they'd had some pretty spectacular fights, even before Ivar had tried to kill her.

More than once in the aftermath of those brawls, she'd found Alerio watching her, his gaze steady, questioning. Silently telling her he was there if she needed to talk. Or do something really stupid, like file a complaint.

Yeah, *that* would have gone over well. Kind of like taking a tachyon beamer on a temporal Jump. By the time Ivar got through expressing his opinion, the resulting crater would have been visible from space.

Seven hells, she'd been a fool. But after what happened with Colonel Kavel, Dona had been determined she'd never have an affair with another commanding officer.

Unfortunately, Alerio Dyami was a hell of a lot more tempting than any commander she'd ever had. Including the colonel.

Especially the colonel.

So instead she'd focused her passions on Ivar Terje . . . and what a clusterfuck that had turned out to be. Her taste in men sucked liked an air lock venting into space.

Dona found Main Briefing packed with Enforcers. Every chair in the cavernous room was occupied, wide rows of them sloping down to Alerio's massive black podium. The elegant obsidian stand stood center stage on a platform that ran the width of the room.

Above that was an enormous trid screen that displayed the blue and silver Temporal Enforcement shield. The ancient scales of Mother Justice hung superimposed over an hourglass that in turn floated above the Galactic Union's star field.

A sharp bark drew her attention, ringing over the murmur produced by a thousand chatting time cops. Frieka stood on his hind legs in one of the seats, forepaws braced on its back. The chair next to him was empty; he and Riane had held it for her.

Oh, hell, she thought. *They'll want all the details, and I'd rather eat my shard pistol.*

Too bad she couldn't run. *Fuckit. Might as well get it over with.* With a mental sigh of resignation, Dona strode down the stairs to drop into the seat next to Frieka. It squirmed around her until it cradled her backside comfortably. "Thanks," Dona told her friends. "I was afraid I'd have to stand all the way through the briefing."

Riane frowned, assessing her face with that habitual Vardonese attention to detail. *Probably analyzing the bags under my eyes and the accompanying ghostly pallor.* Dona hadn't slept worth a damn the night before; she'd been far too busy mentally flogging herself for stupidity above and beyond the call of duty.

"You look like hell," Riane told her bluntly. "Dammit, when are you going to get it through your thick head—you are not responsible for the actions of your psychotic ex!"

That was the trouble with cyborg friends. Dona was a talented liar, but she'd never been able to fool Riane's sensors. "It's not that."

"Then what is it?" The redhead glowered. "I swear everybody's gone nuts! First Frieka staggers in at too-fucking-early after getting plowed with the chief—" She broke off, eyes widening.

Dona silently cursed, watching her too-clever friend put the facts together. The same instincts that made Riane an excellent investigator also made her a real pain in the ass to any friend with a secret. "Oh sweet Goddess!" She turned the heat of her glare on her furry partner, whose ears flattened defensively against his skull. "And you didn't *tell* me?"

"Kid, I realize this is hard for you to grasp, but the chief's love life is not your business."

"It is when he's boning my best friend!"

"And if she wanted you to know, she'd tell you."

Riane switched the glare to Dona, who managed not to cower. She relaxed fractionally when the Warfem's glare dissolved into a salacious grin. "I've got to say, your taste in men has definitely improved. So how was he? I want details!"

"Can we not do this in front of every Enforcer at the Outpost?" Dona hissed, feeling her cheeks blaze.

"What, you think they aren't going to figure it out on their own? You work with *detectives*, you twit. Cyborg cops with sensor implants. The half-life of an Outpost secret is about fifteen seconds." Riane grimaced, obviously thinking the same thing Dona was. "Well, except for Ivar."

Luckily Dyami picked that moment to stride to the podium.

"There's the chief. Briefing's starting," Dona whispered. *Thank the gods.*

"Don't think this means you won't have to spill," Riane hissed. "You and I are going to have a long talk. With details. Lots and lots of details. With illustrations. And . . ."

"*Hand puppets*," Frieka put in, and snickered.

"Okay, fine," Dona grumbled. Maybe her friends could help her find a little desperately needed perspective. They always had before, even when Ivar had been doing his best to break her like a Soji egg. Come to think of it, they'd urged her to dump him; both agents had hated his cyborg guts long before he'd been unmasked as a traitor.

And I should have listened to them.

"We," Alerio announced, jolting her back to the present, "have a problem."

As Alerio played his neurocomp's recording of Ivar's gloating threats, the gathered Enforcers listened in complete silence. Dona could almost taste their collective rage. It seemed to fill the huge room, a fog of raw fury.

She couldn't help but cringe when their eyes locked on her during Alerio's vivid description of Ivar's attack.

"Fucker," Frieka growled. The word seemed to hang in the air, silently echoed by every agent in the room.

"Yeah, that's a pretty damned good description of Ivar Terje," Alerio agreed dryly. "Obviously, we're not going to hand anyone over to the Xerans' dubious concept of justice." His eyes narrowed, and a muscle flexed in his jaw. "But we're also not going to allow Terje and his band of psycho priests to murder any more tourists. Even if we have to kill every last one of the hornheaded bastards."

CHAPTER FIVE

Cold determination filled Alerio's dark eyes as he scanned Main Briefing and its rows of Enforcers. "As of now, we're all on bodyguard duty. I have assigned everyone to teams of three at a minimum to ensure you can counter any Xeran terrorist squads.

"If any of you *do* encounter Xerans, you are to immediately courier the Outpost for backup. Obviously, you should report the number of attackers so we can respond in sufficient numbers to neutralize the threat. A trid of the attacking force would be useful. Are there any questions?"

Wulf put up a meaty paw. Genetically engineered for life on a planet with three times Earth's gravity, the agent was built like a human tank. Yet, big as he was, Wulf was also a damned good criminal investigator, with an instinct for solving temporal crimes that was almost psychic. "What about our current caseload? I'm still working on that da Vinci theft . . ."

Frowning, Alerio leaned an elbow on the podium. The motion made his biceps bunch. Dona stared in hypnotized longing before jerking her eyes away.

". . . we're all going to have to back-burner other investigations until Terje and his priests have been apprehended, along with any assassins the Xerans may hire," Alerio was saying. "The safety of temporal travelers has to take precedence over solving crimes that have already occurred."

Wulf sat back in his seat, but the big man did not look happy. From what Dona had heard him say over beers in the Outpost Mess, he was tantalizingly close to apprehending the thief responsible for the disappearance of thirty-eight legendary paintings. Leonardo da Vinci's *Leda* was the most priceless of the lot; it had vanished sometime during the eighteenth century under mysterious circumstances. Wulf thought that was the work of a time-jumping thief, and he was probably right.

"You'll get him anyway, Wulf," Alerio told him. "Even if it takes a little longer, you'll track the bastard down."

Wulf's cheeks went pink at the chief's praise. In a man the approximate size of an interstellar frigate, the effect was oddly charming.

"I've also managed to arrange the temporary transfer of a few more Enforcers from the European office," Alerio went on. "These are cyborg agents specializing in historical undercover work. I think they'll prove effective as we counter whatever nasty little tricks the Xerans try." The chief bared his teeth in an expression more snarl than smile. "I intend to give Terje a surprise he won't forget."

The Enforcers rumbled agreement. There was something so feral in those growling voices, even Dona felt a chill. *Seven hells, they're pissed. But then, so am I.*

"I've sent your assignments to your respective comps," the chief continued, "along with details of where you'll be going and who you'll be guarding. I'll expect reports on how you intend to cover your protectees by Gamma shift. Include any logistical problems you anticipate so we can address them before you jump. Any questions?"

He nodded at someone behind Dona.

"What are we telling the tourists about this?" the agent asked.

"Not a damned thing," Alerio said. "And no, I don't like it either, but Headquarters is concerned about triggering a media shit storm we don't need. We've been lucky so far. If the journos had gotten wind of the Hardin Tours massacre, we'd be ass-deep in trid bots right about now. That's a headache we do not need. It's going to be hard enough keeping all those tourists alive without tripping over journos every time we turn around. Not to mention that Terje would just love to kidnap some well-known head-talker he could torture on vid."

Dona frowned. She understood the chief's point—even agreed with it—but this situation felt like a sonic grenade. It could easily explode in all their faces . . . And if it did, it would take their careers along for the nasty ride.

She didn't want to go through that again. She'd barely survived the last time.

I have received a com from Chief Dyami with your orders, her neurocomp announced.

Yeah, she'd been wondering where that was. *Display.*

Instead of the usual dossier file, a trid image of Alerio appeared in her mind stage. "Enforcer Astryr, you will be assisting me and a nonstandard agent in guarding Geneva Kamil and her tour guide as they attend a ball in nineteenth-century South Carolina." Alerio's tone was matter-of-fact, but there was a note of steel in his voice that suggested dissent would not be welcome. "Both computer simulations and my gut indicate this party is a high probability target."

Well, yeah. Geneva Kamil was a trid star with both money and influence. Which explains how she'd acquired visas for such a small party; tour groups usually numbered at least ten, all of whom paid handsomely to visit whatever time period they intended to tour.

A quick mental calculation told her Geneva would probably

pay half a million galactors for this trip, between visa fees, hiring a tour guide, and the charge for tube travel there and back.

Dona frowned. Guarding the woman was going to be a hazardous pain in the ass. Alerio was right; Ivar would cream his armor at the thought of capturing the actress. Murdering her would make him famous. Or rather, infamous.

So yeah, Dona could understand why Alerio would want to personally provide the star with protection. Callous as it sounded, Geneva would make the perfect bait. Ivar wouldn't be able to resist.

The only thing Dona didn't understand was why Alerio wanted *her* as his partner. The emotional situation between them could easily become an ugly distraction when they could least afford it. "What the hell is he doing?"

Riane blinked in surprise at her growl. "What is who doing?"

"The chief. He wants me to partner with him to protect Geneva Kamil."

"Geneva?" Frieka's vivid eyes widened. "I love her. She kicked ass in *Time Slip*."

"Oh, come on—that ridiculous piece of crap?" Riane scoffed. "She fought off four Tevan warriors in that trid. Count 'em. Four! There is no way in hell a light battleborg like the character she played could have done that. Hell, one Tevan damned near cleaned my clock, and I'm a Warfem!"

"Yeah, yeah, but it was still a great scene." Frieka displayed every one of his many teeth in an appreciative canine grin. "Remember when she kicked that Tevan in the 'nads?"

"And you cheered like a fourteen-year-old girl." Riane rolled her eyes. "Goddess, I was so embarrassed!"

"Oh, like you weren't rooting for her, too." The wolf sniffed of disdain. "I heard that sob when she sacrificed herself for the ship."

"I did not sob," the Warfem objected. "I don't cry at trids."

"Yeah, right." He turned to Dona. "You should have heard the kid during the climax. She cried so hard she soaked my fur. Damned near caught a cold."

"Hey," Riane protested, "the wolf sidekick reminded me of you. Of course I cried."

Dona grinned, absently enjoying the pair's bickering. But no matter how welcome the distraction, it still didn't address her current problem. Her gut insisted partnering with Alerio on this job was a really bad idea. And over the years, Dona had learned her gut was usually dead-on.

The trouble was, Dyami was her commanding officer. He could order her to do any damn thing he thought necessary to accomplish their mission: protecting innocent people from temporal criminals. Which meant she couldn't refuse the assignment, not if she intended to remain an Enforcer.

And she did, because Dona loved her job. True, she'd become an Enforcer in the first place because she'd had no choice, but she'd soon discovered just how much she loved being a time cop. She loved analyzing temporal crimes, finding patterns even the Outpost computer missed, gathering evidence to prove she was right, and capturing the perpetrators before they could steal another priceless work of art or rape another temporal tourist.

You couldn't change history, but sometimes, history was a lot less cut-and-dried than it seemed. You could never really be sure which crimes were fated, and which you could solve because you were *supposed* to solve them. Over the years, she'd learned that uncertainty only added to the spice. Besides, there was nothing quite as sweet as preventing some abusive bastard from preying on innocent civilians.

Solving temporal crime had given Dona a purpose when she'd thought she had no reason to live. *That* was why she wouldn't say one damned word to Alerio.

The meeting finally broke up. Enforcers flowed into the aisles, discussing their new assignments as they headed for the room's four double doors. As more agents filed past, Frieka braced his paws on the arm of Dona's seat. "Want to head to the Concourse with us? I've got a yen for a big plate of *chiva*."

Like Frieka, Dona loved the meat strips swimming in tangy *chiva* sauce. She was opening her mouth to accept the invitation when a familiar voice spoke up from behind her.

"Perhaps later," Alerio said. "Dona and I need to plan our next mission."

She turned to meet the Warlord's calm black gaze, and just resisted the need to snarl. "Aye, sir." Dona stifled the urge to give him a sarcastic salute. Enforcers didn't salute; he'd know it was a substitution for a gesture far more vulgar.

With an effort, Dona wiped any trace of anger from her face. Fortunately she'd had plenty of practice. Neither the colonel nor Ivar had appreciated any demonstration of how she felt about the way they treated her.

Why are you so surprised? that nasty reptilian whisper hissed from the darkness in her skull. *Did you really expect him to respect what you wanted? You're his subordinate, idiot. You're nothing to him.* True, Alerio had been an attentive and sensitive lover compared to the others. The most sensitive she'd ever had, in fact. *Maybe bedroom performance is a bigger indicator of character than I thought...*

You truly are a fool, aren't you?

She blinked, suddenly recognizing that papery whisper. It sounded a lot like the colonel...

And Alerio is watching me. His big body stood utterly still, his cool gaze locked on her in a way that sent a chill up her spine. It reminded her far too much of her first commanding officer. The colonel in a frigid rage didn't even need a shockcane; the man could leave frostbitten welts with every word. She hadn't thought the chief had that in him. *Oh, this isn't good.*

"We need to discuss the case in more detail—in my office,"
Alerio told her coolly.

She nodded, this time making sure her expression was utterly
empty of anger. "Yes, sir."

Definitely not good.

Alerio's office was just down the hall from Main Briefing, occupying a prime position on the Admin Deck. Surprisingly spacious,
it was dominated by one of those Outpost windows that ran the
entire length of the room. The view it offered was nothing short
of breathtaking: mountains kissing the horizon clad in vivid spring
splendor. Elms and maples, oaks and cottonwoods, their leaves
incandescent with countless shades of green. Above them hung a
sky so blue, it made her eyes ache. A pair of black couches stood
before the window, angled to make the best of the view.

Alerio's desk offered a stark contrast to that extravagantly sensual window. A curving shape in reflective black polycarbonate,
the desk looked as if it belonged on a warstar's bridge. Alerio could
control every system on the Outpost from that desk. The chair
behind it seemed to grow directly from the floor, thickly uphol-
stered in some kind of gleaming black material. A pair of smaller,
far less comfortable-looking chairs crouched before the desk as
though waiting for any hapless Enforcers who'd earned the chief's
wrath.

Alerio ignored the desk, instead waving her toward the pair
of couches. "Unlock that stiff spine and sit down, Enforcer," he
told her in a dry tone, dropping into one of them himself. "Permission to speak freely granted."

She lifted a brow and sat down cautiously. "I wasn't aware I
asked for it."

"Oh, you did. Just not out loud." He raised a black brow. "Go on. Tell me exactly what you think before you explode from the sheer pressure of your disapproval."

This, perversely, made her determined not to say one word. "It is not my place to tell my commanding officer my opinion of my assignments." *Damn, I sound like I have a stick up my ass.*

"No," he agreed, without cracking a smile. "But tell me anyway."

There were any number of things she could say—if she were stupid enough. Which she wasn't. Colonel Kavel had taught her the perils of taking a commander at his word.

＊

Well, you fucked this one up, Dyami, Alerio thought in disgust as he watched Dona's pointedly expressionless face. *Now you're going to have to fix it.*

When she remained stubbornly silent, he sighed. "Fine, then I'll start. As you're aware, we are painfully shorthanded when it comes to protecting all the scheduled tour groups in numbers sufficient to fend off a Xeran assassination squad."

He paused, but she only looked at him with polite interest. Containing his growing impatience, Alerio continued, "I don't normally participate in fieldwork, of course, but the only way we can cover the schedule is with the addition of a new team. And since you no longer have a partner, this logically leaves the two of us working together. Unless you want me to break up an existing partnership . . ." Some of those Enforcers had been working together for years.

His sensors told him her temper promptly began to cool. *That's right, Dona. I didn't pair us just to force you into something you don't want.*

"That's not necessary," she said.

"I didn't think it was. But I'm aware you may find the situation uncomfortable, considering what happened the other night."

Dona sighed. "If we avoid a repetition of that . . . incident, it won't be a problem."

"Making love to me was an 'incident' to you?" *Yeah, that's helpful,* he snarled to himself. *You sound like a spurned lover.* Which was basically what he was. Wrestling his temper back under control, he made a negating gesture. "Forgive me. That was not appropriate."

"There's nothing to forgive. This is a trying situation." Despite her gracious words, Dona's frigid expression didn't warm.

Which was a bit like tossing a flamer into a tank of thruster fuel. It was all Alerio could do to contain his fury as he bit out, "Thank you for your understanding." *Damned if I'll touch you again. Even if you beg. Warlords do not crawl.*

Not even a violet-eyed cop who made him ache to stroke and taste and kiss. A woman whose smile flashed as bright as her intelligence . . .

And whose courage was going to get her killed if he wasn't damned careful.

"Is it true what I've heard about Vardonese Warlords?" Geneva Kamil's lids dipped over the golden eyes her fans adored. "That you're all very . . . *aggressive* lovers?"

Dona's hands curled into fists in her kidskin gloves, though she kept her face expressionless. The closed carriage they rode in jolted over a bump hard enough to click her back teeth together. She damned near bit her tongue.

"Don't believe everything you hear," Alerio told the actress, flashing even white teeth in his best charm-the-asshole smile. "People are prone to exaggeration."

Dona couldn't help but notice that was not precisely a denial. She tried not to be intrigued.

"Pity." Geneva's gaze ran down his body with unblushing hunger. "I do like an aggressive man. Particularly one so very . . . large."

To be fair, Dona couldn't really blame the actress for her carnivorous interest. Alerio in Victorian evening wear was nothing short of mouthwatering. Of course, his facial tattoo would have been a problem, but Chogan had injected his skin with a drug that made the ink temporarily vanish.

He'd also removed the beaded Vardonese combat decorations from his long hair, which he'd then braided and bound flat to his skull. A dark wig in the short style worn by men of the period finished off the disguise.

"I did this all the time when I was a field agent," he'd told her back at the Outpost, apparently in response to her fascinated gaze. "I could have had my comp project an imagizer disguise, of course, but if some temporal accidently touched my long hair . . ."

"We'd have a problem, because trids don't fool the sense of touch."

Which explained why they both wore the clothing of the period; a T-suit did not feel anything like nineteenth-century evening wear. As much as Dona secretly loved how Alerio looked in temporal armor, he made a luscious Victorian. The fit of his tight black trousers drew the eye to his long, impressively muscular legs, and his well-tailored jacket made his shoulders appear impossibly broad while simultaneously emphasizing his narrow waist. Yet he looked as comfortable as if he really were a Victorian aristocrat.

Far more at home than Dona in her gold ball gown, with its hoop skirt and layer upon layer of horsehair-padded petticoats. Adding insult to injury, the dress's dainty cap sleeves revealed arms far too muscular for a woman of the period; most plantation debutantes never did anything more strenuous than embroidery.

Dona was a bit happier with her hair. She'd gathered it at her nape in an intricate arrangement of braided coils and a few deliberately disheveled curls. Best of all, it was secured by clusters of needle-thin quantum stilettos that would hopefully be mistaken for combs.

Armed or not, she had no idea how to fight in all this fabric. Not to mention the corset beneath the gown, with its tight lacing and the whalebone stays that made mere breathing an effort. She had no idea how the women of this time tolerated such torture devices. Or more to the point, *why* they tolerated them.

Goddess help me if I have to fight, she thought gloomily. All these skirts would probably wrap around her legs and dump her on her face the first time she attempted a kick. Seven hells, she wasn't all that sure how to get her hoops through a doorway.

Geneva, by contrast, looked every inch the Victorian debutante as she perched demurely on the carriage's red velvet squabs, surrounded by a cloud of sapphire blue silk. Her pale skin seemed to glow in the soft light of the oil lantern, while her hair blazed in every shade of red from warm copper to shimmering flame. Once they reached the ball, the imagizer in her pearl necklace would dull the metallic gleam of her irises to a more human amber. Not that the change would blunt her incredible beauty.

Geneva's tour guide sat beside her, swaying gracefully with the carriage's bumpy progress. Julia Reginald wore an elaborate smoke-gray evening gown tiered in black lace. Jet earbobs swung at her ears, while a matching jet necklace looped around her neck and draped over her impressive breasts.

Dona wondered how the guide had secured invitations for all of them to the ball Mr. and Mrs. Kevin Northram were hosting at their rice plantation. According to her dossier, Reginald had an impressive network of plantation social connections she could call on whenever she needed to indulge some rich client's fantasy. In this case, Geneva Kamil wanted to experience the life of a plantation deb, right down to the carriage ride.

"This should be a pretty boring trip," the guide had told them before the Jump. She seemed a little puzzled at Alerie's insistence about providing them with an escort. "Especially con pared to my usual jobs."

Well, yeah. According to her dossier, Julia's main business was conducting tours of Civil War battlefields—*during* the battles. True, the groups were sheltered by a camo shield that rendered them invisible while they watched what had actually happened, but that didn't make the tours precisely safe. An invisible tourist was as vulnerable to a rifle bullet as anyone else.

Abruptly the guide stiffened. "Lose them!" Leaning forward, she fisted her hands in her skirts, twisting the fabric in agitation. "Whip the horses up and outrun the bastards!"

Must be using a com unit to talk to the carriage driver, Dona realized.

"You . . . might want to go easy on the whip," Alerio murmured. "The horses won't like it."

Geneva stared at the guide in dawning horror. "Outrun *who*?" When she got no answer from Julia—whose expression now verged on outright terror—the actress turned to Alerio. "Gods and devils!" she exploded. *"Who are we running from?"*

"Highwaymen," Dona told her absently as she scanned their pursuers. To the chief, she added, "I count twenty-four. Twenty with shard pistols, two with tritium rifles, two more with Winchesters. And what's with the gunpowder tech?"

Alerio shrugged. "Maybe they didn't have enough guns to go around." He frowned. "Scans make them as Xerans, none with horn implants."

"Not priests, then. Monks, maybe. No battleborgs, either, which evens the odds a little."

The chief snorted. "Considering we're going up against twenty-four of them, we need every advantage we can get."

"At least there's no sign of Ivar either."

"Actually, I'd feel better if he *was* here. Instead of say, getting ready to ambush us from behind a camo field."

Dona grimaced. "Good point."

Over the rumble of the wooden wheels, a whip snapped once, then again and again as the coachman roared curses at his laboring team. Their pounding hoofbeats drummed faster, as the animals ran with everything they had.

Bracing both hands against the vehicle's jouncing walls, Dona breathed deep, readying herself for the fight she knew was coming. The carriage rattled over ruts and rocks in the wake of the four-horse team. A particularly hard bounce clicked her back teeth together. She tasted blood and braced her feet, wedging herself deeper into a corner.

A hard jolt flung Geneva across the carriage. She choked off a scream as Alerio caught her with casual Warlord strength and stuffed her back into her seat. Julia absently steadied her wild-eyed client while listening to her coachman, who was evidently giving her a play-by-play.

A blast of fléchettes hissed overhead, punctuated by a male scream. Alerio swore as the carriage rocked wildly and the thunder of hooves began to slow.

"What was that?" Geneva demanded, one hand clamped over Julia's with a white-knuckled grip.

"Shard pistol," Dona told her, frowning as she scanned through the carriage's wooden walls. The tritium shards had sliced into the driver's torso, leaving him slumped and bleeding in his seat, the reins dropping from his lax hands to flap loose over the team's sweating backs.

"Jorge?" Julia snapped. "Jorge, dammit, answer! Jorge!" She turned to stare at Alerio. "They shot my coachman. I don't think he's conscious." One hand shot out to grab the chief's knee, nails digging in painfully. "You're supposed to protect us, Enforcer!" she spat. "*Do* something. Jorge's dying!"

"I will if I can." Alerio's eyes flicked back and forth as he swept sensor scans over the carriage's surroundings. "Unfortunately, I'm about to have my hands full keeping the rest of us from joining him."

"But he's been *shot*! Jorge could be dying while you sit on your . . ."

"Calm down," Dona snapped coldly, silencing the woman in mid-rant. "Look, once we're all safe, I can Jump him back to the Outpost. Our doctor can bring him back from the dead if she has to."

"How?" the guide demanded, her voice spiraling into a wail. "Our return Jump isn't scheduled until Monday! And if the coach is damaged . . ."

"It'll be fine, Julia." Dona flipped up her gold skirts to reveal the gleaming blue scales that covered her thighs to the knee. The abbreviated suit of temporal armor was designed to be worn under civilian clothes; the ball gown's layers of fabric provided the perfect camouflage. "It doesn't have sleeves or boots—and wearing it with this corset is a pain in the ass—but it'll get me and your man to the Outpost. Five minutes later, he'll be in regen."

The two women gaped at her T-suited legs. "How did you . . ." Geneva began.

"I suspected we'd run into trouble," Alerio explained. "We've got courier bots, of course, but I like to hedge my bets." A gesture indicated his trousers. "Unfortunately, this getup is a little too snug for armored underwear."

The guide laughed, the sound high-pitched with hysteria. "If I lose Jorge . . . I don't think I could stand it." A tear rolled down her cheek.

"I'll get him into regen, Julia. He'll be okay." Dona braced herself as the carriage jolted to a stop. Her sensors painted a vivid image of the four horses snorting and stamping, tossing their heads, tack jangling. One bay mare half-bucked, kicking out at the carriage as if panicked by the scent of the coachman's blood. The big white horse harnessed beside her snaked out his neck and nipped her hard on the shoulder. She squealed and shied away before subsiding, cowed by her teammate's teeth.

As the team heaved and blew, the highwaymen began to steal closer. One of them flipped down the hinged carriage steps . . .

Dyami surged from his seat, ducking his head to accommodate the carriage's low roof. One foot slammed into the coach door, kicking it open with a screech of rending wood. It crashed into the highwayman who already had one foot on the carriage steps, sending him tumbling with a startled yelp. As he hit the packed dirt of the road, the shard pistol flew from his hand to disappear into the thick brush.

Alerio leaped from the carriage, producing a derringer-sized shard pistol from his sleeve with a flick of his right hand. A quantum combat knife chimed in his left. In the same blurring, graceful move, he shot the first highwayman, kicked another in the face, and whirled to slit a third's throat.

As the chief charged his next target, Dona sprang from the coach, skirts wadded in one hand. Jerking one of the quantum stilettos from her coiled braids, she sent the thin knife flying. The weapon thunked into a fourth killer's barrel chest. Gasping, he clutched at the blade and collapsed. His shard pistol thumped to the dirt beside his dying hand.

A plump, graying man snarled at Dona as he brought his weapon up to aim it between her eyes. She spun aside like a bulldancer, avoiding the pistol's hissing tritium spray. As she whirled to face the gunman again, her forearm snapped out. A quantum dagger thudded home in the gunman's left eye. His mouth gaped in a silent scream as he toppled into the roadside weeds.

Dona's neurocomp filled her brain with a sensor image of a tall whippet of a man drawing a bead on the back of her head. She whirled, jerking her hoopskirt up to her thighs, and kicked upward in a merciless arc. Her heel crunched into the thin bones of his nose, driving the resulting splinters into his brain. Pain lanced up her calf, and she grimaced, silently cursing her too-thin dancing slippers. *That move is a hell of a lot easier in armored boots.*

Drawing another stiletto from her hair, she scanned the surrounding trees. Her eyes narrowed as her neurocomp pinpointed a man aiming a shard rifle at Alerio. She killed him before his finger could tighten on the trigger.

You may call yourself an Enforcer, but under that pretty armor you're still Kavel's Killer. Just another assassin with delusions of morality.

Shut up. She slid another blade from her tightly braided bun. The needle-thin length of tritium felt cool and familiar in her fingers before she sent it on its way with a snap of her wrist.

Out in the ring of trees, someone screamed. The cry drowned in a gurgle, but she was already tracking her next target. Thinking nothing at all, she killed one Xeran after another in a bubble of silence and peace.

Monster.

Shut. Up.

Alerio's reinforced fist crunched into bone, shattering the would-be kidnapper's skull. The Warlord had gone to *riaat* as he'd leaped from the coach, and now his blood burned with cold biochemical fire. As the berserker state amplified his strength by a factor of ten, it numbed his awareness of pain and exhaustion. He could fight until he dropped. His lips stretched in a wild wolf grin. He'd missed the feral pleasure of cutting loose, of giving no quarter and expecting none.

This mob of killers deserved anything he did to them.

Relentless as a machine, he ground through his foes with punches, kicks, and ripping thrusts of his combat knife. He'd lost count of the number he'd killed.

Need to leave one alive. I've got a few questions . . .

Dona raced by, and his eyes flicked to follow. Even deep in a berserker haze, he was acutely aware of her. Skirts bunched in one hand, she punched and kicked, flattening every Xeran in her way. Now and then she paused to reclaim one of her knives before plunging it into someone else.

There was no rage on her face, no bloodthirst or desire for revenge. Just calculation, blinding speed, and the flash of steel. He had to suppress the urge to grab her for a kiss whenever she went by.

A pistol roared once, twice, a third time, followed by three booming shots in rapid succession, the gunfire deafening at close quarters. Alerio jerked his head around to see Julia Reginald reloading a revolver, grim concentration on her face. She'd evidently decided to stop panicking and start fighting.

"That's enough!" an unfamiliar voice shouted.

Eyes narrowing, Alerio turned, his sensors locking on the last remaining Xeran. The one they'd have to leave alive.

"All you fuckers throw down your weapons and get the hell away from my men!" He had a thick Xeran accent, all slurred vowels and harsh glottal stops.

And he had a hostage.

CHAPTER SIX

The Xeran's fist was wrapped in Geneva's glorious hair as he jammed a shard pistol against the thin white flesh of her temple. Her golden eyes rolled in animal panic.

Dona and Alerio started easing toward the hostage-taker in tandem. One step. Two. Three. Slow and stealthy as a pair of wolves.

"Stay back!" the Xeran shouted, grinding the gun against her head. She cried out, cowering while simultaneously trying to pull away. He jerked her in close again, glaring at the two Enforcers as he backed toward the carriage. "Stay the fuck back!" His face twisted in the furious terror of a man who'd thought he'd had the situation in hand, only to see it sucked right out the air lock. *"We had you outnumbered, damn you!"*

"Not on your best day," Dona muttered.

The highwayman jerked Geneva by her hair past the horses, ignoring her yelps of pain. Tears rolled down her perfect cheeks, and her shoulders began to shake. She was terrified.

"He's trying to drag her into the carriage," Dona murmured to Alerio. "Must have spotted the enhancements."

"Yeah, well, I'm damned if I'll let him . . ."

Which was, of course, when the Xeran finally got a good look at the chief's face—and the hot *riaat* glow of his eyes. His eyes widened in horrified realization.

"Oh, shit." Dona tensed. "Alerio . . ."

"Fuck me!" the man howled in tones of outraged betrayal. "You're a goddamn Warlord! The botfucking priests didn't say nothing about no gods-cursed *Warlords!*" Jerking his pistol from Geneva's temple, he aimed at Alerio and started to squeeze the trigger.

The lead carriage horse kicked him right in the ass.

Howling in astonished agony, the Xeran fell on his face, both hands flying back to cradle his abused butt. The forgotten pistol fired as it fell, forcing Dona and Alerio to duck.

With a growl, Alerio pounced on the hapless kidnapper, smashing him into the dirt as he jerked a set of restraints from a pocket of his coat. Ignoring the man's writhing, he started tying the Xeran's wrists together with the thin magnetic cable.

Before Dona could join them, Julia shouted at her from the carriage box. "Enforcer, Jorge's bad! If you don't get him to the Outpost now . . ."

Dona veered toward the couple and began to run. "Alerio . . ."

"Go!" Alerio snapped.

Reaching the box, she bounded up beside Julia and bent to lift the injured coachman into her arms. He didn't stir.

"Save him," the guide begged. "Please." A tear meandered down her cheek.

"There's time, Julia. But you have to move back so I can Jump."

The woman jumped down from the box and backed away, watching them with desperate hope. Dona gave her a tight smile, gathered the injured man closer, and Jumped.

The temporal warp flared as bright as a star as the sonic boom made the carriage rock on its great wheels. The three mares jumped and bucked, whinnying in panic. The white horse that had bit the Xeran barely flicked an ear.

Alerio straightened from the hog-tied kidnapper to give the big animal a nod. "Good work, Enforcer Pendragon."

The stallion shook his mane in a jangle of harness. "Botbangers fall for that trick every time," the horse grumbled, his deep voice resonant. He had a distinct cockney accent. "Gods' truth, the idea of a cyborg horse never even crosses their tiny ape minds. It's bloody insultin', it is."

Alerio watched Geneva Kamil waltz past in the arms of some planter's son, a beaming smile of pure delight on her inhumanly lovely face.

He'd taken both women back to the Outpost so he could interrogate the captured Xeran; leaving them alone was obviously not an option. Actually, he'd half expected Geneva to abandon her dream of dancing at a Victorian ball, but evidently she was made of sterner stuff. The break had given the actress time to recover her composure, and they'd returned with a backup coachman. This time, though, they'd Jumped in a great deal closer to the Northram rice plantation—as they would have done in the first place if Alerio'd had his way. Unfortunately, at the time, Geneva had refused any change in her half-million-galactor itinerary, and he'd been unable to explain because of Colonel Ceres's ill-conceived orders.

Unsurprisingly, Geneva had turned out to be the belle of the ball, which had done a lot to return her confidence. The moment she'd walked in her dance card had started filling with the names of visibly stunned bachelors. They'd all insisted she was the most beautiful woman they'd ever seen, which was probably no exaggeration, considering the lack of Victorian genetic engineering.

Much bad poetry was composed on the spot in praise of her flaw-less face. She'd proved her acting chops with pretty blushes.

Alerio scanned the intricate pattern of dancers as they spun beneath the cavernous ballroom's glittering crystal chandeliers. A four-piece string ensemble strove to be heard over the chatter-ing, laughing crowd. The crowd won.

He blinked, noticing a trio of—to his eyes—underage debu-tantes staring at him, whispering behind their fans. Wondering what the hell they wanted, he gave them a polite nod. They burst into giggles and fled.

"It seems you have a fan club," Dona observed over the mission's com channel, probably just so she wouldn't have to shout over the crowd. *"If you spoke to them, they'd probably faint dead away."*

"Witless little femmes." They reminded him of the Vardonese aristocrats back home: certain the universe revolved around them, on the grounds it wouldn't dare do anything else.

And Alerio intended to make sure the universe didn't prove them wrong. At least not tonight. He did another crowd scan, searching for anyone whose body contained molecular traces alien to nineteenth-century Earth. Like Borka Czigany, highwayman, would-be kidnapper, and hired assassin in the pay of the Crystal Fortress.

It had taken Alerio less than five minutes to crack the Xeran's cheap neurocomp and use it to give Czigany an irresistible com-pulsion to confess his crimes. Which would have been a violation of his civil rights, had it not been for the fact that he was an enemy combatant caught trying to kidnap a temporal tourist on nineteenth-century Earth. Galactic Union's courts took a very dim view of that kind of thing.

Especially since Czigany wasn't exactly a blushing virgin. The bastard had done everything from stealing priceless temporal artifacts to assassinating the leader of the Xeran political under-ground. In fact, Alerio gathered that if a hornhead priest told Czigany to commit any crime against anybody, anytime, anywhere, he'd never think twice. Not exactly a man who suffered from an overactive conscience.

Firmly in the grip of the chief's compulsion, Czigany had cheerfully admitted he and his Jump gang had decided to kidnap Geneva Kamil because they'd wanted to collect the bounty the priests were offering for captured temporal tourists: a quarter of a million galactors. Czigany had figured they could probably get half a million for Geneva, given her fame.

If the hornheads had realized Alerio would assign Enforcer escorts to the tours, they'd neglected to share that information with Czigany.

Half a million galactors, Alerio thought. *Oh, sweet Goddess, we're going to be ass-deep in these idiots.*

"I owe you more than I can ever repay," Julia Reginald told Dona and Alerio as they sipped mildly alcoholic punch from crystal glasses. Geneva and the two Enforcers were posing as Julia's guests from a fictional Germanic principality; anyone who overheard them would hopefully think they were speaking a foreign language. Though come to think of it, a language didn't get more foreign to nineteenth-century South Carolina than Galactic Standard. "If not for you, Jorge would have bled to death."

Dona smiled; it was nice to be appreciated. "I'm just glad we made it to the infirmary in time. Dr. Chogan said if we'd been ninety seconds later, he wouldn't have made it."

"So she told me." Punch in one hand, Julia waved her fan at her glistening face with the other. Too many sweating people dancing around a room without climate control was a lot less romantic than it sounded. "Jorge has worked for me for twenty years, and he's become quite dear to me. More than I ever realized, in fact."

"Close calls do have a way of making a lot of things clear," Alerio observed absently, still eyeing the crowd like a professional bodyguard.

"And they don't get much closer than the one we had today." Julia shook her head and sipped her punch. "We're all fortunate you decided to provide us with an escort, Chief Dyami. Otherwise I'd likely be dead, and Geneva . . . The gods know what they'd have done to her."

"It's better not to waste your energy imagining all the things that didn't happen," he said. "What matters is that you, Geneva, and Jorge are safe."

"Very true." Julia's hazel eyes sharpened as she studied him. "But I'm curious, Chief Dyami. Why *did* you decide to escort us on this trip?"

Somehow Dona managed not to freeze. *If he can't divert Julia now, she'll run to the media the minute she gets back. The cover-up will blow wide open, and we'll all be fucked.*

Alerio didn't even look away from the crowd. "Geneva's wealth is well-known, and she mentioned her plans to dance at a nineteenth-century ball on one of the Interstellar Data Hubs. I had a feeling the comment would attract the wrong kind of attention." He shrugged those broad shoulders. "It seems I was right."

Julia's fan froze in mid-wave. "I told the little twit not to brag about this trip!"

Dona sipped her own punch and shrugged. "Yeah, we always give tourists that warning. And there's always somebody who doesn't listen."

"Good thing we avoided such a tragedy today." Julia studied Alerio over her fan, her gaze still a bit too sharp.

Dammit, Dona thought in disgust. *Looks like she still hasn't bought it.*

"While you were questioning our would-be kidnapper, I ran

into a friend of mine." The guide's fan waved a little faster, reminding Dona of the twitch of a cat's tail. "Perhaps you know him—Kangse Wei? He's a documentarian. Quite famous. Kangse told me he was assigned an escort, too. In fact, he said every tour going out this week will have Enforcer bodyguards."

Alerio lifted a brow. "Do you often listen to rumor?"

"Not as a rule. But I've been a temporal guide for twenty-six years, and I have never known of an Outpost chief playing body-guard." She smiled sweetly. "Surely you're not that shorthanded."

"Of course not." Alerio gave her one of those charming smiles he did so well, but Julia's eyes didn't even glaze. "I haven't had field duty in so long, I worried I'd gotten rusty." He returned his attention to the crowd as if barely interested in the conversation. "As for the other tours this week, I felt your fellow guides could use more experience in working with Enforcers. A little practice now will keep everybody alive in the event of crisis."

"Yes, that does make sense." Julia's waving fan slowed. She'd probably hoped she'd uncovered a scandal she could parlay into free media advertising for her agency. "Actually, I'm surprised no one thought of it before now."

"Oh, we did." Alerio shrugged. "We just haven't had a chance to implement the training before." As the string quartet swooped into another waltz, he turned to Dona and gave her a credible bow. "May I have this dance?"

Good idea, get us the hell away from her before she thinks of another question. "Of course."

As Alerio led her out onto the dance floor, Dona told him over the mission com channel, *"Actually, the training thing sounds like a good idea."*

"I'll have to come up with a suitable program." Taking her into his arms, he spun her out among the swirling crowd of dancers. And damn, it felt entirely too good.

Neither Enforcer had ever waltzed before, though the German aristocrats they were pretending to be would definitely know their way around a dance floor. Which was why the mission's required Educational Data Implant had included popular dances of the period, along with an English language refresher, Victorian slang, and the finer points of nineteenth-century etiquette in the Deep South. Having absorbed the EDI's package of skills before the Jump, they could probably dance rings around anyone else in the room.

Gazing up into the chief's handsome face, she found herself acutely aware of the warmth of his palms even through her evening gloves. His eyes should be glowing now, judging by the arousal her sensors detected. Luckily his comp's imagizer concealed the effect.

Dona swallowed and licked dry lips as her own need rose. His gaze tracked her tongue tip with heated interest. *Yeah, definitely glowing.* And if Dona had been a Warfem, her own would be lit with the same red blaze.

Unable to hold his stare, she aimed her gaze over his shoulder.

His sensor implants were probably telling him exactly how she felt. A memory flashed through her mind: the last time they'd made love.

Dyami, black eyes flaming as he drove his cock into her with long, driving thrusts that sent corkscrews of pleasure twisting along her nerves . . .

I could have that again, she thought. *Tonight. When we return to the Outpost, we could make love. And then I'll lie awake cursing my lack of self-control.*

She couldn't afford to keep giving in to her desire for Alerio; that would only make it harder to resist the next time. In the end, it would be like the colonel all over again. Her life would sail out the nearest air lock as she was forced to turn her back on everything. Her home, her career, her rank, the skills she'd spent years developing . . .

Though she'd been able to join Temporal Enforcement after Kavel got through wrecking her existence, that wasn't the sort of second chance that came around more than once. Which was why she'd been devastated when Ivar had turned out to be a traitor. She'd come so close to being charged as his accomplice, she'd figured she was well and truly screwed. She had been wrong.

Then.

But if she didn't stay away from Dyami, she might find herself in the same sort of ugly mess. Like Temporal Enforcement, Arania's military had been small. Rumors could travel through its ranks at light speed. Whispers about her relationship with Kavel had dogged her like ghosts, until she'd had no choice except to leave.

If she was stupid enough to make the same mistake with Alerio, she could expect the same result.

Assuming Alerio treats me the way the colonel did. True, the chief seemed to be a fair man, especially compared to Kavel, who'd thrown her to the wolves the minute he'd needed a scapegoat. Alerio would never do that.

You didn't think the colonel would prove to be a conscienceless shit, either, but you were wrong then, too.

Then there was Ivar, surely the worst mistake she'd ever made. At least the colonel hadn't committed treason.

Every man you fall in love with turns on you. Watch your step, or Alerio Dyami will be next in line.

Still a little nauseated from the return Jump to the Outpost, Dona closed her eyes and braced her armored boots apart. She'd changed back into her T-suit the minute they were far enough from the plantation, having grown thoroughly sick of that gown. *Especially the corset.*

The familiar light blast and thunderous crack announced Julia and Geneva's return. *It's a good thing Mission Staging has good shielding, or everyone on the Outpost would be permanently blind and stone-deaf.*

Opening her eyes again, Dona found the carriage and its horses on the Jump pad. The three mares whinnied and danced. Pendragon just looked bored.

Despite its fragile appearance, the reinforced carriage was equipped with temporal generators powerful enough to drag all four animals along for the ride. Still, Jumping would have been hard on the animals if not for the nanotech harnesses that compensated for often ugly side effects of temporal warps. Not quite as effective as a full T-suit, but you couldn't dress a horse in armor.

Alerio appeared with the standard thunderclap, as usual Jumping last. He shot Dona a probing look as if to make sure she'd arrived with mind and body intact. That wasn't always a given; warps could sometimes have unexpectedly ugly effects for no apparent reason.

She nodded at him, silently acknowledging his concern.

Geneva's voice rang out from inside the carriage, edged with a distinct whine. "Lost gods, that was sickening."

"The wages of time travel, my dear. One gets used to it." Despite the offhand words, Julia sounded deeply relieved to be back.

The carriage rocked as the substitute coachman jumped from the driver's box to the staging pad, then moved to unfold the steps and swing open the carriage door. Still playing his role to the hilt, he offered Geneva a half-bow and a hand down. She accepted it and descended the steps, twitching her skirts into place.

"Why can't we have T-suits?" the actress demanded when she had both feet safely on the pad. Glancing up, she spotted Alerio and stalked toward him. "Armor would make the whole thing a lot less stressful. Besides, then we'd be able to escape any sodding kidnappers."

"Except the government couldn't control where you'd go," Alerio explained patiently. "We can't have tourists Jumping wherever the hell they want. We tried that a couple of decades ago, and it was chaos."

"Besides," Julia added, "Galactic Union law states no one can legally possess a T-suit except TE agents."

"Too bad that never actually stops anybody," Dona said over the com channel. No matter what steps TE took to curb the practice, bootleg suit manufacturers always found ways to sell their wares to temporal criminals.

"Good thing, too," Alerio replied dryly as he moved to join her. *"Otherwise you and I would be out of a job."*

Geneva headed for them, skirt swaying like a great bell with the roll of her hips. She looked as ethereal as a fairy queen as she rested one hand on Alerio's armored chest and raised her huge, famous eyes to his. "Thank you so much for taking such good care of me." Dark lashes dipped as she rose on her toes to press a lingering kiss on his tattooed cheek.

Dona managed not to grind her teeth.

Just.

Alerio's gaze flicked warily in her direction before he gave the actress a coolly professional nod and stepped away. "That's what you pay us for, Ma'am."

With a wistful sigh that verged on tragic, Geneva dropped her heels to the deck and offered Dona a limp hand. "Thank you, too. Dona, isn't it?"

Enforcer Astryr. She managed to bite back the correction and shook the actress's disinterested hand. *Good Enforcers don't break a tourist's fingers. Even when she richly deserves it.* "We're delighted to have been of service," she lied.

Geneva's smile was strictly perfunctory. "I'm sure."

"Thank you so much for protecting us, Chief." Julia glided over, taffeta petticoats rustling. "You too, Enforcer." True gratitude lit the smile she gave Dona, who smiled back. "You're welcome to escort my tours anytime."

"I only wish it hadn't been necessary," Alerio said, "but I'm glad we were able to inconvenience your kidnappers."

"Not as glad as we are." Geneva slid an arm through Julia's as she turned the guide toward the door. "Fabulous tour, darling. I can't wait to do it again—without the highwaymen. That was a bit more entertainment than I had in mind."

"Truer words, darling." Julia laughed, a tinkling sound she must have learned from a Victorian debutante. "Would you care for a tour of the Outpost? There's the most amazing restaurant on the Concourse level, The Dark Nebula. You really must try it. Chef Marie makes a beefer filet over asparagus tips and wild seabloom that's simply . . ." She kissed her fingers in an extravagant gesture.

"Sounds delightful. But how's the bar?"

"Fabulous. I recommend the Slingshot Orbit . . ." The pair rustled out.

Glad to be rid of them, Dona turned to find the coachman unhitching his team. Enforcer Pendragon sighed in relief as the human hauled the harness off his sweating back.

"Glad that's done." The stallion's vocalizer flashed blue through the silken strands of his mane. He looked around the cavernous room. "Where's Frieka? He promised to take me pub-crawling."

"Hold your horses." The wolf trotted through Mission Staging's double doors. "If you'll pardon the expression."

"What an *amusing* little fleabag you are." Pendragon tossed his head and clipped toward the big wolf, only to break step as if a thought had occurred to him. "I assume you have had all your shots?"

"Kiss my bushy tail, Glue Trap," Frieka retorted equitably. "Let's go. Getting *you* plowed will take all night as it is." The two wandered out, exchanging good-natured insults as they went.

"Awww . . . Frieka's found a friend." Dona grinned up at Alerio as they brought up the rear of the little parade.

"Pendragon would be a good friend to have," the chief agreed. Ahead of them, the unlikely pair headed for the Concourse level and gods knew what exotic alcohol. "I'd love to have him on staff permanently. We could use him. I've put in a transfer request, but since the two previous ones were turned down, I'm not particularly optimistic."

"Why not? I thought the European Outpost had a whole herd of cyborg horses."

"They do. Unfortunately, Chief Tadhg hates my guts. I get the distinct impression that he knows exactly how badly I need a horse-borg, so he'll do everything in his power to keep me from getting one. He only agreed to let us borrow Pendragon this time because the situation is so dire."

"Sounds like a case of Warlord envy." Some TE commanders actively hated Vardonese officers, viewing them as glory hounds who stole rank and accolades from more deserving agents.

Alerio shrugged his broad shoulders. "I don't have the evidence to make a bias complaint stick, but Tadhg does make a point of being a prick."

"Maybe Frieka could convince Pendragon to pressure his chief for a transfer," Dona suggested. "The fuzzball can be surprisingly persuasive for somebody with four legs and a tail. He's certainly talked me into all kinds of things." She grinned wickedly. "Some of which I shouldn't have done."

"I don't want to know." Alerio grinned back before his eyes narrowed with calculation. "Though you make a good point about Frieka's powers of persuasion. I'll com him and suggest it."

They walked along for a moment as the chief's expression grew distracted by his silent conversation. "Okay," he said at last, "Frieka says he'll work on it."

"I'm not surprised. Frieka would love nothing better than to get a new sidekick. Especially with Nick and Riane emitting 'choking clouds of pheromones.'"

As they stepped into a lift for the ride up to the Residence Deck, Alerio leaned his broad back against the compartment's rear wall. He gave her a crooked smile that sent a pleasant little zing through her heart. "Would you like to have dinner? I thought we could discuss our next mission."

Dona opened her mouth to say no, only to hesitate. He was right about the mission. "All right. Let me change out of this armor, and you're on." *I just hope I won't end up regretting it.*

CHAPTER SEVEN

The setting sun backlit the Blue Ridge Mountains in fire. Sitting at the small dining table positioned before the room-length window, Dona listened to the hum and click of the vendser as Alerio programmed their meal. Like her, he'd dressed in duty blues, as though to remind both of them this was a working dinner. Minutes later, he put a pair of steaming, fragrant plates on the linen tablecloth. Rare beefer filets, roasted tul, and a slaw of credwan and pearlies. She smiled across the table at him as he sat. "Looks delicious."

"With any luck it will be—though you never know with a vendser." Alerio picked up his knife and fork and started slicing into the thick slab of beefer. "Well, it's definitely tender. How's the ale?"

Dona took an unwary sip and gasped at the blazing path the alcohol burned down her throat. "Delicious. It could strip the paint off a warstar," she wheezed.

The Warlord's teeth flashed in a white grin against the green and gold of his facial tattoo. "Good. I just got in a case of it."

"A *case?*" She took a bite of the pearlies and sighed at the smoky crunch.

"Yeah. Frieka and I killed the last bottle I had." He grinned at her over a forkful of steak. "That furball can drink. Good thing I'm a cyborg, or I'd *still* be hung over."

She laughed. "Sounds like Pendragon's in for an interesting night."

"He's a horse, Dona. I doubt even Frieka could drink him under the table." He ate the bite of beefer, blinked in approval, and started cutting another.

"Never underestimate the ale-guzzling skills of a cyborg wolf." Dona paused to enjoy her own mouthful, chewing reverently. Swallowing, she asked, "About this bounty the Xerans are offering. You do realize every asshole with a T-suit is going to be gunning for temporal tourists?"

"Now that you mention it, yeah. And you're right, it's going to be a problem. We can cover all the tours for a while, but sooner or later the guides are going to realize something serious is up. Judging by what Julia said, rumors have already started to circulate." He shook his head as he took a bite, swallowed, and added, "It won't be long before the lid blows off."

"Yeah." Dona stared thoughtfully out over the violet-shaded mountains. For a long moment, they were both content to eat and watch the sun sink behind the rolling horizon. "What if we set a trap?" she asked suddenly.

"For whom? The Xerans have a lot more priests than the Outpost has Enforcers. Now, if all we were talking about was Ivar, that we could do. Unfortunately, our real problem is the Victor. How the hell do you trap a god?"

"Well . . ." Dona considered the problem as she ate. "We know the Victor wants the T'Lir pretty damned bad. And Wyatt almost killed him with it six months ago. What if we got Nick another shot?"

"I don't think the Victor will be that easy to sucker again." Alerio frowned thoughtfully. "He's crazy, not stupid. Besides, what if he got away with the bait? I don't think I want to risk handing the Victor that kind of power. He's dangerous enough as is."

Dona glanced up from her beefer. "That's the gods' own truth. First thing he'd do is declare war on the Galactic Union. If he could use the T'Lir to actually win, he'd demand we all worship him—and he doesn't take 'no' well. When the Xerans invaded Arania, they tried to convert every town they took, and killed every colonist who refused."

"Did the same thing on Vardon." Swirling the ale in his glass with slow circles of one big hand, Alerio gazed broodingly into its depths. "I was only five when they invaded, but I remember the killing. I was almost one of their victims more than once, even before I became a compcracker." He threw back a swallow of the ale as if it were water. "They didn't much like Warkin children. And we didn't much like them."

Dona stared at him, feeling a sudden kinship with Alerio she'd never suspected. He stared back until she cleared her throat and looked away. "That kind of thing does tend to stick with you. Especially if you're a child."

Alerio picked up the bottle of ale and held it out toward her in offering. When she nodded, he topped off her glass. "So. The Xerans will try to convert the worlds of the Galactic Union if they can. And they'll get *really* pissy with anyone who says no."

"A lot of people will end up dead. There's way too much riding on this, Chief. We've got to stop the bastards, or it's all going to hell." She frowned and took a burning sip. "What about the government? They could . . ."

"Yeah, they could. But they won't. I've been exchanging courier bots with Colonel Ceres for months. They seem to think if they ignore the Victor long enough, he'll go away."

"Yeah, 'Gutless' is basically their mission statement. Meanwhile, Ivar's running around butchering innocents with psychotic abandon." Dona plunked her chin on her palm and brooded as the woods went dark beyond the window. "Bastards. Stupid, stupid bastards. Nothing ever changes. Ever."

Alerio frowned, looking into her eyes.

So I'm drunk, she thought rebelliously. *And depressed. I've got plenty of reason to be both.*

After a moment's hesitation, he rose from his seat and walked around the table. Extending a hand to her, he said, "Come on, Dona. Join me."

Somewhat to her own surprise, she put her hand in his and let him pull her to her feet. She followed him to the couch knowing very well she was making a mistake. *Probably the ale*, she decided, as the floor dipped under her boots. *A smart woman would leave.* She sat down anyway. *What the hell. I've never been particularly smart.*

Sliding an arm around her shoulders, Alerio drew her against his side. "Fuck Ivar."

She laughed, and heard more than a little boozy bitterness in the sound. "I did. That's the problem."

"Look, Ivar is an arrogant little prick. But he's also sloppy, and he's definitely not as smart as he thinks he is. Sooner or later, he's going to screw up. And I promise you this: before we throw his cyborg ass in the nearest penal colony, I will personally beat the shit out of him. Just on general principles."

Dona found herself settling into his warm hold. "That works— as long as you let me get a couple of shots in. I owe that bastard for blindsiding me."

Alerio smiled down at her. "It's a deal." His arm felt entirely too strong and warm around her shoulders, his big body hard with tight muscle and redolent with the scent of aroused male. Her head buzzed pleasantly. *Gods, how Ivar would rage to see me cuddling with Alerio Dyami.*

And who gives a fuck what Ivar would think? He's history, and you can't change history. Alerio is now.

Okay, definitely drunk. But fuck it, Dona decided with a sudden euphoric recklessness. *I'm tired of tiptoeing around my fears. Alerio is not Kavel, and he's sure as shit not Ivar. I want him—I've always wanted him. If I'd had the guts to go after him to start with, I wouldn't have gotten screwed by Ivar. In the worst possible sense of the word.*

She'd spent two years giving in to her fears, and that wasn't like her. *It's time I act like a warrior instead of a victim.*

Turning to face Alerio, Dona rose to her knees on the couch. He glanced up, surprised, and she took his mouth with greedy heat.

Gods, he's delicious. Tasting of Vardonese ale and masculine heat, his lips felt incredibly soft as they parted under the pressure of hers. His tongue met hers in a spiraling mutual stroke. One big palm cupped her face, fingers brushing back and forth over her cheek as they kissed. Deep, lazy. She heard herself moan.

Suddenly greedy, Dona flung a leg across his lap and settled astride him. He instantly went hard under her ass, and she purred into his mouth. The hand stroking her face sank into her hair and fisted, drawing her even deeper into the kiss.

By the time they broke apart to breathe, Alerio's eyes burned in full Warlord blaze. "Sweet Goddess, I want you," he said in a hoarse rumble. "I've wanted you for two empty years. I'd watch you endure that psychotic bastard, watch him treat you like shit, and it drove me insane."

"I know," Dona told him, aching for the loneliness she could almost feel in him. A yearning so strong she could see it even through the glow. "I'm sorry." *I should have been braver.*

"Why did you put up with Ivar's crap? You could have filed a complaint. I would have stopped him. I *itched* to stop him."

"I was afraid." Shame heated her cheeks, but she didn't let her gaze drop. Didn't let herself take the easy way out. "I didn't think I deserved any better. And he was so subtle—all those stinging little barbs. I wondered if I was being oversensitive."

"You weren't," Alerio growled. "Ivar was a prick. I'm just glad we finally got the treasonous asshole out of your life." Stroking her jawline with his thumb, he stared into her face, his expression brooding. "And I'm going to make him pay for everything he's done. To you. To that poor guide he raped and murdered. To Jessica Arvid." Galar's wife had survived Ivar's murder attempt only by using Sela psychic powers she hadn't even known she had. The chief's glowing eyes narrowed as his face hardened. "That bastard is going to wish he'd never drawn breath. On my honor as a Warlord."

"You don't have to swear an oath to me. I *know* you." Dona sighed. "I just wish things were different. Wish I didn't have the shitty history I have . . ."

"History's the one thing you can't change, Dona. It doesn't have to keep us apart if you don't want it to." Alerio cupped one breast through her uniform top. His thumb flicked back and forth over one nipple. The sensation was so hot, so delicious, she sucked in a breath. "Do you want things to be different? Between you and me, if nothing else."

"Gods, yes. I want you. That I do know."

He smiled in one of those heart-stopping grins. "And I want *you* naked. Now."

Hot arousal flooded her sex as she grinned back in delight. "All right."

They undressed each other with impatient hands, stripping off duty pants, shirts, jerking down briefs, and tossing aside socks and boots.

When Alerio settled back on the couch again, he was extravagantly naked, his chest wide and brawny, his legs long, muscle working along them. His cock stood thick and proud above the furry weight of his balls.

Dona was just as bare, laughing as she climbed back into his lap, trapping his shaft beneath her butt. "Gods, your cock feels incredible." So hard, yet covered in skin like hot velvet. She gasped, and let her eyes close. Enjoying the warmth of his skin against hers, all that hard strength contrasting with soft body hair.

Alerio's mouth closed over a nipple and sucked in a demanding pull. Her eyes popped open and she exhaled, shuddering as pulses of pleasure stabbed from the rose tip, flashing to her brain and swelling cunt. Caressing the other breast, he tugged its budded nipple, sending waves of keen sensation rolling through her with every hard beat of her heart.

Yet there was something she had to tell him. Now, despite the rising tide of blinding pleasure. Now, before they went any further. She caught his head in her palms and stared down into his eyes. Willing him to listen. "I'm not a victim, Alerio. And you're not going to treat me like one."

"I've *never* thought of you as a victim." His stroking hand stilled as his expression hardened. But when she tensed, his gaze softened. "And I would never hurt you, Dona. *Will* never. On my honor as a Warlord."

That was not an oath his people took lightly. If he said he wouldn't hurt her, he wouldn't. Period. Which is why it shook her to the core. "I believe you, Alerio." Deep within her, something scarred and vulnerable began to unwind from its tight, defensive ball.

"How about this one, then?" He caught her around the waist and tumbled her down on the couch. "I've never wanted another woman the way I want you." Stretching out on top of her, he claimed her mouth in fierce demand as he settled over her like a cloak of solid male muscle.

Sighing into his mouth, Dona relaxed into boneless surrender, stroking the powerful tendons and muscles of his body, fingertips savoring their smoothly working contours. Her free hand slid around his thick rib cage to caress his back, drifting down his spine to grip his powerful ass. "Mmmm," she purred, enjoying the banquet of sensation that was Alerio Dyami. "You feel incredible."

"Thank you." Alerio grinned in a white flash of teeth, his glowing eyes watching her nipples dance on the rise of her breasts. "I can definitely return the compliment. Gods, your skin is soft. Like silk and fur and rose petals." He laughed softly. "Well, I never claimed to be a poet."

"Hey, I'm not complaining. Though if you'd like to . . ." Before she could finish the sentence he slid down and covered a nipple with his hot, wet mouth. Dona gasped at the darts of heat, squirming as he teased with stunning skill. "Have I mentioned . . . you have a very, very nice mouth. And tongue. And hands . . ."

Alerio looked up to grin. "Why, thank you." Bending down again, he suckled a nipple back into his mouth. Dona tasted delicious, smelled even better, and felt nothing short of amazing. Gently, carefully, he scraped his teeth over the nubbin and listened to her moan of delight.

"Ohhh, that feels so niiice."

"Just what I was thinking." He laved her nipple with a swirling lap of his tongue.

She arched, catlike, sleek and soft and warm. Her legs parted. Alerio caught his breath as she slid a long, lean leg up the length of his to hook a graceful calf over his ass.

His cock twitched, trapped between her belly and his. Soft flesh teased its shaft until it jerked in hungry longing. Dona moaned again, so softly. Like a plea. The sound sent a bolt of erotic hunger through his brain as he inhaled the rich scent of her arousal: rich with such erotic promise that his mouth went dry.

"Goddess Mother, I want you," Alerio whispered against her breast.

Her fingers curved into claws and dug into his broad back. "Yes. Oh, yes . . ."

Goaded, he released her nipple and began to string a nibbling path down her body. Biting here, licking there, swirling designs with his tongue until she squirmed and sighed. Silken legs stroked up and down his hairy thighs as her nails dug into his back, raking just hard enough to make his blood race hotter.

He started alternating nips and tiny, careful bites as he worked down her torso, stopping to lap her belly button and nibble until she giggled, squirming. Satisfied—well, not yet, but soon—he slid between her long runner's legs. She spread them eagerly wide and dug her nails in his shoulders. He growled at the tiny, delightful sting and kept sliding.

Until he could see the plump lips of her sex, covered in a neatly trimmed triangle of dark hair that was soft as a kitten's fur. He could smell her arousal, and his mouth flooded with saliva. Parting her nether lips with his thumbs, he admired the slick red petals shimmering under a coat of erotic cream. He groaned in anticipation and leaned down to taste. Salt and woman, and greedy arousal. *Just wait,* he told her lower lips. *I'm a long way from done with you.*

Dona ground her head back into the couch cushions as Alerio lapped in greedy strokes, pausing to probe or swirl or thrust. Fingers, tongue—he had equal skill with both. Pleasure pulsed through her body, making her feel more drunk than the ale had. "Gods, Alerio," she gasped, writhing. "Your tongue . . ."

He paused halfway through a figure-eight pattern around her clit. "What about it?"

"What about what?" She sounded pleasure-stunned even to herself.

"You were saying something about my tongue." He gave her another flickering stroke with its tip.

"It's demonic." She arched her back, grinding shamelessly against his face. "*You're* demonic . . . making me so *hot.*"

"Should I stop?"

She dug in her nails. "Only if you want me to kill you."

"We can't have that." He went back to teasing her, but now he worked his fingers into her cunt, pressing them deep, parting them in scissoring thrusts. Delicately ruthless and utterly irresistible.

Dona squirmed, hips pumping helplessly. Her panting moans sounded so nakedly erotic, Alerio's cock bucked. *Almost ready.* He drew back to slide an index finger into her depths. Tight muscles gripped the digit.

"Goddess, you're delicious," Alerio rasped, imagining the sensations awaiting his aching cock. "And incredibly wet."

"So when are you going to do something about it?" Dona growled, sounding just as impatient as he felt.

"Now." He pushed up on hands and knees, then crawled up her body to settle into the arms she opened wide for him. "Right. Now."

Alerio planted one hand on the pallet and used the other to position his cock at the opening of her sex. His first thrust made him freeze, afraid he'd come too early. She was just so incredible, slick, swollen tight as her inner muscles clamped down on his cock. Delight flared across his consciousness in an exquisite starburst.

"Oh gods, Alerio!" Drawing up her knees, she wrapped her legs around his waist, using the leverage to grind up to meet his stroking cock.

He breathed in desperate pants as the pleasure built and built even more. Dona ground up at him in an eloquent demand for more. More heat. More friction. More shimmering pleasure.

He fucked harder, pumping into the cradle of her body, watching her face with absorbed fascination as he gauged her pleasure and fought his own. Waiting for his moment, *the* moment.

He saw it arrive when her face went slack with what could have been pain or pleasure. Sliding a hand between them, Alerio thumbed the jutting button of her clit, circling it as he rode her with deep thrusts. Fending his own orgasm off with sheer will and concentration.

Dona gasped as inner muscles suddenly clamped tight in the first deep pulses of orgasm. He growled back, teeth grinding as he fought to give her the time to peak. He circled his hips to corkscrew his way deep, rolled his thumb over the tiny erection of her clit.

And watched her fly. She screamed, her body lashing against his, inner muscles tightening and releasing, tightening and releasing. Something about that sound made him buck against her and come, pulses shooting into her depths. Refusing to fight the shaking delight. She screamed, teeth gritted, writhing beneath him as he lost it and roared, shooting up into the blazing heights . . .

The final rolling spasms faded. With a spent groan, Alerio collapsed over her, panting and hot and so incredibly male. Catching her around the waist, he rolled onto his back, pulling her tight against his side.

Dona blew out a shuddering breath, one arm curving across his chest while easing a possessive leg over both of his.

For the first time in far, far too long, she felt at peace.

Pleasantly exhausted, they lay wrapped around each other, heartbeats slowing with their slowing breath, bodies still buzzing in the aftermath of their shared climax. Dona rested her head on his shoulder and closed her eyes, breathing in his musky spice as she savored the taste of him lingering on her tongue. Ale and salt and distilled Alerio. The lighting dimmed, probably responding to a command from his neurocomp. Full darkness settled in around them, warm and comforting after the violence of their pleasure.

"I really should go back to my quarters," Dona murmured against his shoulder.

"You really shouldn't," Alerio corrected, without opening his eyes.

She started to pull away, then groaned and gave up. "I can't move."

"Then don't." He opened his eyes and gave her a sleepy grin. "Please."

So she nestled deeper into his arms and relaxed at last. Feeling, despite everything, that they were both precisely where they ought to be. Smiling into his sweat-damp shoulder, Dona drifted off to sleep.

Dona slipped through the darkness like a ghost, her R-34 tachyon rifle slung across her back. She glanced down and discovered she was wearing Aranian combat armor. Its stealth field was activated, projecting a pattern of leaves and dirt that slid across her body until it seemed she wasn't there at all.

A child whimpered in pain.

Dona froze in mid-stride. Five years of war had hardened her, but a child's pain always had the power to punch through her protective numbness.

She'd been a child, too, when she went to war. A cyborg child, but a child nonetheless. She, too, had once cried in the dark, knowing no one gave a damn.

I'm coming, Dona thought and strode silently in the direction of the cry with a combat 'borg's smooth, liquid strength. I'm listening. I heard you, and I'm coming.

Nobody had ever listened to her.

Grunts. A rhythmic slapping that was all too recognizable. The child's voice grew louder, building toward a scream. It cut off when a hand hit flesh in a brutal slap. A male voice snarled a curse.

Dona's stride lengthened. Oh, now you're dead, you son of a bitch.

Sobbing. Pitifully, painfully muffled, as if the child cried into her arm. Silently, Dona began to run.

She found them lying across the trail. A Xeran, judging by the ring of horns glinting on the man's head. The pants of his armor hung over a nearby bush. He'd pinned the girl beneath him, her dirty shirt hiked up, trousers tossed aside. She whimpered again, the sound soft and hopeless with despair. She looked so tiny, especially compared to his meaty heft.

Gods, *Dona thought, for a moment stunned motionless.* How old is that child?

And how did she get all the way out here to become this Xeran bastard's prey?

Based on skeletal maturity, she is approximately twelve, *the neurocomp said.* As to how he captured her, there is no way to tell. However, there is a village a kilometer farther along the trail. It is the closest habitation, so I calculate there is an eighty-five percent probability it is her home.

Dona could guess what had happened far too easily, though she couldn't guess the details any more than the comp could.

The so-called priest, lurking just beyond the town's perimeter, perhaps reconnoitering. Planning an attack. Spotting the girl as she left the village, gods knew why. And the Xeran . . . Sickened, she cut the thought off.

Standing over them, Dona began to tremble as a storm of fury hit her without warning. She started to grab the tachyon rifle slung across her back, bring it around . . .

She stopped. At this range, the blast would go right through him, killing the child Dona wanted so desperately to save.

One hand fell to the combat blade on her belt. She drew it, the oiled steel sliding silently from its sheath. She didn't intend to use it, but something unforeseen could always happen. Better to be prepared.

Clenching the other hand, Dona silently called up the code knife. Letting her eyes slide out of focus, she searched for the flaw she'd discovered in the Xerans' firewalls. She'd discovered the tiny flaw in their neurocomps two years before. Every one of the hornheads had it.

The Xeran's plunging hips stopped. Dona was so focused on cracking his comp, she didn't react in time when the priest jerked out of the girl, leaped to his feet, and spun toward Dona, face twisted in frustrated rage. "You stupid Aranian whore," he snarled. "I'm going to take that knife and ram it into your . . ."

She almost heard the mental click as she broke through.

Dona lunged, driving the code blade into the Xeran's forehead as if it was a physical weapon. The code punched through the priest's defenses to inject its virus payload into his implant. It froze him as though he'd been cast from plastium, mouth still open to spew more filth.

Dona drove her combat knife into the bastard's chest all the way to the guard. He reeled back, falling flat on the trail like an axed sapling. His body convulsed beside the cowering child who'd been his victim. Dirt smeared the small, elfin face, eyes swollen almost closed from weeping. Bruises distorted her features, and her nose was broken above bloody lips.

Dona wanted to stab him again. Kill him over and over. Cut him into chunks and scatter them from one end of this jungle for the wild dogs.

But the girl was staring at the knife, her eyes huge, not moving. Barely even breathing. Making Dona feel like a monster. "Look, I . . ."

"Don't kill me!" The child snapped into a protective ball, one arm wrapped around her bloody, naked torso, the other around the head she'd tucked into her chest, eyes squeezed shut.

Dona knew that pose. She'd once held it herself.

She swallowed. The smell of the Xeran's blood suddenly made her stomach heave, though she'd long since grown used to that.

Plop. Plop. Plop. A slow, steady patter on the leaves next to her feet. Dona looked down. The combat knife she held was dripping. She opened her fingers and let the knife fall.

"I'm not going to hurt you," she said softly, but the shaking child

only curled into a tighter ball. "Look, I just want to take you back to your village."

The kid's eyes squeezed shut as she wailed, "Don't hurt me!"

"I won't. I wouldn't. Not ever." Dona's voice dropped, shaking. "I was a little girl once."

A long, terrified pause. "He hurt me."

"I know."

"Is he dead?"

"Yes."

"Good." A sniffle. "I'm glad. I'm glad you killed him." Another sniffle, this one somehow defiant. "He was evil. He deserved it."

"Yeah, he was evil. And yeah, he deserved it." Crouching, Dona picked up the child's pants and offered them. The girl hesitated a long moment, one swollen eye staring up into Dona's face. At least she'd stopped crying.

Finally Dona put the pants down and backed away. The girl snatched them up and jerked them on, then dragged her shirt down where it belonged. When she was finally covered again, Dona extended a hand. The child shrank away. "I'm sorry I scared you. Look, let's just . . . go."

The doubt in those enormous eyes hurt worse than taking a blade herself. Dona gestured down the path. "Your village is that way. Don't you want to go home?"

The child snuffled and scrubbed a dirt-smeared hand across her runny nose. "I . . . guess."

Dona forced a smile. When the kid flinched, she realized her face was probably covered in blood splatter. With a mental sigh, she started up the path toward the village. "Come on, I'll walk you home."

She didn't turn around, but after a pause, she heard the crunch of small feet walking through the leaves in her wake.

"Caroleen?" A male voice cried in the distance. "Caroleen? Caroleen, where are you?!"

"Papa!" The girl darted past Dona, racing down the trail like a

startled thing. Dona followed at a slow jog, wanting to make sure she made it back to her father.

"Caroleen!" The voice came closer. He was running.

"Papa! I'm here, Papa! I'm here!"

Dona stopped to watch her vanish around a cluster of crownferns. "Papa!"

"Caroleen! Oh, gods, what happened?"

Hysterical sobs followed, along with a frantic spill of words. "I went looking for Mr. Whiskers because he was lost, and I couldn't find him anywhere, and I looked and looked, but . . ."

"Damned cat," Papa muttered. "Where have you been, girl?"

"A hornhead grabbed me! He hurt me, Papa!"

Her father gasped as if he'd just taken a mortal wound. Dona winced.

Incoherent murmurs, soothing whispers.

The next words sounded quite clear. "But then the 'borg lady came, and she killed him! She killed him dead, Papa!"

Dona turned and walked back into the jungle to look for her knife.

The dream shifted, wrenching into another place, another time.

Dona strode through the Aranian compound, headed for her own tent at last, wanting only to forget the night in sleep.

A group of soldiers staggered out of the Enlisted Club, half-supporting each other, laughing. Drunk.

"Gods!" one of them said, peering at her. She could almost see the haze of alcohol fumes wreathing the woman's head. "That girl's got blood all over her. Is she hurt? Shouldn't we . . ."

"Naw. That's Kavel's Killer, dumbass," one of the others interrupted. "She always comes back wearing somebody else's blood."

"That's Astryr? Shit! I thought she'd be taller."

Then the dream jumped again, and she stood in the shadow of a tent, a soothing pool of darkness. She knew the darkness, and it knew her.

A soft, high voice began to whimper to the sound of flesh smacking on flesh . . .

"Bastard!"

The scream of rage jolted Alerio awake to see Dona roll off the couch, bare feet thumping to the floor. He hit the deck an instant after she did, scanning for whatever threatened her. But there was nothing there.

Yet she stared around at his quarters with a snarl twisting her face, her body coiled to fight.

She's asleep.

Sleepwalking, his neurocomp confirmed. *It would be best not to touch her. Doing so would only increase her disorientation.*

"It's all right, Dona," he murmured soothingly, keeping his distance as his comp ordered the room's illumination increased to full. "You're in my quarters. Everything's all right."

Dona blinked. Awareness returned to her violet eyes as she stared at him in bewilderment. "Alerio?"

"That's right. It's me." He held out his arms and waited.

She paused, before throwing herself into them. Her arms wrapped around him with desperate strength. "Gods and demons, that was a bitch of a dream."

"Ivar?" Alerio stroked her back.

She laughed, but it sounded more like a sob. "He's only my latest boogeyman, Alerio. I've got a whole collection to choose from." Dona pulled free. Despite his inclination to draw her tight again, he let her go. "Most of 'em are Xeran. I killed a *lot* of Xerans." Her delicate face hardened. "And every one of them deserved it."

He paused, remembering her file. "That was when you were with the Aranian military?"

"Yeah." Dona glanced around, spotted her T-suit top and snatched it up. "I'd better go."

He already missed her warmth. "I like having you in my arms, Dona. Stay."

She looked at him in pain and longing before she jerked her uniform top over her head and started searching for her pants. "I need to be alone right now. That dream . . ." She broke off. "It's better if I go."

"All right." *Trying to stop her would be a really bad idea*, Alerio told himself, though the haunted look on her face made his chest ache.

Dona sat down on the couch to drag on her pants and stomp her feet into her boots. Without another word, she rose and headed for the door.

When Alerio stepped into her path and leaned down for a kiss, she dodged without looking at him. "I'll com you in the morning."

His big hands fell to his sides. "All right." Feeling helpless, Alerio watched her escape from his quarters like a woman fleeing a potentially fatal mistake.

Have I lost her again? Did I ever have her to begin with?

Alerio went back to bed and tried to sleep. After a fruitless half hour staring at the ceiling, he gave up and rolled out of bed. His comp could put him to sleep in seconds, but too many problems nagged him. If he didn't solve at least one of them, he knew he'd only end up wrestling them all in his dreams.

Naked, he dropped into his chair and palmed the top of his desk. Instantly, a glowing grid sprang into place above its smooth obsidian surface. Alerio reached in and drew out a three-dimensional golden box.

Dona's dossier.

He leaned back and stared at it. He'd last read the file—or at least most of it—two years ago, when Dona was first assigned to the Outpost. She'd only just graduated from the TE academy, having requested to become an Enforcer after a decade with the Aranian military.

He'd approved the request, of course. She had an impressive list of qualifications, including combat skills and a dazzling collection of military decorations for bravery in some very ugly operations.

She could also hit any target with any weapon, and her hand-to-hand combat skills made even Alerio raise an eyebrow. Arania didn't have a great reputation when it came to producing combat 'borgs, but Dona had upgraded her tech at her own expense before attending the academy. During her four years there, she'd amassed a respectable file of glowing recommendations.

But there was one section of her dossier he'd never read: the complete psychological report prepared by one of the staff psychiatrists at TE Headquarters.

He'd read Dr. Pjam's medical conclusion about Dona's mental health, but the rest of the file was under a privacy block. Her conclusion said Dona was intelligent and mentally stable, with strong interpersonal skills and a keen understanding of the motivations of others. But there was one offhand line that had nagged at Alerio for years.

"Despite whatever challenges Dona Astryr encountered as a child and a teen, I believe she will make a skilled and capable Enforcer."

"Despite whatever challenges"? Now, what the hell did that mean?

Though his curiosity had been piqued, Alerio had no reason to probe deeper. He could have cracked the privacy block and read the file anyway; he'd spent his boyhood compcracking Xeran cyborgs and dodging homicidal priests. He'd left the rest of the file alone because reading it would be a violation of Dona's privacy.

Two years later, he still felt that way.

Thing was, Dona's behavior since then—such as putting up with Ivar's abuse—suggested that whatever childhood trauma she'd suffered was still a problem now. If he had a better idea of just what had happened to her, maybe he'd be able to help her resolve the issue.

Alerio frowned, eyeing the three-dimensional file box icon as it floated above the desk. *Am I rationalizing a lover's curiosity?* It was possible, but his gut insisted there was something in that file he needed to know.

Even if he had to invade Dona's privacy to do it.

She was going to be seriously pissed off when she found out what he'd done. And she would find out, because he would have to tell her. Otherwise, it really would be a betrayal.

A cold ache in his heart told him what he was considering could destroy any hope of a relationship they had. Yet something had gone badly wrong in Dona's childhood that was still throwing a shadow over her life today. Unless he found out what it was, they had no chance.

Which may be beefershit, he thought grimly. *But one way or another, I'm about to find out.*

Taking a deep breath, Alerio went to work cracking the privacy block.

The block shattered in five-point-three minutes. "Must be losing my touch," Alerio grumbled as he tapped the first image, activating it.

Dr. Javen Pjam had skin the smooth honey brown of caramel. Her coloring made her jade green eyes even more startling. They matched the spun-gold hair that reminded Alerio of a Spanish doubloon he'd once seen. Her medical robes were cut like a kimono, the elegant fabric a rich bronze swirled with green and gold.

She studied a younger Dona across the width of a massive teak desk, her gaze probing. Dona looked oddly informal dressed in a dark brown civilian tunic and trousers. Her hair was cropped to shoulder length. "So your parents were gene-gineers?" Pjam asked.

Dona nodded. If she felt any nervousness at the power the doctor had over her future, it didn't show. "Yes. They specialized in gene-gineering children for the wealthy. I gather they made a very good living at it."

The doctor made a note on her desktop with a stylus that matched her eyes. "I'd imagine your sisters' respective careers helped them attract business."

Alerio drummed his fingers on his desk as he searched his memory of Dona's background dossier. One sister had been a six-time gold medal winner in anti-grav gymnastics at the GU Olympics. The middle sister was a trid actress who'd been famous from the age of five.

Dona nodded, expressionless. "My parents were very proud of them."

The doctor looked up. "They 'were'? You mean they're not anymore?"

She shrugged. "I'm sure they still are, but I haven't spoken to any of them in eighteen years."

Pjam blinked, visibly startled. "Since you were eight?"

"Right."

She looked down at her desk. Alerio suspected she was giving herself time to think. "You were six when your zero-grav dance teacher told them that though you were technically proficient, you had no talent for the artistic aspect of dance."

"I didn't." If the judgment stung, it didn't show.

"And whose fault was that?"

"My parents argued about that. Who was supposed to alter whatever gene it was, and hadn't. Who was responsible."

"They didn't blame you?" The doctor lifted a shining blond brow.

"Why should they? I didn't gene-gineer myself."

"Ah. No, I don't suppose you did." Pjam scribbled a few more notes. "How did they react to learning about the . . . problem?"

"I was born to be a marketing tool, and I was worthless." Oddly, she didn't sound angry. If Alerio hadn't known better, he'd have thought she was talking about someone else. "Worse than that, really. I was evidence they could fail. Not the kind of kid you wanted hanging around."

"That must have been painful."

"It's been twenty years. All that stuff doesn't really matter to me anymore."

The doctor gave her a skeptical stare. Alerio didn't think he believed her either. He was beginning to understand why Dona tolerated Ivar's abuse. Apparently, she'd rarely known anything else.

"Why did your parents decide to send you to the Aranian academy?"

"I had the intelligence, the physical strength, the agility, and the discipline. And at the time, the government paid families a quarter of a million galactors to let them implant a child with tech and send him to the 'borg academy." You had to implant the biocrystal net when kids were young, before their brains matured. Otherwise their bodies would reject it.

"A quarter of a million is a lot of money," Pjam observed.

"Well, it's not an easy process, and it wasn't particularly safe. Especially given the quality of Aranian tech at the time. Kids suffered hallucinations and a host of physical side effects. You had officer candidates dropping from heart attacks and tech rejection strokes at the age of ten."

Pjam looked appalled. "And your *parents* let the government do that to you, knowing all that?"

"I have no idea whether they knew it or not, but I'd assume they did. It was common knowledge, which was why the government was so desperate for implant candidates. They had a hard time getting parents to agree."

"Yours did. How did that make you feel?"

Dona jerked one shoulder in a half-shrug. "We were at war. I was needed. And they had to do *something* with me."

"You were eight. Most parents don't require their children to turn a profit before the age of ten."

"Most parents aren't genetic engineers."

"Actually, I know a great many genetic engineers, none of whom sell their children like poverty-stricken Mithran peasants." The doctor sighed. "Never mind. What was the academy like?"

Her expression eased slightly. She almost smiled. "I learned a great deal."

"Yes, I'd imagine becoming a government assassin would require mastery of all kinds of skills."

Dona gave the doctor a long, cold look that barely missed contemptuous. "We were at war, Doctor. And the Xerans were trying to steal our lisium mines, the only thing Arania had that was of any value." She curled a lip. "And that wasn't even their worst habit. Not by a long shot."

Well, I can definitely agree with that sentiment, Alerio thought, remembering life as a very young Warkin child under the Xeran occupation.

"The Xerans do have an ugly reputation," the doctor agreed. "Did you hate them?"

"I didn't feel guilt over killing them, if that's what you mean." Dona stared absently out the office window, watching flitter lights swoop over the capital in the dark. "And at least I was somebody."

"And who was that?"

"Kavel's Killer." Something flickered across her face, there and gone so fast, Alerio wasn't positive what emotion he'd seen.

"What was your relationship with the colonel like?"

There was that emotion again. This time Alerio was fairly sure it was pain, or perhaps anger. Or possibly both. "He gave me things I didn't even know I needed."

"So it was a good relationship?"

"I thought so at the time."

"But not now?"

Dona turned to study the doctor, irritation flashing through her cool violet gaze. "I can't tell whether you're asking these questions to see what I'll say, or whether you genuinely don't know the answer."

The woman sat back in her seat in a rustle of bronze silk. "Assume I don't know the answer. Then you're safe either way."

"Fine." Dona gave her a jerky nod.

When she said nothing more, Pjam raised a blond brow and pushed. "So was it a good relationship?"

"He was my lover."

The doctor looked down at the desktop, nodding. "When did that start?"

"A couple of weeks after I arrived at the base."

The doctor frowned. So did Alerio; they were probably doing the same math. "I thought you were fifteen when you were sent to help defend the mines."

"I was."

The psychiatrist looked so shocked, Dona evidently decided to elaborate. "The war was going poorly, so headquarters decided to throw all available personnel at the problem. They gave me a few tests and concluded I had the emotional maturity to handle combat at that age."

"So I understand. I also understand that commanding officer raped you."

Like Dona, Alerio had assumed Pjam knew far more than her apparent lack of a therapeutic poker face would suggest. But judging from her obvious shock now, he decided she'd really had no clue.

But then, neither had he. He felt sick.

Alerio tapped the desktop, stopping the vid file as he fought to control the white-hot fury steaming through his blood.

Jolting to his feet, he heaved his desk chair up and threw it at the room-length window. The plastium screen bonged like a great bell. It didn't crack, having been designed to withstand fire from a tachyon cannon battery.

The chair fell on its side, looking a bit warped. Alerio stalked over, pulled it upright, and straightened one badly bent tritrium-cored arm. Carrying the chair back to his desk, he dropped it into place and sat down again. He tapped the file to resume play.

"I was flattered," Dona said in a low voice. Shame flickered in her eyes, and Alerio ground his teeth. He didn't get up to throw his chair again, but he came close.

"The colonel gave me the approval I never got from anyone else," she said softly. "And after the first few times, the sex really wasn't all that bad."

Alerio stared at the playback. *I never thought I'd say this, but Ivar Terje must have seemed like a fucking improvement.*

CHAPTER EIGHT

"Did you realize Colonel Kavel was an abuser, Dona?" Dr. Pjam asked.

The cyborg raised her chin, defiant. "I was young, not stupid."

"I never thought you were."

"Yes, well, your question implied otherwise." She rose and strode to the window, staring out at the night beyond. "I told myself he loved me. He certainly said as much often enough."

Turning away, Dona began to pace. "For the next five years, I was . . . happy. I'd never really been happy before, not even when I lived at my parents' home. Even then, I'd had expectations to live up to." She grimaced. "Or to fail to live up to."

"And Kavel didn't expect anything from you?" There was a note of contempt in the doctor's voice. Dona looked up sharply, and Alerio realized she thought Pjam's anger was aimed at her. Instead of that evil fucker Kavel.

"No." The cyborg paused, her mouth curling into a smile that was just a little twisted. "Well, yes, come to think of it. He wanted me to stay fifteen forever, but I couldn't seem to pull it off."

"Did he tell you that?"

"No. But I gathered as much when a sixteen-year-old was

assigned to the base. He made her his personal clerk." Dona's smile was cool and bitter. "I'd just turned twenty."

"I'm sorry." To do the doctor credit, she seemed to mean it.

A muscle rolled in Dona's jaw as if she was grinding her teeth. "I didn't much enjoy being bitterly jealous of a teenage kid who wasn't even remotely the fighter I was."

The doctor watched her, sympathy in her rich jade eyes. "Humiliating."

"Intensely. But for the first time, I began to see I'd been manipulated. It became obvious when I heard him say the same things to the new recruit that he'd once said to me. But even then, I didn't understand the situation." Rage flashed through her eyes, burning in the violet like a storm. "Not really."

"Didn't you report it?" Pjam's knuckles had gone white around her stylus.

"Yes, when it finally hit me what he'd really done." She sat down and crossed her booted feet, studying the toes as if she'd never seen them before. "I was on my way back from a mission when I found a Xeran priest raping a twelve-year-old colonist. I killed him and rescued her."

"She must have been so grateful."

Dona shot the doctor a look. "She was fucking terrified of me. I took her back to her father and returned to the base. And found Kaven and the girl . . ."

"Oh."

"That's when I knew he was a monster."

"I'm sorry." Pjam sounded as if she really meant it. Alerio found himself thinking a little better of her for that.

"I reported him to Aranian central headquarters. He claimed I was a jealous psychotic bitch who had made up vicious lies to smear his reputation out of a craving for revenge." Again, she sounded so icily controlled, Alerio ached for her.

"Surely they didn't believe that? But your record . . ."

". . . Meant nothing. He had plenty of witnesses willing to provide him with an alibi. I've got a feeling some of the officers who served with him suspected what he was doing with all those young interns. Nobody did anything because he was a military hero."

"A hero?" Pjam looked incredulous.

Dona spread her hands. "I don't know. There was something about rushing into one of the lisium mines to prevent a Xeran saboteur from blowing it up. He saved half a billion galactors' worth of lisium. The government gave him a medal."

Which explained a great deal. Lisium was a key component in low-cost tachyon field generators. Without the mineral and the weaponry it made possible, the Galactic Union would be easy prey for the Xerans. Which was why Xer had tried to conquer Arania.

"So nobody believed you?"

"I was Kavel's Killer, doctor. A sniper and assassin. Not exactly an ideal witness."

"You were also his victim," Pjam said hotly. "A victim with a computer implant. All they had to do was check your neurocomp's account of the incidents, and they'd have known you were telling the truth."

Dona dropped back into her chair to sprawl with boneless grace. "Except it's not unknown for 'borgs to use their comps to plant false memories in their own brains."

"True, but a decent forensic hacker can prove a fake like that without even breaking a sweat."

"Yeah, assuming the brass brings one in, rather than just assuming the accuser is lying."

"But . . ."

"Kavel had a lot of friends," Dona told her, almost gently. "And I didn't have any at all."

"So you're telling me he got away with it," the doctor snapped hotly. "He's still out there, abusing other children?"

A faint, cold smile lit Dona's face. "No. Headquarters didn't take action against him, but the Xerans did."

The doctor stared at her, eyes widening. "The . . . Xerans did?"

"It was a war. People get killed in wars."

"So I'm told."

"He'd left the base one night, headed to a meeting with the parents of a young girl. I'm told he was planning to make her his intern."

"Intern." Now Pjam looked almost as expressionless as Dona.

"Yes. A Xeran patrol ambushed him on the way, and he was killed. From what I gather, it was a very unpleasant death."

Pjam studied her. "Which you had nothing to do with."

"No, and I can prove it." Dona's smile was faint and cold enough to induce frostbite. "*Did* prove it, at the inquest one of his five-star buddies called. At the time Kavel died, I was a hundred kilometers away, having dinner with a fellow officer. And she'd have had no reason to lie." Her lips curled very, very slightly. "After all, she'd been his intern."

Alerio wondered how she'd done it. He was a little surprised to realize he was glad she'd found a way to kill her abuser.

Dona hated being a victim.

The chief pulled the cork out of the bottle of ale. It was almost four in the morning. He promised his conscience he'd only drink one glass before he'd make another attempt to sleep.

He didn't expect to have much luck. Not after what he'd learned about Dona.

"*Chief? Chief Dyami? My sensors tell me you're awake in there . . .*"

Alerio answered the com. "*Frieka? Why aren't you in your bunk? Still pub-crawling with Pendragon?*"

"Unfortunately, none of the pubs have Frieka's precious Vardonese ale," the stallion put in. *"And I'm dying for a sample. It can't possibly be as good as the fleabag says."*

Alerio laughed. *"Hell, why not? I could use some company right now."*

Pendragon was a little too big for Alerio's quarters, so the three of them decided to head outside to the chief's favorite picnic spot. The Warlord spread a blanket on the flank of the moonlit mountain, then poured bowls of ale for his four-legged friends. Toasting each other, they drank.

"This is good stuff," the horse said, lipping ale with an expression of deep concentration.

"Told you." Frieka looked at Alerio. "Okay, Chief, what's up with you? And don't say nothing, because I know damn well there's something. Is it Dona?"

Pendragon raised his head. "That's the female Enforcer with the purple eyes, right?"

"That's the one." Frieka settled down on the blanket. "She and the chief have been trying to ignore each other for the last couple of years."

"Now there's an utter waste of time." With a gusting snort, the stallion dropped his head again and drank. "I'll never understand humans. They have to make everything so damned . . ."

". . . Complicated!" Frieka finished, shooting Alerio a triumphant look. "Ha! He agrees with me."

"Now *there's* a surprise."

"So what's bothering you about Dona?" Frieka asked.

Alerio hesitated. "I can't really talk about it without violating her privacy more than I have already."

Frieka gave him an assessing look. "Finally hacked Pjam's file, did you?"

Alerio stared at him. "Are you saying you already have?"

The wolf flicked an ear in a lupine version of a shrug. "Two or three months ago. I knew there was something ugly in that file, and I was right."

Alerio opened his mouth to chew out the lupine Enforcer, only to snap his mouth closed in frustration. "There's not one bloody thing I can say about your violating her trust that isn't just as true of me."

"Well, I *haven't* violated anybody's trust, and my curiosity is killing me." Pendragon pricked his ears. "What happened?"

"Dona had a very complicated and ugly childhood." Frieka thumped his bushy tail on the blanket. "By the way, if Temporal Enforcement ever offers you the services of a psychiatrist named Javen Pjam, turn them down. She's an idiot."

"Know her," the horse said shortly. "And you're right, she is an idiot. Apparently nobody ever told her mental health professionals are not supposed to pass judgment on their patients' lives."

Alerio blinked, wondering what aspect of Pendragon's life had drawn the doctor's commentary.

"So." Frieka turned to study him again. "Now that you've learned all Dona's ugly secrets, what do you intend to do?"

The horse gazed at Alerio, ears pricked, before lowering his head to his ale. "He's going to dump her."

"I'm not going to dump her," Alerio snapped. "I'm concerned about her, and I don't want to make things any worse."

"You're right, Pen," Frieka said thoughtfully. "He *is* going to dump her."

"Dammit, Frieka, every single relationship that woman has ever been in—including the one with her parents—was pure poison. What if I fuck it up? I'm a Warlord, dammit. We kill people. We don't nurture them."

"Best nurturer I ever met was Baran Arvid," Frieka observed, referring to Riane's father. "But you're damned near as good at it. Judging from what I've seen, you take good care of your people."

"That's different," Alerio growled. "I'm not sleeping with them."

"I'd hope not," Pendragon said. "Frieka's been trying to get me to ask for a transfer, and I'm not interested in being sexually harassed."

"You're not my type."

"You have no idea how relieved I am to hear it."

Alerio glowered at him. "Just what we need—another smart-ass talking animal."

"Which is better than a dumb-ass talking human."

"Isn't he quick?" Frieka gave the stallion an admiring look. "I love the way that kind of shit just rolls out of his vocalizer."

Alerio grunted.

"Seriously, Chief," Pen said. "Obviously I don't know exactly what problems your female has, but I don't see how a breakup with you would make it any better." He flicked his tail across his haunches. "You strike me as the sort of commander who wants to actively improve the lives of those under his command. Especially an agent you . . . feel something for."

And that's putting it mildly, Alerio thought.

The next day, Alerio ordered his implant to compensate for his sleepless night and too many glasses of ale while he prepared his gift for Dona.

Maybe it would make up for his sins.

Surveying the results in the golden light of the morning sun, he decided he'd accomplished his goal. "If I'm really lucky, it will at least put her in a good mood." He grimaced. "Maybe she'll even let me live after I tell her I hacked that damned file."

A mental order activated a camouflage field, hiding his work. It wasn't really likely that a temporal native would stumble on it, but he didn't want to take chances. The field was a bit of added insurance.

Fifteen minutes later, he arrived at Mission Staging, where two different tour groups were scheduled for Jumps.

Eleven historians surrounded their temporal guide, Masoud Gertsenzon, arguing about the best way to observe the December 20, 1803, French handover of the city of New Orleans to the United States. At the opposite end of the room, a team of Enforcers inspected their baggage for contraband—items that were illegal to transport into the past for various reasons.

Alerio stopped long enough to introduce himself, shake hands all around, and wish the group luck with their trip.

Striding across the room, he found Kangse Wei fidgeting while his equipment was inspected. The slender young documentarian wore a canvas duster, black pants, boots, and a white shirt with a string tie. According to the trip description he'd filled as part of his visa request, he planned to shoot a trid about the gunfight at the O.K. Corral. Which meant Wei would spend most of the next week concealed in an invisibility field so the temporal natives wouldn't know he was there. Just like the fleet of invisible camera bots he'd use to shoot the scene.

Wei was fidgeting from foot to foot as Alerio walked up, almost dancing as he watched the agents searching his equipment. "Come on, Forcies, get it *done*. I want to Jump."

Alerio raised a brow. "What's your hurry, sir? Wyatt Earp isn't going anywhere. And you've already done everything you're going to do."

"Maybe, but it sure doesn't feel that way. And the gods alone know how many doc-jocks are shooting in Tombstone right now." The young man glowered as he drummed his fingers on his thigh. "I need to tell *my* story."

The inspection team started flipping the cases closed. "Looks like they're finished," Alerio told him. "Good luck with your story, Mr. Wei."

"Thanks. Happy times, Forcie." With a farewell wave, the documentarian strode toward his waiting pile of gear.

Shaking his head, Alerio started toward the other end of the room, where another group of Enforcers stood talking in low, intense voices.

Wulf, a heavy-world agent who was ten centimeters shorter than Alerio—and thirty kilos heavier—was partnered with Tonn "Bear" Esso, equally massive, though considerably taller. With them was a tall, strongly built female agent named Irihapeti Aotea with elegant dark features and a regal carriage. Her partner, pale, slim Anzu Genji, was far stronger than her delicate build suggested. The two made a quick and deadly team.

Alerio's fellow Warlord, Galar, had been partnered with Peter Brannon, a deceptively wiry man with a wicked sense of humor.

"Are you agents ready to Jump?" Alerio asked, giving them all a smile.

"We just need to load Wei's equipment on the coach—which may take a while." Brannon jerked a thumb at the stagecoach and its four horses. "Then we Jump."

"While trying to keep the little arteeeest out of trouble," Galar added dryly.

"He does seem a little high-strung," Alerio allowed with a crooked grin. More seriously, he asked, "Is there anything you need that you don't already have?"

Galar shrugged. "No, sir, I think we've got it all covered."

"Good." He slapped the blond on a broad shoulder. "Have a safe Jump."

As the agents chorused their thanks, Alerio headed over to the coach.

Pendragon flicked his tail and stamped. "Get any sleep?"

Alerio snorted. "Hardly. You?"

"Hour's nap. It'll do. My computer's compensating." The stallion lifted his elegant head and pricked his ears. "Hey, isn't that your . . . ah . . . whoever?"

Alerio turned to watch Dona walk in after Jessica Arvid. "Showtime," he murmured.

"Wanted to see you off and give you a kiss," the pretty redhead told her husband. "I hope you don't mind."

"When have I ever minded a kiss?" Galar pulled her into his arms for an embrace hot enough to make her cheeks turn red.

Alerio's gaze slipped past the couple to Dona, who watched him. The erotic intensity of her gaze made him grin.

Then he remembered Pjam's locked file, and the grin faded. Dona's also disappeared, evidently in response. Eyes narrowing, she started toward him.

Oh, fuck, he thought. *I'm not looking forward to this conversation.*

"Something wrong?" Dona murmured when they were close enough to speak privately.

"I need to talk to you."

"What about?"

He hesitated. "Wait until the teams Jump. Then we'll go discuss it in private."

Her eyes narrowed. "You're the chief."

"Yeah." *Whether I like it or not.*

Half an hour later, Dona stopped dead on the trail. She'd initially thought he'd invited her to walk outside the Outpost so they could enjoy a little romantic privacy.

But then, I've always been an idiot. "Let me get this straight— you cracked my sealed medical file?" She couldn't believe he'd do something like that. *Sounds more like Ivar. Only Ivar never cared enough about me to bother.* A fact that only added to her rage.

Alerio glanced away to watch a bald eagle soar over the valley.

"I realize it was a violation of your trust, your privacy. But I knew there was something wrong, and I thought if I understood what it was, I could help."

"How—by waving your magic dick?" Dona glared at his handsome profile. "Oh, that's right—you already tried that."

"I don't blame you for being angry."

Dona ground her teeth. "Thanks so much for your understanding."

Alerio gave her a long, steady look that made her feel like a cosmic-class bitch. "I am sorry for what you suffered at the hands of those who should have protected you." He moved closer. "Your parents. The Aranian military." His lip curled. "Kavel. Especially Kavel."

Dona stared up into his black eyes, trying to read the emotion there. Did she repulse him now—Dona Astryr, ex-lover of a sixty-eight-year-old pedophile? Or did he just pity her?

And which would she hate more?

Alerio watched as Dona spun on her heel and stalked away. Her booted feet crunched through the leaves in long, angry strides.

He'd hoped she wouldn't be as angry as he feared. Instead, she seemed even more furious than he'd anticipated. The betrayal in those lovely violet eyes felt like a blade between the ribs.

Far too many people had betrayed Dona. Alerio hated being one of them. Never mind that he'd only wanted to help, while the rest of the bastards seemed to act from pure selfishness.

For Dona, the end result was the same.

Well, not quite. Cracking her medical file is hardly in the same league as raping her from the age of fifteen. But eyeing those rigid shoulders, Alerio wasn't sure if she'd agree.

She wheeled toward him with such violence, he almost fell

into guard out of sheer warrior reflex. Somehow he managed to suppress his body's wary jerk.

Dona stalked toward him, eyes narrow with calculation. "Just how sorry are you, Alerio?"

"I deeply regret invading your privacy." Honesty forced him to add, "But I'd do the same thing again if I thought it was necessary. In this case, it was necessary."

Temper flashed in her brilliant eyes. "Oh, *was* it?"

"Yeah, it was." He considered putting a hand on her shoulder, only to hastily drop the idea. He'd probably draw back a stump. "The thing with Ivar wouldn't have happened otherwise."

"So now you think I'm a career victim."

"Don't put words in my mouth, Dona." He reined in his own temper with an effort. "Look, I admire the way you've overcome your past. Instead of becoming bitter, you're a generous, compassionate person."

"Right." She snorted in skepticism.

Alerio glowered. "I'm serious. Whenever a case requires empathy, you're the first agent I think of assigning. Even when you were partnered with that asshole Terje, you always treated victims with delicacy and respect."

She blinked up at him, and he realized he'd surprised her. "I knew we got a lot of sexual assault cases. I just thought you'd already . . ." She broke off.

He nodded slowly. "You thought I already knew."

"I had no idea what was—or wasn't—in that file."

Puzzled, he studied her. "If you thought I already knew, why were you so pissed when I told you I'd hacked it?"

"Because it's one thing to get the information because you're supposed to have it," Dona said, folding her arms and rocking back on her heels, "and another to hack a file you know is private. A distinction I'm sure you grasp."

She had him there. "Yeah. That's why I debated doing it for the past six months."

Dona's brows shot skyward. "Six months?"

"What, you thought I hacked your psychiatric file on a whim?" Temper stung him with a quick, hard bite. "You really don't think much of me."

"Alerio, if my opinion of you weren't so high, I wouldn't have gotten so pissed off." Her voice dropped. "And hurt."

"I never wanted to hurt you. That I regret to my soul." Looking down into the violet depths of her eyes, he thought again how incredibly beautiful she was.

Then he was kissing her before he realized he was going to do it.

Alerio Dyami could pack more passion into a simple kiss than any of Dona's other lovers put into the entire sex act. His kiss certainly affected her with more power.

As his mouth claimed hers, Dona had to straighten her weak knees, catch his powerful shoulders, and let her body melt into his.

She had no choice.

The Warlord made a rough sound against her mouth—half growl, half grateful purr. Strong arms wrapped around her, plastering her body against his.

Dona was always surprised at how soft his mouth felt, even during a kiss so fierce. Particularly compared to the thick erection mashed against her belly. She moaned as arousal blazed up in her like a campfire doused in booster fuel.

Alerio released her waist and drew back, cupping her face in his palms. His eyes burned Warlord red, and his breath came too fast. "Tell me to stop. I won't be able to if you don't."

Dona gazed into his angular, handsome face with its bright tattoo. "What if I don't *want* you to stop?"

His eyes flashed red, then cooled. "Are you sure? Five minutes ago you wanted to kick my ass."

She laughed. "I can think of a lot of things to do to your ass, Alerio. Kicking it isn't even on the list."

And it was true. He had wrestled with whether to hack that file for months, had done so only because he was genuinely worried about her. All of which told her she hadn't misread his feelings for her. Unlike Kavel's, Terje's, even her parents.

Alerio Dyami was a genuinely good man.

Dona's sudden grin felt so wide, she suspected it looked a little goofy. She didn't give a damn. Reaching for her uniform's high collar, she traced a finger along the seal and watched his eyes blaze even brighter as the seam parted. "Make love to me, Alerio."

"Okay, you talked me into it." Alerio bent, swept her into his arms, and carried her up the winding path.

Laughing, Dona looped her arms around his strong neck. "Mind telling me where we're going?"

He smiled down at her, his teeth flashing white against his tattoo. "You'll see."

"I love surprises." Settling into his arms, she let herself enjoy the moment.

The ground leveled, and Alerio veered off the path, headed for a massive cliff that formed a sweeping curve. When he rounded the great stone face, a clearing lay tucked against its granite flanks. Flowers ringed it in brilliant shades of red, yellow, and deep, rich violet, along with leafy green cascades of ferns.

As Dona admired the scene, it seemed to ripple like a mirage seen through hot desert air, revealing a tent. Swags of red silk draped from its supporting poles, casting cool pools of shade. Inside the tent lay a thick pallet of white silk piled with pillows.

She blinked at it from the cradle of Alerio's arms. "Where did that come from?"

Alerio ducked beneath the tent's opening and lowered her to

her feet. "I put it up early this morning before the teams Jumped. I wanted to make love to you somewhere more romantic than my quarters." He grimaced. "I also hoped it would put you in a good mood so you'd be less pissed after I told you about the file. Reality had other ideas."

"Either way, it's lovely." She smiled over her shoulder at him and stopped in surprise.

He was stripping off his uniform tunic, revealing the muscled width of his chest. Balancing on one foot, he pulled off his left boot, then his right.

As he opened the seal of his pants, his cock spilled free, thick and flushed dark. Dona stared, her mouth going helplessly dry, as he dragged his trousers down his powerful legs. Stepping free of them, he gave her a grin. "I can't help but notice you're a trifle overdressed."

"Can't have that." Dona finished unsealing her tunic with eager fingers, and let it slide from her shoulders.

Alerio dropped down on the pallet and watched with unabashed lust as she kicked her boots off and wiggled free of her pants. He caught his breath as she straightened to her full height, all graceful nudity, her breasts full, tipped with the tight rose peaks of luscious nipples. A triangle of dark hair lay between the long, strong thighs that swept down to slender, muscled calves and slim feet.

The scent of her arousal teased his acute Warlord senses. The head of his erection bucked against his belly as he remembered the taste of her, the snug grip of her rosy folds wrapping around his shaft.

She licked her lips with her pointed pink tongue. The violet brilliance of her eyes darkened, her pupils expanding at the sight of him.

"You're so beautiful." Her voice sounded throaty, rasping. "I want to taste you. Everywhere."

"Ah . . . Feel free." His balls tightened as his cock lengthened. He wondered if he'd ever been this hard in his life—except for the previous times they'd made love.

She moved toward him in that liquid dancer's stride, then dropped to her hands and knees on the bed. Breath caught, he watched her crawl up the length of his body.

Until she reached his cock.

Slowly, she lowered herself, bending her elbows until her head was mere centimeters from his cock. As she dipped her head, she kept her eyes locked on his in a hot, wild stare that made the blood thunder in his ears. "Sweet Goddess," Alerio rasped. "You're so damned lovely. I've never known a woman so utterly sensual."

"Because you make me feel beautiful." Her cool fingers closed around his hot cock, angled the thick shaft upward. "You make me feel like the most gorgeous woman on the Outpost with those Warlord eyes burning."

Breath caught, he watched her open her mouth, watched the pointed tip of her tongue flick out to swirl over the flushed cap of his erection. Alerio groaned as pleasure thrummed along his nerves. Her fingers tightened around his cock, exerting the perfect degree of pressure as she stroked him slowly. Up and down. Her tongue licked and swirled, each delicate motion seeming to ignite the blood in his veins.

And the way she looked.

That perfect face, intense with arousal that left only a thin ring of purple around her huge black pupils. She shifted to get a better angle on his cock, opened her mouth wide, and swallowed the length of him right down almost to the balls.

Alerio was not a small man, but she didn't choke on his size as other women had. Instead she suckled him with wicked skill, one hand stroking his balls, the other drifting up his chest to find his small male nipples.

He gasped at the pleasure. It took real effort to manage speech. "Let me . . . taste you. Let me touch you."

She looked up at him a moment before she slowly, slowly rose on her knees to give him an evil smile. "Well, if you insist."

Dona rearranged herself, planting her knees on either side of his head, then stretching the length of his torso. Her lush breasts teased his skin as she moved. He reached a hand down, seeking one of those lovely breasts, finding its peak.

As he started to stroke and tease, he slid the tip of his tongue the length of her lips, up and down, then circling her clit. She purred in sensual approval and engulfed him again in a gorgeous erotic rush.

Shuddering in delight, Alerio concentrated on her wet rose folds, savoring her taste and scent as he toyed and licked. Need stormed through him until he ached with it.

Dona's eyes shuttered in bliss as she filled her mouth with Alerio's cock. As she slid the hot, smooth shaft over her tongue, Alerio's fingers teased one nipple while he slowly lapped her sex. The pleasure she felt was so intense and pure, it was like being immersed in heated honey. Floating weightlessly on a golden bed, buoyed by delight.

The orgasm broke free like a champagne cork propelled by a froth of bubbles. It happened to hit just as she raised her head. "Alerio!" she gasped. "Oh, gods, Alerio!"

Strong hands grabbed her waist, picked her up, and tumbled her down on her back. He reared over her, his eyes a solid sheet of fire. He caught her knees and pulled them up until he could hook her heels over his shoulders. Wrapping his hands around her thighs, he aimed his cock for her slick opening. His first thrust was so hard and hot and delicious, her climax spiked even harder.

Watching her face, he reached one hand around to pluck her

right nipple, teasing and flicking as he hunched slowly. His hips ground against her ass, first in long drives, then in grinding circles, then thrusting again, varying the stimulation with perfect skill. Maddened, she threw back her head and screamed her way through the wicked pounding.

His roar rose beneath hers, a raw male bellow of existential pleasure, savage and intense.

CHAPTER NINE

A furious banging jolted Dona awake.

"Chief!" Jessica Arvid shouted from the other side of the corridor door. "Chief, he's taken Galar! That bastard Terje took my husband!" That last word rang with anguish.

"Jessica?" Alerio surged up beneath Dona, rolled her gently aside, and hit the floor, jerking on a robe before striding toward the door.

Dona sat up, swiping her hair out of her face as she stared around them, disoriented. Belatedly, she remembered she and Alerio had returned to his quarters after their adventures in the woods.

"Alerio!" Jessica screamed, genuine panic in her voice.

"I'm coming!" He threw Dona a look. She grabbed her clothing and dove into the bathroom. As she pulled on her uniform, she listened to their conversation through the closed door as her lover let Jessica in.

"What happened?" he demanded. "Did Galar send a courier bot?"

"No, I don't think he had time. It was a vision." Her voice sounded tight with strain, pitched higher than her normal throaty voice. "I was asleep. Next thing I knew, I was watching a gang of Xerans in T-suits attack Galar's coach. He was driving. They shot three of the horses . . ."

"Pendragon?"

"No, him they missed. The others, the mares. Galar tried to brake, but that thing doesn't exactly stop on a dime. The coach overturned when it hit the bodies, and he was thrown. I think he sustained a head injury."

Dressed again, Dona slipped back into the bedroom. "Are you sure it was a vision and not a nightmare?"

"She's had visions before," Alerio reminded her. "Remember when she saw the Xerans capture Charlotte and the two Sela females?"

"Yes, but she told me the other day that sometimes she has nightmares and isn't sure they're not visions."

"Not this time," Jessica told her grimly, whirling to pace. Her velvet robe flapped as she moved, revealing the filmy skirt of her negligee fluttering around slippered feet. "The details were too solid. I could even smell the horses. The blood." She closed her eyes as if fighting for control. "Galar's blood. I don't know about you, but I've never smelled anything in a dream."

Alerio watched her agitated pacing with grim, narrow-eyed attention. "How badly was he hurt?"

"Galar tried to get to his feet, but he could barely stand. Ivar stabbed him in the chest. Right through his T-suit. The blade chimed like one of those quantum swords of theirs, but it looked more like a stiletto." Wringing her hands, she reached the wall and spun to stride the other way. "He tried to fight even then, but between that and the head injury . . . Ivar cuffed him with restraint cable and Jumped, taking Galar with him." Jessica looked so pale, Dona feared she was going to faint. "He's not dead. I won't believe he's dead."

"And he's not going to die," Alerio told her, stepping into her path and catching her by the shoulders. "I'm taking a Jump team and we're going to get him back. Now, tell me exactly what you saw."

"After you sit down." Dona slipped an arm around her friend's shoulders. Alerio stepped back as she guided Jessica to a chair. "Now tell us."

"Chief Dyami?" Nick called through the corridor door.

"What do you want to bet he had the same vision?" Alerio growled as the door opened at his silent command.

"Sorry, but that's a bet you'd lose. I didn't see Galar's kidnapping." Nick paused to allow Riane and Frieka to enter first. The bedroom was growing crowded. "What I *did* see was that Jessica and I have to go with the Jump team, or you'll fail." His handsome mouth tightened into a tight line. "And we may anyway. I didn't see all the details."

"Of course you didn't," Dona muttered. "Because that would make it too easy."

"Goddess knows we never get easy," Frieka growled, the lights of his vocalizer flashing from his fur.

Alerio gestured for the three to take a seat on his bed. "So. Tell me what you did see."

Peter Brannon died defending Kangse Wei, the documentarian the Enforcers had been sent to protect. The two men lay in a bloody ring of five dead Xerans fifty feet from the remains of the coach. As Jessica had told Alerio back at the Outpost, the two had apparently escaped the wreckage and attempted to escape.

"He didn't sell his life cheaply," Dona said quietly from just behind Alerio's shoulder.

"He wouldn't have." Alerio studied the arc of spilled blood and disordered sand around the bodies. "He wasn't as big as Wulf, didn't have the raw power of Terje, but he was a fighter. Intelligent.

Courageous." He winced, remembering Gailisha Brannon, the apple of Peter's eye. "And I'm going to have to tell his daughter she'll have to bury him."

Once Dr. Chogan reattached his head, anyway. One of the Xerans had decapitated him, probably with a quantum sword.

At least Peter had made good use of his own weapon. His fingers still curled around the big axe's handle, and blood soaked the sand. He would have swung the weapon in wide arcs, hacking right through the Xerans' armored T-suits with merciless skill.

But once he fell, there'd been no one to save Wei. The documentarian had been cut nearly in two. "Looks like whoever killed Peter took Wei out with the reverse stroke." Alerio pointed out the sweeping pattern of blood splatter that connected the two bodies. His voice dropped to a mutter. "Poor bastard didn't get to tell his story."

Dona studied the dead men with brooding pity, wiping the sweat from her eyes. The Arizona sun beat down like assaulting fists as flies buzzed around the bodies. "At least it was quick."

"But completely unnecessary." A muscle jerked in the Warlord's jaw. "If Colonel Ceres had let me pull those temporal visas the way I'd wanted, these people wouldn't be dead, and Galar wouldn't have been kidnapped by the fucking Xerans. I should have . . ."

"Disobeyed orders? Committed career suicide?"

He glared at her. "Better that than bury innocent civilians and good agents."

"And the end result would have been more dead, innocent and otherwise." Nick moved to join them. His green eyes appeared out of focus, as if he was looking at something other than the scene around him. A chill brushed Dona's spine as she realized he was having a vision. "The Victor would have declared war on Terran time travel. The deaths . . ."

Riane moved up behind him and touched his shoulder. He broke off so abruptly, his teeth snapped together.

"What do you see?" Dona studied his pale, set face and the green glow of his eyes.

"The dying." He turned away. "Far too many dying innocents."

"Chief!" Chogan called from beyond the wrecked coach. "I've got Pendragon stabilized. I believe he'll be able to talk to you if you get over here before I Jump him back to the Outpost. He needs regen for this wound."

Alerio headed toward them, his boots sinking into the sand. He was conscious of Dona at his heels, her face grim.

The coach lay on its side, surrounded by broken wood that had exploded from it when it hit the horses. Wei's equipment lay among the wreckage, camerabots spilled from broken cases. The chief noticed the vehicle fell on the side with the door. Peter had kicked a hole in the topmost side so the two men could escape.

He hadn't been the only one determined to survive. Pendragon had likewise torn free of his harness and leaped free, avoiding injury when the coach slammed into the rest of the team. The Xerans had managed to wound the great beast anyway. Blood flecked his white coat, much of it from a gash that ran the length of his heaving ribs. Still, judging by his bloody front hooves, he'd gotten in some shots of his own. Apparently he'd tried to stomp a hole in the Xeran who lay on his back nearby, being treated by one of the medtechs.

Frieka sat by the stallion's head, licking the horse's long, elegant muzzle. That bit of uncharacteristically canine behavior told Alerio just how upset the wolf was.

Pendragon raised his head at their approach. His eyes were glazed with pain. "They killed the mares. Why the hell did the bastards kill the mares? They weren't cyborgs. They were just horses." The grief in his voice made Alerio's chest ache.

"They didn't care, Pen," Frieka told him gruffly. "But I'm going to pay the fuckers back for you. They will regret this." His lips rippled, pulling off sharp white fangs. "I'm going to make them bleed."

"And he will, too." Alerio sank to one knee. "What can you tell me, Pendragon? What happened?"

"They were heavily shielded when they hit us. Hell, I was scanning for them, and I didn't have a fucking clue we'd been surrounded. There wasn't even a sensor trace." He dropped his head back to the sand and stared toward the bloody bodies of his team. "Until they shot the mares. Me, they missed. When the girls went down, my neurocomp projected the coach would hit us, and I tore out of my harness." He subsided, his massive barrel rising and falling. "The coach overturned. Galar was in the driver's box—he was thrown. Probably only survived because he was wearing his armor under his civilian clothes. Sensors said he had a severe concussion."

"How many Xerans were there?" Alerio asked.

"Two cohorts of warrior priests, judging by the number and length of the horns. Twenty more monks, varying ranks."

A cohort was made up of five of the most elite, most senior members of the caste. *Thirty Xerans against three Enforcers, one of whom didn't even have hands.* Alerio dropped his head and cursed.

"How did they bring in that many Jumpers without us knowing it?" Dona sounded appalled. "Thirty Jumpers should have created a temporal warp detectable all the way to the Outpost."

"Probably Jumped them in a few at a time," he explained absently. "Dammit, I thought they'd go after the historians, since there were a lot more of them. That's why I assigned Wulf and his three as escorts. Toughest team we have."

"Maybe they wanted to make sure they took one of the Enforcers alive." Dona looked up at him, having dropped to her knees to stroke Pendragon's neck. "They sent an overwhelming force to make sure somebody would survive."

"And *that* means they won't let him die, Jess," Riane told the human as the pair moved to join them. "They'll make sure he gets any treatment he needs."

"And if he can survive, I can fix anything they do to him."

Chogan looked up from her patient to give Jessica a reassuring smile. "He'll be fine."

"I know." Jess forced a smile, but the effort it cost her was obvious. "You've never let us down, Sakari. I know Galar . . ."

"Hey, Chief!" one of the medtechs interrupted. "I've got the captive conscious."

Alerio flashed Pendragon a smile he suspected was savage. "Thanks for leaving me one to question."

"Wasn't my idea. I just couldn't pound through his fucking armor with my hooves."

The survivor was a low-level monk; he had only two horns.

"Well," Alerio purred, looking down at the captive with a stare so predatory, even Dona felt a chill. "I wonder what we can get out of you?"

The Xeran stared up at him in wide-eyed fear. "Don't . . ."

"Let me deal with him, Chief." Dona gave the monk a deliberately menacing smile. "I can get him to talk."

The man shrank against the sand as if he wished it would open up and swallow him. "That's . . . that's not necessary. I'll tell you anything you want to know."

Dona curled her lip. "You mean you'll lie and hope we're gullible enough to swallow your shit."

To her surprise, the monk's gaze hardened. "I'll not stoop to lying for that bastard. Believe me or don't."

"What bastard?" Alerio asked, as if not particularly interested. "Ivar?"

"That puppet?" The monk snorted. "Hardly. The Victor."

Dona glared at him in offended outrage. "What kind of fools do you think we are? I fought you fuckers at Arania. I *know* you."

The captive sneered. "You don't know us now. Not since the rebellion."

"What rebellion?" Alerio demanded.

"The one that *abomination* caused." He jerked his chin at Nick. The big, dark-haired Guardian had moved silently to join them, standing with powerful arms folded. The T'Lir on his arm glinted dully in the desert sun. "After that one broke the Victor, fifty cohorts rebelled, taking half the monks on Xer with them."

"Fifty cohorts?" Dona snorted. "Beefershit. Those bastards are the most fanatical members of the priesthood. Hells, fanaticism is why the Victor picks them to *be* the elite."

"Not after the Victor used Ivar as his refuge following his fight with the abomination. Especially not when the last two cohorts refused to surrender what they held of him." The monk sneered, his expression bitter. "We all knew that 'borg would pollute the Most High, and that's exactly what he did."

"He's babbling." Frieka flicked a dismissive ear. "This is a waste of time, Chief. Crack his comp and make him tell the truth."

Alerio gave the priest a cold glare. "Well? Do I crack you, or do you start talking on your own?"

"I am telling the truth, you stupid 'borg bastard. The cohorts held part of the god, and they refused to give him up," the monk spat. "Ivar led the loyalists against them—I was stupid enough to follow him—and we killed them all. He took the pieces back, but when the Victor reformed from the 'borg's body, he was mad." His gaze shifted away, staring into the distance as if at some horrifying vision. "Mad and corrupted. He ordered the captive priests burned in Ponichi Capital Square, babbling about medieval Earth kings. So no, I don't care to become a martyr for the Victor."

Alerio was still trying to get more useful intelligence out of their captive when a voice spoke over the mission com channel. One Dona knew far too well.

"Missing your boy Galar, Dyami?" Ivar asked in a laughing

purr that sent a chill down her spine. Everyone in the party simultaneously stiffened. "Want him back?"

She exchanged a look with Alerio. "What do you want, Ivar?" the chief demanded coldly.

"You know what I want. Otherwise you wouldn't have brought Wyatt. Get the T'Lir and bring it to me. Alone. No Nick. No Jessica. No Dona. No fucking backup whatsoever. Or Jessica gets to bury her Warlord."

Alerio's handsome face looked as if it had been cast in plastium. "Where am I supposed to take it?"

Ivar rattled off a string of coordinates. "That's your first stop. There'll be others. I'll give you the next one when you get there. On foot. If I get so much as a whiff of anybody other than you, I'll send Jess poor Galar's head in a box. We don't want that, do we?"

"No."

"Of course not. Not with you being such a 'hero' and all. You have fifteen minutes. Just possible if you haul ass. Otherwise . . ."

"I'll be there."

"Of course you will." Ivar's tone lost its edge of mocking humor. "And don't think you can fool me with a fake. I'll know, and Galar will get a whole lot shorter. By a head. Maybe part of his neck, too, but definitely by a head."

Com link broken, Dona's neurocomp told her.

She swallowed, fighting a cold wave of panic that filled her throat with greasy nausea.

Alerio turned to Nick. "I need the T'Lir."

The Sela Guardian looked at him for a long, silent moment.

"Nick . . ." Jessica stared at him, desperation putting a tremor in her voice. "He's not bluffing. We both know that."

"No, he's not bluffing." Nick pulled the silver band off his biceps and handed it to Alerio.

Accepting it, the chief met his gaze. "Whatever Terje's got in mind, I'm not going to let him get away with it."

"If you can stop him."

"I'll stop him."

"Alerio . . ." Dona had to stop and lick lips gone painfully dry. Her heart pounded so hard, she could barely hear herself speak. "You can't do this. Ivar hates you. He's going to kill you."

"He's going to try." Alerio turned away. "But he will definitely kill Galar if I don't. And I've lost all the agents I mean to lose today."

Ivar watched the black speck that was Alerio Dyami run toward the fortress the Victor had created in the heart of the Arizona desert. It wasn't a very big fortress, true. It didn't need to be, with only twenty-four priests alive to man it. But it still resembled a medieval castle, complete with towering stone walls and battlements.

The Victor is insane. Obsessed with medieval kings and crazy as a Soji Dragon in season. The thought zipped through his mind before he had time to suppress it.

Pain! Agony raced across his skin as though he'd been sprayed with acid. His knees buckled, and he cried out before he could clamp his lips together.

I am not mad, the Victor growled from Ivar's feet.

For once, he hadn't assumed his towering golden form. Instead, he wore what Ivar now knew to be his true appearance: that of a roiling black amoeba, glistening in the throbbing sunlight and heavily shielded from the Warlord's sensors.

I. Am. Not. Mad. Say it!

"Of course you're not mad," Ivar wheezed. It took everything he had to remain on his feet, but he didn't dare fall in front of the Victor. He had an ugly feeling the thing would eat him. "I meant no offense!"

See that you remember it. I still know your every thought.

"Yes, I know!" *Gods help me.*

I am your only god now, cyborg. With one last flaming wave of pain, the Victor ceased the torture. Ivar sagged against the battlements, acutely aware of the two warrior priests watching him with stony contempt. The bastards hated his guts.

Almost as much as I hate Dyami.

Glancing over the battlements, the battleborg blinked in surprise. The Warlord was damned fast; Dyami had almost reached the castle in the short time Ivar had been . . . preoccupied. Though he'd been going full-out in the blistering heat for over an hour, he still ran with the smooth, relentless power of a combot.

Those Vardonese bastards knew their nanotech and genetic engineering. Ivar wasn't sure even he would have been able to survive a trek like that without collapsing from heatstroke. Any ordinary human would have dropped dead almost an hour ago. Which of course was the whole point: to run Dyami so hard, the Enforcers didn't have a chance to follow.

Too, all that exercise should have eaten into even the Warlord's impressive physical reserves. He would still put up a fight—he wasn't even in *riaat* yet—but he wouldn't be able to resist long before his body finally gave out.

The fucking idiot. The chief must know he was a dead man. Must realize the Xerans had no intention of surrendering Galar and every intention of killing Dyami himself once he turned over the T'Lir.

Ivar shot a sullen look over one shoulder. The blond Warlord lay on his back, spread-eagled in anti-grav fetters that held him immobile. The knife wound he'd suffered had finally stopped bleeding, thanks more to his neurocomp than any treatment the Xerans had given him. Even so, Galar was only half-conscious. The concussion he'd suffered during the coach crash had taken a heavy toll.

He was lucky to be breathing at all. He'd be dead by now if

Ivar'd had his way. Arvid had always been almost as big a pain in Ivar's ass as Dyami himself.

Another vicious blast of pain. *I told you, I will bend the Warlord to my will. Dyami, and that one down there.*

They're Warlords. The thought flashed through Ivar's mind before he could stop it. *They don't bend, and they'll gut you if you try . . .* A blast of pain brought tears to his eyes. Frantically, he toed the line. "But it will do them no good, Great One," he wheezed. "You'll blow out their minds like a match." *Like hell.*

This time the thought zipped past too quickly for the Victor to catch it. Mollified, the oily bastard stopped inflicting that crippling pain. *Too bad I can't do that all the time.* Luckily the Victor didn't catch that either.

"All right, Ivar, I'm here!" Alerio bellowed from the base of the wall. "Now I want to see Galar. Alive." He held up the T'Lir, fingers closed around the green gem. "Or I'll shatter this, and your god gets nothing."

"He lives." Ivar gestured dramatically and stepped aside. The anti-grav fetters dragged the blond upright and up into the air. The blond Warlord groaned in pain, head lolling forward on his shoulders.

"Barely," Dyami snarled. His fingers tightened on the gem. "Put him in regen, dammit, or . . ."

"Put him there yourself!" Ivar spat back, in no mood for Dyami's alpha male bullshit. "*After* you hand over the T'Lir."

"Bring him down and get it!" The Warlord's eyes flared so brightly red, they were visible even at this distance in full desert sunlight.

Ivar hesitated. Damned if he wanted to get in range of those fists with the chief's eyes that color. True, the Victor had upgraded Ivar's own tech yet again—the process had been just as agonizing as it had been the first few times the "god" had worked on him— but even that was no guarantee against Dyami in a mood. The

Warlord could do more damage through sheer strategy and a suicidal refusal to surrender as anyone else could with raw power.

This is a trap, Ivar thought. *Got to be. Dyami isn't this damned stupid.*

He did another sensor sweep, but once again, he could detect no sign of the shielded Enforcers he'd expected to arrive in Alerio's wake. Though Ivar wouldn't have been able to punch through their sensor shields, he should have been able to detect the energy trace of the fields themselves. Yet there was absolutely nothing there.

Because he didn't bring them, the Victor told him, roiling impatiently around Ivar's feet. *I told you the weak fool wouldn't risk his underling's life. I would sense the Enforcers' minds if he had, and there is nothing there.* A dark anticipation surged through the link. *Now I will take what is mine. At last!*

A massive spike of power buckled Ivar's knees as the Victor sent his energies swirling over the ramparts downward toward the Warlord waiting below.

Alerio was still staring up at the battlements when the three-meter-tall golden giant appeared, almost in his face. He threw up an arm block in sheer spinal reflex. It did him no good as a fist the size of his head slammed into his skull.

The next thing he knew, he was staring up at a painfully cloudless blue sky through a field of dancing sparks. His head was full of his neurocomp's shrieking alarm Klaxons, but he had no idea where he was or what had just happened.

The Victor hit you, the comp told him. *GET UP!*

Years of experience had taught Alerio never to ignore that tone in his comp's voice, no matter how bad he felt. He reeled to his feet, but the world swung around him so violently, he almost fell again. He looked down and felt a chill.

His hands were empty.

The bait. Where the fuck is the bait?

He took it, the neurocomp said. *He's stopped to drain it, just as you expected.*

The world stopped spinning as the implant compensated. Glancing around wildly, Alerio spotted the Victor kneeling at the base of the fortress wall a good ten meters away. Last he remembered, he'd been standing *beside* the wall.

Wait. He knocked me ten meters with one punch?

Yes. He's incredibly powerful.

Let's just pray he's not all that bright.

The giant held the T'Lir in both hands as he studied it in obvious fascination. Alerio licked lips left painfully dry by his enforced desert run. *If he spots the trap, we're fucked.*

So far Nick had done a good job creating the dummy T'Lir. The counterfeit looked exactly the same as the silver armband with its embedded green gem, but the real thing was still locked around the Guardian's arm. Apparently the Victor didn't know the T'Lir couldn't be removed until Nick died—and then it would immediately disappear off to whomever the sentient gem had selected to be the new Sela Guardian. Damn sure wouldn't be the Victor.

The trick had been faking the aura of power that clung to the T'Lir even in its half-drained state. The Victor had seen the gem during the battle with Nick six months back, and they'd known he'd spot a substitute.

Nick had proposed the solution back at the Outpost, since it was obvious what the Victor would demand as Galar's ransom. It seemed the spirit of Nick's dead mother had volunteered to inhabit the phony gem and serve as the conduit for the catlike guardian spirit that inhabited Nick. But the cat had warned Nick it didn't have the power to fool the Victor for long enough.

So Jessica and Riane had linked with Nick, adding the psychic abilities the Sela had given both women months before. Nick suspected the Sela had somehow known this day was coming, which was why they'd empowered Jess and Riane to begin with.

The next step was to fool the Xerans at the coach, which they'd managed to do. The only thing they hadn't anticipated was that Ivar would demand Alerio bring the T'Lir; they'd expected the Victor to require them to turn over Nick instead. Still, the psychic attack they'd planned should work, assuming the Victor took the bait.

Alerio frowned. What was that ancient military saying they taught at the Vardonese academy?

"No plan ever survives first contact with the enemy."

From the cool confines of the grav-sled, Dona watched the Victor examine the counterfeit T'Lir. Her guts laced themselves into intricate knots of nausea.

"He'll be fine," Frieka told her, sitting strapped in the seat at her side. With Pendragon back at the Outpost in the equine-sized regenerator the European Outpost had sent along with him, the wolf had decided to accompany the rescue party. "Dyami can plot rings around those bastards."

"He'd better." Dona frowned, shooting a concerned look at Jessica, who sat in the back of the sled with Nick and Riane. The human's eyes were glassy, and sweat streamed down her face as she sat with her hands gripping the couple's. Without the grav-sled, Jess never would have survived the trek across the desert.

The sleds were illegal for use on Jumps, of course. If a temporal native happened to spot one during an invisibility shield failure—unlikely, but theoretically possible—the teardrop-shaped vehicles would be too obviously alien. They were only supposed to be used to transport supplies and equipment on the Outpost, but Alerio had ordered the three units along on the Jump anyway.

"Let the bastards court-martial me," he'd growled. *"I don't give a shit as long as this works."*

The sleds were crucial to the plan; their sensor shields made them completely undetectable. Unlike those created by T-suits, sled shields produced no ghosting, thanks to their more powerful onboard generators.

Better yet, Ivar would never expect Alerio to violate regs by bringing one along on a Jump.

The problem was they couldn't be sure what the *Victor* could sense. Alerio had decided to take the chance anyway.

The other issue was that the three sleds couldn't detect each other. The only way they'd been able to avoid colliding as they followed Alerio was by triangulating on the Warlord and flying in rigid formation.

"Get us closer," Nick said to the sled pilot.

Enforcer Carrie Jones gave him a short nod as her hands glided over the controls, bringing the craft to within meters of the Victor. They watched the tridscreen as the "god's" golden lips peeled back, exposing his white teeth in a grin.

Nick's broad shoulders tensed under the dove-gray scales of his civilian T-suit. Beside him, Riane tightened her grip on his hand. "Now!" he snapped to his companions. The sled flooded with blinding green light as he, Riane, and Jess began to glow, pumping their collective energies into the stone. The Victor stared down at the faux T'Lir in fascination.

Dona reached across to Frieka, her fingers sliding into the wolf's thick black fur and curling into a fist.

Alerio looked up, silently praying to every goddess he could think of. Right on cue, two grav-sleds popped into view, swooping downward at the battlements to begin Galar's rescue.

He whirled and glanced around, searching for Dona's sled, which should be waiting nearby behind its own camo field. Exactly as planned, the big dark blue sled popped into view as its shield dropped. Its silver-trimmed door slipped open silently, and he raced toward it to fling himself aboard. "Get us up there!"

Carrie Jones sent the craft shooting skyward on pulsing blue anti-grav fields before swooping in to land on the fortress's flat stone roof. Alerio popped open the weapons locker, revealing the shields and quantum axes inside. Without a word, he took one weapon and tossed another to Dona as she and the wolf moved to join him. Jones would remain with the sled, guarding their rear.

Jess, Nick, and Riane didn't move; they were busy channeling power to the spirit of Charlotte Holt. The pilot gave Alerio a sharp nod. It was her job to protect the three while they did theirs.

The Enforcers leaped out onto the ramparts as the sled's door snapped shut and locked behind them.

CHAPTER TEN

Images flooded the Victor's mind, visions so hypnotically real, he could only watch in fascination. All of them featured six-legged creatures that looked vaguely familiar. It took him a moment to remember where he'd seen one before.

Ah. There'd been an old Earth animal called a *tiger*: huge, brawny, and striped. These creatures had six limbs, though. The first pair looked like thin, disproportionately long human arms with agile fingers like those of primates, but the other four were nothing short of massive, with claws as long as human fingers. Their feline heads had outsized pointed ears, short muzzles, and huge, intelligent eyes.

Despite their animalistic appearance, they were star travelers. Aggressive, too, conquering every race they encountered, then stealing their technology. The cats killed any individuals stupid enough to resist and enslaved the rest. The Victor could only admire their bloodthirsty efficiency.

It crossed his mind to wonder if these were some version of the Sela, who were also six-legged and catlike. But the Abominations were dainty pacifists, nothing like these brawling brutes who killed and died with equal abandon.

They also sang alien songs the Victor found he could somehow understand, though he'd never heard their language before. Songs that gloried in bloodshed and conquest as proof of their worthiness to rule.

He watched entranced as one of the aliens' huge ships approached a green and blue gem of a world. It disgorged a smaller craft that landed in a clearing near a crowd of creatures that looked like wheel-shaped crabs, except with fur and a greater number of legs. *They call themselves the Di'jiri*, said a soft, androgynous mental voice.

What the hells? the Victor wondered, but then the doors opened on the felinoids' lander. One of the big cats leaped out, followed by fifty or so armored feline soldiers. The lead cat demanded the Di'jiri surrender in a tone the Victor interpreted as acute boredom. He didn't seem to care whether they understood his threat to kill them all if they didn't immediately surrender.

Victor suspected they didn't, since the Di'jiri only blinked their faceted eyes and trilled in polite interest.

The felinoid leader reared on his back legs and lunged, striking out with both powerful mid-legs. His claws ripped through the nearest Di'jiri, which died in an explosion of orange life fluids.

Roaring in joy, his team fell on the survivors and killed them all. The Di'jiri made no attempt to flee or resist as they fell beneath the warriors' claws.

The Victor frowned in restless disappointment. Where was the glory in killing creatures so utterly lacking in fighting spirit?

"*That,*" something growled in the felinoids' tongue, "*is quite enough of that.*"

A creature five times the size of the others melted into view as if it had dropped a camo shield. *The mother of the Di'jiri*, the psychic voice told the Victor. *And she is most wroth.*

The felinoid captain and his warriors froze as though suddenly unable to move, though rage flashed in their enormous eyes. *The*

Di'jiri Mother has done something to them, the Victor realized, outraged.

She circled the team, scuttling on her ring of jointed legs, trilling and clicking her claws as if talking to herself. Finally she switched to the felinoid tongue. *"My children did nothing to you. Nothing! And yet you murdered them!"*

"Not murder," the Victor corrected under his breath. "Conquest. The strong have a right to rule the weak."

"It's time you share the suffering of your victims, monstrous ones." The Mother's ring of eyes began to glow a bright, all-too-familiar green. The same glow he'd seen in the depths of the T'Lir.

The felinoids began to scream in terrified anguish; the pain the Mother felt at her daughters' deaths and the grief of her surviving children. The psychic suffering of thousands of Di'jiri crushed down on them like the gravity of a black hole.

And the Victor shared that pain.

Though no stranger to the thoughts of others, he'd never experienced the agony of his victims. Now he discovered exactly what it was like as visions flooded his skull: disorienting images of the Sela captain and his soldiers fleeing back to their mothership at maximum speed.

And yes, they were Sela. Apparently the events he was seeing had happened centuries before.

Every captain and his men infected every Sela they encountered with the same psychic abilities the Di'jiri Mother had forced on them. It was like some horrific mental plague.

In the weeks that followed, the contagion flashed from one end of the Sela empire to the other, carried by the mothership *Conquest Song*. The psychic plague drove warriors mad as they shared their victims' horrific deaths, tasted the grief of sundered families, felt the helpless fury of being forced to serve sadistic conquerors.

Eventually the Sela could take no more. They began to slay

themselves in an effort to escape their guilt. Their vast empire collapsed within months.

Those who survived retreated into hiding as they struggled to learn how to control their psychic abilities. Eventually they decided they had to atone for their actions, but they also knew their lives wouldn't be long enough to make amends for so many crimes.

They created the first T'Lirs as a repository for their souls and power. They would be reborn in each Sela generation that followed. Though their new bodies did not consciously remember their past lives, they still felt the compulsion to devote themselves to peace.

And the Victor didn't give a shit. He only wanted the pain to stop.

Roaring in agony, the Xeran god colony sent his life force streaming upward, toward the enemies he sensed battling his soldiers on the ramparts of his fortress.

They did this to me! And they're going to pay . . .

An axe in one hand, a shield in the other, Alerio battled the hulking cohort leader who'd attacked him when he'd stepped from the sled. The big priest carried a two-handed quantum sword that chimed like an ancient church bell. The weapon was fully as long as the Xeran was tall, but the bastard knew how to use the awkward blade. The hornhead whirled the enormous sword in blurring figure eights, blocking Alerio's axe swings between attempts to decapitate him. Alerio leaped back, blocking the hornhead's latest swing with a thrust of his shield. He felt the impact in his back teeth; if the shield hadn't been made of the same quantum steel as the blades, it would have been hacked in two. "Arrrrgh!" the Victor howled, the rooftop shaking under his big gold feet as he fell out of the sky. Alerio instinctively jumped back just as the giant hit his own priest in the side of the head. The man's skull exploded like a melon blasted with a shard pistol. As the Xeran fell, the Victor leaped over his corpse, huge hands reaching for Alerio, eyes bulging, black as deep space and flecked with stars. His mouth gaped in a silent shriek of madness.

Oh, fuck, the chief thought. *That doesn't look good at all . . .*

Something naked and golden hurtled through Dona's peripheral vision, but she didn't dare take her attention off the monk she fought. The wiry bastard had a cat's speed and a sword longer than she was tall.

Thank the gods for sensors; she could ask her neurocomp. *What the seven hells was that?*

The Victor just killed a priest. He's attacking Chief Dyami.

A hideous male scream rang out, sounding as if someone were being gutted. Before Dona could whirl to defend Alerio, the monk she was fighting shouted, "No, Most Glorious! He's one of us!"

Instantly Dona swung her axe, severing her distracted foe's head. It spun away, spraying blood across her helmet visor as his body crumpled. His quantum sword struck the rooftop with a high, pealing note. She glanced around to check for nearby attackers. Her immediate surroundings were clear, so she slid her axe into the armored sheath designed to hold it across her back.

She bent and snatched up the monk's enormous sword. If she intended to help Alerio fight the Victor, she'd need the longest weapon she could get her hands on. The giant had too much reach otherwise.

Leaping into a run, she headed for the Victor, now stalking Alerio. The giant swung his own quantum sword in figure-eight swings that flashed in the harsh sunlight.

Alerio retreated, blocking his enemy's pounding blows with his shield and a speed born of *riaat*. Despite his three-meter height, the Victor was unbelievably fast. He must have been equally strong, because every blow of his sword drove the Warlord back.

Dona broke step, studying the pair. For all his terrifying power, there was no control, no strategy to the Victor's attacks. His swings left him wide open, but Alerio couldn't take advantage of his wild assault because the giant's reach was so damned long. The Warlord simply couldn't get close enough to hit him.

She swallowed as fear clamped needle claws into her stomach. Though *riaat* multiplied Alerio's strength, she knew the effect was only temporary. A Warlord could maintain the berserker state no longer than a half hour before he collapsed from a lethal combination of overheating and exhaustion.

How long has Alerio been in riaat*?* Dona demanded.

Eight-point-three minutes, the neurocomp replied. *But the run through the desert drained his reserves. I estimate he has no more than six-point-four minutes before he suffers system collapse as his body overheats. There is a ninety-six percent chance the Victor will kill him the moment he goes down.*

Screw that, Dona thought. *That golden son of a bitch is not killing Alerio Dyami. I'll gut him first.*

There is only a fifteen percent chance you will succeed.

Shut the fuck up. Eyes narrow, teeth clenched, Dona focused on the two fighters and waited for her chance.

Maybe she didn't have the chief's berserker strength. Maybe she lacked his height and muscle. She was going to find a way to save him anyway . . . assuming he didn't find a way to save himself.

Either way, the man she loved wasn't going to die today.

If I don't wrap this up in six minutes, I'm completely screwed, Alerio thought grimly.

Normally, six minutes was an eternity in a fight like this. Even gene-gineered warriors could burn through their reserves with deadly speed in all-out battle. The priests and Enforcers around him had visibly slowed from the speed of minutes before.

All but the Victor. *That* fucker seemed just as deadly as he'd been to begin with.

Alerio ducked a swing of the giant's sword and threw himself into a rolling dive. Slamming to a halt, he leaped up and swung his axe in a vicious diagonal arc. His blade hit the Victor's naked golden flank . . .

And bounced off in a shower of sparks.

Fuck, Alerio thought, flinging himself clear. He felt the wind of the Victor's sword as the Xeran giant tried to cut him in two.

Hitting the ground, he rolled neatly to his feet—just in time to see the Victor turn on Dona and swing. Alerio's heart stopped in his chest, but Dona moved to parry with the instantaneous skill of a trained duelist, swinging her own enormously long weapon into position. He instantly realized what was about to happen.

"No!" Alerio shouted, leaping toward her, trying to get between her and the Victor. "He's too damned strong!"

As he'd feared, the Victor's sword met hers, the blades chiming as the giant angled his weapon and sliced across Dona's slim back. She made no sound, but Alerio sensed the spill of blood down her back. The Victor had sliced right through her T-suit.

With a roar, Alerio rammed the toes of his right boot against the Victor's knee, forcing the giant to stumble into a monk trying to off Frieka. Snarling, the Victor whirled and cut the Xeran in two.

Someone roared a Xeran protest, but the Victor was already charging Dona again.

"Stay out of this, dammit!" Alerio snapped at her as he threw himself into the giant's path. "And that's an order!" Shouldering her backward, he rammed his shield into the Victor's swinging sword, deflecting it.

The giant was out of reach for an axe-swing—curse those endless arms—so Alerio ran at him, shield held high to protect his head. The Victor bellowed.

Enforcer Astryr is circling, seeking an avenue of attack, Alerio's comp observed.

Of course she is. Just because I gave her a fucking order, that doesn't mean she'll obey it. "I told you to get back, Astryr!" he shouted, blocking the relentless blows. "Unless you want to spend the next month mucking out the Outpost stables!"

"A little horseshit never hurt any—" Dona broke off with a startled cry.

Thrusting his shield to meet the Victor's weapon yet again, Alerio dared a quick glance back at her.

Ivar had Dona pinned flat on her back while trying to shatter her helmet faceplate with repeated blows of his fist. She bucked and cursed as he hammered the plastium visor.

Alerio whirled, but before he could intervene, the Victor's fist slammed into the side of his head. The impact batted him through the air like a spiked grav-ball. He tumbled across the roof and hit the parapet wall so hard he saw stars.

The Victor snatched him up by one ankle and slung him right over the parapet. Something snapped, and he cried out in agony as he fell.

Six stories straight down.

The Victor just threw Chief Dyami off the roof, Dona's neurocomp said. *The chief's leg is broken.*

Dona couldn't even spare the breath to curse as she threw up block after block, trying to keep Ivar from beating her head in. *Any other injuries?*

His comp says he's badly concussed, but his T-suit absorbed the impact of his fall. But the Victor just leaped after him . . .

And that's not going to end well. Dona missed a block, and Ivar's fist rammed her faceplate, shattering the plastium. Unable to see past the broken visor, Dona punched Ivar with all her strength, making him stagger. Using her sensors as a guide, she pivoted and kicked one foot out from under him. Dona flipped to her feet as Ivar almost tumbled over the parapet after Alerio. He grabbed the edge and caught himself as Dona snatched off her ruined helmet.

And sensed a monk swinging his sword at her from behind. Dona spun, slicing her great sword across the bastard's gut. The man screamed in agony, then screamed again when she kicked him ruthlessly off her blade. "That's what you get for jumping me from behind, botfucker," she muttered.

Damn, she ached to go after Alerio, but she had to take care of Ivar first. Terje was wearing his best crazed psychopath's expression, complete with bulging eyes and a fixed rictus grin.

She knew that look. He often wore it whenever he was trying to unnerve gullible . . .

Oh, fuck. She stared at him, feeling a chill rolling through her blood. There was something in those eyes, something icy and insane. *That's no act.*

Alerio blinked. He was on his feet and circling the Victor, his feet scuffing smoothly through coarse sand. Somehow they'd moved to the *base* of the fortress, but he had no idea how they'd gotten there.

You have a concussion, his implant told him. *The Victor punched you in the head and threw you over the parapet. The fall broke your leg. I used my emergency control of your body to get you back on your feet.*

Wait, my leg's broken? Alerio thought, confused. *But I'm walking, and I'm not in any . . .* Realization hit. *Oh. Pain block.*

I also ordered your T-suit to go rigid over the injured tibia. It's taking the majority of your weight, so you should not make the injury worse. I have accelerated your body's healing, but the break will require regeneration.

If I live that long. Alerio had to keep fighting until he brought the Victor down.

However the hell he was supposed to accomplish *that* neat little trick.

He was calculating his next attack on the Victor when his neurocomp spoke. *Message from Riane Arvid.*

Alerio frowned. Riane was supposed to be on one of the sleds with the team attacking the Victor. *Which obviously hasn't gone so well, or the bastard wouldn't be trying to pound my head in now. Never mind, put her through.*

"Chief, we need your help." Her mental voice rang with urgent tension.

"You've got it, though last time I checked, I'm not exactly psychic."

"No, but you are the best compcracker I've ever known."

Alerio ducked with all the speed of *riaat*—just barely avoiding the Victor's vicious sword swing. *"I'm also a bit busy. But your efforts to drive him insane . . ."*

"Backfired. Badly."

"Well, he has *killed several of his own people."* Spotting an opening, Alerio charged in, swinging his axe at the giant's knee. Laughing like a Savannah Hopper, the Victor leaped straight up. The axe missed as he swung his sword.

Alerio threw up his shield and blocked it, then threw himself backward, landing on the shield's inner curve as he kicked upward with both feet. His armored heels caught the giant in the balls. The Victor howled in pained outrage.

"Good shot, sir!" Riane enthused.

"Yeah, if the fight judge doesn't deduct points for poor sportsmanship. So what can I do to help take this bastard out?"

"The Victor's basically one big computer. No organics at all any-

more. *Nick, Jess, and I have created a . . . well, you could call it a spell. We think it'll kill him . . .*"

"*You* think?"

"*It should work. We already got the first half of it loaded, but his firewall is blocking it. I've been battering at his defenses, but I can't seem to get through. We thought if you could hack his firewall, you could load the other half . . .*"

"If he doesn't kill me while I'm distracted."

Alerio's neurocomp spoke up. *I can direct your body while you attempt hacking the Victor.*

He hesitated. Comps weren't particularly creative fighters, lacking the instincts humans used in combat—or in penetrating antiviral defenses. On the other hand, an implant's reaction time was faster. Considering the Victor was basically a computer, that advantage might allow the comp to succeed where Alerio had so far failed.

Fine. Just don't get me killed.

Alerio let his comp take full control over his body. It instantly sent him soaring upward, somersaulting over the Victor's sword stroke.

Reassured, Alerio relaxed and sent his mind into virtual space. It was a very old mental skill, one he'd been practicing since he was a boy infiltrating the hated invaders' computers.

Alerio released his hold on his body until his mind seemed to float skyward like a grav-sled. For an instant, he watched himself dodge and leap, somehow avoiding the Victor. Viewed in virtual space, the giant was surrounded by a glowing mesh that looked impossibly intricate: the antivirus shield designed to keep out hackers. He frowned. The mesh appeared even more complex than the firewalls he'd cracked as an adult Temporal Enforcer.

But complex or not, he had to find a way past the Victor's defenses. Reaching out, he sent a delicate sensor probe sweeping over the Victor's virtual shield.

The giant's head snapped back, the star-flecked eyes finding his virtual body as if he were visible. The Victor's eyes narrowed.

Oh, shit, Alerio thought.

"Your lover thinks he can crack the Victor like some cheap colony comp." Ivar barked out a laugh, his voice spiraling into a shrill register that didn't sound quite sane. "The master's going to burn out his brain and leave him with the mental power of a hand-calc."

"The 'master'?" Dona smirked, though the side of her face was so swollen from his punches, her muscles could barely form a smile. "The Ivar Terje I know wouldn't call anybody 'master.'"

That wiped away the grin. His fist blurred at her head.

She tried to block, but her aching arm didn't respond in time. His knuckles rammed her nose. Blood flew. Dona stumbled back, almost tripping over her own feet. Somehow she regained her balance, shaking off the impact.

Ivar laughed in her bleeding face. "You're fucked, cow. If you give up now, maybe I'll feel merciful enough to spare your life."

She spat blood on the rooftop. "Yeah, right."

"Why not? You always were good with that hot little mouth. Guess Kavel managed to teach you something."

Dona felt her face wipe clean of expression.

"Did you really think I didn't know?" There was that crazy laugh again. "Baby, I cracked your psych file a year ago. Poor little Dona. A dirty pedi's sex slave. No wonder you fell for me. You were all but programmed to be *somebody's* victim."

The icy shock shattered like a scum of ice over a puddle. Dona snarled in rage.

She'd always wondered if Ivar knew her secret, but she'd never been sure.

"Kept you guessing, didn't I?" Ivar taunted. "Even when I all but *told* you I knew everything, I'd toss in some little comment to make you wonder. I could see you struggling to puzzle it out. Stupid little . . ."

In her fury, Dona automatically let her eyes slide out of focus, just as she'd once probed the computer defenses of the Xeran priests Kavel sent her to kill.

Once Ivar's comp had been typical Galactic Union tech, but all those Xeran upgrades he'd boasted about had changed that. Now his neurocomp was more Xeran than not—and so was its software.

As she studied the glowing mesh of his firewall, Dona's heart sank. *It's so much more complicated than their old tech.* So complex, in fact, it took her a moment to spot a familiar weakness she'd used against the priests all those years ago. *Still there*, Dona thought in amazement. *The lazy bastards just built the new software over the old code.*

She'd never realized it before because she no longer needed to use her old code knife. Her tech had been upgraded with Enforcer systems that were a match for the priests'.

And *that* meant . . .

It had been years since she'd generated a code knife, but some skills you never forgot. She curled her fist around the imaginary blade.

"Last chance, slut," Ivar sneered, drawing back his quantum blade. "Are you going to beg for mercy, or are you going to die?"

Hiding her delight, Dona snarled, "Fuck. Off."

He shrugged. "Too bad. I was looking forward to fucking you up the . . ."

Dona stabbed the code knife right into his forehead, where the firewall mesh originated. The firewall shattered. His eyes went wide just as the priests' had every time she'd used that trick on them. He froze, just as unable to move.

Grinning in triumph, Dona slid into his neurocomp. This would be a great opportunity to raid his comp for useable information . . .

Then she spotted what appeared to be a twisted cable of code leading off through virtual space. She stared at it, puzzled. The cable burned far brighter than the rest of Ivar's software. In fact, it was brighter than any priest's she'd ever seen, though it also looked kinked, as if something had twisted it. She followed it . . .

Right to the Victor.

Wait. What had Ivar said? *Your lover's trying to crack the Victor* . . . Alerio must be trying to help Nick and his team infect the giant; nobody was better at compcracking than Dyami . . .

Except Dyami didn't know about Dona's code blade. It had never occurred to her to tell him, since she'd never suspected the flaw would be usable. Five years, after all, was plenty of time for the Xerans to discover and repair it.

Yet they hadn't. And that meant Dona could use it like a back door, not only to Ivar's mind, but to the Victor's. *I can destroy the Xerans' god.*

Do you really think it'll be that easy, bitch? Ivar commed, guessing her intentions. *He'll destroy you. He'll make you his puppet, just like he did me.* There wasn't a shred of doubt in the traitor's mental voice.

He was probably right, much as it galled her to admit it.

It didn't matter. She couldn't let the Victor kill Dyami, even if it meant making herself vulnerable to cyber attack.

Ignoring her shrieking instincts, Dona threw open every com frequency she had. *"Alerio!"*

Alerio circled the Victor through virtual space, trying to find a way through the giant's firewall. His own Warlord body had begun to overheat, despite his comp's protective systems. He watched his body stagger, then regain its balance with a jerk. If he didn't find a way past the Victor's firewall in the next . . .

"Alerio!" Dona's desperate scream cut through his preoccupation. *"Here! Come this way!"* He felt her drop her own firewall.

Ivar, Alerio realized, absorbing the blast of information she sent him. *Ivar is the Victor's weakness.*

Alerio shot through the gate Dona held open for him, slicing through her mind and into Ivar's. The traitor howled and tried to launch his own cyber attack, but Dona blocked it. Ignoring him, Alerio headed for the tangled connections Dona pointed out between Ivar and the Victor. Connections that seemed to be breaking one by one. The Victor must have detected their invasion of his puppet's mind. Unfortunately for the Victor, he was having trouble breaking all the links.

When Alerio reached the thick glowing cable, only one strand remained intact—but one was all he needed.

Sinking virtual fingers into that last strand, he fired Nick's virus into it. The strand turned bright green as it carried its payload into the Victor. . . .

The knee of Alerio's broken leg hit the sand, triggering a blinding flash of pain . . . *Wait, I'm back in my body? But that means . . .*

Terror spiked through him.

He jerked his head up. Face contorted in madness and rage, the Victor towered over him, one huge fist drawn back for a blow that would doubtless shatter his skull.

Then the giant just . . . froze. Utterly immobilized.

As Alerio watched, a wave of black rolled outward from the giant's star-flecked eyes. Faster and faster, the rot surged over the golden skin, until it reached the feet planted wide on the sand.

Is he about to turn into that oil he became when he fought Nick?

But no. Looking closer, he realized the substance shone in the light of the setting sun with a dull crystalline gleam, something like quartz.

No, his neurocomp whispered, *it's much more fragile than quartz.*

He froze, scarcely daring to hope. Biocrystal became fragile when it died. He'd just never seen it outside a cyborg's body afterward . . .

A nerve-wracking hesitation, as if his comp was running a series of scans. *Yes, it's dead.*

Maybe. Or maybe not.

It took Alerio three tries to struggle to his feet. His *riaat*-fueled strength was almost gone. Ignoring the pain of his broken ankle, Alerio braced himself and slammed his fist into one of the giant's black crystal thighs.

It shattered, exploding into massive chunks that pelted down around him, bouncing off his shoulders, hitting the sand around his armored boots. Deprived of the leg's support, the giant toppled and hit the ground. Its own weight shattered it, the dead crystal breaking into chunks.

But that wasn't good enough.

Grimly determined, Alerio started stomping the chunks, breaking them into rocks, then pebbles, walking back and forth as he relentlessly crushed every piece of biocrystal into sand, despite the pain of his broken leg.

As he worked, the wind swept up the fine black particles and spun them into obsidian dust devils, then carried them away.

CHAPTER ELEVEN

Dona watched Ivar's eyes roll back in his head. He crumpled like a marionette from a Punch and Judy show she'd once seen.

All around them, the rest of the priests were doing the same. Keeling over, one by one.

Dead, Dona's implant told her. *They're all dead.*

The virus must have spread from the Victor to his priests, she realized. Which meant . . . that would only have worked if he'd been linked to all of them, but he was just paranoid enough to do it. *Alerio!*

Heart shoving its way into her throat, she ran to the parapet and looked over it.

Six stories below, the Warlord lay sprawled on his back in the midst of a circle of blowing black sand. *What's wrong with him?*

He's unconscious, her implant told her. *His body overheated from a combination of the heat and* riaat, *and he lost consciousness.*

"Dona!"

Riane and Nick and their pilot hurried down the grav-sled's ramp. She ran toward them—and kept going right on by. "Come on! We've got to get Alerio on that sled so we can Jump him back to the infirmary before he dies from heatstroke!"

Aboard the sled, Jessica hovered anxiously beside a regeneration tube.

"Galar?" Dona demanded, dropping into the sled's pilot seat.

"Badly hurt, but he'll survive," Riane said.

Jessica managed a tremulous smile. "Once we get him back to Dr. Chogan."

"So let's get the chief and Jump," Frieka growled, entering behind Nick, Riane, and the sled pilot. "I want to check on Pendragon."

Riane grinned at Dona and Nick. "True love is a wonderful thing."

Frieka glared at his partner. "Oh, you're as bad as your mother, implying some disgusting relationship between me and that cat of hers."

Two more Enforcers boarded just before Dona got the sled in the air.

Five minutes later, they Jumped for the Outpost, Alerio safely inside a second regen tube.

Alerio woke when Chogan popped the tube lid. She gave him a smile as he levered himself out. "Good to have you back, Chief."

"And it's even better to *be* back." Studying her, Alerio frowned in concern. The doctor was visibly exhausted, which didn't bode well. "Did we get everyone else back?"

"Yeah." She put a hand between her shoulder blades and stretched wearily. "Some with nasty sword wounds. Jonelle Cartye died, but I was able to resuscitate her. She'll be in regen at least two more days, healing all the damage." The doctor grimaced. "Then I'll have twenty-six autopsies to do."

Correctly interpreting his widening eyes, she added hastily, "All Xerans. Plus Ivar, of course. Evidently the virus you planted spread to everyone the Victor was linked to. Which was all of them. According to my preliminary med-scans, everyone you hadn't already killed died within seconds from biocrystal-death-induced aneurisms."

"Couldn't have happened to a more deserving bunch of assholes. What about the Victor?"

She gave him a tired smile. "Several evidence bots managed to vacuum up what was left of his dead crystal."

"But he *is* dead?" Alerio thought he remembered as much, but things were a bit fuzzy. And what he did remember . . .

"Very dead. There's no way even the Xerans will be able to bring him back."

He searched her face. "But are you *certain?*"

Chogan shrugged. "I scanned what was left of the biocrystal . . . sand. There were just enough fragments of petrified memory to prove it was him, but that's about it. There definitely isn't enough to re-create him, even if such a thing were possible. He's dead and gone."

Alerio closed his eyes in relief. That was why he'd been so determined to crush every last biocrystal chunk into powder, even when it became evident the wind was carrying the dust away.

"Of course," the doctor said, giving him a significant look, "you'd have had no way of knowing the wind would carry off the dust, you being unconscious by then."

He opened his mouth, about to correct her assumption.

"And even if you *hadn't* been unconscious," she continued firmly, "nobody would consider you responsible for deliberately losing all that crystal in nineteenth-century Arizona, since you were half-dead from *riaat*-induced heatstroke." Her narrow glare warned him not to disagree. "As my medical report concludes beyond any doubt whatsoever."

In other words, Chogan covered my ass. Otherwise Headquarters would have all the excuse they need to court-martial me.

Actually, she has a point, his implant said. *You did have heat-stroke. Even Colonel Ceres could hardly call your thought processes optimal.*

Oh. He blinked.

"It's a good thing Dona got you into regeneration so fast, or you might not have made it home," Chogan continued. "There are limits to what even regen can do, once brain damage gets severe enough."

Muscles relaxed that he hadn't been conscious of tensing. "So Dona's okay?"

"Just fine." The doctor's tired eyes crinkled in a smile. "Oh, she had a few cuts and a whole lot of bruises, what with one thing and another. But I took care of most of that, and her comp healed the rest. In fact, she should be walking through the infirmary doors right about . . ."

"Alerio!" Dona's voice rang with delight.

He turned to watch her hurry in, her eyes bright with joy. "Goddess, I'm glad to see you. Are you all right?"

"Better than all right." She gave him a sunny grin. "Ivar's dead, and so are his priests. I don't think we'll have to worry about the Xerans kidnapping any more tourists."

Turning away, the doctor strolled toward the ward exit. "If you two will excuse me, I've got work to do . . . somewhere else."

They barely noticed, too busy staring at one another hungrily. The moment the corridor door closed behind Chogan, they were in each other's arms, mouths meeting in a ravenous kiss.

Alerio's mouth tasted like distilled sex. Hot, thick with some exotic Vardonese spice. Gods knew where it had come from; the man had just gotten out of regen. Yet there it was, that blend of sweetness and sharp bite she'd always associated with him. He drank from her mouth just as thirstily, his tongue stroking and swirling around hers, his teeth catching her lower lip in a slow, seductive tug.

All the while, he held her plastered against the length of his body as if trying to absorb her through the skin. He felt so damned big—so tall and broad and hard. The rolling contours of his muscularity shifted under those gleaming navy scales, unbearably tempting.

And too damned far away.

She hooked an arm around his neck and lifted herself until she could wrap both legs around his waist.

That's better.

The core of her sex ground against the rigid length of his delicious erection—through two layers of armor scales, gods curse it. She growled in frustration against his mouth.

Still too far.

Alerio laughed, puffing warm breath and spice into her mouth. "Dry humping in combat armor is an exercise in frustration, love."

She drew back just far enough to speak. "So let's take it off. I'll bet we could figure out how to put up a privacy bubble around one of these ward beds . . ."

"You know, I'm almost desperate enough to do it."

Dona grimaced, picking up on that "almost." "But not quite."

"Almost, though."

With a moan, she rolled her hips against that unbearably distant erection. "I'm not sure I can make it back to either of our quarters."

"Neither am I." He flashed a wicked smile. "But I do have an idea . . ."

The room was one of the biggest on the Outpost, so much so that it took up most of one entire level of the Enforcement wing. Poles of varying heights jutted from its soaring dome, each supporting a hoop ranging in size from teacup to several you could fit a regen tube through.

Just beyond the dome, rows of seats rose in concentric rings. Dona gave Alerio a smirk. "Why, Chief Dyami, I had no idea you were so kinky."

He gave her a hungry stare. "I could say the same, Enforcer." Both wore nothing but grav-generation belts. "Though this isn't really kinky."

Dona lifted a brow. "No?"

"Kinky would be inviting spectators."

She laughed. "And selling tickets." Her eyes dropped to his cock, which promptly hardened even more. "Come to think of it, that would be really easy to do."

Alerio gave her a heated stare. "I'm afraid I'm far too possessive for that. I don't share." The arena's dome darkened, turning black as it polarized on command.

"Think of the possibilities." Dona gave him a teasing look. "Nude grav-ball could really take off."

"Only assuming all-female teams. There isn't a man alive who'd let anyone swing a grav-stick around his pride."

Dona pretended to cower, crossing her arms over her bare breasts. "Hey, I have no desire to take a stick across *my* delicate bits either."

Alerio gave the anatomy in question a long, admiring look. "I don't think the word 'bits' does them justice." A slow, wicked smile spread across his face. "But I can think of something that would." He reached for her.

A silent command activated Dona's grav-belt, while reversing its axis of attraction. She fell upward. Grinning downward at him, she called, "Only if you can catch me first!"

"Oh," he growled, "I can catch you."

Alerio launched after her like a spear. *Damn, I think I'm in trouble.* Her lips pulled into a grin of pure anticipation. *Good.*

A small hoop jutted off to her left. She shot out an arm and grabbed it. Her momentum whipped her around, and gravity shifted as she flipped the belt's axis so that its field sent her shooting the opposite way just before Alerio gabbed for her. He growled, his eyes flashing red with lust and temper, caught the nearest hoop, and flung himself after her.

Dona sailed across the chamber, her body held as straight as a blade. Alerio admired the luscious view: the sight of her delicious ass muscles working, her thighs together, toes pointed. Her perfect breasts drew upward in the direction of "gravity," their nipples like furled roses.

Lust prowled through him, hot, primitive, fierce with the animal need to have her. The same feral instincts that made him a Warlord put a burning edge on his hunger. He knew his eyes glowed.

Which gave him a wicked idea. Lips pulling into a fierce grin, he shot a command to the Outpost main comp.

The arena went completely dark as a sensor-blocking field descended over the entire dome.

"Hey!" Dona yelped from somewhere ahead of him. He heard a vibrating thumb as she caught one of the hoops and halted her flight. "No fair!"

"Since when do Enforcers care about 'fair?'" He grinned in the dark. He'd never have pulled this stunt on a human, of course. Anyone but a 'borg would have ended up hurt by running into one of the jutting hoops.

Fortunately, he and Dona knew the location of every goal in the arena. Thanks to their neurocomps, they could maneuver in the dark by memory and computer calculation alone.

As he flew through the darkness, his comp revealed the location of an approaching ring. Around it hung a forest of additional circles, all of different sizes: the goals. He caught the hoop, dragging himself to a halt. It was one of the bigger ones; he swung around and crouched inside it, gripping its rim with fingers and toes. Nostrils flared, he drew in air, tasting the scent of her.

Thump. Thump. Thump.

He cocked his head, listening to the soft rasp of breathing as Dona leaped from hoop to hoop, the vibrating hum of the plastium as she hit each one in turn. His neurocomp displayed another hoop, superimposing a glowing red box on the darkness.

Dona.

He gathered himself, flicked his belt's gravity on just behind her, and leaped to sail through the darkness. The belt's field wasn't true gravity, so it affected only the one who wore it. Otherwise the game would have never have been possible.

Dona sensed him coming, and bounced from her perch with a yelp of alarm. The target followed her.

Sweet Mother Goddess, I can't wait to get my hands on her.

He wanted to feel Dona's firm muscled legs and kitten-soft breasts, ached to taste her mouth and her sex. The cream and salt, just slightly astringent . . .

He loved the taste of her, adored the distilled eroticism, the slick texture of soft female folds just begging for his cock. The hot grip around his shaft, clinging with every hard thrust . . .

His mouth flooded with saliva and the head of his cock stretched upward until it brushed his belly. His hands felt hot with the need to touch. He licked dry lips, focused on the red target.

~

Dona watched the hot glow of Alerio's eyes as he soared toward her. Her nipples ached, and she savored the rush of wet heat in her sex. For a moment, she was tempted to wait for him and let him claim her here now.

No, she decided, *I'm going to make him work for it.*

Dona sprang, heading for a tight cluster of hoops, her speed increasing as she pinpointed the belt's gravity field just behind them. Catching a hoop, she let her momentum swing her around . . .

Fuck! He's right on me! She leaped, flinging herself toward another perch, trying to keep the game going as her body thrummed with eager anticipation. *When he catches me, I want him hot.*

Alerio hit the hoop she'd just left with a vibrating *thump*, before flinging himself at her. She leaped for another hoop, gripped it, and powered herself toward a fourth, kicked a foot into that one, and kicked off into the dark.

She felt the heat of Alerio's body the moment before his arms snapped around her waist like the jaws of a trap. Instinctively, Dona twisted, fighting his grip, shooting punches into any part of him she could reach—if carefully, to make sure she didn't actually hurt him.

"Oh, I don't think so," Alerio purred in her ear as he contained her struggles despite her cyborg strength.

Gods, he's strong. Even stronger than she usually realized. Growling and bucking, Dona got exactly nothing for her effort but his low, triumphant laugh.

"You might as well give up." He bit the lobe of her ear in a tender nip that sent a shiver up her spine. "You're not getting away from me."

Wrapping both strong thighs around her waist, he pulled one of her arms back and wrapped her wrist in a length of restraint cable. Spitting a curse despite the arousal jolting through her, she shot an elbow into his ribs. He ignored the blow and captured that hand, too, looping it in more of the cable.

Dona gasped. Her nipples ached, and she felt her cunt go hot.

"Ahhhhh," Alerio rumbled. "I thought you'd like that." He relaxed the clamp of his thighs just enough that he could turn her to face him, her wrists gathered tight against her spine. His eyes blazed in the darkness. "You *like* being tied. And you'll like this even more."

His mouth closed over her left nipple in a startling erotic assault that tore a gasp from her mouth. Alerio rumbled in satisfaction and suckled her lazily, simultaneously scraping his teeth across the furled bud. Sparks blazed up her spine in pulses with each teasing bite.

By the time he lifted his head again, she was squirming helplessly in her bonds. "You taste delicious." He transferred his mouth to the other breast as he cupped and squeezed the first, rolling the nipple with lazy fingers. "How do you like that, hmmm?"

"You know exactly how much I like it . . ." Dona had to stop to pant.

He laughed. "Well, yes, actually I do." She couldn't see a damned thing when he lowered his head again, though she caught one last triumphant flash of red.

Then he closed his eyes and seemed to vanish.

Darkness surrounded her, thick as tar and smelling of aroused male. Dona wanted to run her fingers through the rough silk of his hair, but her cabled hands refused to obey. The sense of helplessness heated her simmering arousal until it seemed to smoke through her like hot oil.

Desperate to touch him, she lowered her head until her lips found the thick cords of his neck. She feasted there, running her tongue over his skin, gorging her senses on the taste of him, drinking in his Vardonese musk. Masculinity and raw sex made her head spin. She buried her nose in the thick fall of his hair and closed her eyes. His mouth did wicked, delicious things to her breasts, pointed tongue flicking her erect nipples, each pass making her body ring in sweet reverberations. *Ping ping ping.* Crystalline shivers of delight.

He began to bite her, careful teeth pressing delicate skin, sending erotic shivers rolling over Dona in sweet waves. She found his ear and bit him back.

To her satisfaction, he growled, so she caught his lobe and bit him again—slowly raking her teeth across that soft bit of flesh, then flicking her tongue into the sensitive channel of his ear.

"Pushing it," he rumbled.

"I like pushing it," she breathed.

"I noticed." He wrapped one powerful arm around her and flipped them both, grabbing the hoop with his free hand to stop their rotation.

Silk lashing her thighs as he caught her knees, spread them wide, and nudged his face between them. Red eyes flashed at her up the length of her body. She felt his fingers part her wet, soft lips.

Sensation stormed her, so fierce she shivered. His tongue traced a burning path from her clit to her hot cream core. His stiffened tongue stabbed into her depths, then softened to explore and lick. Pleasure flared through her body, jolting, electric shocks of delight. His fingers teased her sex, strumming her clit, thrusting deep into her core.

Orgasm flashed through her like lightning in dark clouds, blazing across her senses. The hot power of the climax was so intense, she didn't even feel him let her go, leaving her floating helpless and stunned. She only became aware again when he drew her close, one hand catching her ass, his narrow hips settling between her legs.

Aiming his cock for her opening, he thrust deep, all the power of his brawn behind it.

Dona threw her head back, moaning at the stark erotic power of the pleasure.

The lights came back on, obeying some soundless order of Alerio's. She stiffened, blinded by the blaze of light beyond his broad shoulders. She clenched her eyes shut as her comp implant worked to compensate. By the time she opened her eyes again, she could see Alerio's fiery eyes gazing down into hers from the elegant planes of his face.

I forgot how damned handsome he is.

"Goddess," he murmured as if somehow reading her mind. "You're so beautiful." He sounded almost . . . awed.

She found herself believing him. "Gods, Alerio," she burst out, "so are you!"

Laughing in genuine amusement, Alerio began to thrust, slowly, carefully, without his usual hammering power. His glowing gaze never wavered from hers. She wrapped her legs around his waist, pressing up to meet his thrusts.

Making love in zero gravity meant they couldn't use body weight to pump to climax. They had to rely on muscle power.

Dona tightened the grip of her thighs as he cupped her butt and shoulders, pumping lazily at first, gaining speed gradually as the pleasure overcame his control. She watched his face in absorbed fascination as he threw his head back, clenching his teeth, fighting not to come. Fighting to wait for her.

Meanwhile she could feel the strong throbbing pleasure building in her sex, gripping and releasing over and over . . .

"Come," he growled at last, as if unable to wait anymore. "Come for me now!"

That feral growl triggered the storm that had been building in her. Her climax seemed to detonate, a ferocious explosion, fierce and hot.

Dona convulsed in Alerio's arms, her back arching hard as she shouted in triumph and delight. Alerio echoed her with a primal male roar.

They floated, wrapped in each other, basking in the lazy aftermath. Alerio reached beneath her and freed her wrists. She gave him an approving purr and curled her arms around his neck, snuggling closer against him.

He felt delightful wrapped around her, hard muscle gleaming with sweat, his hair floating to tangle with her own. Dark chest hair teased her nipples. She sighed into his shoulder, on the verge of drifting to sleep.

"I love you." He said the words the way he'd comment on the strength of gravity, as if the astonishing comment was nothing more than simple fact. Undeniable.

Dona froze, her eyes flaring wide, her breath catching.

His eyes searched hers, irises still blazing with the strength of his emotion. "Marry me."

She swallowed, a lump of raw emotion choking her. Astonishment? Pain? She didn't even know herself. "But I've got psychological scars that go all the way to the bone."

"And it's time you healed them." He stroked one hand up and down her back. "I can help you with that." He began to float downward as he gradually cut power to his belt. Automatically, she followed suit, frantically trying to think.

"But . . ." She was having so much trouble processing the idea of Alerio loving her, she couldn't put together a coherent argument. "You . . ."

"Not that you need much help," he told her calmly. "You're the strongest woman I've ever known."

"You . . . *want* me?" There was more wonder in the question than she knew there should be. It made her feel naked—more than she had when they'd made love—so she made it a sentence, trying to sound certain. "You want me."

He smiled down on her. Somehow those flaming eyes of his looked kind, warm as a campfire on a cold night. "I don't just want you, Dona Astryr. I *love* you. And that will never change."

There was such certainty in that last sentence, she found herself grinning back at him. "I love you." God, it felt good to finally say it. To finally admit it, both to him and to herself. *"I love you!"* She threw her arms around him, a bubble of laughter spilling from her. "I love you, love you, *love you!*"

He laughed. Her back touched the floor as full gravity kicked in. Alerio's big body came to rest on hers. "So you'll marry me?" he asked, his gaze searching hers with a trace of worry.

"What a question." Dona grinned, happy tears stinging her eyes. "How could I do anything else?"

PERFECT MATE

Jennifer Ashley

For all my readers who love the Shifters
and ask for more.

CHAPTER ONE

A bear needs her beauty sleep.

Nell stifled a groan as a rhythmic banging dragged her out of profound slumber, the kind she found only in the depths of wintertime. Never mind that she lived now in a city in a desert rather than deep woods—in winter, her wild nature let her submerge into long, dark sleeps.

But the rest of her family wasn't going to cooperate this morning. The headache that had begun in her dreams penetrated to her waking life, and she cracked open her eyes.

Who in the hell was doing all the pounding out in her kitchen at . . . *five o'clock in the morning?*

Nell dropped the clock with a clatter, swung out of bed, grabbed her pink terrycloth robe, and jammed her feet into some kind of footgear—whatever happened to be on the floor; she couldn't see through bleary eyes in the dark.

If Shane or Brody were working on motorcycle parts in her kitchen or some idiotic thing like that, she'd whack her cubs up the sides of both their heads. It was winter. The boys knew to leave Nell alone in the dark of night in winter.

She stomped out of the bedroom, down the short hall, and into the kitchen.

A huge Shifter male she'd never seen before perched on top of a short stepladder, reaching up to nail a strip of wood onto the wall. The hammer *banged, banged, banged* into her headache.

Nell's kitchen was a wreck—the counters and cabinets had been ripped out, the drywall broken, wires and pipes sticking forlornly out of the walls. In the middle was this Shifter—a bear—she didn't know, his hammering jamming pain through her already throbbing head.

He stopped, mercifully, and laid the hammer on the one counter that was still intact. Not seeing her, he picked up his next weapon—a power drill—and prepared to attack the innocent wall.

Nell ducked back down the hall to her bedroom, silently scooped up her keys, stepped into the back hall that ran between bedrooms and kitchen to the laundry room, and unlocked the padlocked broom cupboard. She removed the double-barreled shotgun from its place, snapped in cartridges, and headed for the kitchen.

The Shifter in the kitchen had turned on his power drill, its whine cutting into Nell's brain. He never heard her until she slammed the shotgun closed, aimed it at him, and said in a loud voice, "You have ten seconds to tell me who you are and what the hell you're doing."

The drill stopped. The bear Shifter glanced at her, blinked once, and carefully set the drill onto the counter. Then he smiled.

It was blinding, that smile. The man was big, like all bear Shifters, solid muscle under a torso-hugging shirt and paint-stained jeans. His arms were huge, like her son Shane's, this man's covered with wiry black hair. The Collar around his throat, black and silver, winked under the overhead fluorescent light.

His hair, which he'd tried to tame by cutting it short, was a mess of a mottled black, brown, and lighter brown strands. A grizzly.

Instead of having dark eyes, like Nell and her sons, this man's eyes were a brilliant blue. Paired with the smile, the scrutiny of his blue eyes sent Nell's heart pounding, which did nothing good for her headache.

"I'm Cormac," the man said. His voice rumbled like a low wave of thunder, one far off enough to be comforting, not worrying. The sound filled the room and wrapped around everything in it. "You must be Nell."

Nell tightened her grip on the shotgun. "This is my house. Who else would I be?"

"Shane gave me the key and told me to get started." He waved a hand at the empty walls but never took his gaze from Nell. "He wanted to surprise you."

"Consider me surprised. You still haven't told me who you *are*. As in, where did you come from? What clan? What are you doing in our Shiftertown? How does my cub know you, and why don't I? I'm ranking bear in this town, and no new bears come here without my say-so. Or didn't Shane bother to tell you that?"

His look was unworried. "I got here last night. I'm from the Wisconsin Shiftertown, but I'm transferring here. Eric introduced me to Shane. Shane was excited about putting in the kitchen, and he told me to go ahead and start."

Logical answers, perfectly straightforward, coming from an intoxicatingly good-looking Shifter who never lost his smile or the sparkle in his eyes.

"*Eric* introduced you to my cub? Without telling me first?" Questions blared through Nell's mind, which was still clouded with sleep and pain. "And what do you mean, you transferred here?"

"Paperwork went through," Cormac said. "Guess I'm the new bear in town."

Again the wonderful rumble, with a hint of laughter. Nell wanted to hold on to the noise, to wrap it around her, and because of that, she clutched the gun a little tighter.

"Oh yeah? I haven't been asleep *that* long. No new bears transfer here without Eric our fine Shiftertown leader discussing it with *me* first."

Cormac reached to the counter and lifted a screwdriver—a quiet tool at least. "Eric said he didn't want to bother you with it."

"He did, did he? That smug little pain-in-the-ass Feline . . ."

Nell trailed off, hurting too much to think of some really good names to call her next-door neighbor, a wildcat and the leader of the Southern Nevada Shiftertown. Feline Shifters always thought they were smarter than anyone else, probably because the damn cats never went to *sleep.*

Nell opened her mouth to launch another string of questions at Cormac, who wasn't bothered in the slightest that he was staring down a loaded shotgun, but the back door burst open to admit both her sons.

The door really did burst—it flew back into the wall, the glass in the upper half rattling alarmingly.

Shane stopped, taking in Nell, Cormac on the stool, the shotgun in Nell's hands. Brody, his younger brother, nearly ran into the back of him.

"Mom," Shane said in the voice Nell had come to know meant *Come on, Brody, we need to calm down our crazy mother.* "Please don't shoot Cormac. He's all right."

"Fine, I'll shoot you instead." But Nell didn't move the gun, because she'd never, ever do anything that might come close to harming her cubs, even if her cubs were full-grown, seven feet tall, pains in her behind, and could shape-shift into powerful grizzlies.

"You're not even supposed to have that gun," Brody said from around Shane's back. He wisely hadn't come all the way inside. "Eric told you to return it. Remember?"

Yes, but what Eric didn't know wouldn't hurt him. "Obviously I need it for defense, since you two insist on handing out the keys to our back door."

"Didn't need them after all," Cormac said. "The door was unlocked."

"That's not the point!" Nell yelled. Most Shifters didn't lock their doors. "The point everyone's *missing* is that there's a new bear in town, and no one consulted me about it. That's never supposed to happen. *Why* are you new in town? Did the other Shiftertown kick you out? Why did you want to come here? Tell me your story, handyman."

Cormac settled in comfortably on top of the stepladder and rested his arms on his thighs, the screwdriver hanging from his relaxed grasp. He looked like the kind of man who could be comfortable anywhere—on a stepladder, on a lawn chair in a backyard, on a rock on the edge of the woods, overlooking the beauty of an endless lake.

"I requested the transfer," he said. "I'm looking for something. I visited the Austin Shiftertown, because I had clan there. The leader there told Eric about me, and Eric said I could try my luck out here."

"Looking for what?" Nell asked, her eyes narrowing. "And why couldn't you move to the Austin Shiftertown? What's so special about the Nevada one?"

Brody laughed. Maybe he wasn't so wise after all. "Oh, you're gonna love this."

Cormac looked Nell full in the eyes. He wasn't supposed to do that, because she was dominant, but this smart-ass bear held her gaze and refused to look away.

"I'm looking for a mate," he said. "The Wisconsin Shiftertown didn't have any more unmated bear females not related to me, and the only bear females of mateable age in Austin are in my clan." Cormac spread his hands, still holding the screwdriver, his shirt moving with his muscles. "So, here I am, continuing my search."

Nell lowered the gun, still angry, and broke it open. She wouldn't shoot Cormac. Much more satisfying to go at him tooth and claw when it was time to teach him who was top bear around here.

"Don't know why Eric told you to come here then," she said. "There are no unmated female bear Shifters in this Shiftertown."

Cormac just looked at her, his sunshiny smile getting wider. Brody guffawed from his relative safety behind Shane's back, and Shane's face was painfully straight.

"No?" Cormac's question was soft.

"No," Nell said firmly. "Except for . . ." Her heart plummeted, down through the shoes she'd managed to slip on—combat boots, she now realized. Her headache flared with a vengeance.

"Except for me," she finished.

Cormac kept his casual position on the stepladder so he wouldn't leap down, embrace Shane and Brody, then grab Nell, throw her over his shoulder, and run next door to demand that Eric perform the sun and moon mating ceremonies then and there. It was nearly dawn—there would still be a moon, and the sun would be up soon.

He'd found her. At last, at long last.

Even with the shotgun, Nell was perfect. Her hair, mussed from sleep, was black streaked with light brown, not a thread of gray in it. All bear Shifter females were tall, and Nell, at six feet and change, was no exception. But she had fine curves to go with her height. Nothing in Cormac's experience ever looked more sexy than the towel-like pink bathrobe embroidered with dark pink roses, hastily belted over those flowing curves.

Even more sexy were the round-toed combat boots that rose halfway up her shapely calves. She'd put them on the wrong feet. She was adorable.

He'd gotten the letter a hundred years or so too late. If Cormac had known about her all those years ago from his clansman who'd abandoned his clan, he would have gone to her, helped her, made her life—and his—more bearable all this time.

No matter. He'd found her now. He'd make up for the lost time, for Magnus's sake, for Nell's sake, and for his own.

"I'll give you ten more seconds," the siren beauty said, "and then you're out of my kitchen."

Nell's eyes under her scowling brows were velvet brown, the flash in them, behind the temper, that of a desperately lonely woman. Nell had her cubs, and she had her position as alpha bear in this Shiftertown, but Cormac knew and understood resigned loneliness, and Nell possessed it.

"Mom, if he leaves, he can't help put in the new cabinets," Brody said. "Don't make Shane and me do it all by ourselves."

Nell switched her glare to her youngest. "You two are perfectly capable of . . . Wait a minute, what new cabinets? When did I have time to buy a new kitchen?"

"You didn't," Cormac answered. "It's a gift from Eric."

New rage blazed in her eyes. "Eric again? What the *hell* is he up to? Brody, go next door and tell Eric to get over here. I want to talk to him. Now."

"Are you kidding me?" Brody's brown eyes widened. "You want *me* to go tell Eric what he needs to do? I'd like to keep my head on my body, thank you very much."

Nell growled, the flash of her Shifter beast curving her fingers into claws. Cormac watched her fight her instinctive alpha temper, watched her tell herself that her cub was right. Shifters didn't rush to a dominant and give him commands, or even make requests, even on behalf of another dominant Shifter.

"Fine," Nell said, her voice guttural with her bear beast. "I'll tell him myself."

She shoved the shotgun at Shane, then stomped past Brody, who moved hastily aside, and out the kitchen door into the dark

morning. The porch lights shone on her hair, moving in a sudden
January wind, and the pink embroidery of the roses on her robe.

"How far before she realizes what she's wearing?" Brody asked
Shane.

"All the way into Eric's house," Shane said.

"Nah," Brody said. "Bottom of Eric's porch." They shook on it,
then watched. "Ha. Too bad, Shane. I win."

Nell appeared again in the light of her own porch, though Cormac's Shifter sight had let him observe her entire journey to Eric's
porch and back again. Nell pushed past her sons, snarling low in
her throat, and made for her bedroom, slamming the door so hard
that flakes of loose drywall fluttered to the kitchen floor.

Eric made the problem of who would fetch him moot by walking over the next minute.

Cormac hadn't known Eric long enough to make a full assessment of the man, but so far Cormac was impressed with what he'd
seen. Eric was a Feline whose family tended to snow leopard.
Leopards were not the largest of wildcats, but they were fast and
smart, which made them dangerous fighters. Cormac had fought
leopards in the rings at Shifter fight clubs, and while Cormac had
been several times their size, they'd made him work to win the
match.

Eric walked unhurriedly across the yard toward Nell's house,
hands in the pockets of his leather jacket, gaze on the ground, as
though he didn't much care how fast he got anywhere. He looked
up as he hopped onto the back porch and stopped just outside the
open back door, not offering to come in without invitation.

"How's it going?" he asked.

He directed the question to all of them, but Cormac knew Eric
addressed him personally. Eric's jade green eyes showed no
rancor—in fact, his stance was so laid-back that any human might
dismiss him as harmless, despite his height and obvious physical
strength.

Deceptive. Cormac was a little older than Eric, but not by much, and he could see how Eric had carefully crafted his nonchalant bearing to hide razor-sharp awareness. As Shiftertown leader, Eric needed to engender trust across species, and he'd never be able to use force to do it. He was dominant, but if a bear like Shane really wanted to take him out, the leopard in Eric would be hard-pressed to survive. Fighting in the ring was one thing—the fight club had rules. Battles in real life were a different story.

The door down the hall slammed open again, and Nell came out, this time dressed in a sweatshirt and jeans. She still wore the combat boots, but she'd put them on the correct feet.

Nell shoved her dark hair from her eyes and focused her glare on Eric. "You'd better have a damn good explanation for this."

"I do," Eric said, his tone mild. He remained on the porch, despite the cold wind, carefully coming no farther into Nell's territory. "I need Cormac to be here, and I need you to go along with it. You two mating will help me, and help you, and help all the other bears as well." He relaxed enough to smile, but his green eyes were watchful. "In fact, Nell, you'll be doing it for the good of all Shiftertown."

CHAPTER TWO

On a narrow street off Charleston Boulevard, in a twenty-four-hour club that was much more like the old, seedy Las Vegas than the slick new one, a man studied four snapshots he'd laid out on a somewhat damp table. His beer bottle, along with another empty, stood beside them. Across the room, a stripper—a tall, well-built Shifter woman, complete with Collar—danced her provocative dance.

Shifter strippers were popular, because Shifter women, apparently, never minded stripping all the way down to what was legal. They were also tall and curvaceous, with large breasts that were all natural, and equally great asses.

Josiah Doyle—Joe to his friends—occasionally watched the stripper, but confined himself mostly to memorizing the photos, which he'd burn tonight.

The first was of a man, Hispanic or Latino, with black hair and brown eyes. Joe's notes on the back of the picture said that the man was a former cop who now ran a security company. Probably a dangerous guy to screw with. Joe was pretty dangerous himself, but he wasn't completely stupid.

He sipped beer and set the still-cold bottle down again. The next photo was of a gorgeous honey of a Shifter woman, blond with light green eyes, tall and sweet like the stripper. She was the wife—or *mate* as they called them—to the Latino. Another potentially dangerous target, because the ex-cop Latino would protect his wife.

The third photo was another human, this one tall and thinner than the first man, with pale skin, black hair, and eyes so dark they might as well be black too. Joe flipped over the photo and reread what he'd written: Stuart Reid, another former cop, now employed by DX Security—the Latino ex-cop's firm—and living in Shiftertown.

Joe let out his breath in a slow sigh. That Shifter bear from Mexico who'd contacted Joe had to be crazy to go after these targets. But a job was a job, money was money, and Joe had promised himself he'd look into it.

The first three were no-goes, however. Joe didn't kill humans, no matter how high the price. Killing humans was murder, and murder brought with it a long prison sentence. Joe had never gone to prison in his life, and he never intended to. He'd never even received a speeding ticket, and all his weapons were licensed and legal.

Besides, if he stooped to murdering humans, his mother would freak. Any break in the Ten Commandments meant a long lecture over Thanksgiving dinner, Christmas dinner, or Easter dinner—whichever holiday happened to be closest to the offense. For Joe, the breach was usually taking the Lord's name in vain or coveting something. Joe had learned to keep his mother happy so he could eat his bird and stuffing or ham and greens in peace.

The stripper up on the little stage was baring it gladly, and Shifter females could *bend*. His mother didn't have to worry about Joe committing adultery with her, though, or even coveting. She was a Shifter, for crying out loud. He might get fleas or something.

He bent to the photos again. The female Shifter in the photo was a better target, but again, if the Latino guy and maybe even Reid, who worked with her husband, protected her, then hunting her would be too risky. Joe might have to kill the two humans to get to her, or kill them to defend himself if it came to it. Nope. Best stay away from them.

Joe pushed their photos away and drew the fourth one to him. This one, now . . . This one had potential.

The photo showed a huge male with muscle on muscle and dark hair streaked with brown. The Collar around his neck proclaimed him Shifter, as did the look in his brown eyes. Shifters always had a certain look, as though they really did want to knock you down and kill you the first chance they got, never mind the Collar programmed to shock them if they became violent.

This Shifter wasn't married to any human, and he'd never been a cop—Shifters weren't allowed to join law enforcement. He wasn't related to the Shifter woman target either. She was a wildcat and he was a bear, and from what Joe had heard, different Shifter species didn't get along that well with each other.

Shifters could be killed without a stain in the eyes of God, or even in the eyes of Joe's mother. Shifters were animals. Sure, they walked around in human guise, but how did that make them different from circus animals dressed up and paraded around in front of kiddies?

The bounty on the Shifter male was set at twenty thousand. A hundred thousand for the four, or twenty thousand for single kills. The Shifter doing the hiring obviously wanted to encourage Joe to go for the collection.

But then, Joe had never been greedy. An honest day's living was better than six figures earned by deeds on the other side of legal. If he could pay his bills, help out his mom, and enjoy his life, he was happy.

Twenty thousand was a nice chunk of change. The target looked tough, but Joe liked a challenge.

He turned the photo over and studied the info on the back. The bear seemed to have only one name, but Joe had heard that the bear Shifters never took last names. Weird, but whatever.

This bear lived in the heart of Shiftertown, with his mother and younger brother, and his name was Shane.

"See, Mom?" Shane said. "You'll be doing us all a favor."

Cormac watched the stare-down between Nell and Eric. Nell could have invited Eric inside at any time, but she stood with her arms folded and kept him outside the door. Cormac liked that, because the arrangement put him between the two of them, Cormac in a good place to protect her.

"For the good of Shiftertown," Nell repeated, ignoring Shane. "Go on, Eric. Explain that."

"I've put in for a grant," Eric said calmly. "You know we're still cramped for housing. We have all the new Lupines plus the extras we can't tell the humans about."

Cormac didn't know who these extras were, but the others seemed to, so he kept silent.

Eric went on. "We need more space for the Lupines alone, but the humans will pay for only so much housing. Even with Iona—she's my mate, Cormac—cutting costs for us at her mom's construction company, it's tough to get more funding approved. Bears are the most difficult Shifters to place. If I show I'm willing to have more bears live here, I can qualify for a grant for more housing. So when I heard that Cormac wanted to come here, I figured it was a good start. He can help me bring in more bears from his clan, I can get my grant, and we solve the housing squeeze."

Officially, he meant. Unofficially, Shifters had more room than they let on. Still, Eric's Shiftertown had recently had another Shiftertown-full of Lupines shoved in with them, the humans having closed one in northern Nevada to save costs. Even with the extra underground rooms humans didn't know about, ten Shifters to a small house was still a tight fit.

"Speaking of housing," Nell said. "Tell me he's bunking with you." She jerked her chin at Cormac.

Eric gave her a smile. "Nope."

Nell's brown eyes widened with anger. "Oh, no, you don't, Eric. I have barely any room as it is. Shane and Brody take up a lot of space, and I have Reid staying here."

"Yeah, Mom, but notice Reid's *not* here," Shane said. "He's spending nights down the block with his girlfriend, and you know it. We can give Cormac Reid's room—good incentive for Reid to move in permanently with his sweetie. Who's a bear," Shane added to Cormac. "In fact, she lives with the Shifter females we rescued from a crazy Shifter down in Mexico. Peigi is the only bear, but I know the others must be ready to find new mates—mates who are sane, that is. So if it doesn't work out with my mom . . ."

"Shane," Nell snarled. "Zip it."

"I'm just giving the poor guy options," Shane said, undeterred. "Since you're not welcoming him with open arms."

"Cormac stays in your house, Nell," Eric said. "It's a good plan. Reid can move in with Peigi and her roommates—he can help protect them against unwanted attention, and I'm guessing I'll be doing a mating ceremony for him and Peigi soon." He gestured at the torn-up kitchen. "Besides, looks like Cormac's handy for putting up the new cabinets."

"Why do I even have new cabinets?" Nell asked. "Are you trying to bribe me with a spontaneous kitchen makeover?"

"This is courtesy of Iona's construction company," Eric said. "Your old kitchen was falling apart. Iona got the new cabinets and the countertops at cost. You can thank her later."

"I'm sure your mate and I will have a big talk later," Nell said.

"Yeah, well, you and Cormac talk it out first." Eric stuck his hands back into his pockets. "Then come see us."

Eric turned around, an alpha's signal that the conversation was over. He walked away, back into the growing dawn, and no one said a word or tried to stop him.

The others watched Eric, but Cormac kept his gaze on Nell. Behind the anger in her eyes, he saw confusion and even terror. He'd have to go slowly with her, reveal the other reasons he'd been looking for her when the time was right. The letter in his back pocket burned him, but Nell could only take so much. The letter had been hidden this long. What was another few hours?

Nell had retreated into a hard shell, and Cormac would have to crack it, little by little, to show her how warm it could be outside. But he could be patient. He'd learned patience at an early age, because patience meant survival.

Nell didn't look at him. "Shut the door, Brody," she said. "It's cold."

She turned on her heel and walked back into her bedroom, once more slamming the door.

Nell was going to skin Eric, and then Cormac. Maybe even her sons, the grinning idiots.

The banging and drilling had resumed in the kitchen, Shane's and Brody's voices added to Cormac's. Since when were her two terrors so anxious for their mother to mate again? They'd pretty much driven off any other male Nell had cast her eyes on since they'd all moved here.

No, to be honest, Nell had driven them off. But she'd had her sons' approval every time.

Of course, all the males she'd tried to date had been Felines, Lupines, or even humans, when she could meet a human tall enough. No bears, because this Shiftertown had a shortage of unmated bears. Eric hadn't been wrong about that.

A grant, my ass. Eric did what he wanted and didn't wait for humans to give him the money to do so.

Nell peered into the mirror as she brushed her unmanageable hair. At least she didn't have many lines on her face, in spite of having raised her sons on her own, alone for most of that time. She didn't look a day over a hundred.

Shifters didn't show age much until close to the end, and many never made it that far—at least, they hadn't in the wild. Hunters, starvation, and death in childbirth had taken out most Shifters before they ever reached their third century.

Nell was nearing her hundred and fifty year mark, her sons both just at their first century. Cormac was younger than she was. While Shifter bodies didn't show age, there were other ways to tell. Scent, body language, and the eyes.

Cormac's eyes said he was older than Shane but not as old as Nell. About halfway in between probably—say a hundred and thirty. And he was mateless. She wondered if he'd had a mate before and had lost her, but she hadn't had time to look at him long enough to search for traces of a broken mate bond.

Another way Shifters died in the wild was by giving up. Surviving became too much for them, especially for a male who'd decided to forsake his clan. Young Nell had found it romantic at first—she and Magnus hiding from humans, fighting to stay alive, relying on each other as mates.

Bears were pretty solitary anyway, but Magnus had quarreled with his clan, and so was completely alone. Nell had been too far from her own clan to be able to rely on them. No good roads or airplane travel in those days, and trains came nowhere near where Nell and Magnus hid themselves, and so they'd strived to make it on their own.

Fine until the stress and fear had wearied Magnus. And so he'd found a way to end his pain, leaving behind a frightened female grizzly, only ten years past her Transition, to raise two small cubs all on her own, hundreds of miles from anywhere.

Nell's anger and grief at Magnus's betrayal was as sharp today as it had been a hundred and thirteen years ago. Nell remembered her wails of despair when she'd stumbled across his body, how the bear in her had come out without her being aware that she'd shifted. She'd howled long into the night, holding her dead mate, thinking nothing would ever stop the pain that flooded her.

Nothing, that is, until she'd heard the terrified cries of her cubs, hunting for her, calling for her. Brody and Shane had given Nell a reason to live, a reason to bury her grief and get on with life.

Nell thunked down the hairbrush and scowled at herself. She was getting maudlin, and she didn't have time to wallow in the pain of the past.

She left the bedroom, striding down the hall again, pretending to ignore everyone in the kitchen, even when the three stopped and silently watched her go by. She walked out the back door into winter sunshine, the air cold but not icy, and turned her steps down the common land that ran behind the houses, heading for Peigi's.

She sensed as well as heard Cormac come out the back door and follow her. He didn't bother to be stealthy about it. Cormac's even stride told her he was coming after her because he wanted to, and he didn't care if she knew it.

"Thought you were anxious to get my kitchen fixed up," she said when he reached her.

"Plenty of time to get it done today, with your sons' help. I wanted to see more of Shiftertown."

"Why? This place isn't much different from any other Shifter-town."

"Sure it is," Cormac said. "The one in Austin is full of bunga-lows about a hundred years old. In Wisconsin, half the Shiftertown is in thick woods. More bears and wolves up there than Felines. All this open desert makes me crazy."

"You'll get used to it." Nell scowled at him. "Why'd you really come here?"

"Told you. Looking for a mate."

"Humans don't like Shifters moving from state to state on a whim. Did you get kicked out of your Shiftertown?"

Cormac didn't answer. Nell glanced at him again, to find him looking around at the houses, which were small rectangular homes built in the '70s, common in towns in the west. Cormac's face was a careful blank, but something in his eyes made Nell uneasy.

"Does Eric know the real reason?" Nell asked him. "Or only what you told him?"

Cormac's blue eyes flicked to her for a brief instant. "You know, jeans look sexy on you."

Nell didn't hide her snort. "Do you say that to all the bears whose pants you want to get into?"

"No." Cormac had such an expressionless face, guileless. He must have practiced a long time to achieve that look. "What do you call those pants I see women wear, the ones that stop just below the knee?"

"Capris."

"Capris. I bet you'd look sexy in those too."

"It's too cold for capris. It's January."

"Compared to Wisconsin, this is a balmy summer day."

"Well, not for me. I left cold winters behind twenty years ago, when I got rounded up and transported here."

"Eric says you came from Canada. The Rockies."

"Eric talks too damn much."

"Only because I asked him," Cormac said. "I want to know all about you."

Nell faced him, and they both stopped. Gray dawn was turning to pink, the undersides of the few high clouds stained brilliant fuchsia. "I'm not looking for a mate," Nell said in a hard voice. "I'm sorry you're lonely, and I'm sorry you came all this way, but I'm done with all that. I have my boys, I take care of the other bears here, and I don't need a change."

"Don't need it, or don't want it?"

Nell made an exasperated noise. "Goddess, this is why I don't go out with bears anymore. All of you think you're so big and strong, so you expect everyone to do what you say. I have news, grizzly." She tapped his chest. "I'm plenty strong myself. Plenty strong without you. Without anyone."

Cormac looked down at the fiery woman poking his chest. She truly believed what she said.

Eric had told him, *Nell's been alone since she got here, finding every excuse not to connect.* She'd gone out with other Shifters and a few humans, but nothing had come of it, no matter how hopeful the male might have been.

Cormac had searched the country for Nell and her cubs, and he wasn't about to stop now that he'd found them. He had a mission to fulfill, one too long in the making.

"I can see that you're a big, strong woman on your own," Cormac said. "Where are you heading, by the way? Or are you just walking around in a snit?"

The flash in her eyes could have burned down a building. "I'm doing my job. I look in on the females and cubs we rescued to make sure they're all right. They went through a rough time."

"Shane said something about them being taken from a Shifter in Mexico?"

"Yep. An un-Collared Shifter mate-claimed these females and kept them sequestered in the basement of an abandoned factory. Trying to set up his own little Shiftertown. Eric's sister Cassidy with her mate Diego, Diego's brother, and Reid and Shane, rescued them. The poor cubs the Shifter fathered on the females never saw the light of day until they were brought here. They're still traumatized." The lines around her eyes relaxed. "But getting better."

"Because of you."

"Because of me, and Cassidy, and Iona, and others helping out. I'm not some Lady Bountiful. Like I said, I'm just doing my job."

"Sure you are." Cormac grinned at her.

Nell growled, the rumble of an annoyed she-bear, before she turned her back on him and kept walking.

Cormac followed, chuckling to himself. Nell was prickly, but he'd get past her spines. He'd made the promise. Just because his old clansman was in the Summerland—the afterlife—and couldn't hear him didn't matter.

Nell headed for a house that didn't look much different from any of the others around it. The house had a long back porch with a sliding glass door that looked into a kitchen and family room. A cluster of kids—six, seven?—were sitting around a table in the family room. One of the cubs jumped up when he saw them and slid open the patio door.

"Aunt Nell!" the cub shouted, and flung his arms around her waist.

Nell rumpled the little boy's hair as she hugged him back. He was a bear cub, brown bear possibly, though Cormac found it hard to tell bears other than grizzlies until they shifted.

"How are you, Donny?" Nell asked.

Donny started to open his mouth and eagerly answer, but then he caught sight of Cormac behind her. The other cubs at the table, who'd been digging into a pile of breakfast, also froze, forks and spoons halfway to their mouths.

Donny ripped himself from Nell and fled blindly to the kitchen, where he dove into the small space between refrigerator and kitchen wall. He squeezed himself as far into the shadows as he could and cowered there, making whimpering noises.

Two of the other kids started to yowl, the remaining three sitting motionless with terror.

Nell raised her hands. "No, it's all right. He's not—"

A female bear Shifter, as tall as but not as curvaceous as Nell, ran into the room, her eyes wide in a fear not far removed from

Donny's. A man followed her—a tall, thin man with black hair and eyes so dark they looked as though they'd sucked the blackness of every moonless night into them. His scent slammed its way into Cormac's nose and triggered a primal and long-buried instinct.

Cormac snarled, his hands sprouting the razor claws of his grizzly. He had to fight to keep himself from changing to the beast, the best form in which to fight the . . .

"Fae," he spat. "You have a *Fae* here—with cubs?"

"*Dokk alfar,*" the tall man said immediately. "Dark Fae. Not high Fae."

"What the hell is the difference?" Cormac's rage surged. He shouted at Nell, "What is he doing here? Why hasn't someone killed him yet?"

"This is Stuart Reid," Nell said, cutting across his words. "It's his bedroom you're taking over, so show some gratitude."

"*This* is the Reid you said was living in your house? Are you insane?"

Nell put her hands on her shapely hips. "*You* are the one terrorizing the cubs at the moment, not Reid. Stifle it." She turned to the kids at the table, her body language relaxed so they'd calm down. "It's all right. This isn't Miguel. He won't hurt you. I promise he won't, because if he does, I'll smack him over the head with a frying pan."

The girl cubs at the table started to giggle. The males, more wary, didn't laugh, but they settled a little, forks moving back to pancakes. Only Donny stayed wedged beside the refrigerator, the scent of his terror sharp. This feral bear—Miguel—must have scared the shit out of him.

Poor kid. Sympathy made Cormac withdraw his claws, shutting away the in-between beast. Whatever nefarious reason had brought the Fae here wasn't as important as reassuring the cubs. Cubs came first.

"You see what you're doing?" Nell said to Cormac as the other female Shifter went to coax Donny out from behind the refrigerator. "You charge in here unannounced and scare the cubs half to death. Where did you learn to be Shifter?"

"From myself," Cormac said. "I had to raise myself, in the wilds of northern Wisconsin. Been alone since I was about an eight-year-old cub." Not much older than these kids.

The female Shifter looked around. "Since you were a cub?"

"Yep. My parents were killed by hunters, and it was just me left. I had to learn to get by on my own. Never even saw another Shifter for almost a decade and a half after that."

Nell stared at him in shock that Cormac pretended to ignore. He didn't want to win her on the pity card. But it had been rough, a bear cub wandering by himself not sure whether he was beast or human.

"The blessings of the Goddess on you," the female Shifter said. "I'm Peigi. This Fae, as you call him, helped rescue me and the other females Miguel had stolen, plus all our cubs. So Stuart's welcome in my house."

Hmm. The Fae man looked defiant, and Cormac decided to let it go for now. Weird shit happened in Shiftertowns, and Shane had indicated that Reid and Peigi were now a couple.

"In case everyone was wondering, this is Cormac," Nell said. "He's a grizzly, he moved to this Shiftertown, he thinks he needs a mate, and he thinks that mate is me."

The whole room perked up. Donny finally came out from his hiding place, though he stayed behind Peigi.

One of the girls at the table said, "Are you going to have a mating ceremony, Aunt Nell? I love mating ceremonies. I can't wait until mine."

"That'll be *years* from now," Donny scoffed from behind Peigi's legs. "Aunt Nell is much, much older than you, so she'll have to have hers right away."

"Do we get to dance in the inner circle?" the girl-cub asked. "I know Aunt Nell's not our real aunt, but she takes care of us, and we're practically family."

Shifters formed two circles at rituals and ceremonies—immediate family and close friends on the inside, the rest of Shiftertown on the outside. The slow dancing, each circle moving the opposite direction, called the Goddess and the God to be present at the festivities. Or so it was said. The stately dancing usually degenerated into a raunchy party within minutes of the mating.

"Fine by me," Cormac said. "You can all be in the inner circle. Maybe even the Fae." Cormac's nose wrinkled. Reid's slightly acrid scent was stirring his killing instincts.

"Uncle Stuart is okay," the girl said. "Even if he stinks."

"Excuse me!" Nell lifted her hands, and everyone stared at her. "No one's doing any mating here. Cormac barged into my house this morning declaring he wants a mate—that he wants *me*—and he still hasn't told me why."

It was time to tell her the truth. Cormac caught and held Nell's gaze. "Magnus sent me."

Cormac watched the shock course through Nell's body, her pupils swiftly contracting to pinpricks. He knew he'd dealt her an unfair blow, but he didn't have time to woo her gently. Eric had said Nell would be tough, but Cormac saw that unless he broke through, and broke through quickly, she'd shut him out forever.

He'd broken through all right. Nell came for him, claws sprouting from her hands. Her body met his with an audible slam and took him backward through the open sliding door.

The two of them tumbled off the porch to land in the dirt and dried grass below, Nell's huge claws going for Cormac's throat.

CHAPTER THREE

Nell pummeled him blindly, old anger and grief surging from the past, wrapped in Magnus's name. Cormac couldn't have known him, had no business saying he had.

She was shouting that as she bashed at his face, but Cormac blocked every blow with rapid efficiency.

Finally Cormac grabbed her wrists and rolled over with her, pinning her against the cold ground with formidable strength. His blue eyes had darkened into near-blackness; Shifter eyes, willing her to be still.

Nell scented the distress of the others on the porch, Reid's Fae scent heightening as he debated what to do. Cormac held Nell down without quarter, but his hands on her wrists were surprisingly gentle.

"You never knew Magnus," Nell snapped at him. Her mate had never mentioned anyone called Cormac—not that he'd mentioned many people from his past. Magnus had liked isolation.

"I didn't say I had," Cormac said. Damn him, he wasn't even breathing hard. "He was of my clan, but he was gone from them by the time I found them. He'd abandoned them."

"I know." Nell couldn't stop growling.

Shifters, especially bears, could live apart from their clans, and often did in the wild, but they still had deep ties, and the clan leader could call on them when he needed to. Clan leaders even had a spell that could drag clan members to him in times of desperation—useful in the days before cell phones.

A Shifter who cut all ties, including the blood bonds that made the spell work, was unusual, and the clan declared said Shifter dead to them. Magnus had cut ties, because he disagreed with his clan leader's very old-fashioned and rather severe form of ruling.

Nell had been young and so soppily in love she'd thought it romantic that he'd decided to strike out on his own. She'd had no trouble traveling with him until they'd found a place where they could be utterly alone—herself and him—to start a new clan.

The problem was, when a Shifter severed himself from his clan, he lost part of himself. Magnus had regretted his action almost at once, but hadn't known how to undo it. He'd certainly have been punished if he'd gone back, maybe even with death. He hadn't been wrong that his clan leader had a cruel side.

If Magnus had lived long enough, he might have found a way to reconcile and bring Nell with him, but he'd grown more and more remote and depressed. Nell had seen the signs, but hadn't really understood them until too late.

"They didn't know about you," Cormac said. His hands softened on her wrists, his eyes returning to the deep blue. "Magnus never told anyone he'd taken a mate or had cubs. No one knew until about six months ago. Then I knew I had to find you."

"What do you mean, you knew you had to find me? If Magnus never told anyone, how did *you* know?"

"He wrote a letter before he died, all about you, but it was lost. Not until a Shifter I knew in Canada found it, in a museum in Winnipeg of all places, and sent it to me, did any of the clan know of your existence. Magnus confessed he'd taken you as mate, and asked one of us to look after you when he was gone. So I decided to find you and carry out his wishes. Better late than never."

"So that bullshit about searching for a mate was just . . . bullshit?"

"No." Cormac's smile came back. "But it was a good excuse to get transferred out here. I didn't tell my clan leader about you or the letter, because he's still old-school. Now that Shifters are civilized, he might not try to kill a cast-off Shifter's cubs and mate, but he might make life very hard for you. If I take you under my protection, that won't happen. And I didn't lie about wanting you as mate. After I read that letter, and Magnus's description of the incredible woman you are, I knew you'd be the perfect one for me."

"You are so full of . . . Get *off* me."

Cormac climbed to his feet so quickly that Nell was left, stunned, in the dirt, on her back. Then he reached down with his big hand and pulled her up, strengthening the tug at the last minute so she landed against him.

He was warm, solid, comforting. Her emotions were in turmoil—Magnus, abandoning her as he'd abandoned his clan, but permanently. Magnus writing a letter, telling his clan all about her, begging someone to come and take her as mate so she'd be cared for when he was gone. The letter lost so no one had come, and Nell had been alone. Now Cormac was here, proclaiming he'd come for her. A hundred years after she'd needed him.

But it was tempting to lean against him, to let him take her weight. She'd carried so much weight on her shoulders for so long.

Nell started to pull away. Cormac tightened his arm behind the small of her back and pressed her closer, his mouth coming down on hers for a searing kiss.

Cormac knew how to kiss. Knew how to tease her lips open, how to soften on the corners of her mouth. He gently drew her lower lip between his teeth, tugging it a little, a hint that he could take her with wildness if he let himself go.

The cubs on the porch cheered. Nell jerked away. She took a step back, missed her footing, and started to fall. But Cormac's arm was there, keeping her on her feet.

Peigi looked a little more concerned than the kids she took care of—none of them hers, because she'd never conceived with Miguel. Reid simply watched with his enigmatic expression.

"Do you and Cormac have the mate bond, Aunt Nell?" Donny asked.

Nell suppressed another growl. She didn't want to talk about the mate bond, or mate-claims, or mating *at all*.

She yanked herself away from Cormac. "Don't even try to follow me," she said, and marched away down the green.

Behind her, she heard the cubs asking questions in concern, and Cormac's rich voice rumbling in answer.

He *didn't* try to follow her. Now why was she disappointed?

Screw this. Nell kept walking, going nowhere, her feet taking her there fast.

Joe started stalking the bear Shane by going to another bar. This one was called Coolers, popular with Shifter groupies—humans who wanted everything from the opportunity to gaze at Shifters to multiple-partner sex with them in the parking lot.

Not all groupies dressed up with fake Collars or wore fake cat's ears or whiskers, thank God. Many looked normal, and Joe pretty much blended in.

Joe was good at blending in. He'd observed the people who came here, and had bought clothes they'd wear—in this case, jeans from a higher-end shop at the mall and a Harley T-shirt.

He knew from careful observation that Shane came to this bar quite often. Sometimes Shane left with a woman; sometimes he left with his brother or Shifter friends; sometimes he worked here as a bouncer. Only a matter of time before Joe would have the chance to corner Shane, maybe when the bear snuck out for a bit with one of the groupies. A drunk groupie woman could be taken out with a mild tranq before Joe tackled the harder job of tranquing and hauling away the bear.

Hardest of all would be lugging the bear carcass someplace out into the desert to dump it after the kill. He'd slay the bear in one of his cabins, which he'd already prepared, complete with plastic for keeping the blood off the floor and walls.

The Shifter paying the bounty said he'd take the head as proof of death. Joe would make sure Shane was in bear form when the bullets went into him. He knew a taxidermist who didn't ask questions, so he could get the bear head stuffed before he tried to drive it across the border into Mexico. Less messy.

Shane walked into the club while Joe was going over his plans for about the hundredth time. He'd come with his brother, plus another bear Shifter Joe hadn't seen before and a dark-haired Shifter woman who didn't look too happy.

The table next to Joe's had cleared out moments ago, and Joe kept his gaze on his beer bottle while Shane and friends approached that very table. Shane's brother peeled away to go to the bar, and the Shifter woman sat heavily on the chair that the third Shifter man pulled out for her.

Joe took up his beer and concentrated on two sexy human women in tight red dresses gyrating on the dance floor, pretending not to notice the bears at all.

"I don't even know why I'm here," the Shifter woman was growling.

"Because Cormac wanted to see the place," Shane said, sitting down. His back was about three inches from Joe's chair. "You like Coolers, Mom. You come here all the time."

"Sure, to talk to my friends. Not to get all dolled up like I'm just past my Transition. Why did you want me to wear this? You wanted to see if a large woman could stuff herself into a tight dress?"

She was glaring at the Shifter who must be Cormac. If she was Shane's mother, Joe's research put her as the bear Shifter Nell.

Nell didn't look bad in her black, slinky dress. She called herself large, but she meant she had breasts the stripper he'd watched early this morning would envy, and hips that drew attention to her nicely shaped ass. If Joe were into Shifters, he might give Nell another look.

Nell's entire attention was on Cormac, and Cormac's on her. Shane got to his feet. "I'll just go help Brody with the drinks."

"You stay right where you are, Shane," Nell said, in the tone of a person using anger to cover fear.

"If Brody has to carry more than two drinks, he'll spill something. Better this way."

Shane shoved his chair aside, backed up a step, and ran straight into Joe. Joe's beer jolted, but Shane grabbed the bottle out of Joe's hand in a swift move and set the beer down before it could spill.

"Sorry, man," Shane said. "Want me to get you another?"

Joe shook his head, waving to indicate everything was fine. He didn't want to talk, didn't want to give the bear too many points of recognition. Shane shrugged and went across the floor in search of his brother.

"This isn't going to work," Nell said, as soon as Shane was gone.

The blue-eyed Shifter leaned back and sent her a smile. "Having Shane and Brody get the drinks?"

"Don't pretend to be obtuse. I've been thinking about this all day, while you and my sons made so much noise in my kitchen. You felt some kind of obligation to find me when you read Magnus's letter? It's irrelevant now. He's been gone for more than a century, and I didn't even know about the stupid letter. It doesn't mean you need to be my mate. Even if you are good at putting up shelves."

Cormac listened to her adamant words, his expression one of interest and concern. When she finished, he casually draped his arm over the back of her chair. "When he died, why didn't you go back to your own clan? You must have been out of your mind with grief, and scared witless."

"Because they were about eight hundred miles away, and I had two little cubs and no money. All I could think about was survival, right then and there. Besides, no one had been happy with me accepting Magnus's mate-claim, and we'd never gone through the sun and moon ceremonies. Magnus didn't think they were necessary." She sighed. "You know what it means that I couldn't go back to my clan? Means I couldn't have a Guardian send his body to dust. I had to burn him."

Joe knew that when Shifters died, a Shifter called a Guardian stuck a sword through the dead Shifter's heart. Apparently, they believed that this released the soul to the next life. Burial or cremation in the human form was anathema to them. Joe imagined the poor woman, two little kids clinging to her, having to make a decision to dispose of the body that went against all her beliefs. Must have been rough.

Cormac came forward and put his hands over both of Nell's, his engulfing hers. "I am so, so sorry. I wish I could have found you then. But at least I've found you now."

"Yeah? Well you're about a hundred and thirteen years too late."

"No." Cormac's voice was steady. "It's never too late to not be alone."

Nell studied Cormac with a kind of wide-eyed daze that was almost panic. "I'm used to being alone. I've done everything alone."

"You might be used to it, but you don't like it. You can't lie to me, Nell. I can read you, and I can scent you. What I'm sensing is a Shifter who likes to take care of everyone, but doesn't do many things for herself."

"Hey, I get out. I come here. I've had a sex life, thank you very much. My boys are embarrassed about it."

"Not the same thing as letting yourself look for happiness. Before you kick me out on my ass, give me a chance to help you find that happiness."

Nell went silent. Shane and Brody sure were taking a long time fetching the drinks, and Joe saw the pain in Nell's eyes when she glanced at the bar as though looking for her sons.

The guy Cormac was pouring out his heart. In Joe's opinion, he was rushing Nell a little—sounded like he'd read some letter her mate had written and he'd showed up here because of it. Amazing how they talked about a century here, a century there, like humans talked about years. Must have been hard on her, being Shifter way back then, when Shifters had hidden their true natures, especially with kids to take care of.

Joe watched them out of the corner of his eye as he took another sip of beer. Both the Shifters wore Collars, and both were larger than humans, but they looked right together. They fit. With their fingers entwined, Nell looking at their joined hands, Cormac's gaze fixed on Nell, Joe figured it was only a matter of time.

Cormac tugged Nell a little closer. "Tell you what. Why don't we dance a little?"

Nell looked up, not liking that. "If we leave before Brody and Shane get back, we'll lose the table."

"There are other tables." Cormac laughed. "You know half the people here. I'm sure they wouldn't mind sharing."

"I do know half the people here. And they'll see me dancing around like a fool."

"Not like a fool." Cormac pressed a kiss to her hair. "Come on. There's nothing to be afraid of."

Nell looked up at him, then took on a look of defiance. "All right. See if you can keep up."

"I love a challenge, darlin'."

Cormac led her away, walking in front of her—Shifter males always went first to scope out any danger. But he held her hand all the way.

Joe lifted his beer in a silent toast. He hoped they worked it out. They made a good couple.

As they disappeared into the mass of dancers on the floor, Joe's thoughts returned to his plans to kill Shane. Nell's story was heartbreaking, but twenty thousand dollars was twenty thousand dollars.

CHAPTER FOUR

Cormac could dance. He could dance, he could kiss, and he had a smile that lit up the room. It wasn't fair.

The dance was a quick one. But instead of shaking himself around like the humans or the younger Shifters, Cormac kept hold of Nell's hands, pulled her close, and spun around with her. He swung her out and then back to him, never missing a step.

Nell found herself against his chest again, with his hands on the small of her back. He was a solid wall of male, strong and steady, a rock in a whirling maelstrom.

Raking up her pain about Magnus was breaking something open inside her. It was too long ago—she'd moved on. She'd managed to survive after Magnus's death because she'd had to. Shane and Brody had needed her.

Once humans had discovered that shape-shifters existed and herded them into Shiftertowns, Nell's past had receded, becoming a distant world. She'd found a new life, her sons had better chances of finding mates, and she looked forward to settling down and dandling her grandkids on her knees.

Now Cormac was messing with her head. She hated thinking about Magnus lying dead, shot multiple times through the head with the large revolver he'd bought. One shot wasn't always enough to kill a Shifter. Magnus had shot himself until he'd collapsed, and then he'd bled to death on the bank of a river.

The pain of that was nothing Nell wanted to remember.

Cormac swung her around again in the dance, then she ended up once more against his chest.

He smelled of perspiration and himself, warmth and spice. Nell's anger wound through her still, and she wanted to lash out at him, claws and all, for causing it.

At the same time, she wanted to sink into his warmth, where nothing mattered but the music and the dance. The noise was a cushion of sound, isolating them, the darkness keeping everyone else in shadow.

Nell risked everything and let her head rest on his shoulder.

Cormac rubbed his hand through her hair, slowing the dance. Nell moved with him, closing her eyes.

Nice to have someone to lean on. Nell had relied on herself alone for too long.

The music faded, segued into another song, and blared again. Faster this time. Shifters yelled and started whirling, including her son Brody, who'd snagged a young Feline for the dance.

It was too much. Too much sound, too many scents, too many bodies.

Bears were meant to live in the quiet of deep woods, near the cool of a mountain river. What the hell was Nell doing in Las Vegas, in the middle of a pile of Shifters, dancing at a club?

"Want to get out of here?" Cormac said, his voice warm in her ear.

"Please," Nell said breathlessly.

His hand closed over hers, sure and comforting, taking her out of this place into the chill darkness and blessed quiet of the winter night.

"You all right?"

The parking lot outside the club was freezing, and Nell had nothing but the little wrap that came with the dress, but Cormac was beside her, his warmth cutting the cold of the January wind. This was the Mojave desert, blistering in the summer, but it could turn bone-cold in the winter.

"What do you think?" Nell asked.

"I know what you need."

"Don't you dare say a good roll in the hay."

Cormac frowned, as though that had been the last thing on his mind. "No, you need to get away and go for a run. Come on. I know a place."

"How can you know a place? You just got here."

He shrugged. "Eric and his mate told me about a place. In case we needed somewhere to be alone."

"Eric is an interfering pain in the ass."

"He's Shiftertown leader. Being an interfering pain in the ass is kind of his job."

Cormac kept hold of Nell's hand but walked her on toward his truck, a secondhand F-150 he'd picked up just today. Shane had insisted they all come here in it. They'd looked ridiculous, three large bear Shifters in the cab, Shane lounging in the back. Nell was sure the drivers they'd passed had laughed their asses off.

"How will Shane and Brody get home?" Nell asked as Cormac unlocked the door.

"Somehow, I think your sons will be just fine. Half of Shifter-town is here. They'll catch a ride."

Yes, Shane and Brody were pretty good at taking care of them-selves. Brody was one of Eric's trackers—he helped Eric look into problems and acted as a bodyguard if necessary. Shane performed similar tasks for Nell, the highest ranking bear in Shiftertown.

Where would Cormac come into the hierarchy? Dominance shifts were a huge problem when new Shifters moved into Shifter-towns. Things still hadn't shaken down from the Lupines moving in. The Lupine leader was a big wolf Shifter called Graham, who'd been his Shiftertown leader before that Shiftertown was closed. Graham and Eric had come to an agreement not to battle for dominance, but the tension still ran through Shiftertown.

Cormac didn't seem worried about dominance, hierarchy, or any other annoyances of Shifter life. He drove confidently away from Coolers and up the Boulder Highway to 95 and north out of town, before turning onto a smaller highway that led toward the mountains.

In January, Mount Charleston and the surrounding peaks would be packed with snow, and Nell was in a close-fitting black party dress with a tiny shawl, and heels. She was already shivering.

"I didn't bring my skis," she said as Cormac started winding to higher elevations.

"Bears don't ski." Cormac laughed, a warm sound that filled the truck. "But I'd love to see it. Wouldn't *that* video go around the Internet?"

"Don't be stupid." Nell growled because she wanted to laugh. The vivid picture of Shane, in his bear form, his Collar around his neck, skiing downhill with poles and everything—maybe a little woolly hat on his head—flashed through her thoughts. Knowing Shane, he'd wave a big bear paw at her as he went by. *Look at me, Ma!* He'd always been such a show-off.

Nell folded her arms over her chest and pretended to be grumpy. "You haven't told me exactly where we're going."

The pickup bumped over ruts, the piles of snow on the side of the plowed road growing larger as they climbed. "Cabin that belongs to Eric's mate. Iona said if we needed to get away and be alone, I could grab the key from her and come up here anytime. I like her."

"Yes, Iona is very generous."

Cormac looked sideways at her. "You know, someday, you're going to break down and enjoy yourself."

"I enjoy myself all the time. I'm the queen of enjoying myself. Driving up the mountain in a deep freeze while I'm wearing a small dress isn't my definition of enjoyment."

"You're a bear, Nell. You love the cold. Don't tell me you don't miss northern winters." He let his hands relax on the wheel, head back on the headrest. "Snow like a layer of cloud, unbroken, untracked. Stillness so vast you can hear snow sliding from a tree branch two miles away. Curling up in a den in blissful solitude, warm and safe, while the world falls silent around you. I love hibernation—great time to catch up on reading."

Nell did remember the emptiness of the land in northern Canada, the cold that destroyed and yet was beautiful at the same time. She'd lead Shane and Brody through the winter wonderland, where they'd ice fish and then cook it in the little brick house they'd built themselves. In spite of Nell having no mate to help her out, there still had been some good times. Her sons were bundles of love, and as little cubs, they'd been adorable.

They still were adorable, and didn't they get embarrassed when she said so?

Cormac left the main road behind and drove along a half-plowed road, his tires spinning a bit about every ten yards. He finally pulled into a clearing, parked in front of a cabin with large windows and a deep porch, and turned off the truck. All was darkness and silence. Peaceful.

Nell followed Cormac into the cabin, where he adjusted the heat settings and built a fire in the fireplace.

The cabin had a large living area and one bedroom downstairs, and a second floor with two doors—bedrooms with a bathroom between them. She knew that Eric and Iona often drove up here for privacy, which was hard to come by in Shifter houses, and he invited others up here when they needed quiet time, but Nell had never come. This was Eric's territory, and Nell wouldn't invade it.

Apparently, Cormac had no such worries. He coaxed the fire

to start, then rummaged in the refrigerator and freezer, finding beer, water, and plenty of frozen dinners.

"Iona keeps the place well stocked," he said admiringly.

"Iona and Eric come up here a lot, as do Cassidy and Diego, and Iona's human family. In fact, I'm surprised to find the place empty."

"Eric said he'd keep everyone away."

Nell planted her hands on her hips. She opened her mouth to yell at him, then she exhaled, letting her body unclench. Why bother? Cormac and Eric had obviously planned this little excursion, probably had laughed about how Nell would react.

"Eric is going to be picking his teeth out of the carpet for a long time," Nell said.

"Eric's a good guy, for a Feline."

"Felines are sneaky," Nell growled. "Too sneaky for their own good."

"That's why I prefer bears." Cormac came around the kitchen counter to her and rested his hands on her waist. "Especially a sweet, lovely, warm female bear who tells it like it is."

"No one tells it plainer than I do," Nell said.

"Glad to hear it."

His hands on her waist were warm, distracting. Somehow there was less distance between them, his body an inch from hers. Nell's breasts touched his chest when she took a deep breath.

"I don't want to talk about anything," she said. "I don't want to talk about Magnus, or why he killed himself, or what happened to me after that. Or the letter, or why you decided to find me. All right?"

Cormac's eyes had darkened to his bear's, his smile gone but his mouth still soft. "All right."

"You agreed easily."

"I know when to shut up."

Nell swallowed, her voice softening. "All this digging up the past, it hurts me."

"I know." Cormac skimmed his hands up her arms to her shoulders, his face now closer to hers. Unshaved whiskers, black against his tanned skin, glistened in the growing firelight.

"I don't want to have sex with you," Nell said, the words difficult. "Not right now. I'm too upset."

"I know."

Cormac's hands warmed her, and so did his eyes. The heating system came on, brushing toasty air through the cabin, and the fire started to crackle.

Cormac's lips warmed her even more. Nell let him kiss her, not fighting, not pulling away. Kissing was fine. Not dangerous. Not heartbreaking.

At least, it never had been before.

Cormac coaxed her lips open as his hands moved to her back. Nell clenched her fists at her sides as his skilled tongue dipped inside her mouth, licking the moisture from behind her lower lip.

The taste of him, a new sensation, heated her, opened her. Her body warmed as the room lost its edge of cold, her muscles relaxing whether she liked it or not.

She was too old for this. Nell was in command of her body, her mind, her emotions. Always. She had to be. Fun was one thing. Becoming a blubbering idiot was something else.

As he kissed her, Cormac's hands closed over hers, caressing, easing them open. He twined his fingers through hers—blunt, callused fingers that held the strength of ages.

Heat gathered at the base of her spine. She wanted to flow against him, to reach for him with her whole body.

"No," she whispered.

"I'm only kissing you." Cormac's breath was hot on her lips. "That's all, Nell."

She liked how he said her name. A plain, short syllable, but his voice rumbled it and filled the empty spaces.

"All right," she said softly. "Kissing only."

Cormac smiled, his eyes glittering in triumph, and Nell's heart squeezed.

Cormac kissed like he danced. He started a rhythm of small kisses across her lower lip, gentle ones on the corners of her mouth, nibbles where he'd kissed her.

His whiskers rubbed her chin, then her cheek when he took the kisses to her cheekbone, the bridge of her nose. Nell struggled to breathe. When she inhaled, she got the scent of him, a male wanting a female, and the nice, clean smell of his breath.

He kissed her cheek again, and she felt the touch of his tongue. He brushed kisses and little licks all the way to her earlobe, then came the small prick of his teeth.

She sucked in another breath. "Kissing only, I said."

"This is kissing." His voice tickled deep inside her ear. "And this." He touched kisses to the shell of her ear, then her temple, her forehead.

Nell closed her eyes. He'd released her hands somewhere during the kissing, and she now clutched the fabric of his shirt. She tried to make herself let go and couldn't.

Cormac kissed the tip of her nose, smiling as he did it. The man smiled too much. He had to stop that, because he made her want to smile back.

He touched kisses to her mouth again, this time interspersing them with little licks. Every lick sent a stream of fire through her, her female spaces responding with answering fire.

Nell's mouth opened for him, her lips shaping to his. Cormac swept his tongue into her mouth, continuing the dance. He licked behind her teeth and under her tongue, tangling with her, tasting her.

He gently pulled back, taking away his talented mouth, leaving Nell bereft.

"Now *you* kiss *me*," Cormac said.

"What?" Since when did her voice shake so much? "I have been."

"No. I kissed you. It's your turn."

"We aren't cubs," Nell tried.

Cormac's laugh was soft and low. "Do you see anyone here who cares?"

They were alone. Quite alone. Up here on the mountain, shielded by a blanket of snow, there was no one to see them, no one coming. Eric, the rat, had probably warned everyone in Shiftertown to stay away.

Cormac waited. He had laughter in his eyes, which crinkled in the corners. Nell read loneliness in those blue eyes, remembered how he'd described being left brutally alone as a cub. But she also saw that his loneliness had not defeated him.

Nell drew a breath, put her hands on his shoulders, and kissed him hard on the mouth. Cormac's lips firmed under her brief assault, and he chuckled when she drew back.

"That the best you can do?" he asked.

"Oh, you ain't seen nothing yet, honey."

Nell wrapped her arms around his neck. She opened his mouth with hers, darting her tongue inside. She licked him, tasted him, played with him, nipped him. She slanted her mouth across his, taking him in, their lips meeting and parting, the soft sounds of kissing blending with the crackle of the fire.

Cormac's large hands pressed the small of her back then moved down to her buttocks. He scooped her up to him, his mouth strengthening on hers, as she kept on kissing him.

More sliding of lips, tangling tongues, biting, kissing. When Nell started to back off, Cormac pulled her closer, his mouth commanding.

Something changed in that kiss. The playful Cormac became serious, a Shifter male commanding a female. Nell felt the change, scented it . . . wanted it.

If she knew what was good for her, she'd push him away, storm back to the truck, and drive it down the mountain, leaving Cormac behind. If he and Eric were so chummy, Eric could come and get Cormac.

All right, so Cormac probably had the truck's keys in his front pocket, and Nell digging into the pocket to take them out would be dangerous. Good thing she knew how to hotwire a pickup.

She shivered. His pocket would be a warm place, and his cock would be just within reach.

Nell broke away, struggling for breath. "Kissing only."

Cormac's eyes held less laughter and more desire. "Was anyone doing anything else?"

"You were thinking about it."

"Of course I'm thinking about it. I'm here alone with you, and you're wearing that sexy dress. I want to peel it off you and lick every inch of your body. I want you down on that soft rug in front of the fire, so you and I can do what Shifters were meant to do."

"Fight off the enemies of the Fae?"

"Yeah, funny."

"If I give in and make love to you, you'll use it to persist with this idea that you want me as your mate."

Cormac shrugged. "I'm going to persist anyway, so we might as well have some fun."

"I can't have sex with you!" Nell's words rang up to the high ceiling of the cabin, circled around the balcony on the second floor, and came back down.

"If you've forgotten how, I'm happy to teach you. You put your arms around me . . ." Cormac demonstrated.

"Will you stop joking? I have full-grown cubs, for the Goddess's sake."

"Why should I stop joking because you have full-grown cubs? They both have good senses of humor. Shane, in particular."

"I barely know you."

"Nell." Cormac slid his hands under her hair, closing the few inches of space between them. "I know I scared you. I know I upset you. I should have been more careful. But reading that letter tore me up inside. I needed to find you—I couldn't rest until I found you. It was like the Goddess had sent me straight to you. When you walked out in that pink fluffy bathrobe with your shotgun and your boots on the wrong feet, I knew I'd been right to search for you."

"I wanted to plant one of those boots right up your ass. Still do."

"No, you don't." Cormac massaged the back of her neck. "If you did, you wouldn't be kissing me."

"Can't I want both?"

His smile returned. "Then you admit you want to kiss me? Good."

"Kissing you has its good points." Nell hadn't felt so thoroughly kissed in a long, long time.

Cormac closed more space between them again, still gently kneading the back of her neck. "What else are you willing to do? Besides kiss me and boot me in the ass?"

"No sex."

"You keep insisting. All right, I can live with that for now."

"And take off your shirt."

Cormac's eyes widened, and his hands stilled. "What?"

"I said, take off your shirt. If you're talking about becoming my mate, I want to see what I'd get."

CHAPTER FIVE

Cormac thought his heart would stop. The lady of his dreams was looking at him with her fine dark eyes and telling him to undress.

No problem. Shifters were used to getting rid of clothes to become beast. If they didn't, clothes ripped to shreds as bodies expanded, and that could hurt.

Cormac unbuttoned his shirt, slid it off, and tossed it to the couch. His T-shirt followed. He put his hands on his hips and faced Nell, pretending he wasn't quivering like a cub nearing his Transition.

Nell stood with one hand on her waist and let her gaze rove slowly down his torso. She took in his pectorals and abdomen, the black hair on his chest, the indent of his navel. She traversed every inch of him, and Cormac itched as though she'd run her fingers very lightly over his skin.

"What happened there?" Nell stepped close and touched the long scar that ran from Cormac's abdomen to his back.

He found it difficult to breathe. "Hunter. A long time ago, in the wild. Just grazed me."

Concern flickered in her dark eyes. "You got away. What happened?"

"I ran back behind some trees, shifted to human, and then charged out, yelling at him. I thought the guy would shit himself. He figured his bullet had gone wide and winged some crazy kid screwing his girlfriend in the woods. I laughed my ass off."

Nell stroked the line of the scar. "You laughed while you were standing there bleeding?"

"I found a doctor who stitched it up. Healed fast. Like I said, the bullet only grazed me."

Nell kept stroking the scar. Her fingers were warm, gentle. His fiery woman could be sweet.

She drew her hand from the scar and put her palms on his chest, pulling her fingers together over his flat nipples. The fire of the movement made him shift his weight.

"Everything all right?" she asked.

"I have a hot woman touching me, driving me crazy."

"Yeah? Deal with it."

Her voice went low and throaty, a warm contralto that wound heat through Cormac's bones. When he loved her, it would be good. It would be incandescent.

Nell tugged his nipples with the tips of her fingers. Cormac balled his fists and made himself not touch her. From the little smile on her face, she was enjoying making him insane.

She moved her hands again, this time to smooth them all the way down his front. "Good muscle tone."

"I like to keep in shape." Hard for Shifters *not* to be in shape, but Cormac could play along.

Nell fanned out her hands around his abdomen, then came back to poke his navel gently with one fingertip. Cormac jumped. "Devil woman."

She tickled him, while he grunted a laugh, then she took her hands around to his back and stepped close. Nell ran her hands up his spine, then drew her fingers around his waist again, retracing the scar.

Cormac held still, not wanting to scare her away. His cock was firm inside his jeans; the bulge must be more than obvious.

But though the mating frenzy had called him from the moment Nell had laid her head on his shoulder on the dance floor, Cormac wouldn't push himself on her. Nell was like a wild bird—tough in many ways, but too fragile in others.

His fragile bird skimmed her fingers around his navel again, then popped open the button of his jeans. "I mean I *really* want to see what's in the package."

Nell's eyes sparkled with wickedness. Behind the wickedness, though, Cormac saw fear. She wanted to play but didn't want it to burn.

Fair enough. He could play.

"So, unwrap it," he said. He touched an openmouthed kiss to her cheek, following it with a little lick.

"You sure?"

"We're alone, the fire is warm, and my best girl wants to undo my pants. Of course, I'm sure."

Her eyes flickered again when he said *best girl*, but she tugged his zipper down. Then in one swift move, Nell opened the jeans all the way and slid them down Cormac's hips.

"Hmm," she said. "Boxers."

"Disappointed?" The thin cloth of the boxers hid nothing, the fabric tenting straight out with his arousal.

"Thought you'd be commando," she said.

"I was dancing, and it's cold. Didn't want to chafe."

"It's promising." Nell lifted her gaze from his cock. "But I need to be certain."

"Woman, you're killing me."

Cormac ended the game by shoving his boxers down with the jeans. He ended up with everything pooled around his ankles, but before he could kick anything away, Nell gave him a little shove. Cormac overbalanced and went back onto the sofa.

Nell stood above him, her hair spilling forward, her breasts pushing up from the confines of the tight dress. Cormac held still, folding his hands over his stomach. She had to notice how much he was shaking.

Nell roved his body with her gaze again, lingering on his cock. "That *might* be satisfactory."

"But you're not sure."

"As my grandma used to say, the proof is in the pudding."

"Fresh out of pudding, love," Cormac said.

"Not from where I'm standing."

Nell slid her fingers down his chest, his abdomen, over his hands in the way, and down to the base of his cock.

Cormac closed his eyes, his own fingers digging into his stomach as Nell closed her hand around his hardness. He clenched even tighter when she squeezed his cock and started to stroke.

"No," Cormac said, voice strangled.

She paused. "No?"

"I mean, no, don't do that while you're standing over me. Come here." He reached up and took her arms, tugging her down to him. She overbalanced as he had done, and fell full length on top of him.

Didn't hurt a bit. Cormac found himself with his arms full of lush, full-bodied woman, his hands finding every curve.

She squirmed at first, but that only added to his joy. Cormac kissed her lips, and Nell stopped to slide into the kiss.

Let me stay here forever with you. Not alone anymore. You and me, we were meant to be.

Cormac wanted to say the words out loud, but not yet. He wouldn't rush her.

The dress proved to be supple for its clinginess. The top eased downward without much effort on Cormac's part. Sweet rounds of Nell's breasts came into view, no bra in sight.

"So *you* are commando," Cormac said, his hands full of warm weight.

"Only on top. The dress looked lumpy with a bra."

"Good thing for me." He drew his thumbs over her nipples, which hardened nicely under his touch. He wanted to lower his head to them, to suckle, but later. He slid his hands up under the skirt and found the elastic of panties.

Nell didn't fight him pulling them off. The skirt shimmied upward as he did, and then Nell stilled. His cock lay between her legs, he feeling the tickle of her wiry hair and the liquid heat there. But he made no move to slide inside.

Nell's throat worked. The look in her eyes was one of almost panic. Cormac watched her fight to master it, and then she slid one hand between them and found his cock, forming her fingers around it.

Cormac couldn't stop his noise of pleasure. Nell fixed him with her gaze, eyes daring him to do anything but lie there and let her pleasure him.

Hey, if that's what she wanted . . .

Cormac wrapped his arms around Nell and drew her down for another long kiss. He tasted her mouth, played over her lips, held her while she stroked him, her hand bringing him to life.

His vision began to cloud. All he saw was Nell's beautiful face, her lovely brown eyes, her full lips, red with his kisses. Cormac pulled her closer still, wanting to drown in her softness. He kissed her throat, her clavicle, then down between her breasts.

He kissed her breasts, one at a time, pausing to lick, then nibble. Nell went on playing, pulling, stroking, every touch bringing Cormac closer to ecstasy. He heard the noises coming from his throat, but he could only revel in the taste of her, the warmth of her on his body, her hand on his cock, palm cupping his balls.

A groan filled the room. Cormac thrust against Nell's hand, catching part of her heat under the skirt. His arms were full of gorgeous woman, his mouth full of her too.

"Holy shit." The hoarse words were his. He was coming, holding her, thrusting, smiling, kissing. The panicked light had gone from Nell's eyes, and now she smiled back, a woman knowing her power.

Cormac dragged her down to him, kissing her lips, biting her mouth, his cries of joy turning to growls. He crushed her lush body to his, never wanting to let her go.

"I thought you said no sex," he rumbled as his wild ride eased down to a relaxed, wonderful glow.

"And there wasn't."

No, Nell had grabbed him and unmanned him before he could throw her to the ground and force himself onto her. Not that he'd intended to do that. He knew he had to go slowly with her, to bring her to tenderness over time.

He pressed a soft kiss to her mouth. "But you didn't get any pleasure, darlin'."

"Yes, I did. That was fun." Nell's big smile and shining eyes told him so.

"Don't play with fire, sugar." Cormac slid himself off the couch out from under her, leaving her half sitting up and staring at him, startled.

He showed her then how strong he was. In a few seconds, Cormac had Nell flat on her back on the sofa, her skirt pooled on her belly, his hands parting her legs, thumbs stroking the petals of her opening.

"What are you doing?" she asked, sucking in a breath.

"I thought that was obvious." Cormac grinned at her before he bent down to kiss her damp hair. "I'm giving back."

Nell gasped again as Cormac gently blew on the curls at her opening, then licked her. Sweet, amazing taste of woman poured into his mouth. Cormac's heart pounded for joy as he fastened his mouth over her and proceeded to drink.

It didn't last long. Nell's frenzy began soon, she bucking against his mouth while Cormac savored all he could of her. Then he was back on the sofa, in her arms, both of them kissing and touching, stroking, licking, growling, laughing.

No sex. Not at all. But oh, such intense and astonishing pleasure. Cormac was in love.

A cell phone pealed loudly in the darkness. Nell jumped awake, finding herself lying across a hard male body, his arms around her. His cock, not ramrod-stiff any longer, lay heavily against her bare thigh.

Clarity hit her, and Nell tried to roll to her feet. Jeans tangled her—Cormac's—then her bare feet hit the carpet and her skirt slithered back down her legs.

Her cell phone kept ringing from the tiny purse Cassidy had lent her. Nell usually relied on pockets, but this slinky dress had none. She was breathless by the time she wrestled the purse open and snatched out the phone.

Shifters weren't allowed to have voice mail, so they either answered the phone or missed the call. But almost all phones had caller ID these days, so she could see that it was Brody's number.

"What?" she bellowed into the phone.

"Mom, seriously, I don't want to bother you, but I think there's a problem."

"Problem? What problem?" Shiftertown burning down? Eric dead in a dominance battle? Rogue Shifters trying to take over?

"I can't find Shane," Brody said.

Nell flashed back to when she'd been a scared thirtysomething, barely into adulthood for a Shifter, with small cubs who kept getting lost. *Mama, I can't find Shane* had been a common refrain. Those little bears had gotten themselves into so much trouble.

She let out a long breath, holding on to her patience. "We're talking about *Shane*. He probably ran off with something female. Where are you?"

"Still at Coolers. He's not with a woman. I'd know that. I mean, he's really gone. You didn't send him on an assignment, did you?"

"When would I have found time to do that?"

"I don't know. I'm asking on the off chance. I'm worried."

He sounded it, and Brody wasn't often worried. Nell felt Cormac behind her, his body heat on her back. He'd put on his jeans, but not his shirt.

"When did you last see him?" she asked Brody.

"Sitting at the table we all snagged in the first place. You and Cormac were dancing by the time Shane and I got back with the drinks. Then you two left, and Jace and a human girl came to sit with us. The human girl was way more interested in Jace than us. Shane went off to see if he could find someone for himself, and Jace and the girl went to dance. I sat there for a long time. Shane never came back, so I started looking for him. He was just gone."

"How do you know he didn't find someone to be with? Or a friend to talk to? Or didn't give up and go back home?"

"Because he would have told me. Plus, he would have had to catch a ride, since you and Cormac took off in the pickup. I never saw him leave with anyone, and neither did anyone I asked."

Nell's concern started to pick up, but she tried to stay calm. "He could have gone out to find a bus. Or a taxi."

"I'd have picked up the scent if he'd walked to a bus stop or even got into a taxi in front. There's nothing. I can't find his scent at all, but there's so many here it's confusing. He's not in any of the back rooms, or in any of the cars in the parking lot. I looked. He vanished into thin air, and Shane's pretty big. Hard for him to do that."

Nell's palm sweated where she clutched the phone. She knew Cormac had heard every word, Shifter hearing being what it was—not that Brody was being quiet.

"Don't worry yet," Nell said. "There's no reason anything should have happened."

Even as she said it, her heart squeezed with fear. Human hunters were allowed to hunt and kill un-Collared Shifters for bounty, and sometimes they didn't bother checking whether the Shifter they'd caught had a Collar or not.

Then again, most hunters went out to the wild places, where feral Shifters were more likely to be found eking out an existence. Hunters didn't hang around parking lots of dance clubs in the middle of the city.

"Who's there with you?" Nell asked.

"Jace, for now. Looks like Graham and that girl he likes, plus a couple of his Lupines. I don't see anyone ranking except Graham and Jace."

"Well, don't raise the alarm for now. We can't start a major panic and then find out Shane's in a broom closet making out with his latest conquest."

"I know. But I thought I should tell you, even though I know you're . . . busy."

"I'm not writhing in a naked sexual frenzy, Brody."

"Goddess, Mom, *please* don't talk about naked sexual frenzies. I'm upset enough about Shane without that picture in my head."

"Tough. I have a life. But my cubs come first. I'll be right there."

"No, no." Brody's words came in swift distress. "You don't have to. I'll find him. Don't interrupt your date. I just thought you'd want to know."

"Why do you assume I'm on a date? I could have dumped Cormac by the side of the road and be home alone in a bubble bath."

"I know you didn't, because I saw how you were looking at him when you two were dancing." He raised his voice a little. "Good job, Cormac."

Cormac leaned over Nell's shoulder. "Thank you. I'll come back with her. I think you're right that we need to find Shane." He looked at Nell, his blue eyes close. "Even if he's only making out in a broom closet."

"No, really . . ." Brody began.

"We're coming," Nell said firmly, and clicked off the phone. She looked up at Cormac, who hadn't moved an inch. "Sorry."

"You're right. Cubs come first."

"Shane's a hundred years old and bigger than I am. When am I going to believe he can take care of himself?"

Cormac slid an arm around her waist. "Not until he's taking care of you." He kissed her cheek. "Come on. I'll drive you down."

CHAPTER SIX

A light snow had fallen while they'd been in the cabin, and white dusted the roads. Cormac took it slowly, the narrow ribbon of road with its hairpin turns and no guardrail at times heart-stopping.

They made it back to the main road, the snow vanishing as they wound down to the desert floor. The air was still cold when they made the turn to the 95, but less icy.

The parking lot at Coolers was still full. The place closed at two, and it was one thirty, but Shifters would linger until the last minute, before taking their party back to Shiftertown.

Brody came out the front door when Cormac pulled up before it. The bouncer—tonight a large Lupine who worked for Graham—watched as Brody half-dragged, half-helped Nell from the truck.

"I seriously can't find him, Mom. And yes, I checked the broom closets."

"I never saw him leave," the bouncer said. "Ma'am."

"Let's not panic," Nell said, adjusting her wrap. "We're talking about Shane. He's not stupid."

She walked inside past the bouncer as Cormac roared off to

park the truck. The club was still going strong—plenty of dancers, loud music, and Shifters at the bar.

After the safe, snug cabin alone with Cormac, the weight of all the people crashed into Nell's senses. Too many sights, scents, sounds. She wanted to find a nice quiet den somewhere and hole up to think about what had just happened with Cormac.

She kept walking, scanning the dark crowd, hoping she'd spot her tall oldest son dancing in slow interest with a female. She knew that Brody would have been thorough, though, or he wouldn't have called.

Nell smelled wolf before she saw him—Graham, the leader of the large group of Lupines who'd joined their Shiftertown in November.

"Haven't seen him," Graham said before Nell could speak. "We've all looked. Brody's pretty sure he didn't leave with a woman."

"What if he left with a man?" the young woman who'd walked up to Graham's side asked. She had brown hair in a French braid and wore a dress similar to Nell's, except it was bright red. Graham slid an arm around her waist, and the Lupines who had approached with Graham subtly widened the space between themselves and the young woman.

Graham answered, "If you mean Shane decided he's gay, I doubt it."

"I meant, maybe he didn't necessarily leave for nookie," the girl—Misty—said. "People can talk to each other without having sex."

Graham grunted a laugh. "People, sure. Shifters, not always. Mating frenzies hit hard."

Misty shrugged. "Still, you should find out who he was talking to before he left. Maybe he went off to another bar to play pool with someone."

Brody heaved a long sigh. "I thought of that. I've been asking. No one noticed. *I* didn't notice."

Nell sensed a tingling warmth at her back, and she looked over her shoulder, expecting Cormac to be right behind her.

No, he'd only walked in the front door. Holy Mother Goddess. She felt his presence all the way across a crowded room, over blaring music, and above the scents of Shifters who'd been sweating on the dance floor. Nell was aware of every step Cormac took from the door to her, the tingle growing the nearer he came.

Bad sign. Very bad sign.

Cormac stopped an inch behind Nell and slightly to her right, his warmth encompassing her. His position would let him easily move in front of her to block an attack by Graham, or swing around to guard her back if necessary. Protective and efficient.

The significance of his stance wasn't lost on Graham, who raised his brows and looked at Cormac then Nell with new assessment.

"Get them to close the club a little early," Cormac suggested. "Easier to look for Shane if the place empties out."

"You want to tell Shifters and Shifter groupies that they have to go home early?" Graham asked, his voice a grating rumble. "You value your life?"

"If they think Shane might be in trouble, they can help," Cormac said. "Recruit them to look."

Nell adjusted her wrap, Cormac making her too warm. "Shane will be so embarrassed."

"Better embarrassed than dead," Cormac said. "Did anyone call Eric?"

Brody shook his head. "I didn't want to bother him if it turned out to be nothing."

Graham glowered down at them, but he didn't growl that he was as good as Eric, that they didn't need the Feline. The fact that Graham *didn't* snarl and complain worried Nell. When things mattered, Graham took the chip off his shoulder and got the job done. Which meant that Graham was concerned about Shane too.

"I got this." Jace, Eric's full-grown son, pushed past them and wove his way to the sound system. A moment later, he was standing on the small stage, microphone in hand. The music died away, the lights came on, and Shifters and humans looked up from the shadows, blinking.

"Hey," Jace said.

The Shifters began to growl and mutter, but Jace stared back at them without worry. His stance was as easygoing as his father's, and his presence started to fill the room. Nell felt it as the Shifters quieted, watching him—the need to notice this man, young as he was, and find out what he wanted them to do.

"I'm looking for Shane." Jace's tone said both *We're all friends here* and *Shut up and listen* at the same time. "I want everyone to look at the person beside them and check that it's not Shane. And then leave—slowly. And if you see Shane on your way out, tell him his mom's looking for him."

Soft laughter rippled over the crowd, but they obeyed him.

Jace had them filing out without rushing or snarling. Nowhere did Nell see Shane.

Once the club was empty, and the humans who worked there started closing for the night, Jace returned to Nell. "We can sweep the place for scent now."

He broke them into several groups—Graham with Misty to check the front, the Lupine bouncer to help Jace check the far reaches of the parking lot. Brody would take the rooms inside the club, and Cormac and Nell would check outside the back door.

"He's going to be challenging his father for leadership one day," Graham said as Jace took off to search. He showed his teeth in a cold smile. "I want to be there to watch."

"I'll make sure you have a front-row seat," Nell said. "For now, can we find my son? I hope we *do* embarrass him. He can work it off for the next twenty years."

Cormac said nothing as he led her away to start their search. Nell found his silence comforting. No condescending reassurances—no *We'll find him, don't worry.* Cormac knew they wouldn't have emptied out the club to comb it for scent if everything was fine.

The hall that led to the back door behind the kitchen was full of conflicting odors. The human workers and many Shifters had been this way, and one of the humans had dragged a large amount of garbage out here.

Cormac opened the heavy back door and led the way outside. The frigid air struck Nell, seeming even colder after the overheated club than it had on the snowy mountain.

Plenty of people had come this way as well, including the human with the garbage. The scent trail of bathroom and bar trash blazed brightly to the Dumpster, so brightly that Nell had to turn away from its obvious path and concentrate on the less intense scents.

Cormac crouched down and examined something on the broken asphalt. A feeble light above the back door didn't help much.

"What is it?" Nell asked.

"Not sure." Cormac stood up and scanned the now mostly empty parking lot. "I'm going to go bear. I can scent better."

"Makes sense."

"Want to join me?"

"No," Nell said. Her bear wasn't as sensible as Nell in human form, at least when it came to males. She might find Cormac irresistible and do something stupid like agree to curl up with him for the rest of her life. "I can think better in this form."

"Suit yourself. But I bet I'd love your bear."

"Don't say I'll be sexy."

Cormac's grin widened. "I'll keep it to myself then."

He toed off his boots as he spoke, then stripped out of his leather coat and shirt beneath. He didn't flinch from the January air, but unbuckled his pants and slid them off, letting his underwear follow.

He was breathtaking. Nell didn't pretend not to look as Cormac straightened to his full height under the yellowish glow of the backdoor light. Shadows played on his tall, naked body, and the light glistened on his unshaved whiskers and dark hair. He was a beautiful man, full of strength.

Cormac stretched his arms above his head, and let his bear take over.

Cormac always wondered how humans could stand seeing the world from only one perspective. Maybe that's why they had such short lives, and why so many lived those short lives in misery. Wouldn't hurt humans to be able to see things from an animal's point of view once in a while.

The power of the bear flowed through him, giving Cormac confidence in strength. He was very aware of Nell standing near him in her slinky dress under the weak light. Aware of the warmth of her, and the scent of a woman who'd found pleasure this night.

The light haloed her, as though the Mother Goddess touched her. His bear didn't feel the erotic connection to her as he had in human form, but Cormac saw to the heart of her—a strong woman who'd endured much and yet never let it break her.

He wanted to spend the rest of his life with her.

But if something had truly happened to Shane, Nell would spend the rest of that life grieving. Cormac could not let that happen.

He butted Nell with his head, and she gave his back a stroke. She didn't hide what was in her eyes, which she tried to do when they were both in human form. She was scared, and she was vulnerable, but she was also determined.

Cormac put his head down to sniff what had puzzled him. At Nell's feet, the patch of asphalt had long since broken and never been repaired. In the dry gravel, he'd scented a drop of something he couldn't place.

His bear nostrils widened as he sniffed, and gravel dust went up his nose. He sneezed, but in that moment, he understood the scent.

Tranquilizer.

The tiniest drop, which might have fallen from a hypodermic. A shot from a tranq rifle might be heard, even over the din of the club. But someone coming up to an unsuspecting Shane and sticking a needle into him—that would make no noise. The perpetrator could have done it in the hall, or right here outside the back door.

And then what? Cormac lifted his head and scanned the parking lot. Once that human or Shifter had tranqued Shane, he or she would have to lug Shane's unconscious body out to a vehicle to get him away. Someone would have seen him do that.

Or would anyone have? If the tranq had only had enough juice to put Shane mostly out, then Shane would stumble around like he was drunk, not unusual at a bar, even if it took a lot to get Shifters drunk. Any observers in the parking lot would assume they were seeing a human or Shifter taking home a blotto Shane.

Not that anyone had reported seeing them, but witnesses might have gone home before Brody had become alarmed, and therefore wouldn't know there'd been need to report it.

Cormac lowered his head and snuffled around again. There were many footprints and many scents, but now that he was in bear form, he could take the time to sort them out.

Nell waited beside him while he worked. Her warmth gave him an anchor, and his human senses, buried deep, observed that the view of her legs wasn't bad either.

Not far from the back door, Shane's scent suddenly unfolded from the others, a layer that smelled a bit like Nell, even more like his brother Brody. The scent held the fiery hint of Shifter bear, and a bite that was all Shane's own.

Now to figure out where the scent went.

He felt Nell come alert. "Have you got him?" she asked.

Cormac grunted. He very carefully traced Shane from the scent pool, in a line that moved from the back door toward the Dumpster.

Cormac followed, one step at a time. The trail of the garbage was cloying and distracting. Cormac closed his eyes and forced himself to focus on Shane alone.

If someone had put him into the Dumpster . . . No, the trail moved beyond that.

A vehicle had been parked behind the garbage containers. Cormac smelled exhaust and oil, a drip of antifreeze. The car or truck had been parked here, away from the bulk of the parking lot, in a place with easy access to the alley that ran behind the club. Whether the driver had understood that stopping the truck near garbage would confuse the scent, Cormac couldn't tell.

Cormac inhaled at a spot on the pavement where he calculated the driver's side door might have been, then moved from there in an expanding circle, nose to the ground. Nell walked next to him, carefully keeping her heeled shoes out of the noisome puddles around the trash containers.

He caught scent of someone else, froze. Wait . . .

Cormac lifted his head. The scent was familiar. Wasn't it? No, he couldn't place it.

Cormac stretched his body, willed himself to rise again to his human form, muscles and sinews crackling.

"What?" Nell demanded.

"Shane was tranquilized and brought out here to a car or small truck. By a human." Cormac inhaled again. "I swear I've smelled the human before."

"Where?"

Cormac knew what she meant. He guided her to stand where the vehicle had been and kept his hand on her arm as she inhaled. Nell tested the cold scents a good long time before she shook her head.

"No one I recognize."

"But it's familiar."

"Lots of humans come to this club. Maybe we brushed by them on the dance floor."

Cormac thought about that, playing over his scent memory of the night. The problem was, he'd filled every one of his senses with Nell, especially on the dance floor—her warmth, her scent, the feeling of her body against his.

Cormac still scented her on himself. He took a step closer, right against her back, and wrapped his arms around her.

"I can't remember," Nell said. He heard the tears in her voice.

"It will come."

Cormac closed his eyes, not fighting his need to melt into her. Fighting the senses only clouded them.

They stood together, locked as one, comfort and need twining them. Nell's scent filled him again, covering the stench of the garbage, and everything else but Shane and the . . . *Ah.*

Cormac opened his eyes. "He was here. In the club with us. The guy at the next table."

Nell's eyes also came open, and she looked up and back at him. "I remember. He was sitting alone, and Shane bumped into him. Nearly spilled his beer. Please don't tell me he's out for revenge because a Shifter almost spilled his beer."

"I don't think so. This was well planned. The guy didn't just happen to have a syringe full of tranquilizer in his pocket."

"But why Shane?" Nell's voice rose toward panic. "Or is he a hunter who'll take any Shifter?"

"Hunting Collared Shifters is highly illegal. Even the human cops wouldn't look the other way for that. Too touchy."

"Then he wanted Shane specifically."

"That's my guess."

"Why?"

Cormac closed his arms more tightly around her. "We'll find him, and we'll ask."

"Do you remember what he looked like?" Nell said, worried.

"Yes. Every detail."

Nell looked at him in surprise. "Every detail? I barely noticed the guy."

"Habit I picked up growing up. I notice everything around me at all times, every scent, sight, sound, feel—taste if necessary. I learned to live like an animal long before I understood what it was like to live as a human. I was nearly twenty before I found the rest of my clan."

Life had been . . . interesting. The true bears had given him a wide berth because he'd smelled wrong.

Cormac had wandered alone, a cub calling for someone, anyone to help him, and realizing finally that there was no one to come. He'd learned survival on his own, hunting and killing his own food, eating it raw.

"I'm sorry," Nell said.

"What I learned comes in handy," Cormac said without self-pity. He released her from his arms but took her hand. "Let's use it to find your cub."

CHAPTER SEVEN

The human employees still inside the club went bug-eyed when Cormac walked in naked, but the Shifters didn't notice.

Nell noticed, but then, she'd become hyperaware of Cormac. His scent was on her and hers on him. Scent-marked—the first step in the mating game.

Cormac became bear again to sniff around inside, and he was joined by Jace in his Feline form. Jace and Cormac hunted around the tables, while Graham looked on, his human girlfriend watching with her fingers steepled at her lips.

They found nothing at the table. The guy had left no trace of himself but his scent.

Nell vaguely remembered the man nursing a bottle of beer while she'd sat at the next table trying not to pour out her heart to Cormac. But the bartender confirmed that the table had been cleared a long time ago, any beer bottles left there now in the gigantic pile in the recycle bin.

"We could get fingerprints from the chair and table," Brody suggested. "See if he's got a record, anyway."

Cormac shifted into his human form as Brody spoke. "Then

we'd have to involve the police." He looked at Nell. "You want to do that?" Cormac knew from experience that getting human police interested in Shifter problems complicated matters more than they helped.

"We don't have to," Nell said. "We have a secret weapon."

Cormac raised his brows, unsure what she meant, but Brody relaxed. "Diego and Xavier," he said. "I'll call them."

"Take it easy," Joe said. "You're groggy."

The Shifter-man's eyelids fluttered as he tried to open them, then Shane gave up and slumped back into the chair—the sturdiest chair Joe possessed.

Joe had been driving out to his cabin, keeping with his plan to kill the bear there then decapitate him, when his cell phone buzzed. The man on the other end had been Miguel, the Shifter who'd hired him.

"How's it going?" Miguel had asked.

"I got one," Joe answered. "You'll have proof in the morning. Twenty grand, right?"

The voice took on a Shifter snarl. "I want them all."

"Can't promise that. Too problematic. I think a hundred grand's even too low for all four. I can give you this one, and you hire someone else to go after the others."

"I want all of them, especially the Shifter bitch and her mate. I'll give you the hundred thousand for just those two."

"No thanks. If I capture and kill a cop, even an ex-cop, even one who's shacked up with a Shifter, I'll never live to enjoy the money."

There was a moment of intense, furious silence. "I hired you because you were good. Or said you were."

"I am good. I'm just not stupid. You'll get one of the four. I have him right here." Shane had been out, slumped against the truck's door, his hands and feet chained. The second tranq, delivered when Joe had gotten him into the truck, had knocked him cold.

"Keep him for me," Miguel said. "I want to make the kill myself. And then *I'll* go after the other three, and you will help me."

No way. But Joe didn't argue with him. People who hired bounty hunters or ordered hits weren't always stable.

"Now you want me to keep him alive?" Joe asked. "For how long? I only have so much tranquilizer."

"For as long as it takes. I'll call you when I make it to town."

Joe had hung up in irritation. He'd really wanted to get some sleep tonight.

Joe had continued to the cabin he'd already set up for the kill. Easiest to keep Shane there, and it was far enough out of town that if the Shifter gave him too much trouble, Joe could simply shoot to kill without any neighbors hearing. Miguel would have to suck it up. The money Miguel offered wasn't good enough for Joe to take extra risks.

Shane's eyelids fluttered again. Joe shoved a sports bottle of water between Shane's lips and upended it. Shane coughed, but Joe didn't relent.

"Don't need you dehydrating. He wants you alive."

Shane swallowed the water and licked droplets from his lips. "Who the hell are you?" His voice was still scratchy with dryness. "Wait, I saw you at the club, didn't I?"

"The name's Josiah. My friends call me Joe. Now I have a little dilemma. I'm starting to think I'm not going to come out of this very well, no matter if I give you to the nut-job who wants you or negotiate with you for your release. So do me a favor and don't ask me any more questions while I sit here and think about what to do."

"Huh," Shane said, letting his eyes close again. "If you think your only problems are me and the nut-job, it just means you don't know my mother."

Joe didn't laugh. "You say that because you haven't met *my* mother. Your mom was the Shifter lady sitting at the table with you tonight?"

Shane opened his eyes again. This time they were more focused. "Yeah, that was her."

"Nice-looking woman. Hope it works out for her and that other bear Shifter. It's tough for widows to find someone new."

"Ain't you sweet?" Shane's hands moved under the chains that wrapped his body, and one spark leapt from the Collar around his neck. "How about we talk about this on more even terms?"

Joe lifted his tranq rifle, loaded and ready to go. Another rifle lay next to it, that one with .30-06 bullets. "If you sit there calmly, I'll let you stay awake," Joe said. "If you move too much, I'll put you out again, or shoot you with real bullets. Either way I wouldn't be able to let you in on the decision-making process." He smiled at Shane, who didn't smile back. "So shut up, and let me think."

Diego Escobar, the mate of Eric's sister, and Diego's brother, Xavier, ran a security firm called DX Security. They showed up in response to Brody's call for help, along with Reid, the guy who called himself a dark Fae. Apparently Reid worked at the security firm with the two humans. Weird.

Cormac liked Diego, who looked over the scene without fuss, listening to Brody, Nell, and Cormac tell him what they'd found. Xavier said fingerprints were a long shot—there'd be a lot of them, if they could even get clear ones, plus the waitress would have wiped down the table when she'd cleaned up. Even so, Xavier got started checking out the chair in which the guy had been sitting.

Diego opened a laptop at another table and had Cormac describe the man. Brody and Nell put in what they remembered, but Cormac gave Diego the most detailed description.

"I'm impressed," Diego said. "How long have you had perfect recall?"

"It's not perfect recall," Cormac said. "I just notice things."

Not that he didn't recall every touch, every kiss, every breath of himself and Nell up at the cabin. The time with her had eased his heart, allowing a new spark of warmth to grow. Cormac hung on to that spark in hope. Mate bonds were precious and didn't happen to everybody.

Diego had software that quickly rendered an image, then he and Cormac made adjustments. Another laptop with more software let Xavier scan the fingerprints he'd managed to lift and look for a match. He didn't find anything, but said he wasn't surprised. If the man had been careful, he'd have touched as little as possible and wiped everything off before he left.

Diego's facial recognition program had more luck.

"He doesn't have a police record," Diego announced. "Or an FBI file. But I have access to more information than that." He tapped keys and brought up a photograph of their man. It was a casual snapshot, a man of average human height with brown hair, standing in a hunting vest in the woods. "His name is Josiah Doyle." Diego tapped the arrow key to move to more information. "He's a bounty hunter. Goes after bail jumpers, escaped convicts, and un-Collared Shifters."

Nell's hand tightened on the back of Cormac's chair. "Why would a bounty hunter go after *Shane*? He's not an un-Collared Shifter."

"I think we should ask him," Diego said. "I have the addresses of his house and a couple of cabins. I'd bet he took Shane to one of them."

"To kill him?" Nell asked, her lips white.

Cormac squeezed her hand between his. "I'll never let that happen. We'll find him and bring him home."

"Don't worry, Nell," Diego said. "Xav and I have plenty of firepower and know how to use it. And we have Reid."

"And me," Graham rumbled.

"Don't even think about it," Nell said. "I don't want my cub getting caught in the cross fire."

"And he won't," Diego said. He had a kind voice, soothing, even with his overtone of authority. That the human man wasn't intimidated by Shifters like Graham, Nell, and Jace said a lot about him. "We know what we're doing, Nell. We'll go, we'll get Shane, and we'll bring him back."

"I'm going with you," Nell said. "I'm not sitting at home waiting and wondering if you'll find him before it's too late."

"Graham sent Misty home," Diego pointed out.

"She's human," Nell returned. She fixed Diego with a steely stare. "Don't argue with me, Diego. I know what you did when it was your mate and cub in trouble."

"Yeah, and I also took the help I was offered," Diego said.

"But you didn't wait at home."

"No," Diego admitted. "I didn't."

"Well, then."

"Nell's right," Cormac broke in. "We need her. We'll have to split up and check each location—we don't have time to check them all in turn." He pointed at the locator map on Diego's computer. "I think his house is the least likely place. We should check it in case but put most of our might on the cabins. Graham and Jace can scope out one cabin with Xavier; and Nell, Brody, and I will scope out the other."

"While I grab backup and go to the house?" Diego asked. He grinned. "You're good at giving orders, but I'm modifying them. Xav and I will go to the house. Less fuss if only humans drive up to see Mr. Doyle, no Shifters in sight. Two teams of Shifters will check out the cabins, but I'm sending Reid with one."

Cormac blinked. "The Fae? Why?"

"It's all right," Nell said. "Reid is useful, and he likes Shane. I trust him."

Interesting. But whatever.

"Good," Brody said. "Let's head out. Anything's better than hanging around here sweating."

Nell put her arm around her son. Cormac rose and joined them, and the three closed into a warm, comforting huddle. Cormac had no inclination to step away, to let Nell and Brody be private. The encompassing hug meant they accepted him, that Cormac was part of them now.

Cormac brushed his hand over Brody's hair and kissed Nell briefly on the lips. Then they broke apart to go hunt for Shane.

~

Nell knew Shane was in the cabin at the end of the track as soon as Cormac stopped the truck out of sight on the mountain road.

The sun was rising, touching the folds of land flowing down from the woods that all but hid the cabin at the end of a clearing. The tiny cabin had a wide front porch that overlooked the clearing, its back wall shadowed by ponderosa pines.

Josiah's second cabin, the one Graham, Jace, and Reid were checking, was a small house in the middle of a desert valley, reachable only by a narrow dirt road. Such a setup, Nell had noted when Xavier showed them the map, would allow the bounty hunter to spot anyone approaching from miles away. On the other hand, Josiah would never be able to get himself away from that cabin without being seen.

No, *this* cabin was the better candidate, with its escape route into the woods, which was why Nell insisted that her group come to check it out. Graham had understood that and hadn't protested, and Nell had been silently grateful to him.

"We should shift," Brody said. "Come at him from three sides."

"So that way he can shoot only one of us?" Cormac asked dryly. "I would guess he has a good rifle with a scope, plus rounds big enough to take out a Shifter. One of us would be very dead."

"You have a better idea?" Brody asked.

"I go myself. I'm good at woodcraft."

"I'm a grizzly who grew up in the northern Rockies," Brody countered. "I know from woodcraft. And that's my brother in there."

"You lived in a house and wore clothes," Cormac said. "I assure you, I spent most of my growing-up years sleeping on leaves and eating raw fish. He'll never see me coming."

Nell briskly stepped between them. "Will you two stop playing king of the woods? I have the best chance. I can walk right up and knock on the door. The bounty hunter is human, and the majority of human males have taboos against shooting or hurting a female."

Cormac turned on her. "And some humans see females as beings who should be treated like crap. Even if he doesn't shoot you, he might take you hostage."

"And then we'd have two of you to rescue," Brody said.

"No, he'd have a snarling mama bear ready to kill for her cub," Nell said. "I hope I rip this stupid dress when I shift to beat his ass."

"Aw, Mom, you look pretty."

Nell ground her teeth. "I don't know who I thought I was kidding, wearing this thing. It's not *me*."

The look Cormac gave her would have seared her to her toes if she hadn't been so scared for Shane. "I for one prefer you *out* of the dress, but we'll talk about that later."

Brody briefly closed his eyes and shuddered. "Goddess," he said. "They don't stop."

Cormac stripped off his coat and shirt. "I can get behind the cabin and inside before the hunter knows there's a danger."

"Want us to provide a distraction?" Brody asked.

Cormac slid out of his jeans. "What, dancing up and down saying *Shoot me, shoot me*? I don't want him knowing *anyone* is out here yet. You'll know when to come assist."

"When he hangs your dead bearskin out the window?" Nell demanded.

"Nell, honey." Cormac came to her in nothing but his boxers, the cold not concerning him. He slid his arms around her waist, his skin so roasting hot he warmed the January morning. "You'll know. I already know everything you feel."

Nell went cold, then hot again. She'd felt it, though she'd been trying to deny it, the tiny seed in her heart, the minute tether that could grow into something amazing if she let it.

"Cormac." She shook her head. "Too soon. Too fast."

Cormac smiled at her. "Nell, under the Father God and before a witness . . . I claim you as mate."

Brody stared at them a second then broke into a wide grin. "Yes!" He pumped both fists, but his shout was a whisper.

Nell's throat closed up in panic. "That's a dirty trick, Cormac."

"I've waited too many years to find a mate of my heart," Cormac said, his hands warm on hers. "But there's no time like the present. I've mate-claimed you, love. Promise you'll at least think about it?"

"This isn't the time or place," Nell said.

"Stop arguing with him, Mom," Brody said. "Just go with it for now." His huge grin broke through again. "This is awesome. Now we need to get Shane, so we can celebrate."

Cormac moved with newfound speed. He knew the mate bond was forming between him and Nell—it had started in Cormac when he'd found the letter from Magnus and read the words across the decades. *Find Nell. Care for her in the way I haven't been able to.*

Cormac had felt the bond grow when he and Nell had been alone in the cabin—the spark had jumped like the flames that had leapt from the kindling in the fireplace.

The mate-claim was the first real step in making her his. A mate-claim meant Cormac had declared his intentions to fully mate with her, that he wanted her to join with him in the official ceremonies under sun and moon, which would bind them together forever. It meant that all other males had to back off, that Nell was *his*.

Cormac wished he could have found her all those years ago, so she wouldn't have had to make her way in the world alone, truly alone. But at least he was here now, and he could get Shane back for her.

Whether Nell refused his mate-claim later, or denied that she felt the mate bond, Cormac could at least make sure her cub was safe. He'd been too late to help Nell in the past, but he could help her now.

Cormac skirted the clearing under the cover of the trees, keeping to the shadows and making his way around to the back of the cabin. This low in the mountains, the snow had melted, but clouds hung over the peaks, and the cold breeze from them said that snow was on its way.

The cabin looked quiet, but Cormac knew that two living beings were inside. He could scent them clearly—one human, the other Shifter, injured and overlaid with the strong scent of unhappy grizzly.

The porch wrapped all the way around the cabin, the interior one story. Probably two rooms—kitchen and living room combo and one bedroom with a small bathroom. Compact, tidy, great summer getaway.

The cabin had too many windows. Cormac couldn't be certain

in which room the hunter and Shane waited—living room or bedroom. Bathroom might work as an entrance if Cormac went in human. That is, if he could figure out which window led to the bathroom, and if the bathroom had a window at all.

He kept to the shadows as he drew as near to the cabin as he dared. One corner was shaded by a huge pine, but that corner also could fully be seen by the wide windows across the back porch.

The side of the house was more exposed to the clearing but had fewer windows. Cormac shifted back into human, lowered himself to a crouch, and ran from the edge of the trees to the house, pressing himself down under the windows.

The bare ground beneath the windows was littered with junk, but nothing as helpful as a periscope or even a mirror presented itself. There was, however, broken glass and rusty nails to cut Cormac's bare feet.

He risked a quick look into the first window, but a shade had been drawn, showing him only a blank white. A window shade would mask what was inside, but if Cormac stood up outside it, his silhouette might show. A shooter needed only the silhouette.

He went at a crouch to the next window and darted another look inside. A shade had been drawn down on this window as well, but one inch above the sill had been left exposed. Through that gap, Cormac saw a dim bedroom with junk strewn across the floor and piled on the bed.

The room was empty of people, though. No Shane, no bounty hunter.

Cormac checked the windows for wiring that would mean an alarm system. Nothing. The windows were newer than the cabin itself, panels of thick glass that slid sideways to open, screened to keep out bugs.

Cormac carefully removed the screen from the bedroom window. The window itself was sturdy, double-paned, and though there wasn't a lock or alarm system, the window was definitely latched.

Old windows in decent condition were much easier to pry open than new windows engineered to withstand fire, high winds, and burglars. On the other hand, windows could be taken apart from their frames if a person knew how, and Cormac knew how. The one job the humans had let him have in Wisconsin had been construction. He hadn't been allowed to use the big boys' tools, but he'd been very good at carpentry and component installation.

Cormac fished around the litter on the ground for nails that weren't too far gone, and pushed these around the frame as shims. He'd need to find something flat and sturdy to use as a crowbar. He had a tire iron back at the truck but running there and returning unseen was too much of a gamble.

He also had to work as quietly as possible so no one would hear the *snick, snick* of him trying to remove the window. He would have to—

Boom!

The window shoved itself outward under his hands. Cormac dropped the nails and covered his face as fire lit up the room inside. Fire engulfed the front windows of the house as well, and a line of flame zipped down from the porch and headed for the propane tank, used for the cabin's winter heat.

Cormac was shifting to bear even as he ran for the propane tank and its safety valve, his half-shifted claw-hand slamming off the propane just before the fire reached it.

He lunged away from the tank and back to the house, which was burning merrily. Another explosion rocked it deep inside, the roof now in flames.

Coming across the clearing were Nell and Brody, both in bear form, both running all out.

Nell would try to burst in there to save her cub. She'd get

herself burned all to hell, and maybe shot by the hunter, if he was still alive.

Before Nell and Brody made it halfway across the clearing, Cormac turned and dove through the broken front windows and into the fiery room.

CHAPTER EIGHT

Cormac couldn't see anything. Fire raged, and smoke choked the room. Cormac's full grizzly body had shoved the broken window out of the frame, and glass cut through his fur, but he barely felt it.

His claws snagged on a rug on the floor. Shifting to the beast between human and bear, Cormac seized the rug and flung it across the sill, creating a temporary break in the flames.

Something moved in the shadows of a corner. Cormac ran that way, blinded by smoke. He found chains, too strong to break, a limp body on a chair, the hot liquid of blood.

Cormac stayed his bear-beast, a creature nearly eight feet tall, head bumping what remained of the low ceiling's beams. He grabbed the body, chair and all, and half carried, half dragged it to the window and the rug across it.

He heaved the chair and Shane outside. The chair landed on its back on the porch, breaking the porch's boards. Shane lay unconscious, covered with blood.

One of the grizzlies running toward the house shifted to become Brody. He seized his brother and pulled him off the porch and away from the house.

The second grizzly came barreling into the cabin after Cormac.

"Nell!" Cormac tried to yell, but there was too much smoke for a breath.

The hunter was in a corner in the living room, his rifle in his hands. As Nell charged him, her Collar arced electricity around her neck, trying to slow her down. The hunter's rifle came up, the barrel pointing at the center of Nell's chest.

Cormac bellowed. He became grizzly all the way as he leapt at Nell, shoving her hard aside. The gun went off, the bullet catching Cormac full in the belly.

As pain erupted in his stomach, Cormac heard Nell roar. She reared on her hind legs, mouth open to flash her insanely huge teeth, an enraged grizzly ready to kill.

When she came down a second later, her great paws broke the rifle into three pieces. Then Nell went for the hunter, her Collar sparking like crazy.

She would have savaged him, killed him, and ripped apart his body, if a tranq dart hadn't thwacked into her side.

Nell screamed a horrible snarling scream. She came down, missing the hunter, her form swallowed by flame and smoke.

Cormac leapt after her, feeling like his insides were falling out. He found Nell's slow-moving body in the smoke as she tried to heave herself to her feet.

The tall form of the Fae called Reid stood just outside the front window, a tranq rifle in his hands. Diego and Xavier flanked Reid, and behind them were Graham and Jace.

Reid handed Diego the tranq rifle, swung in through the window, and moved to the human hunter. Reid grasped the hunter by the shoulders, and then he and the human . . . disappeared.

Cormac's bear blinked, then coughed, pain buckling his legs.

"Out!" Diego shouted. "Before it comes down on you." Cormac tried to climb to his feet, slipping again to the floor. Xavier whipped inside, wrapped wiry arms around Cormac's backside, and hauled him up.

"Move your ass," Xavier shouted. "Before I move it for you."

Graham and Jace went for Nell. Nell swatted at Graham, but Cormac growled at her.

Nell wouldn't go with Graham. She staggered to Cormac, her muzzle dripping blood, her eyes as red as the flames around them. Cormac put his shoulder to hers, leaning on her strength.

Together, supporting each other, encouraged by Jace and the cursing Graham, Cormac and Nell pushed through the rug-draped broken window, half tearing out the wall with them, and staggered out into the cold, fresh breeze of the mountain morning.

Brody made sure everyone had shifted back to human before the fire trucks arrived. The cabin was beyond saving, but the danger that the fire could spread to the forest beyond had multiple fire trucks there within minutes.

Diego and Xavier stayed in the clearing to talk to the firemen. Brody and Graham had gotten the rest of them all into the pick-ups a little way up the road, out of sight of the fire.

Graham did some quick first aid on Cormac's gunshot wound, saying it had been a clean shot, and Cormac should be all right if he didn't move around too much. It hurt like hell, but Cormac knew it could have been worse.

Nell was fine except for coughing up smoke, but Shane was more of a worry. He was still out, lying flat in the bed of Cormac's pickup. Graham had picked the padlock on Shane's chains and was now performing his quick patch-up on the bear, but Shane didn't wake.

Reid had the human hunter locked in a pair of handcuffs and now stood over him, training a pistol on him. Dimly Cormac reflected that pistols and handcuffs were made of steel, and Reid, a Fae, shouldn't be able to touch either of them. Iron made Fae sick, could kill them even. Reid showed no sign of weakness, however, as he continued to point the semiautomatic at Joe Doyle.

Nell had squeezed back into her little black dress. She had to be freezing now that light snow was starting to fall. But instead of huddling in the pickup's cab with the heater on, she sat in the bed next to Cormac, very close to him.

Cormac put his hand on her warm thigh and let it stay there. They needed to talk, but not now.

Now was not the time for words. It was time to let the mate bond silently grow while Cormac and Nell healed and took care of Shane. They'd speak of forever later.

"Last time I work for a Shifter," the bounty hunter muttered. He shifted his weight, trying to get comfortable in the cuffs, but he made no move to run away. "How'd you get me out of there?" he asked Reid. "Did I pass out?"

"Yes," Reid said.

He lied. Cormac smelled the lie, plus he'd witnessed Reid grab Joe and vanish. Another thing to talk about later.

"A *Shifter* hired you?" Nell asked sharply. Her voice grated with inhaled smoke, but Cormac's throat didn't work at all.

"He must have rigged my place to blow up," Joe said. "Then called me and told me to stash the bear and wait for him, so he could make the kill himself. But he never intended to pay the bounty. He just wanted to slaughter. Didn't care if I went up too. Bastard."

"What Shifter?" Brody prodded, voice hard.

"Dick-wad who calls himself Miguel."

Graham looked up from where he was bandaging Shane, eyes narrowing. "Isn't Miguel the Shifter who kept Peigi and the others sequestered in the old factory in Mexico? Until Diego blew it up?" He chuckled. "I'd have paid money to see Diego do that."

"I thought Miguel had been caught," Brody said.

Reid shook his head. "About half those Shifters got away. The Austin Shifters have been trying to round them up, but they've only caught a few of them. Miguel is resourceful."

"So he's taking out his frustration by putting a bounty out on Shane?" Nell demanded.

"Not just Shane," Joe answered. "He also wanted Reid here, plus Diego Escobar and Cassidy Warden. I guess he blames them for his problems. If Escobar blew up Miguel's home base, I'm guessing Miguel thought he'd blow up the perpetrators in return. He has a serious screw loose."

Reid gave him a hard stare. "What about you? You nabbed Shane and were going to hunt me, Diego, and Cass."

"No, I'd pretty much decided on just the bear. You and the other two were too risky, even though the money was good."

Cormac felt Nell tense, ready to come off the truck bed. "*Just* the bear?" Her voice held a warning snarl.

"He seemed like the easiest target," Joe said without worry. "I don't kill humans. Guess I was wrong about the bear being easy though. No way I would have gotten through all of you to collect the bounty, even if Miguel hadn't exploded my place all to hell."

"Where is Miguel now?" Graham asked.

Joe shrugged. "Don't know. We only communicated by cell phone, and I bet his is a burner."

"If my son dies," Nell said clearly. "I'm taking it out of your hide."

"I think he'll be all right," Graham said, tucking in Shane's bandage. "Anyone got any booze? I'm going to try to wake him up, and he'll need something for the pain."

"We're fresh out," Jace said, coming back from Diego's truck, where he'd been on the phone. "Reid, can you get Shane home safe? My dad can look after him. Tell Dad everything that happened, but assure him that Graham and I have got it on this end."

Reid nodded. He handed Jace the pistol, climbed up on the truck bed next to Shane, wrapped his arms around the unconscious bear-man, and vanished. Displaced air stirred the ends of Nell's hair.

"Shit," Cormac croaked, at the same time Joe's eyes widened. Joe stared at where Shane and Reid had been. "Hey, did anyone else see that?" he asked.

Reid, Cormac decided, for some reason could teleport. He'd never heard of a Fae being able to do that, but then, they weren't supposed to be able to touch iron either. Cormac shuddered. "Do you ever get used to him doing that?"

"No," Graham said.

Nell ignored them. She was twitching, fighting her instincts to kill Joe and rush off to be with Shane. Cormac gave her thigh a weak squeeze, trying to soothe her. Nell's face was smeared with soot, her hair wild, her neck singed by her Collar going off. Cormac thought she'd never looked more beautiful.

"Tell me what happened in there," Nell said to Joe in a hard voice. "How did Shane get hurt?"

"A little homemade bomb under the kitchen counter," Joe said. "I spotted it right before it went off. It had a cell phone trigger—Miguel called me. The second bomb was in my fireplace, and Shane was sitting right next to it. I guess a lot of shit flew into him. Not my intention. My instructions were to keep Shane alive."

"So that Miguel could kill him?" Nell's Collar emitted three bright sparks. "I'll make you pay for that in so many ways, little human."

"Settle down," Jace said, an edge to his voice. "We can't murder a human, much as we want to." He looked at Joe. "Do you have a way of getting in touch with Miguel?"

"If my cell phone isn't fried, his number will be on it. I have another phone in my truck—would be on that one too."

"You're nice and cooperative," Jace said.

"I'm a businessman. And this deal was a bad business decision—I get that now. If you want to take down Miguel, you go for it. He's too crazy for me."

Graham went in search of one of the phones while Jace continued to watch Joe. Brody climbed into the truck bed to hunker on the other side of Nell. Surrounded by the warmth of Cormac and her second son, Nell began to relax, a little at a time. But her eyes still held rage and terrible fear.

"Shane's in good hands," Cormac said to her. "As soon as Diego and Xav are done here, we'll go to him."

"I know that." Nell gave him an impatient look. "Shane's resilient, and Eric knows what he's doing. I'm worried about you, you idiot. Why did you push me away like that and get shot?"

Cormac growled. "So I wouldn't have to watch you be mowed down by a rifle, woman. Why do you think?"

"I can take care of myself."

Cormac heaved himself onto his elbows, anger giving him strength. "Don't spout that bullshit at me. Of course you can take care of yourself—under normal circumstances. But don't stand in a burning building with the Goddess knows how many more incendiary devices in it, with a bullet coming at you, and scream, *I can take care of myself.* The bullet doesn't care. Sometimes we can't do it all by ourselves. Sometimes we need other people. Doesn't mean you're helpless. Just means you're alive."

Nell blinked at him, her Shifter fury still in her brown eyes. "Since when are you an expert at togetherness? You decided to sneak into a cabin to find a Shifter bounty hunter who had who knew how many weapons—*by yourself.*"

"Best way at the time."

"Well, jumping in there and dragging out your ass and Shane's was the best way for me."

"You almost died!" Cormac roared, which hurt his throat like hell.

"So did you!"

"Sheesh," Brody said, half rising, his hands up. "Could you keep it down? Explosions give me a headache."

"They can't help it," Jace said. "They're mates. The ceremonies will be only formalities at this point."

"He is not my mate!" Nell shouted.

"Yes, he is," Jace, Brody, and the bounty hunter said together.

Nell growled and snapped her mouth shut, but at least her terror had left her.

Graham returned with a phone, plus Diego and Xavier. Diego studied Joe without expression. "Miguel, huh?"

"Yep."

"Wonder why he didn't take out a bounty on *me*," Xavier said, looking a little hurt. "I was there too."

"You were unconscious, with a broken arm," Diego said.

"True," Xavier said. "Now I remember. All the pain, the thirst, the stink. Good times."

"I should have shot him when I had the chance." Diego took the phone from Graham. Joe indicated which of the unnamed numbers was Miguel's, and Diego tapped it.

"Miguel," Diego said in a cheerful voice when someone clicked on at the other end. "This is Diego Escobar." He went into a string of Spanish Cormac didn't understand. Diego was still smiling, but his eyes were hard. Joe must have understood the words, because he winced.

"The easy way would have been to surrender to the Shifters looking for you earlier this year," Diego said to Miguel, switching to English. "The hard way is going to be me and every Shifter I know coming after you. You'd better keep an eye over your shoulder, day and night, waking and sleeping, because we'll be right behind you, Miguel. And when we find you this time, we're not going to be so nice. No, that's it. You don't get to talk." Diego clicked off the phone, tucked it into his leather coat, and kept his smile as he turned to look at Joe.

Joe's body tightened under Diego's scrutiny. "Let it be known I was cooperative," the man said quickly.

"I haven't decided what to do with you yet," Diego said. "The human police can be obtuse, which is why I started my private firm. DX Security is more open-minded. I don't think any of us want a bounty hunter willing to kill Shifters running around loose, do we?"

"Nope," Graham said. He smiled too, and his smile held evil.

"I could let Graham explain a few things to you," Diego said to Joe. "He's thorough. I don't know Cormac well, but I expect that when he gets a little better, he'll be just as thorough. But I think I'll have you talk to Eric. He'll be nice and let you have a beer, but Eric's little chat will stick with you. Forever."

Jace grinned, looking much like Eric at the moment. "Good idea."

Joe had gone pale. The man still didn't fear Shifters enough, but Cormac suspected that after today, he'd learn to fear them as he should.

"We done here?" Cormac asked, his voice scraping. "I love a good early morning woodland snowfall, but right now I'd rather have a roof over my head and a mattress under my back. And then a good breakfast. Pancakes. With honey. Lots and lots of honey."

"Bleh," Graham said, the big man's nose wrinkling. "Bears."

"Brody can cook," Nell said. She slid down next to Cormac, snuggling up to him, the tension easing from her again. "Take us home, Diego."

Nell knew that Cormac was worse off than he claimed. When she and Brody got him out of the pickup and into Nell's house—and onto her bed—he collapsed against the pillows. His eyes half closed, he remained motionless for a long time.

Nell got him undressed—he'd resumed a shirt and jeans in case any humans saw them after the rescue. Exhausted, she sank down onto the bed next to him. She still wore the black party dress, now torn, burned, and stained with soot and blood.

Cormac had refused to go to a clinic, and said Graham's patching up would do. The wound had been clean, the bullet exiting without touching anything major, and Shifters were good at healing. Plus his Collar had never gone off, he said, because he hadn't attacked anyone. He'd have no Collar fatigue to slow down his recovery.

Stupid bear.

Nell closed her eyes, but the image of Cormac leaping inside the burning cabin had seared into her. She'd thought her heart would stop. Then Cormac had found Shane and shoved him out— had done everything to keep Shane safe.

If Cormac hadn't been there, if he'd never come out to this Shifertown looking for Nell, he wouldn't have been in place to save Shane. The enormity of that made Nell open her eyes again, and they stung with tears.

The house was quiet now. Shane had come out of his stupor when they'd returned, annoyed he'd missed everything. He was hurt, but not as bad as everyone had feared, and was already demanding food.

Nell lay down next to Cormac on the small bed and pulled a quilt over them both. She should ask Cassidy or Iona to watch Cormac while she showered and ate breakfast. But she didn't move.

Brody had appointed himself Shane's caretaker, and Reid had gone to Eric's to help deal with the bounty hunter. Last Nell understood from Reid, they planned to use the bounty hunter to assist them in finding Miguel. Eric was already scaring Joe into working for them voluntarily.

Eric had said that Nell and Cormac had done enough for now—the hunt for Miguel would go on, and Eric wanted Peigi and Reid to be there to confront Miguel when they found him. Peigi had earned the right to decide what was to be done with Miguel herself.

Now Cormac needed to heal, and Nell had a need not to leave his side. The new bond wouldn't let her.

"Stupid bear," she whispered out loud.

Cormac's eyes opened a slit and blue gleamed out. "Could say the same about you."

"Don't start in again that I should have stayed home knitting."

"I never mentioned knitting. Knitting never came up." Cormac's voice sounded terrible, so far from its pleasant rumble that Nell wanted to cry.

"Stayed home cleaning my shotgun then." She faltered. "Which I'm giving back to Xavier. I never want to see a gun again."

"I'll be fine, woman."

"And stop calling me *woman*."

Cormac opened his eyes a little more. They were red from the smoke and exhaustion, but Cormac managed to look bright and alert. "Do you know why I'll be fine?"

"No, but I know you're going to tell me."

Cormac moved his arm over Nell's abdomen, warm strength. "The touch of a mate. It speeds up the healing." His voice grew softer. "At least, I've always heard that. Never had the chance to try it until now."

CHAPTER NINE

Nell swallowed on dryness. "Neither have I."

They lay shoulder to shoulder, faces turned to each other. Cormac caressed her waist. "I'm sorry about Magnus, love."

"Can we talk about it later?"

"We can talk about anything you want, anytime you want. For the rest of our lives."

"Stop." Nell touched his lips. "You made that mate-claim when I couldn't deny it."

"Yep," Cormac said. "No time like the present."

"I haven't accepted it yet."

"I know."

He didn't insist, didn't do the dominant thing and try to beat her down with his stare. Cormac lay quietly and simply watched her, his eyes heartbreakingly blue.

"You can deny it if you want to," he said.

She clung to that safety line. "I do deny it. I'm not ready yet. Please, don't rush me."

Cormac's eyes darkened to his bear's color, and his arm tightened around her. "Are you sure?"

"Yes. No. *I don't know.*" Nell was confused, stunned by the events of the day, worried about Shane, and scared to death that she was forming the mate bond in her heart for Cormac.

The mate bond meant they'd be bound together forever, ceremony or no ceremony, and pulling the bond apart would mean unimaginable grief. Nell had already gone through grief, and she'd almost had to go through it again today. She never wanted to know grief again.

"Are you very sure?" Cormac asked.

"For now. Later. When you're healed, we can sit down and talk about it . . ."

He stopped her words by touching his hurt hand to her lips. "I don't want to talk about it later." Cormac exhaled, warm breath on her cheek, then he raised his head and bellowed, "Brody!"

His voice was broken, but he could still be loud.

Nell half sat up. "What are you doing?"

Brody nearly fell into the room, his eyes round with fear. "What? What's the matter?"

Behind him, down the hall, Nell heard Shane ask, "What's going on?"

"Nell refused my mate-claim," Cormac said. He sounded calm. Too calm.

"What?" Brody said, dismayed.

"Mom," Shane called, "the guy saved my life. Give him a break."

"And you need someone to be with," Brody said. "You know, for the next half of your life."

Nell sent him a glare. "Thank you very much for your concern."

Brody raised his hands. "I'm just saying."

Cormac was the only one who'd remained silent. "It's your decision, Nell."

"I know it's my decision. You all need to stop badgering me. I need time to *think*."

"That's your final word?" Cormac asked.

Was he trying to drive her straight to insanity? "It is."

Cormac drew a long breath. "In that case . . . Nell, under the light of the sun, the Father God, and in front of witnesses, I claim you as mate."

The words weren't loud, but they moved full force. Brody started to laugh.

"*What?*" Nell half shouted.

Cormac kept his gaze intent on her. "Is that a refusal?"

"Yes!"

Cormac shrugged, the movement tired. "It's your decision." He looked at Brody, who was grinning like a fool, then back at Nell. "Nell, under the light of the sun, the Father God, and in front of witnesses I claim you . . ."

Nell screamed and sat up. She slammed her hands over her ears. "Out!"

"Get back here, Brody," Shane said from down the hall. "Obviously, those two need to talk."

"And shut the door behind you." Nell took her hands from her ears to point at the door.

". . . as mate," Cormac finished.

Nell balled her fists. "You double-crossing, sneaky . . . *bear.*"

"Go on," Cormac said to Brody, who didn't bother to hide his laughter. "We need some privacy."

"Take all the time you need," Brody said. "Hang a sock on the door or something. We'll keep away until it's gone."

"Brody," Nell said in a furious voice.

"Good luck," Brody said to Cormac. He started to go, then he swung back and came to the bed, leaning down to enclose Cormac in a careful embrace. Cormac returned it the best he could. "Thank you," Brody said. "Seriously."

"Anytime, cub of my mate. I know you and Shane are the most important things in the world to her."

Now Brody looked embarrassed. "Yeah, well." He broke the embrace and headed for the door. "Have fun, kids."

And he was gone, a giant draft and house-rattling door slam in his wake.

"You're not going to take no for an answer, are you?" Nell asked, her heart fluttering with the beginnings of panic.

"Nope."

"You're not following the rules."

"I'm following the rules to the letter." Cormac put his arm around her shoulders and eased her back down to him. "You don't need time, Nell," he said. "You've had too much time. So have I. I know you're scared. I am too. But we'll go into it together, figure it out together. No more games, no more time alone. Let's take the rest of time . . . together."

Yes! Nell wanted that. Someone to live with, someone to laugh with. Shane and Brody might have mates soon, their own families. She and Cormac could be here, anchoring them.

"You've done nothing but rush me and confuse me since you came into my house," she said. "You started banging in my kitchen at five in the morning to get my attention, didn't you? You could have waited for a civilized hour."

"I believe in being direct."

"Direct this, bear brain." Nell growled at him, a she-bear at her most formidable. At the same time, she slid the torn dress off over her head and dropped it on the floor. "You need to finish what you started."

His eyes sparkled with interest. "Yeah?"

"I'm talking about my kitchen. I want it finished, and looking as good as the ones in those fancy magazines. And then I want you in it with me, cooking my cubs dinner, or giving our friends a party, or taking me in a mating frenzy on the countertop. Got it?"

Cormac gave her a quiet smile. "I think I do."

Nell drew a breath. "In that case, Cormac—I accept your mate-claim."

He caressed her cheek. "But there aren't any witnesses."

"My ass. They're listening outside the door." Nell raised her voice. "Did you hear me? Cormac, mate of my heart, in front of my nosy, can't-mind-their-own-businesses sons, I accept your mate-claim."

The cheer from the hall and the bedroom beyond confirmed that her cubs were there and listening hard. Then they were laughing, their rumbling filling the house. Brody moved off, back to Shane's bedroom.

Cormac caught Nell in a kiss that stole her breath. She held him, her lips warming with his, while the rest of her body trembled.

Cormac eased back from the kiss, his eyes beautiful blue again. He ran his fingertip down her nose, then he turned away and rolled out of the bed.

Nell gaped up at him from the quilts. Cormac was stark naked, the bandages white on his dark skin. His cock, uncaring about wounds, lifted in readiness.

He started to bend to the floor, then he grunted and tossed something up with his foot to catch in his hand.

"What are you doing?" she asked.

"Putting a sock on the door." Cormac opened the door, quickly draped the sock over the doorknob, and closed it again. "I don't want anyone in here until I'm done."

"But you're still hurt. We can't possibly . . ."

Cormac grinned. "No time like the present."

He came back to the bed and looked down at Nell where she lay on the quilt in nothing but her panties. His sinful look made her shiver.

"I'd love to dive right into you," he said. "As it is . . ." He lifted the quilt and slid carefully under it, grunting again.

"You should sleep," Nell said. "We'll celebrate later."

"No." Cormac lost his smile, the word sharp. "I almost lost you today. I almost lost *me*. I'm not waiting another second." He jerked the quilt out from under her, enclosing her in it with him, and moved himself on top of her. "Mmm," he said, lowering his head to kiss her. "This doesn't hurt."

"But you could start bleeding again."

"I don't think so." He took her hand and put it on his abdomen. "Graham is good, and I've been lying here basking in the warmth of my mate. I think I'll be fine."

She exhaled. "Thank the Goddess."

"Yes, the Goddess sure has been good to me."

Cormac stopped talking then, his smile leaving him, his eyes stilling. Nell touched his cheek, but he simply looked at her.

Their bodies wanted to come together, the mate frenzy rising in Nell and beginning to blot out other thoughts. She moved against him, rewarded by the weight of his cock slipping between her legs.

Cormac's jaw tightened, as though he held himself back, as though he feared hurting *her.*

"My love," she whispered, hands moving to the small of his back. "Yes."

Cormac growled. And he let himself go.

His kisses fell on her flesh, brands of fire, then he took her mouth in a kiss that broke her, lightened her, and seared into her heart. At the same time, Cormac slid inside her, opening her with his thick, blunt cock.

Nell pulled him down to her, excitement taking her swiftly.

In her heart, the mate bond flared—a sweet, dark pain that made her drag him closer, closer. She drove up to him, and he came down to her with his hands, his mouth, his body loving her as it should.

"The mate bond," he said softly, his broken voice holding triumph. "I knew it would save me."

The note of joy made his voice sound better already. In time, it would heal again, and Cormac would speak her name with the beautiful rumble she'd first started to love.

"Nell," he said, the word caressing. "Mate of my heart. Mate of my life. I love you."

"I love you," Nell said, her own voice breaking. The words were the truest she'd ever spoken.

Cormac brushed the mouth that said them with a long kiss, then he held her in his arms and kept on loving her, first swiftly, then—after a long time—more slowly.

Her touch certainly was healing him. After their first climax, he rested only a few moments before his smile turned wicked again.

Cormac's mouth came down, landing on her breast in an open-mouthed kiss. He licked his way to one nipple, making it stand up in a tight peak, before he suckled it into his mouth. He skimmed hands under Nell to cup her buttocks, raising her hips a little.

He dropped kisses down her abdomen, his mouth hot, pausing at her navel to lick it. Then he pressed his mouth over her belly, and blew, lips sealed to her skin, making a raspberry noise.

"You shit." Nell laughed and pushed at his head.

Cormac laughed with her, deep and dark, before he licked his way between her legs and did the same trick with his mouth there. This time Nell rocked her hips, a moan escaping her. "What are you doing *now*?"

"Savoring you."

No more laughter. Cormac's voice caressed her name, then his tongue caressed *her*. Nell's thoughts dissolved on a wave of intense pleasure.

"Cormac. *I love you.*"

He answered by plying her with his tongue—licking, nipping, kissing, suckling—her hips moving in rhythm. Nell was rising to him, needing him, wanting him.

He licked until another climax swept over her in rolling waves. She cried his name again, savoring the word as he savored her.

Cormac rose up over her, his strength returning, and entered her in one firm stroke. His hardness opened her, satisfied, felt so *right*. He belonged with her, and she with him.

The mate bond began in warmth as he loved her, then it wove around them, binding them as they spun again to climax. Nell skimmed her hands to his buttocks and pulled him to her, feeling herself whole for the first time in such a very long time.

The splinters of herself solidified, Cormac's weight on her, his body in her arms, sealing her into herself, and into him.

Two hearts, two mates, one bond.

THE HUNTER'S CABIN

Jean Johnson

ACKNOWLEDGMENTS

My beta-editors, as always, get my thanks: NotSoSaintly, Alienor, Stormi, and Alexandra. My thanks also to the editors and copy editors at Berkley. I write the story; they ensure it makes sense. This romance is from the world of the Vulland Chronicles, steampunk short stories filled with magic and machinery. Check online at www.JeanJohnson.net for more information about these and other tales. May you enjoy this one as well.

CHAPTER ONE

The cabin was difficult to spot from the air. Vee knew she had the right valley; the hunter's descriptions of the landmarks that were visible even in deep winter were near-perfect, but the actual location of the cabin was difficult to discern thanks to the avalanche that had tumbled down from higher up the slopes. It was the man clinging to her back who spotted the front of the stout stone chimney marking the mound of snow covering the structure.

"There! There it is," Kiereseth asserted, freeing an arm to point at a shadowy cleft and a snow-mounted peak. Around them, tiny flakes drifted down, the tail end of the storms that had plagued this region for weeks. He couldn't fly like Vee could, which meant she had to carry him. Kiers had done his best to be useful, spotting airships to dodge, people to avoid being seen by, and looking for likely places to rest at night in their haphazard travels. "That *has* to be it. Those straight lines aren't the kind made by trees. That one there below it, that triangular bit could be the front of the roofline."

Tensing her muscles, Vee angled their hovering bodies around the ridged mound of rumpled snow projecting out from the mountainside, giving both of them a good look. She then turned to view the jumbled mound of snow blocking everything down to the smallish mouth of the little valley. She shook her head slightly, bringing her body to a hovering stop at just enough of an angle that she could look around comfortably without forcing her piggy-back passenger to clutch at her body for fear of falling off.

"Mister Horgen was right," she stated, her light alto voice echoing slightly off the snow. "This is about as remote as you can get, and still be under the Vull."

"Remote, except for the airships we've seen," he reminded her, his baritone echoing as well. He glanced up, looking for signs of an airship. The clouds obscured most of the sky, but they were high up enough, the rippling, transparent gold membrane that separated the continent of Earthland from the Skylands could be seen through the thinner bits. "Thank the Light they don't seem to have seen us."

"That's why I had you buy that gray overcoat, because you'll look like a bit of cloud when paired with me . . . or in this case, a bit of snow," Vee reminded him. "Air Couriers do know how to hide from our enemies, even if our 'package' is a person. But let's figure out how to unbury this cabin before another airship comes by. We don't know if any shipping routes fly past this exact valley."

Leaning forward, Kiereseth pointed past her shoulder. He pointed the other way, and she obliged by turning them midair, following the thrust of his wool-shrouded, snowflake-dusted arm. She squinted along his arm as he spoke. "Getting in will be difficult. There's been enough snow dusted over everything since the avalanche that any effort we make will be noticeable. Mister Horgen said the cabin's a little over two stories high, and that the front of the roof extends out a bit. That means the snow must be a good twenty feet deep. We'll have a difficult time getting in through that small gap in the front without leaving signs that are visible from the air."

Frowning in thought, Vielle studied the hillside. Off to her right, to the left of the cabin, a thick cluster of trees had blocked some of the heavy snowfall. It had been awhile since she'd flown over lands covered in so much snow. Only a couple of years out of the Courier's Academy, she strove to remember her training about deep winter maneuvers. "Maybe yes, and maybe no. If it's really that deep, maybe we can tunnel in from those trees to the porch? If we use our thon? It's just a twist on building snow-shelters."

"My affinity for Fire thon can melt all that snow, yes, but I won't be able to *shape* it, Miss Vielle," the ex-prince groused. "I come from the southlands, remember? Where snow is only something someone with Air and Water affinities can conjure, because the weather is too warm. I don't know how to make a shelter, as you propose. The drifts would probably collapse on top of us. Forming a stable tunnel requires more than a mere smidgen of Water, which is all I have."

If they hadn't needed a place to hide and rest while the guards looking for them searched fruitlessly down in the lowlands, Vee wouldn't have admitted a single thing. The strength of her abilities was not something the Courier liked to discuss. But they were both exhausted from being on the run, they couldn't stay long in any one town, and traveling in winter—flying in winter—left both of them aching and cold by midday, even with him sharing his thon to keep them warm.

It was now midafternoon, and she had been flying the pair of them low to the ground, which meant a lot of maneuvering up and down as they traversed the folds of the mountains. The cabin was only a few yards away, relatively speaking, but secrecy demanded a more convoluted, energy-draining approach. Her tone was therefore a little snappish. "Well, lucky for you, Mister Kiereseth, I have more than a smidgen. Of *both* Water and Fire. I'm pretty sure that *I* can do it."

"You . . . what?" Kiereseth fumbled to grab her shoulders as she shifted from a low angle to a more vertical position, one better suited for slipping down between the evergreens. "No. Your main affinity is *Air*. The strongest I've ever seen, yes, but you're from the Earthlands. It's only the people in the Skylands who have really strong thon in more than one category," he added, wincing as a few of the tree branches scraped against them, showering them in snow. "So what, are you also that strong in Earth? Are you some sort of . . . of mutant thonist, balanced in all four elements?"

"I'm not *that* balanced. Earth is my weakest affinity, Air my strongest . . . and I'm strong because I am strong, and that's all there is to it. Only Light and Life know why," she muttered, bringing herself upright as her feet touched the snow. Touched, and sank down, and down again, until both she and her passenger were mired up to their waists.

The upper layers of snowfall were a deep, soft, dry powder, with the more compressed layers at least three, maybe four feet deep. The biggest reason they sank so far was that he was still clinging to her, carried piggyback on her shoulders since he couldn't tense his muscles and fly.

"Off. *Please*, Mister Kiers, off you go. I can't do this with you clinging to me. I'm not that strong on the ground, and I can't focus on flying when I'm trying to control two other thons on something I haven't done since the Academy."

"Of course, Miss Vielle." Releasing the young woman, Kieres-eth plopped down into the thick snow in a sort of reclined position as the powder supported his outstretched arms and legs. His disgruntled state gave way before the absurdity of it. Chuckling, he wiggled his limbs in a fruitless attempt to right himself, then muttered, "I feel like I'm in a Weather-be-damned hammock. Ice-cold, but a hammock. If it weren't freezing out, I'd be comfortable."

"Enjoy it while it lasts, Mister Kiers," Vee muttered back,

removing her goggles from her face. She tucked them into the backpack slung across her front. "I'm not sure how exhausted I'll be by the end of this, so I'll be counting on you and your Fire affinity to get that cabin warm."

Arching her arms, she tensed her shoulders and upper arm muscles, gloved fingers clenching slowly into fists. She couldn't bring her arms in close to her chest since she was wearing a backpack in a reversed position, covering her leather-clad breasts, but she didn't need to for this particular thon-focusing trick.

With her body pointed at the cabin, arms arced like she was trying to give the air itself a hug, the snow in front of her gradually started to shift and move. She had to angle slightly uphill to avoid a couple of tree trunks, plus be mindful of where all that melting snow was flowing to beneath the drifts. Not to mention try to make it look like a natural dimple in the snow, rather than a man-made one.

Once she had a tunnel-sized divot formed for the entrance, she was free to send the melted water up in a webwork of curved arches, supporting the snowpack like a crystalline trellis. It wasn't easy work. Without him clinging to her, keeping both of them warm with his Fire thon, the cold had begun to seep through her clothes, and the nearly full-day's flight had exhausted her.

She could have spared a bit of Fire for her own warmth, but juggling the water was just that, a juggle to hold it in place in its webwork of supports while she pulled enough heat back out of the melted snow to freeze it in place, all without melting the layers above into a divot that would be noticeable from the air.

Struggling out of the snow in her wake, Kiers followed her step by step as she moved into the tunnel her quiet efforts made. If he hadn't seen similar displays back home, he might've been astounded beyond words by her strength and control. As it was, he could admit in his head to being amazed.

All this strength and control, after a good six hours of flight just to reach this place . . . and none of it bolstered by a single bite of all that thonite she had bought and packed. Nor had she been born up in the Skylands like him. This much thon strength in an Earthland-bound woman was almost unheard of, back home.

A home he couldn't go back to, thanks to the machinations of his sister.

Mindful of their descent, Kiers spent a few minutes melting some of the snow and dusting more of it over the impact of their landing. It was underneath the evergreen boughs, but he didn't want to make it too obvious. When that was done, he realized she had made several yards of progress.

Following her into the tunnel, Kiers saw her shivering. Only then did he realize she was no longer enjoying the shared warmth of the slight amount of Fire thon he was expending to keep himself warm. Moving up behind her on the cold, grassy path she had made in the snowbank, he gently placed his gloved hands on her back, sharing that heat.

When the warmth finally penetrated her clothes, seeping into her stiff, trembling muscles, Vee had to stifle a moan. She hadn't realized how cold she had grown. Step by step, she continued to craft the tunnel, arms held wide and curved, fingers slowly clenching and flexing. As good as his thon was at keeping them warm, she knew it wouldn't last forever. They needed a real fire, one with wood for its fuel rather than the frailties of mind and body. A real fire, which would allow them to cook the food the hunter said he had stockpiled in the larder of his cabin.

The tunnel broke through to the porch right next to one of the stout tree trunks that had been used as columns to support the deep overhang of the roof, forcing her to swerve a bit. Satisfied with her aim, Vee cleared some of the snow from around the door, where it had piled at least as high as the handle.

The melted water was smaller in volume without the pockets of air trapped between the arms of each little snowflake. Rather than letting it drain through the wooden boards forming the front porch, she shifted it into an icy retaining wall meant to shore up the snowbank looming along the open side. It would be annoying to have to constantly re-clear the front door during their stay here if that snowbank collapsed inward.

"Go on in, Mister Kiers," she urged him, taking a moment to lower and relax her aching arms. Shaping snow used a different, less familiar set of muscles than flying did. "There should be wood inside. Get a fire started in the hearth if you can, or at least find a lamp to light. Mister Horgen said the woodpiles were located just to either side of the house, but it looks like they're completely buried in all this snow. I'll have to dig them out, and give them more of these ice-arches for support."

"You'll have to free the snow from the chimney, first," Kiers pointed out, removing his hands from her wool-covered shoulder blades. "Unless you want me to just blast heat up the flue and melt it off."

"Mister Kiers, I am tired, hungry, and on my last dregs of excess energy. My temper is therefore running short. Since you've professed repeatedly that you cannot cook anything more compli-cated than heating a pot of water, I will have to spare *my* precious reserves of energy to ensure we don't starve to death," she retorted stiffly, feeling the cold closing in once more. "You may translate all of that however you like, but the short version is, *I don't care.*"

Wisely, he sealed his lips against any possible retort, however tempting it might have been, and moved to open the cabin door. Wisely, she turned her attention toward the sides of the A-frame cabin, where it took her a bit more in the way of careful snow-shifting to determine the roofline sloped all the way to the ground. Once she did have enough of the snow cleared away, she explored as far as she could.

That exploration didn't go far. Only a bit of light coming in through the gap high up in the porch roofline, but she could just make out the stacked segments of wood filling the outer eaves, with a narrow path up against the cabin walls on either side. The path was strewn with bits of frozen bark and scraps of wood, dirty and mostly weathered but still suitable for kindling if one didn't have much in the way of Fire-attuned thon.

With the roof extending all the way to the ground on either side, there were no windows cut into the thick timbers forming the side of the cabin. Picking her way back to the porch, Vee wondered how much the ex-prince exploring the interior could see. The sun was still over an hour from setting, but they were surrounded by cloud-covered mountains, and that meant the lighting outside was already growing dim. When the sun did set, it would be as if someone had blown out a lamp, and that meant they needed light now.

Reaching the wooden deck, Vee glanced at the shuttered windows fronting the cabin. A golden glow gleamed faintly through the cracks. Relieved he had found some source of illumination, she opened the door, only to find herself in a dark, modest entry room. It wasn't big, just enough to have a bench on either side with coat hooks above and room for spare boots, snowshoes, and the like beneath the benches, and a pair of steps up to the inner door.

Even as she looked around, the inner panel opened, letting through a large spill of warm lamplight. Kiers poked his dark head into the boot room, grinning down at her. Some of that light danced and crackled behind him, bringing with it the sounds and the scents of a firmly caught hearth fire. Some of it gleamed through his black locks, cut finger-length short in an effort to change his appearance so that the men chasing them wouldn't immediately recognize him without the long braid of a member of the Jade Mountain royal family. Vielle thought the shorter strands looked good on him, balancing the square planes of his jaw with their subtle curls.

"Smart fellow, our host," Kiers praised, dragging her attention back to their surroundings. "It seems he left the house well-prepared for his return. A lamp on the bench down there, and wood already laid in the hearth up here. No alchemical twigs or even a tinderbox in sight, so I suspect our absent host has a fair bit of Fire in him."

Hopping down the distance of the two steps, he worked on unbuttoning his pale gray woolen coat, his gloves already stripped off. Beneath the coat lay a darker gray waistcoat and matching trousers, with two layers of bleached shirt beneath. Shrugging out of the wool overcoat, he hung it on one of the hooks, added his plebeian-knitted wool cap, then moved to help Vee out of her own outer garments.

She was already struggling with the backpack, holding it in place, moving stiffly from hours of holding her muscles tense, channeling her thon so she could fly. He helped set it on the bench, then unbuckled the leather cap on her head while she worked on the buttons of her leather jacket. Pulling it away exposed the coronet of her braided, ash gold hair. Some of the pins came loose as he did so, forcing him to stoop and catch them before they could vanish between the floorboard cracks. That brought him down by her white, trouser-clad legs, and the scuffed white leather boots she wore.

"He also laid out slippers, so off with your boots, too, Miss Vielle," the ex-prince told her, feeling like a valet. "Or do you need help with them?"

"No, I can get them, thank you," Vee replied, pleased that he had offered. Now that she had the chance to rest, her brief bout of temper was fading again. "Sorry for snapping at you. And thank you for helping. And for the slippers."

The reduction in his circumstances had angered him at first, but now it was merely an annoyance at best. Not to mention Miss Vielle expected him to haul his own weight, even if she literally hauled his whenever they flew. Now that he knew her better, he admired her common sense and practicality. He valued her good opinion of him. Claiming the other bench, he worked on removing his own boots.

"You're quite welcome. Apparently, Mister Horgen has a thing for keeping his boots downstairs and wearing lambswool-lined slippers inside the cabin proper. He left three or four pairs lined up just past the door. You should be able to shuffle around in the ankle boots, I think. They'll be a bit big on you, since they looked like they'll fit me without a problem, but they'll be toasty-warm and dry, unlike our boots."

"Then we'll do our best to comply with his wishes, spoken or not." Sitting down across from him, Vee tried not to shiver; the upper level might be receiving some of the heat radiating from that fire, but not down here. Unlacing her boots, she left them with her coat, scarf, cap, and gloves on the bench across from his. Before she could pick up her pack, she found it lifted by one of his hands. The other, he offered to her to assist her to her feet.

"For the record, I've set a pot of water to boil. *Also* for the record . . . if you'll tell me what to do, I'm willing to *learn* how to cook, Miss Vielle," Kiers teased her. "Now that we actually have the facilities and the supplies to do so. I took a quick tour while the fire caught; the larder goes back into a cave set in the mountainside. From the looks of it, Mister Horgen has this place *very* well stocked. Enough for an entire year, I should think. Though I should think it'd only take us a week or two for the men from Jade Mountain to give up on us and move on, thinking that we've moved on as well."

"We'll have to remember to leave a bit more in payment for our host, then," she murmured, accepting the hand. Sitting down in the cold entryway had allowed her sore muscles to stiffen. "Plus set fresh wood in the hearth and return the lamp to the entryway bench, and leave the place as good or better than we've found it. But as to whether or not they'll give up . . . we'll have to fire up the portable aetherometer and try to find the frequency they're using to communicate again. Assuming we can get a signal through these mountains, of course."

"Assuming that, yes," he agreed, leading her into the cabin proper. "They might see that the cabin is occupied, but it'll look like it's been occupied since before the avalanche fell. With no visible tracks leading to or from it, that should discourage them from visiting—and if nothing else, we'll at least know it if they get close. They've been sending out their reports at dawn and dusk. You'll probably want to crank it up soon—do you need a bite of thonite after all that hard work?"

"No, thank you," Vee dismissed. A part of her was pleased he had asked. She found the ankle boots when he pointed at them, and slipped her stocking-clad feet into them one at a time while he toed his way into a pair of lambswool slippers. "I'm not completely depleted yet, and if we're going to be resting here for a good week or so, then I'll have my reserves topped up naturally by the end of it."

"Like we did back in Triskelle as a guest of His Majesty's?" he asked. "The only reason why they found us there is because it was the logical place for us to go next on your little gizmo quest."

"Rest is *always* better than eating part of a cube. We also don't know when we'll be able to buy thonite again," she pointed out. "As for the next logical place, we haven't had a chance to *think* about all the legends we pored over, going through the Trionan king's somewhat confusing, contradictory archives, so we don't know where we're going next."

"Copious and confusing," Kiers agreed. "I'm the one who's been carrying most of the notes, remember?" Stopping her near the hearth, a blue gray stone construct set with a wire mesh screen in front, he gestured at it. "As for our current sheltering spot, this, Miss Vielle, is the single smartest piece of survival equipment Mister Horgen owns. A genuine soapstone fireplace."

She gave him a curious look. Not because she didn't know what it was, but because he seemed so proud to know it. He took that as encouragement to continue.

"Even when the hearth fire dies down at night, the properties of this particular stone will keep this place warm for hours—I only know about it because I chatted with one of the palace servants in Triskelle while he was stoking the fires in the reading hall." Kiers wrinkled his nose as he said it, grinning at her. "There's some strange mix of Earth and Fire affinities in the stone itself; it absorbs heat and holds it inside, never quite getting *too* hot, and then it slowly releases all that kept heat over time. That's a very good thing to know, because we won't have to worry so much about having to get up in the middle of the night to stoke the fire.

"I had to ask the footman what kind of stone it was, since I hadn't seen the like before . . . which is true of a lot of things down here on the ground, under the Vull. I only got to see new things up in the sky when they were painstakingly imported up there, or when I was on a diplomatic trip. Since my exile, I've needed to know these things a lot more than I've needed to avoid looking like an ignorant, pompous fool."

That self-deprecating quip at the end made her smile. He wasn't much of a fussy, status-conscious prince anymore—he still insisted on some formality between them, but he wasn't nearly as arrogant as before. She wouldn't have wished on him the pain of having his own sister frame him for treason if it could have been prevented, but Vee could admit the hardships he'd endured and his efforts to blend in with the common sort were making him a better man.

His comment about needing to know things made her look around, examining their new, temporary home. The front room had two deep bays. One held a sort of crafts nook, with tools scattered over a workbench lining the alcove, and a stool with a clever padded seat that looked like it could rotate so the sitter could face any of the three sides. The windows were also glazed with expensive sheets of glass, she realized. Doubly so, because the hunter would have had to carry them into the mountains by hand, hopefully without breaking any. But if the shutters were open, the window over the bench would have let in a great deal of natural light.

The other alcove, framing the boxed-in space of the entry room, held a padded bench on one side, a paper-strewn table across from it, and bookshelves overhead crammed with tomes, scrolls, and stacks of writing supplies. Some of which were maps, she realized, moving a little closer. Some of the wood on the hearth snapped, and she shook herself out of her curiosity. Turning around, she surveyed the rest of the room.

The hearth of course was central, but above it sat a balcony with banisters and railings made from thick, peeled tree limbs. The A-frame was crossed by antler- and horn-decorated rafters high up, and stout logs served as columns and posts, giving the interior enough structural support to withstand all that snow piled over the roof. But beyond what lay directly overhead, she couldn't yet say because she couldn't see much more. There weren't any lamps up there to illuminate what lay on the floor above. Disappointed, but knowing she would soon find out, Vee lowered her gaze again.

To either side of the hearth, short sections of slender logs had been laid almost to within touching distance of the hearth, dividing the front room from the back by forming two little walls between the stout pillars supporting the upper floor. Flanking them were doorless openings on either side.

Picking the left one, she stepped beyond the wall and found herself in a kitchen. One with a fire crackling away cheerfully . . . in the same hearth, Vee realized belatedly. It had two openings, one to the front parlour, such as it was, and the other to the largish kitchen in the back of the cabin. It also had more of those soapstone blocks, this time forming a sort of soot-stained table over the hearth. An actual cooking stone. She'd heard of such things, but hadn't seen one until now. Most people used sensible iron cook-stoves these days.

Behind the cooking stone, Kiers had hung an iron pot filled with water with a bit of stout chain, since this side of the hearth mouth was bigger than the other side. The support stones for the cooking surface looked to be granite stapled in place with iron bolts, and more granite had been used to form another flat stretch to one side, no doubt meant as a good spot to transfer hot cooking pots to a cooler surface. From the hints of burn marks in the large table occupying the center of the kitchen, she guessed the owner of the cabin hadn't always remembered to do so.

The work-scarred surface of that table held two more lit oil lamps, adding to the light from the open hearth. At the back of the kitchen area lay a stairwell leading to the next floor, and along the right-hand wall, a sink. A real sink, with a built-in metal pump and a set of shelves, one broad enough to serve as a counter.

Odds were, the pump had been frozen before he'd gotten it to work, since it was still cold enough in the cabin for her to see her breath frosting. Still, the sight of that pump, the cauldron of water, and the various washtubs tucked under the stairs reassured her that they would be able to do things like bathe and scrub their clothing while they were here. Kiers, she knew, liked to be clean and tidy whenever possible. So did she, so a bath would be most welcome.

At the foot of the stairs, in the back left corner, was a stout, fitted door. The cabin's owner had taken the trouble to cover it with a narrow strip of polished metal; as far as mirrors went, it was a little blurry compared to a glass mirror, but she could see Kiers in his gray waistcoat and trousers, and herself in her white Courier's leathers, with the black-stitched outline of a winged scroll of parchment on the shoulders. She didn't look very feminine, but she thought he looked rather manly in his shirtsleeves. Like he belonged, rather than like he was trying to hold himself aloof.

He had come far in his exile. She approved.

Kiereseth, watching her look around, nodded at the door when she glanced that way. "That leads to a corridor cut into the mountainside. A little ways inside on the left is another door leading to a small privy room, and at the back is another door leading to Mister Horgen's larder. I've already had a look at both.

"Either Mister Horgen or his predecessor had a fair touch with Earth, since it all has the clean-cut look you'd get from someone used to manipulating stone via thon," the ex-prince added. "Even the shelves in the pantry section were formed out of stone, and the privy hole looks like it goes down a long ways, given there's almost no smell, so be careful you don't drop anything important down there. I doubt we'd be able to get it back up, since I don't know if it ends in a pit, or if it's a sluice that opens up somewhere outside."

"I'll keep that in mind. I think I can see why he was so upset he couldn't get back here through the avalanche," Vielle said, impressed. "I'd be quite content to stay here all winter, too, if I had such a nice home. And I haven't even seen any bedrooms, yet."

"I suspect they're upstairs. I hadn't had time to do more than look around the ground floor when I heard you come in," he said. "You cleared away all that snow rather quickly. I'm impressed."

"Don't be," Vee dismissed, once again feeling awkward about admitting the strength of her abilities. It still didn't feel like a long time had passed since she had been bullied and picked upon for being stronger than the other students. She shook her head. "The roof actually goes all the way to the ground on either side. I just had to clear a bit of snow from the eaves' entrances. But not all of it, of course. If any of those Jade Mountain guards come flying this way in their airship, this place should still look thoroughly snowbound, with no one having entered or left in weeks."

"Yes, but it will look occupied," Kiers warned her. "We won't be able to stop the chimney from smoking or dropping soot on the snow if we keep burning wood for heat."

Vee nodded. "I know. But we need to do it. One of my friends, her father used to say to us kids that a man was warmed once by wood if he burned it, twice if he also chopped it himself, and thrice if he used his thon to keep himself warm . . . because he'd burn through his thon faster than he could burn through a stack of firewood in a single day, and would still have to chop wood and burn it before that day was through. At least, with the average level of Fire-based thon."

"He sounds like a smart fellow, then," Kiers admitted. He looked around the cabin, then shrugged. "Well. Since I've only hunted for sport, not for a living as a furrier as our host does, and as there's only so much sleeping or eating or poring over notes we'll be able to do, I suspect we'll be trading lots of childhood memories like that over the next few days. But before we do that, I believe you'd agreed to teach me how to cook, yes?"

Vee snorted. "I hadn't *agreed* . . . but I'll teach you what I can. I'm not the world's best, though I've managed to make do so far." She started to say more, only to blink at one of the shelves over the sink. "Is that a stack of cookbooks? And jars of herbs? Oh, we definitely did *not* pay Mister Horgen enough to stay here. I could actually cook something with flavor to it, rather than all that crude campfire cooking."

It was his turn to scoff. "We paid that man enough money to leave him in a sated stupor of liquor, steaks, and wh . . . er, women to chat with for an entire month plus," he quickly amended, blushing. "I'm quite sure we're getting our money's worth already."

That made her roll her eyes. Vee picked up one of the oil lamps, aiming for the stairs. "Oh, just call them whores and be done with it, Mister Kiers. I'm not a fragile flower who knows nothing of how the world works. Not to mention that night we escaped, you and I fooled those guards into thinking I *was* one, and that you were just some random client of mine, so that they would overlook us. It was the only way to make them disbelieve that drunken, randy lout you portrayed could not possibly be the stuffy, formal Prince of Jade Mountain.

"I greatly appreciate the fact that you're a gentleman by nature," she added, leaning over the railing for a moment. "But you needn't wrap both of us in wool. Now, let's go see what lies up these stairs."

"I'm almost afraid to," the ex-prince muttered, following her as she continued up the steps. Then winced as the somewhat short woman turned to look back at him, her free hand on her hip and one ash blond brow quirked upward. Clad in two layers of bleached linen shirts and her white leather flight pants, she definitely didn't look like a delicate flower of a lady. She looked strong, competent, and skeptical. She also had a tart tongue at times.

"And what is *that* supposed to mean, Mister Kiers?" Vee asked him.

Kiers cleared his throat and gestured at the cabin around them. "It's quite clear Mister Horgen lives here on his own, Miss Vielle. That means a high probability that there is only one bed upstairs."

CHAPTER TWO

O h." Vee felt her cheeks warming in a blush. "Well," she managed, clearing her own throat. "It's not as if we haven't slept
together before. We'll, ah, just keep wearing our clothes."

"This isn't an inn with only one room left to let," he reminded
her, moving a little closer. "We've nowhere to go while we hide
here for the next week . . . and . . ." His own face flushed. Clearing his throat again, Kiereseth admitted quietly, "And I find you
highly attractive, Miss Vielle. I have since I first saw you remove
your Courier's cap and jacket, back in Father's reception room. I
still do.

"You are smart, beautiful, witty, and wise," he told her, giving
her the unvarnished truth. "Your knowledge of how to move across
the face of Earthland has saved both our hides several times by
now, and our conversations have ranged all over the place without
tedium. I even enjoy the way you smell, which is a good thing
since you've been flying us both across half the continent so far.
I . . . fancy you as *more* than a mere traveling companion, tossed
together by circumstances, but I am *trying* to be respectful about
just how much I do find you desirable, Miss Vee."

His repeated use of the honorific showed he was indeed trying.

His blunt compliments made her blush and want to respond. Vee let him continue without interrupting, however.

"A single, passing night in a crowded inn is one thing, but this is an entire week of hiding in one place, with only one bed," he reminded her, his gaze drifting down over her flight leathers before they returned to her blue eyes. "I'd like to *remain* a gentleman, because I have come to respect you deeply.

"With that in mind, I hope there are a lot of blankets upstairs, because I may have to sleep on the floor down here, to ensure I remain one around you," he finished quietly. "Because I don't think wearing clothing will mean a damn thing to me by day five of our stay, if I get to hold you in my arms every night."

For a long moment, she couldn't speak. Didn't even know what to say, really. But as he lowered those blue eyes in growing discomfort, Vielle knew she had to give him credit for such open honesty. Taking a deep breath, she gave him some honesty of her own, unconsciously tensing her muscles as she did so.

"Well. For my part, Mister Kiereseth," she returned, using his full name instead of his nickname since it seemed the best way to retain some of her dignity in the next few sentences, "I have found you quite attractive from our first meeting as well. On many levels. And . . . that interlude in the alleyway was not in the least repellent.

"I have deeply appreciated you being a gentleman, particularly that night at the inn when we were forced to be pragmatic, but . . ." Blushing, she steadied herself with another breath and finished her sentence. "But I don't think you'll, ah, need to sleep on the floor. Tonight. Or any other night. While we're here."

He stared at her, tanned cheeks flushed, lips parted, eyes widening in realization. Then he blinked and frowned slightly, eyeing her from head to toe. ". . . Are you *floating*, Miss Vielle?"

"What? Oh!" Forcing her muscles to relax, she dropped the few inches she had risen, landing with a soft thump on her feet. One of her borrowed house boots had almost dangled free, forcing her to squirm her toes and heel back into proper place. "Um, yes. I sort of tensed up from nervousness, and I'm so used to tensing up when I want to fly, I guess I just subconsciously . . . I'm babbling, aren't I?" she added, arresting herself. "Let's just, um . . . go upstairs and get this over with—I mean, let's go and *check* what we'll have to deal with in the way of bedding and the like, that's what I meant."

"I know what you meant," he reassured her. He felt a little too tense himself to chuckle freely, though he did smile. He defused some of the tension by pressing his palm to his stomach with a rueful look. "I'm far more starved for food right now, so you've nothing to fear from me at the moment. Unless you suddenly turned into a ration of bacon, of course."

"Hardly," she snorted, relieved the moment hadn't been ruined.

Lamp in hand, she walked—not floated—up the last of the stairs. The glow from the broad wick wasn't overly bright, but it did light up a pair of wardrobe cupboards, a couple of chests, some shelving built into the half-high walls to either side, and the broad bed centered on the balcony. The very large bed.

She stopped on the next-to-top step just so she could stare at it. "Light and Life, that thing's almost big enough for *four* people to sleep in it, never mind our host!"

The opening to the stairwell had been boxed in by solid planks, which meant he couldn't see what she meant just yet. Nudging her forward by a pat on her rump—which made her squeak—Kiers mounted the last few steps in her wake and studied it for himself.

She was right. It was broad and long, mounded high with what looked like a feather-stuffed quilt patched together in colorful blocks of fabric, with a veritable hill of fat feather pillows piled against the headboard. Even if the bedsheets looked to be plain bleached muslin and the quilting material mere scraps of fabric salvaged from here and there, Kiers suspected it was the most decadent thing he would ever see outside of a genuine palace.

"Light and Life indeed," he agreed, studying it in awe. "That is a *huge* bed. I think you could hold an entire . . . Er, never mind," he stated quickly, slamming down on the chain of thoughts that included a mental image of bodies sprawled before him, naked and entwined, using every available inch of that sybaritic bed. He very carefully blocked that thought out, because he was supposed to remain hungry for food right now, not that. He was a prince and a gentleman, and he had to remain that way.

Thankfully, Vee only gave him a mildly curious look, followed by a faint blush. She didn't ask for a clarification on his halted thought. He turned away, seeking a distraction.

What little warmth there was from the fire had already started to gather up here, though the difference was slight, and palpably different over the distance between his head and his slipper-clad feet. Shivering a little, he turned to face the other way, and spotted a door. Moving over to it gave him something to focus on other than the bed, which his erstwhile partner was still studying. Opening it up, he discovered it was nothing more than a large storage room, lined with shelves of rolled-up hides, sticks of sinew, antlers, horns, bones, and yet more tricks and tools of their host's trade.

"I think I've found where he stores the nonfood bits he gets from his kills," Kiers stated, closing the door again. "I don't think we'll need anything from in there, so we'll just leave that alone. It does look like the room goes all the way back against the mountain, though."

"The eaves do, too. It's a good design if you think about it," Vee agreed, dragging her gaze away from the bed. Looking at him didn't help, though, since both views only reminded her of the offer she'd delicately made, downstairs. Needing something to do—like cook them a meal with her limited skills—she headed for the stairs. "Extend the roof all the way back to the mountain, and just as we've seen, an avalanche at this point on the mountainside flows right over this place without dislodging it. I knew the Gullwing Mountains got a fair bit of snow in the winter, particularly up in the northern arc, but I'd never seen an actual avalanche, just heard of them. It looks like he's used to this kind of threat."

Grateful for the distraction, Kiers followed her downstairs. Not that he had much choice, since it was either stay up here in the near-dark, or follow the woman carrying the nearest lamp. "Indeed. Which means the avalanche must have been nigh-impossible to cross on foot, if a man used to wintering up here found it too difficult to navigate."

"It did look rather rumpled from the air," she agreed, reaching the ground floor. "I don't know much about such things, but the other slope of the valley mouth didn't look too stable, either. He might've been afraid of triggering a slide from that side as well . . . and if it can bury a cabin so that it's difficult to recognize from the air, then it could bury a man alive, and no one would ever know." Hearing her stomach grumble, Vee blushed. "Let's have you check on that cauldron of water while I see what I can scrounge out of our host's larder, yes?"

"I shall pray fervently that you'll find enough bacon rations for yourself as well, because I've already claimed the first share," Kiers dared to tease her. "I'll join you in the larder as soon as I've stoked the fire a bit more."

Supper was an awkward affair. The meal itself wasn't too special, consisting of a fry-up of diced venison, root vegetables, a bit of bacon for greasing the skillet, and some herbs from the jars which Vee sniffed at and pronounced vaguely suitable. Plus they had a bit of pan-fried flatbread, which Kiers didn't burn too badly after the first undercooked try. It was the conversation that was awful.

Or rather, the lack of it. First Kiers attempted to discuss the thonite gizmo, which was the main reason they were on the run, but Vee bounced up from the swiveling stool he had dragged in from the workbench nook to the kitchen and grabbed the portable aetherometer. She insisted on cranking it up so they could listen for any possible pursuit, since it was now near sunset. That only produced static, which was reassuring to a degree, but rather monotonous as a background noise.

Then she tried to discuss the legends of antiquity they had researched during their week at the Trionan king's palace, but that only made him bound up and fetch his backpack, where the sheafs of papers had been hastily stuffed in their sudden need to flee. The resulting mess had to be sorted, which left them with the realization a good seven pages of his notes and five of hers were missing, and not all of them from the same chunk. Having to flee in a hurry while His Majesty delayed the guards from Jade Mountain hadn't allowed them the luxury of making sure they had snatched everything.

All throughout the awkward meal, both preparing and eating it, their eyes occasionally met. When they did, both of them blushed a little. Each knew that supper would eventually end, leaving them with just the washing up, and then however long it might take the two of them to decide they were tired . . . which meant each of those little shared glances added an extra layer of tension to the intimacy of sharing the cabin.

The quiet hiss and spit of static from the aetherometer started to die down when they were nearly done scrubbing the dishes. It wasn't until Kiers handed her the last of the scrubbed dishes for drying that Vee realized the noises it made were now fading. The boxy device sat on the kitchen table, no bigger than one of their heads, with the tuning dial still set to the previous frequency they had overheard the guards from Jade Mountain using to coordinate their search efforts.

Wiping the cookpot, she set it on the granite shelf next to the hearth to dry in the heat now radiating comfortably from the bluish gray soapstone, and crossed to the table. A scrub of her hands got them dry enough to shut off the device. The ex-prince—who had briefly wrinkled his nose at the thought of scrubbing dishes like a servant, but otherwise hadn't protested—glanced over his shoulder in time to see her tossing the drying cloth over one shoulder and stooping over the table.

"Did you hear something on the aether?" he asked her, fishing out the silverware they had used from the bottom of the scrubbing bucket.

"More like nothing," she said, opening the little fuel hatch and peering into the square compartment. "It still has plenty of thonite left in the cube. I guess we just didn't crank it enough." Closing the hatch, she gripped the little handle on the side and started spinning it. Then cracked a yawn, belatedly smothering it behind her hand before returning it to her work. "Pardon me. Warm and full and safe, my body is finally beginning to relax, though my brain is still racing . . ."

"I know the feeling. We took so many precautions, walking out of that last town in a completely different direction, hugging the tree line, detouring around anything that looked like it might be a house or a person, hiding from any airship that looked like it might be theirs . . . But I feel safe now. For now," he amended. "It's been a long day, and a long week. We can't stay here forever, but we can stay here for now. And that's a relief."

"Mm, I quite agree," she murmured.

Turning the washbucket of dirty water over, Kiers rinsed the forks in the tub holding the clean, still-steaming water, then turned and moved up behind her. Sliding the towel from her shoulder, he absentmindedly dried the forks while watching her body sway with the effort of charging the device. He made up his mind as she pushed the button, restarting the thing with a fresh crackle of static . . . and smothered another yawn.

Reaching past her hip, he placed the two forks on the tabletop with little clicks of metal on wood, then straightened and stepped deliberately close enough to brush his thighs against her rump. She gasped and straightened up. "Mister Kiers?"

"Yes, Miss Vielle?" he asked. He touched her back with both hands, then slid them around her ribs. The hitch in her breath as he did so made him smile. As she was nearly a foot shorter than him, it was far easier for him to cup the undersides of her linen-clad breasts than it was to wrap his arms around her waist.

"Mister Kiereseth!" she tried to snap, using his full first name. It came out a bit too breathy to be forceful, though. The illicit touch made Vee's head spin, banishing the exhaustion from her body. Still, she tried; the habits of courtly behavior, the ways of polite society, had been drummed too thoroughly into her back in the Courier's Academy. And, ex- or not, he *was* a prince. She didn't want him to think she was taking her earlier offer with the lightness of a professional whore. "What exactly do you think you're doing, now?"

Stooping, he murmured in her ear, "Well, if you're *tired*, then the gentlemanly thing to do would be to carry you up to bed, now wouldn't it?" Gently kneading her modest breasts, he added, "These looked rather heavy, so I thought I'd carry them up first."

The sheer audacity of his preposterous claim, coupled with his bold, ticklish touch, made her burst into laughter. He hugged her for it, cradling her slender form against his body, then leaned forward just enough to turn the aetherometer off. Sagging against him as he straightened, Vee covered her nose and mouth, trying not to snort as she wound down into amused giggles. Only to squeak and tense as he scooped her off her feet, one arm behind her back, the other under her knees.

Kiers hefted her against his chest, then paused and quirked a brow. "Miss Vielle, are you tensing up because you're afraid of my intentions, or are you tensing because you're trying to lighten your negligible mass on my behalf? You don't need to. I am strong."

Cradled against his warmth, she considered his question for a moment, then relaxed. Half of her mass had indeed been negated by her reflexive tensing. It now settled firmly into his arms. She peeked up at him, once again feeling that same stomach-warming tension that had lurked all throughout their meal. "Well, I'm not really afraid of your intentions, per se. I'm just . . . inexperienced. And I don't take such things lightly."

He nodded. "That's understandable. And I am treating this moment very seriously. I hate being kicked out of my kingdom, but I don't regret coming to know you. Although I hope I do not shock you by admitting I have a fair bit of experience. Father and Mother both agreed that their children—male and female— should know plenty about lovemaking, in case anyone should think to sway our minds via seduction.

"It's easier to keep a clear head when you know what to expect. Grab the lamps, will you?" he added, turning so that she could grasp the two lit oil lamps illuminating the kitchen. "It's always best to see what you're doing in a bed, rather than fumbling around in the dark."

"I, er, suppose that makes sense." Face warm at the implications of what they were about to do, she plucked first one lamp, then the other from the table while he carefully stepped around it. Balancing them carefully in her grasp, Vee enjoyed the unfamiliar sensation of being carried upstairs. He had to do so sideways to clear her legs, but once at the top directed her in murmurs to set one lamp on one of the wardrobe cupboards, and the other on the bedside table. Once that was done, he set her gently on her feet at the side of the monstrous, down-quilted bed.

The upper floor of the cabin was by now much warmer than the bottom level, and the temperature difference made the layers of her clothing feel restrictive. She knew enough about lovemaking to know that garments were superfluous in such matters. That prompted her to lift her fingers to the buttons of her outer blouse. A moment later, Kiers covered her hands with his own.

"May I?" he asked, stilling her fingers.

Blushing, Vee nodded. She started to lower her hands, but he drew them up to the buttons of his own layered shirts. The grin he gave her made her smile shyly back in return. Arms interlacing, they pushed the little wooden circles through their holes. He unfastened the waistband button of his trousers, giving her enough slack to start tugging his shirttails free, and she did the same for him.

"So many layers," Vee muttered after helping him out of the first shirt, only to be confronted with the next. "It's a wonder humans even bother with lovemaking in winter."

"Well, I may come from a balmy southern climate," Kiers returned wryly, "but even I've heard that lovemaking is an excellent way to stay warm in winter . . . and while parts of me protest at having to work hard like a common laborer . . . I don't mind playing lady's maid to you."

"We're not that far north, you know. Triona borders the midlands. It's actually just above Heartland, if off to the east a bit, and we're on the southern edge," she pointed out, meaning to be fair, but also trying to distract herself so her fingers wouldn't fumble too much from nervousness. "And I've never played valet to anyone other than myself. If ladies can play the part of a valet."

"I have come to believe through our adventures, Miss Vielle, that you can do anything you like. As for our latitude, midlands or not, we are stuck in the mountains," he said, opening her second shirt. The act bared her chemise-covered breasts. Smirking, Kiers cupped them once again in his hands. "Cold little mountains with pointy little peaks . . ."

"Mister Kiers!" Vee spluttered, blushing brightly. Her chemise wasn't all that thick, and his hands were disturbingly warm.

Almost hot, in fact. The ticklish thrill of his fingers sliding over her modest curves made her feel like she was going to swoon. Air Couriers did *not* swoon. She was sure it was in the handbook somewhere.

"Yes, Miss Vielle?" He didn't stop caressing her, and he didn't stop smiling, either. He did, however, lift a brow at her. "Doesn't this feel good?"

"Well . . . I . . . Yes, but . . ." She knew he had a point, and that this was the purpose for which they had come upstairs, but such a bold touch flustered her. Unable to think of anything better to do, Vee lifted her hands to his chest, popped free the last two buttons of his inner shirt, and pressed her palms to his chest. He hadn't needed to wear an undershirt, so her hands met warm, bare flesh. "Well . . . take that, then! Anything you do to me, I shall do right back to you."

She barely refrained from adding a childish, "So there!" to the end of that statement. She did raise her chin with a touch of defensiveness, though he didn't notice. His eyes had closed at the first press of her skin against his flesh, and his head had dropped back. Even as she looked up at him, she felt his chest swell with a slow, deep breath, his expression lost in a level of sensuality he hadn't displayed before now.

The subtle movement of that breath pressed his firm muscles against her hands. Instinct made her breathe deep, too, until she realized that pressed her breasts into his palms. Unnerving though it was, Vee decided she liked the little thrill that rippled through her body at that thought, so she did it again. Breathed deep, and let her breath escape on a sigh.

That soft, breathy sound undid him. Dipping his head down to hers, Kiers slid one arm behind her back, supporting her as he claimed her mouth in a kiss. His other hand continued to stroke her flesh through her chemise, cupping and kneading with more urgency. Neither of them had eaten a dessert, but she tasted sweet to him all the same. Her soft gasps, her untutored nips, the way she parted her lips, matching him as he deepened their kiss, enflamed his senses. Stronger than a bite of thonite, she went straight to his blood.

Vee did not know how they got onto the bed. One moment she was more or less on her feet, arched over his arm and kissing him back. The next, she was on her back in a mound of softness, struggling for pleasure-laden air as he kissed his way down to the lace-edged neckline of her chemise, tugging at the many tiny buttons sealing the placket.

Belatedly, she realized her fingers were clutching his shirt, trying to pull him closer. That wasn't the right direction. Even she knew his shirt had to come off if they were to get any further. However, he wasn't exactly cooperating; she could only push it down to his elbows at most. "Off . . . off!"

The demand cut through his haze of desire like snow down the back of one's collar. Shuddering with the effort to restrain himself, Kiers shifted back from her. He gave her a confused look. "You don't want . . . ?"

Vielle tugged on his shirt lapels. "Off!" she ordered, flapping the fabric in her hands. "Shirt off, now!"

"Oh! Yes. Of course. Right away," he agreed. Squirming off the bed, he stood and stripped off his shirt, grinning. Standing made him aware of his feet, encased in the wool-lined slippers, and her feet in her borrowed woolly boots. Toeing out of the slippers and pulling off his socks, he unfastened his trousers, eager to get the impediments out of his way.

Pushing up on her elbows, Vee admired his chest, until he pulled off her footwear. Realizing his intent, she struggled off the soft-mounded bed and started stripping off layers as well. She got all the way down to her chemise and knee-length knickers before realizing he was now completely naked before her.

She'd seen drawings of naked bodies, the kind covertly passed around the girls' dormitory, but the real thing was something else. For one, this was in full three-dimensional color, not a sketch in someone's slightly tattered notebook. For another, she wasn't just going to look at his manhood and maybe touch herself under the covers afterward; she was actually going to do things with it.

Vee wasn't quite sure what all could be done with one of them, but the other girls in the dormitory had said that there was kissing and stroking as well as copulating. The possibilities intrigued her.

"See something interesting?" Kiereseth asked as she stared at his erection, her cheeks pink with excitement and an intrigued look gleaming in her blue gray eyes.

Drawing in a deep breath, she nodded. "Why, yes. Yes, I do." Swirling a finger in the direction of his genitals, she asked, "What . . . erm . . . what are the names for all of that?"

The question made him choke on a laugh. "The *names* for all of it?"

"Yes, the names," Vee said. "Look, the girls passed around . . . pictures . . . in the Courier dorms, but we never actually knew the right names for things. We just made up stuff. So unless you *want* me to call it your 'Winky Willy', then I'd like to—oh, do stop laughing!"

He couldn't help it. Great, gut-clenching guffaws escaped him, to the point where he had to sag onto the bed, then flop onto his back, he was so helpless from sheer laughter. In fact, he didn't stop laughing until he felt her muslin-clad thighs straddle his naked ones and her cool fingers wrap around his hot shaft. That made him choke and gasp, panting for breath against the sharp spike of pleasure from her touch.

Merely wanting to get his attention, Vielle blinked at the sudden cessation of his mirth. The wide-eyed look he gave the peaked ceiling was dazed with wonder, and his tanned cheeks had flushed. The thing—obviously not called a Winky Willy, given his reaction—twitched in her grasp. She blinked, surprised, and squeezed it experimentally.

Kiers groaned. His hands flew down to his groin, wrapping gently around her fingers. Pressing them to his aching flesh, he guided her hand up and down, coaxing her into stroking him. "Y-Yessss," he stammered. She squeezed a little as she stroked, dragging a groan out of him. "Light and Life! Oh Light, Vee. Oh, yesss . . ."

Amused, Vee realized this was the first time he hadn't addressed her as Miss Vielle. *Definitely not a formal moment, then*, she decided, squeezing a third time. Finally, she had found a way to get past all that stuffy courtesy he practiced. And from the way he gasped and shuddered, fingers pressing in around hers, he wanted more of that on his . . . thing. She tried again, squeezing and stroking, feeling rather powerful at being able to reduce such a confident man to such a trembling state.

"So what *is* it called, then?" She flexed her grip in emphasis.

"Ah . . . manhood," Kiers managed, thinking his way past the pleasure. "Or shaft, and rod, and . . . oh Light . . . When one is being crude, one calls it a prick," he added quickly, breathlessly, as she rippled her fingers again. "Oh please don't stop . . . please don't . . ."

Vielle didn't even consider it. She was too fascinated by his various reactions to such a simple-seeming thing as her hand on his . . . well, his rod. The word *rod* she could understand since it was shaped like one, and manhood was self-evident, but the other one? Stroking his flesh, she eyed it, then him as she worked. "Kiers . . . why is it called a prick?"

He groaned and scrubbed a hand over his face. She would demand that he think at a time like this. ". . . I don't know! Probably because when a man th-thrusts into a woman, it's like . . . like being pricked by a needle."

Bemused, she shook her head. Her thumb stroked over the tip

of his manhood, where a bead of thick, clear fluid had formed. "This doesn't seem all that sharp to m . . . wait, it's leaking. Is it supposed to leak?"

"Yessss . . ." Hissing the word, he caught her hand, pulling it gently from his flesh. "Enough, woman," Kiers growled, tugging her down beside him. "Or I'll spill all over your fingers before you even have a clue what you're doing to me. That liquid is a warning sign I'm getting close to the crux of my pleasure, and you're not ready for that."

Vee eyed him. "Why should we stop? Why can't I see this crux of yours? I've never seen one in person before, just heard rumors about them, so I'd think I'm ready to know by now."

He shook his head slightly in disbelief. "You're going to be the death of me . . ." Releasing her hands, he cupped her hip, then stroked his palm over her belly, thinking. Finally, he nodded, making up his mind. "Right. Tomorrow, a nice hot bath for each of us, and tomorrow evening, full-on intercourse. But for tonight, we'll use just our hands, and maybe our lips. I don't even know if you've had a crux of your own yet . . . so we'll just start with the basics and work our way up from there, yes?"

That made sense, so she nodded. "Right. And since you're close to your, erm, crux . . ." Vee frowned. "I thought that was called a climax, or an orgrism? Is that the same thing as a crux?"

Kiers choked, coughed, and tried not to grin. From the chiding look she gave him, he hadn't succeeded in covering up his mirth. "Orgasm, not orgrism. They're all the same thing. You can also call it the peak of pleasure. There are plenty of ways to discuss it, just as there are plenty of ways to go about it, because people have been doing it since time began. Even the ancients had a term for it."

"Oh? What did they call it?" she asked, curious.

"The little death," he told her, smirking.

She blinked, thinking back to just a few days ago. "*Ohhh . . .* So when that one archaic treatise was talking about a machine of the ancients that could inspire a *little death* in women, it wasn't talking about *actual* death."

"No, but rather of giving a climax to a woman, yes," he agreed, grinning.

Embarrassment warred with amusement. The giggles won. Covering her mouth, Vee chortled. "No *wonder* you kept blushing every time I wondered aloud why anyone would want to build a machine that could kill a woman and bring her back to life again and again!"

He leaned forward, removed her fingers from her mouth, and kissed her. He couldn't help it; she was just too appealing in her mirth. The eager way she returned his kiss made his body ache for more. Their limbs entwined, soft-worn cotton sliding against skin, until both were clutching and breathing heavily between each nip and lick.

Dragging his mind back up from the ache in his loins, Kiers broke their kisses. He rested his forehead against hers for a moment, stroking back the fine wisps of her ash blond hair, then asked, "Choose. Which do you want to experiment with first? Your crux, or mine?"

CHAPTER THREE

V ee bit her lip. All this kissing and touching and twining had awakened a hunger within her. As much as she wanted to know what sating it would feel like, she was still very curious about his reactions. "Yours," she finally said, sliding her hand from the small of his back. She gently worked it between their bellies, seeking his hardened rod. "I want to see yours."

Light and Life, she'll be the death of me . . . the little death, he thought, amused. Still, a gentleman didn't argue with a lady's requests when it came to pleasure, and he wasn't inclined to start. Scooting fully onto the bed, Kiers lay back somewhere near the middle with his head and shoulders on the pile of pillows, and nodded at his torso. "Begin by caressing me, then. All over. Have fun looking for my erogenous spots."

"Oh, is it supposed to be a treasure hunt, then?" Pushing up onto her elbow, Vielle eyed his muscular body.

"Absolutely," he agreed, tucking his hands behind his head. "Search away."

Mischief prompted her to do it. Without any warning other than a flash of a grin, she tickled his armpits. He yelped and jumped, elbows clamping down against his sides. Delighted in his reaction, Vee giggled and trailed her fingers down over his stomach. His muscles tightened under her touch, but he didn't squirm again until her fingernails ever so lightly scraped the crease between his hip and his thigh.

Not only did he squirm and bat at her hands, his shaft bobbed and twitched, turning a deeper shade of pink at the tip. As curious as she was about it, Vee merely noted the reaction and moved on down his legs. His inner thighs provoked a choked laugh out of the man, and the backs of his knees made him twitch his legs up and out of her grasp. But it was his feet that drew the most interesting responses.

Instead of laughing when she stroked them lightly with her fingertips, he moaned. She did it again, glancing up the length of his frame. His shaft twitched and bobbed as he moaned again, looking thicker and taller where it jutted up from his hips. And when she did it a third time, tickling both feet simultaneously, he groaned loudly, head and shoulders pressing back into the feather-stuffed pillows.

A bead of moisture welled up at the tip of his manhood, clinging to the little slit that had produced it. Experimentally, she stroked both feet again. Kiereseth grabbed a pillow and smacked it over his face, muffling what sounded like a tortured string of curses, but he didn't ask her to stop. Nor did she. Swirling, tickling, even letting her nails lightly scrape, all of it seemed to bring him great pleasure. That bead became a trickle, a pulsing trail of liquid, visible pleasure.

Scooting up on the bed, Vee tried to reach for his shaft and his feet at the same time. The position wasn't going to be easy. Debating a moment, she pushed on his right thigh, bending his knee outward and pulling his ankle up high, then did the same with his left leg, making him look sort of like a belly-up frog. That allowed her to kneel at his side and grasp his shaft, stroking it with one hand and the soles and toes of his feet with the other.

Face buried in the pillow, Kiers complied with the bending of his limbs. Even when it made him tense and groan and feel like he should scream if she didn't stop, it was that arousing, he complied. At least, until he couldn't get enough air. Shoving the pillow aside, he panted heavily, struggling to get enough wind to speak.

"You . . . stop the feet," he gasped, and gestured vaguely with one hand. "That only arouses . . . to madness. Stroke me to . . . to completion . . . *please*."

He did look a bit tortured. Taking pity on him, Vee switched her attention fully to his shaft and the sac at the base. Courier self-defense classes had taught her that the spheres inside were vulnerable to being handled roughly or given harsh blows, but that was information meant for an attacker, not a lover. Instead, she touched them lightly. That made him groan and clutch at the patchwork quilt.

His hips moved, pushing his flesh up against her exploring fingers. That smeared the liquid against them. Vee wasn't an engineer, but she had heard explanations about pistons and cogs and gears from acquaintances who were, and how all those moving parts needed lubrication. The slick feel of it was her clue to its purpose. Swirling her fingers and palm through the sticky liquid, she coated his manhood and continued to stroke.

The pillow flopped back over his face, muffling several more ungentlemanly curses. Where she got *that* brilliant idea, the ex-prince didn't know, but Kiers did know if she stopped, he'd shoot himself. Somehow. Surely there was a rifle or a pistol in a hunter's cabin? *Oh Light and Life spare me, she's doing it again . . .*

He couldn't breathe for long under the pillow. Pushing it aside, he lifted his head and opened his eyes, watching the rise and fall of his hips as they pistoned his shaft through the clasp of those delicious, rippling digits.

A glance from her showed the tip of her pink tongue moistening her lips. That move alone did him in. Feeling the drawing tightness in his loins, Kiers gasped out a warning. "I'm . . . coming! Crux is coming—!"

His hips snapped up in several hard, fast thrusts against her fingers. Guessing he wanted more of that sort of stimulation, Vee stroked faster, doing her best to clasp his shaft, though her fingers and thumb didn't quite meet all the way around. He kept thrusting, hissing her nickname twice—then stiffened, back arched and hips lifted up from the bedding.

With an atavistic thrill, she watched the clear, seeping liquid turn into jets of creamy white. He collapsed for a second, then kept thrusting from the hips, one hand flying down to cover hers, coaxing her into continuing her swift, firm strokes as more and more spurted out. It spattered on his belly and hips, poured over their conjoined fingers, and finally turned back into a seeping dribble.

Patting her hand as his body stilled, Kiers coaxed her into gentling her touch. "Easy . . . be gentle at the end . . . that's it, yes. Light and Life, you are *very* good at that."

She smiled at the praise. "Always was a quick study. And I do love a treasure hunt." Releasing his now softening manhood with a little pat, she wrinkled her nose at the liquid coating her hand. "Er . . . a question, Mister Kiers. Is it always this messy?"

Kiers managed a nod. His breath was almost back to normal, but the sated feeling in his body translated as a bit of post-bliss lethargy. "Usually. If you do it right. And you don't have to call me 'Mister' since I think we've blown right past that point."

She chuckled weakly. "I'd say so. And I insist you call me just Vee. I'd better go get a washrag, I think. I'll be right back," she promised, scooting off the bed with the help of her clean hand. "You just lie there while I fetch everything."

"I'll be waiting . . . Just Vee," he teased. That earned him a mock-dirty look and a mock-swipe at his ribs. "Vee! Vee!" he promised, holding up his hands in defense.

Padding downstairs, she scrubbed her hands at the sink, then eyed the fire. It was starting to die down. Soapstone hearth or no, she didn't think the fire had been burning long enough. Stacking a few more logs so that they would form a decent bed of coals, she dipped some of the steaming water out of the chain-hung cauldron into a bowl, then refilled the iron pot so that there would be a fresh supply of hot liquid to wash with later.

"Do you need help, Miss . . . Do you need help, Vee?" Kiers called down to her, waiting as patiently as he could for the second half of the night.

"No, thank you, Kiers! I was just stoking the fire. I'll be up as soon as I've used the powder room," she called back up the stairwell as she moved that way.

Her detour didn't take long. Washing her hands again at the kitchen basin to make sure they were clean, she carried the bowl and a scrap of cloth upstairs. The moment she cleared the boards blocking in the stairwell shaft, she could see him stretched out on his side, right knee up, left palm propping up his cheek. The sight of her, showing up in her chemise and knickers, made his shaft twitch visibly.

Blushing, Vee carried the bowl over to the nightstand and dipped the rag in it. Wringing most of the hot water from it, she bent over the bed, intending to scrub his stomach. At the first hard back-and-forth rub, he winced and grinned, catching her wrist.

"Easy, woman. I'm not built like a set of floorboards," he teased her. Fingers guiding hers, he helped her bathe away all the streaks she could still see, and all the ones he could feel on his skin. Their mutual touch slowed as the intimacy of the moment grew.

Finally, Vee turned to set the rag on the table. Kiers caught her free hand as soon as she did so, drawing her onto the bed beside him. Without a word, just a long, heated look, he lifted her fingers to his lips and showed her with just a few nibbling, slow kisses that toes weren't the only erogenous extremities in the room. It didn't take much for him to set her heart thumping in her chest, her blood rushing through her veins.

From there, he moved to her wrists, then to her inner elbows. Vee squirmed at that, giggling a little. He smiled, but didn't tickle her armpits; instead, he pressed soft kisses to the bits of shoulder exposed by the broad, lace-edged straps of her chemise. Murmuring compliments, he kissed his way along her neckline to the shallow valley between her breasts.

She knew she wasn't overly endowed; in fact, Vee didn't even need a busk or any staves to support the cups of her chemise. Unlike the sort of woman she had tried to portray that night in the alley, there wasn't all that much for his palm to cup. But the modest curves she did have were sensitive, provoking a soft moan from her lips when he cupped and caressed the left one.

"Ohhh, that feels good," she sighed. Instinct drove her to dip her head and kiss the top of her lover's head. A thought which gave her pause. *My lover. That sounds so . . . thrilling.*

Yes. My lover. Illicit and exciting, and . . . Vee stroked her fingers through his short dark hair, not at all bothered by it when he started slipping the buttons of her chemise through their tight little holes. It just felt right. The right moment, the right person, even the right place.

She sucked in a breath at the feel of his lips closing on the tip of her left breast. Shivered when he circled her areola with the tip of his tongue. Moaned at the sweet ache he inspired when he suckled firmly. "Oh, Kiers . . ."

"Mmm, Vee . . . so delicious," he murmured, nipping lightly at her flesh. His hand shifted to each of her shoulders, drawing the straps of her chemise down and away, one at a time. Palm gliding up and down her arms, he caressed her skin even as he sucked again, making her head swim. Shaking her hands free of the fabric, she sank back on the bedding, uncaring that her chemise was trapped beneath her.

Left arm bracing his weight as he leaned over her, Kiers was free to knead her breast, to caress her ribs with his right hand.

While his mouth worshipped her breast, he skimmed his finger-tips down along the waistband of her knickers, then plucked at the ties holding her last garment in place. He smiled when she lifted her hips, but didn't draw them down her legs.

Catching the curiosity in her eyes, he smiled and slipped his fingers inside the loosened material. Vee caught her breath, watching him with wide eyes. The sensation of his fingers brushing over the tender skin of her abdomen both tickled and unnerved her, stimulating her in unexpected ways.

When those same fingers stroked through the curls sheltering her mound, she whimpered faintly. Not from fear, but from unexpected pleasure. This wasn't her own touch, familiar and safe. This was Kiers' hand, where she couldn't anticipate where or when he would touch. The unknown possibilities lurked in her mind, making her ache from head to toes.

It was a simple touch, a light rubbing along the outside of her folds, yet it stroked free a huge reaction. Bucking against his fingers, she shuddered, thighs parting with instinctive need. Her hands, however, reacted to her inner uncertainties, clutching at his shoulders.

"Shhh, shh," Kiers soothed her, hiding his wince as her strong fingers pinched and dug into his mucles. "You know me well enough by now. You know I'm not going to hurt you. I just want to give you pleasure."

Part of her was annoyed that he'd think that she'd even entertain that thought. "I'm not thinking that! I'm just . . ." Vee blushed. "No one's touched me there but me, for as long as I can remember. It's . . . it's just unfamiliar. I need to get used to it."

He stroked her seam again, grinning wickedly. "Then it would be my pleasure to get you *very* used to my touch, my dear Vielle. After all, familiarity only comes with plenty of practice."

She wanted to laugh at his jest, but couldn't. Not while distracted by his touch. Two of his fingers deftly parted her folds.

The third dipped through the slick wetness between them, sliding it up to coat the pearl of flesh those nether-lips guarded. She choked, stiffening. Her hands pushed at his shoulders, but only because she needed the leverage to lift her hips up into his touch.

"Oh Light! What you're doing—! I swear, Your Highness," she growled between shudders as he did it again, "if you stop and don't follow through, *I* will hunt you down. You'll wish those guards had—oh Light and Life!"

He cut off her tirade with a rub of his thumb and a gentle probe of his middle finger, teasing her entrance. "I assure you, I have no intention of stopping. At least, until you beg me to," he added, smirking. His hand stroked faster, probed a little deeper. "It is said that women have a great capacity for pleasure. In order to prove this theory, I intend to explore your capacity until we find your limits while we stay here . . . and then see if we can expand them."

It was her turn to grab a pillow, thwap it over her face, and curse into its sound-muffling depths. Chuckling, Kiers dipped his head back to her breasts. The combination of lips, tongue, and fingertips sent her over the edge. Wailing into the pillow, Vee tensed in the biggest crux of her life to date. Every little twitch of his fingers on her nethers just added to it, keeping the pleasure rolling through her nerves like little aftershocks from an earthquake.

Only when she dragged the plump, feather-stuffed pad from her face in the struggle for more air did he finally still his efforts. Lifting his lips from her nipple, he grinned. "Enjoyed that, did you?"

A very unladylike retort nearly escaped her. Except the words she would have used would have encouraged more of the same. Settling on a scowling pout, she muttered, "Oh, give me a chance to rest, already! I need to catch my breath."

Fingers still gently cupping her mound under the fabric of her knickers, he shifted up close enough to kiss her mouth. "Let me know when you'd like another go, then. Or if you'd rather be tucked under the covers for a good night's sleep, first."

As much as parts of her body ached with the need for more of that bliss, just his mentioning the word *sleep* was enough to make her yawn. She pouted again when her mouth finally shut. "Don't want to . . ."

Kiers thought she looked utterly cute like that, still flushed and a little sweaty from her pleasure, clad only in her underdrawers with his hand tucked down inside, cradling the wet warmth of her flesh. He could see in her eyes that she didn't want to go to sleep, but that she also needed it. "Right then," he sighed, gently withdrawing his hand. "Sleep first. That way we'll have energy for more, tomorrow."

Vee lifted a brow at his autocratic decision, but the softness of the bed and the post-crux lethargy in her limbs argued that he was right. They'd both feel better after a good night's sleep. She did, however, question the sight of his re-hardened shaft. "What about that?" she asked, pushing up onto her elbows so she could nod at his groin. "Don't you want to take care of that?"

He shook his head. "It'll go away—keep your knickers on," he added, shifting off the bed and casting around for his own under-trousers. "I'd rather be fully awake for our next encounter, rather than play with you in my sleep. Or let you play with me, unawares."

"Mister Kiers, I am hardly likely to . . . to *ravish* you without fair warning!" Vee argued, climbing off the bed as well so they could draw the covers down. Her jaw cracked in a hastily smothered yawn before she could continue. "I mean, Kiers. I *am* an honorable woman, you know. All Couriers have to be."

"I never once doubted that, Mi—Vielle," he promised her, fastening his undertrousers in place. Like her, he was having difficulty *not* using the honorifics of polite society. It was a change in their relationship that would take time to implement. "However, desire is so deep-rooted in our minds, it can manifest itself from the depths of our very dreams . . . and I know I'm going to dream about the feel and the scent and the taste of you, tonight."

"Taste?" Vee asked, thinking of the way he had kissed and licked her breasts.

Lifting his right hand to his lips, he deliberately licked the remnants of her juices from his fingertips, blue eyes gleaming with a mixture of mirth and desire.

Blushing, she tugged on one of her shirts, then climbed back into the bed on the far side from him. "Get the lamps, will you? I stacked extra wood in the hearth to make a good pile of coals and made sure the grates were in place to guard against sparks."

Nodding, he twisted his left hand in a snatching motion, looking at the lamp on the wardrobe, several feet beyond his reach. The flame instantly snuffed out under the power of his Fire-affinity, leaving only a curl of smoke to climb up the glass chimney. Joining her under the covers, he repeated his efforts with the bedside one, plunging them into a semidarkness lit only by the flickering, golden glow of the hearth fire down below.

For a long moment, neither moved, then Kiereseth sighed and shifted a little closer. With a wordless touch, he coaxed her into rolling up against him, sharing their body heat to warm up the bedding, as well as for a bit of emotional closeness.

Vee looked up at him. She couldn't really see him in the dark, but she'd grown used to his presence these last few weeks. "Thank you for giving me pleasure, Kiers."

"Thank you for sharing it with me," he returned quietly. He pressed a kiss to the top of her braid-wrapped head. "Sleep well, Vee."

Nodding, she snuggled into his warmth and closed her eyes, letting her post-bliss lethargy carry her into some very much-needed sleep.

CHAPTER FOUR

Kiers slouched in a very unprincely manner, propping his chin on his palm. His gaze switched back and forth between the slightly incomplete research notes spread over the kitchen table, and the odd, rounded, gun-like device sitting between him and his companion. Vielle had still been sleeping when he had woken, and the air in the cabin had been decidedly nippy. The ex-prince had busied himself with building up a fire, before attempting to re-create a breakfast version of last night's supper. He did all of that while waiting for her to awaken, figuring she would at least approve of the effort, if not necessarily the result.

Vee had kindly refrained from commenting on his efforts when she finally descended after dressing, aside from pronouncing it, ". . . edible enough, I suppose," though she did scrape the blackest bits off the tumble of pan-fried roots before eating the rest. And she had thanked him for joining her in scrubbing the breakfast things. Now, they sat on opposing stools, staring at the work ahead of them. By joint accord, they had decided to do some actual study post-breakfast.

Kiers, however, couldn't focus on the notes he had taken. Not when he had the distraction of the very beautiful, passionate woman across from him, and the enigma of the thing between them. It was either ask her questions about it, or drag her back upstairs.

"So what *is* it, exactly?" he asked her, eyeing the silvery sphere with its crank handle, pistol grip, and three hatches. One hid the cone-shaped muzzle, the other hid the dials and buttons that activated its uses, and a third sat at the back, awaiting a fresh thonite cube. "Your gizmo-thing."

"I don't know." She rolled her eyes and shrugged expressively. "I honestly, truly do not know, Mister Kiers. Aside from what little I've observed, that is. Whatever purpose for which the Ancients made it, they didn't exactly leave any instruction pamphlets lying around."

"Well, I know it can dissolve the membrane of the Vull, *and* restore it," he muttered, eyeing the strange machine. "I observed that much for myself when we escaped from the Skylands. And a good thing, too, since our pursuers haven't hesitated to fire their pistols. But it has four sets of buttons and dials, and I think I saw you using the first two during our escape . . ."

"I don't really know what the other two buttons do," Vee told him. "Except that they all spew different colored mists. Greenish, we both know dissolves the membrane separating the continent from the hexisles lofted into the sky. And golden creates fresh Vull. But there are also a reddish and a purplish pair, and I have no idea what those two do."

"Wait, back up," Kiers interrupted, frowning in confusion. He pointed up at the ceiling of the kitchen . . . or rather at the thin, translucent gold barrier rippling somewhere over the tallest mountain peaks around them. "You said it *creates* fresh Vull membrane. All I saw was it *repairing* the Vull after the greenish mist dissolved a hole we could slip through."

Picking up the gun-gizmo, Vee checked the fuel compartment, the hatch at the back. "Plenty of thonite left in the cube, so let me crank it up and show you what I know."

She spun the side handle a good twenty or thirty times, then gripped the haft and aimed it at the floor beyond the end of the table. Using a small lever he hadn't noticed before, she tightened the cone of the muzzle, then pushed the first button and twisted the dial. Pulling the trigger, she sprayed a stream of golden, mist-like sparks at the floor.

A ring formed on the floorboards, as broad as his leg was long. It rapidly squeezed up into a dome, then started to grow into a bulging bubble as she continued to feed the mist into the membrane. Cutting off the flow, she nodded at it.

"That's the first button." Fiddling with the controls, she depressed the second button and tightened the cone aperture. Greenish mist dissolved a hole in the miniature Vull when she briefly pulsed the trigger. "And that's the second."

As the ex-prince watched, the chest-sized hole started to close in on itself, shrinking the overall bubble back down toward its former, modest dome size. She pushed the first button and aimed the golden mist. Holding it steady, she repaired the hole and more, restoring the membrane to a bulging, rounded form.

"Astonishing," he murmured, staring at it. "This . . . this solves so many questions I've always had about the Vull! We know that the aetherometer can be powered by thonite because it converts the crystallized gas back into an Air-attuned format, converting sound waves into invisible aether rays and back again. But the Vull is solid, like a . . . like a shield. It must attune itself to the Earth element somehow. Or perhaps somewhere between Earth and Water . . ."

"Correction," he amended himself wryly. "It also raises many more questions. What technology the Ancients must have had, to be able to build something like this!"

"I don't think it's an aspect of any one element, myself," Vee stated. She stretched out her leg and nudged the bubble with her boot for several long seconds, then pulled her foot back again. The sphere tried to cling to her toe before popping free. It wobbled and rippled, not unlike the real one outside. "We know it allows pure thonite gas to escape, because the Skylands are rich with the stuff. And that people who fall onto it from an airship or a floating hexisle eventually sink through the membrane. So it's not a complete barrier.

"But I honestly don't know if it's made of any one aspect of thon, or if it's something new. There is a lot more surface area to that bubble than a mere portion of a single one-inch cube of thonite could account for." Vee nudged it again with her boot, then shrugged. "I don't know what it is."

She had a point. Kiers shrugged. "Maybe it thickens the air? That could account for some of the reports of vast windstorms every turn of the century when the hexisles lift off and drift down. To be honest, if thonite gas can make an entire *mountain* float up into the sky, I wouldn't at all doubt its capacity to thicken the air into a protective dome. In fact, if I were to design such a system, I'd pick a combination of thonite gas and natural air, because then it'd be self-healing. Which it does after the hexisles have pierced through on their way up or down.

"Maybe that's why my sister was in a panic over the thought of someone being able to create a fresh membrane at will," he suggested, thinking it through. "Maybe she was worried someone would encase Jade Mountain in one, leaving it cut off from the rest of civilization. Like the floating hexisles used to be, before the advent of airships—I mean, aside from those strong enough to fly themselves from hexisle to hexisle, which you'll admit is pretty rare. Even you have to stop and rest once in a while."

"I don't think these little guns can seal up an entire hexisle," she pointed out, wiggling the one in her hand with the muzzle opening pointed up. "Those are roughly a hundred miles across, on average. This thing can only make a couple bubbles the size of a house before I run out of thonite cube."

"Well, all exaggeration aside, it's the only reason I can think of for her panicking," Kiereseth countered. "Even if all they can do is open a small hole, if you position it right, by logic that should help a hexisle pierce the Vull at the turnover points. And when the isles push through, if you could manufacture these on a large scale and reverse it with the golden spark stuff, they could be used to seal the rifts, cutting off the pressurization differentials and putting an end to the massive windstorms that happen while the world waits for the Vull to naturally but slowly repair itself. None of which should panic my sister. . . . *unless* she knows something about what the other two buttons do.

"So, what *do* they do?" he finished, gesturing at her and her gizmo.

"I told you, I don't know. I do know they produce a reddish mist, and a purplish mist, both of which have no effect on the Vull bubble." Aiming the gun, she pushed the appropriate buttons one after the other. Mist-sparks spat out, first in crimson, then in violet. Neither had any noticeable impact on the surface of the gently rippling bubble. "See? Absolutely nothing."

Bracing his elbows on the table, Kiers rubbed his chin, trying to think of what it could mean. The rasp of his stubble-covered jaw made him remember he had promised both of them a bath today. Sighing, he stood and shook his head. "We're going in circles. We need to take a break and let our minds cogitate. Help me pull out the largest washtub from the stack under the stairs, will you? If we fill it with water from the pump, I can heat it in a trice with my thon, and then we can each enjoy a nice hot bath, and maybe scrub our clothes."

Vee nodded eagerly, rising from her stool as well. "That does sound heavenly. We can also pull out a second tub and set everything we have to soak. Even the woolens can be washed if the water's tepid and we don't scrub too hard. A bit of gentle Air work should dry it all in a trice, too."

Kiers snapped his fingers, pointing at the aetherometer, still sitting on the table amid the papers and the gun-thing. "Ah, right. We should turn on that thing. It's almost midmorning, and the Trionans have a daily broadcast from midmorning to midafternoon on their aetherometer sets. News from the capital and the borders, recitations of poetry, philosophical debates, even a bit of musical performances. I overheard it in one of the palace parlors, and asked about it."

"Like you did the soapstone fireplaces?" Vee dared to tease, grinning at him as she started lifting the smaller buckets out of the tubs stacked under the stairs.

"Cheeky woman," he retorted. He pointed at her. "You be nice to me, or I won't help scrub your back."

She blushed at that. "Er . . . that would imply you'd have to be in the same room with me while I was bathing, Mister Kiers."

Kiers grinned, assisting her. "That it would, *Miss* Vielle. If you'll remember, you agreed last night that we would become lovers, and lovers do bathe together. Even if these tubs aren't quite big enough for that."

She snorted but didn't make a retort. Instead, she helped him heft the two largest tubs into the kitchen. One fit next to the sink, but the other had to be moved over to where her bubble sat. Grabbing her gizmo, she shot a stream of green at it, dissolving the membrane. Kiereseth helped her settle the tub into its place, then went back for the buckets.

It wasn't until his arms were wrist deep in the tub, his back stooped and his heels and knees slowly flexing as if climbing flat stairs, coaxing his thon into warming the chilly water that something occurred to him. "Vielle?"

"Yes, Kiers?" Vee asked, brushing out what dried dirt she could from the next pair of wool trousers destined for the tub of lukewarm, soapy water.

"Would you get your gun thing and shoot me with the red and the purple mists, please?"

She looked up at that, her brows pinching together in confusion. "*Shoot* you with it?"

"Yes," he said, and nodded at the bathing tub. "While I'm using my thon. If it uses thonite for an energy source, then it's possible the Vull is thonite-based, and that means the beams it shoots are able to affect or manipulate thon. So maybe the other two beams affect the use of it?"

The sight of him sticking his hands back into the tub made her wince. "Kiers, if you're going to play with your thon, fetch a bit of wood and light the far end of it afire. Do *not* stick your hands into water which may suddenly turn boiling hot *if* your theory proves correct on one of these settings."

She had a point. He also realized that at times she had a tart way of speaking that the ex-prince just wasn't used to hearing from anyone else. It was actually rather refreshing, and he liked it. He just wasn't going to let her know it right away. Straightening, he lifted a brow at her. "You do realize that, were we still on Jade Mountain, you wouldn't be able to get away with talking to me like that, *Miss* Vielle?"

"That would be because your father was my employer, *Mister* Kiereseth. In *this* venture, we are equals," she reminded him, hands going to her skirt-clad hips, the one outfit she had that didn't need immediate laundering. "Besides, I've been trying to treat you as I would any friend, which means not letting you get away with acts of stupidity. I've come to like you very much, and do not wish to see you get hurt."

That thought was astonishing. *She likes me . . .* It shouldn't have been, but it was. *Miss Vielle really likes me!* She wasn't just putting up with him because they had been thrown together by circumstances. She actually, actively liked him. Kiers didn't realize he was grinning at her until she blushed, smiled back, then rolled her eyes.

"Fetch a stick, you," she directed, "and set it on fire. You can grin and make calf eyes at me later. We have a gun-thingy to test."

He moved to the woodbox, which they had refilled while making breakfast. Selecting a log, he paused as a thought crossed his mind. A chuckle escaped him. "Anytime you wish me to light a fire for you, Miss Vielle, you need only ask. I like you very much, too."

She blushed, catching the innuendo, and flipped her hand at him. Picking up the silvery gizmo, she checked the setting, adjusted the third dial to its lowest, and nodded. "Fire it up, Mister Kiers."

Nodding, he tensed his calves and flexed his toes, focusing on the far end of the thumb-thick, arm-long splinter of wood he had selected. The end darkened and charred for a brief moment, sending up a curl of smoke, then flames snapped up and danced around the tip. They formed a golden-orange halo of moving heat and light, mesmerizing.

"Keep concentrating. Firing in three . . . two . . . one . . ." She aimed the stream of reddish mist at Kiers, not at the burning twig—and gasped in shock as the small, fist-sized flame roared upward, splaying across the underside of the balcony floorboards over their heads.

Kiers yelped and dropped the stick, hopping back. Not since he was a youth had his thon reacted so out of control. The movement disrupted his concentration, snuffing most of the flames. It was still burning when it hit the floor, so he extended his hand and tightened his forearm muscles, clenching his fingers. The flames snuffed out immediately. A glance up showed the boards overhead slightly darkened but thankfully not on fire.

"Well!" he exclaimed softly, turning his gaze to his wide-eyed partner. "I think that proves my theory."

"Pick it up again and try a tiny bit of thon to make a tiny

little flame," Vee suggested, recovering her composure. "Without the gun. I'd like to see if the mist has any lasting effects on you."

Nodding, he scooped up the unburned end of the kindling and curled his toes just a little. A head-sized gout of flame snapped up from the charred end, making him blink. "By the Light! Apparently, it does have an effect." Clenching his fist, he extinguished the flames. Once more, they snuffed out instantly. "Indeed . . . if my sister knew *anything* about this weapon thing—if *Father* knew—then no wonder they wanted to keep it secret. Strongly enough to lay false claims of treason against you and me, in the effort to silence us. This gizmo will *completely* change the face of war!"

"Then we will simply have to decide what to do about it. The two of us, Kiers," Vee clarified. "You and I. Since you and I alone know for sure what this thingy can do."

He nodded. He didn't like it, but he knew she was right. Lifting his chin at the gizmo, he asked, "So what does purple do?"

"Push versus pull, I'd presume. Light it up," she told him, lifting her own chin at the kindling in his hand. He nodded and tensed, heels shifting a little. The end lit up in extra-long, hot flames again. Vee adjusted the dials, aimed, and pulled the trigger with the fourth button depressed. Violet mist-sparks struck his body—and the flame shrunk down to a mere flicker, one not even the length of a thumb.

"Enough—enough!" Kiers rasped, feeling dizzy. She shut the machine off, but he still swayed. Sagging against the edge of the kitchen table, he shook his head. "Light and Life, I could *feel* the energy draining out of me, as if I'd been using my thon for hours, but compressed into seconds." He looked up at her, his face pale under its natural tan, his hands trembling. "This is a *very* dangerous weapon."

Vee didn't like what she had done to him. They had guessed at the weapon's effects, but hadn't known. Closing up all the levers and hatches, she set the sphere on the table and took the still burning scrap of wood from him. Tossing it into the hearth fire, she gave him a regret-filled look. "I'm sorry about that. Would you like some thonite? Would that make you feel better?"

He nodded. "I don't need much, I'd think. Just a bite. Enough to level off the sudden dip in my blood."

Nodding, she headed upstairs to fetch the lockbox from her backpack. There was a partly eaten cube in the box, so she brought that one back down. While he bit into the crumbly, gray, meaty-sweet mineral, chewing on it like it was a block of candy brittle, she took over the task of heating the bathwater. Her Fire affinity wasn't as strong as his, but it could and did get the job done.

By the time the water was steaming visibly, Kiers felt much better. Setting the rest of the cube on the table, he asked her, "So, who's first in the water. You or me?"

"You, I think." Shaking the excess water from her hands, Vee reached for one of the toweling cloths they had found stored in a chest upstairs. "I'd like to take the portable aetherometer up to the ridgeline and see if I can pick up a signal up there. I think the mountains are blocking the aether rays. Earth and Air are opposites, after all. Besides, if you go first, I can have a fresh hot bath to warm up myself when I get back. Just let the woolens soak in tepid water for now. Don't scrub them hard or heat the water, or they'll start to shrink."

That spoiled his plans for having her wash his back, but he had to admit her words held logic. "I'll wait until you've bundled up and set out, then. Take the ice tunnel to the trees, to make sure no one spots you flying up from the cabin itself."

Nodding, she headed for the front room, and the little entryway that held her coat and boots.

CHAPTER FIVE

By the time she came back, almost two hours had passed. Kiers had occupied himself with gingerly cleaning their clothes and hanging them to dry on a rack near the hearth, then dumping the used water down the basin drain and refilling the bathing tub with thon-heated water. When that was done, leaving him with nothing to do but wait, he perused their notes some more and borrowed some of the hunter's paper to write down new speculations of his own, trying not to worry as her absence grew longer.

Finally, he saw movement through the cracks in the window shutters of Mister Horgen's study nook. They had decided to keep those shutters closed so that no one could casually peer in at them. A bit of neck-craning and body-twisting allowed him to see a bit of gray skirt and scuffed white boot just before he heard the front door open. Relieved, he moved around to the entry door and poked his head through.

"Is everything alright?" Kiers asked her.

She shook her head. "Yes and no." Her blue gray eyes were sober as she drew off her coat and cap, hanging them on the pegs above the bench at her side. "I sat up there for a while, searching on various frequencies on the aetherometer to be thorough, and picked up a sending from Najora. You know, the kingdom to the west?"

He nodded, worry drawing up several scenarios. "Have they somehow agreed to declare us fugitives there? Father didn't have very many trade contacts in that land. Not this far north. We only traded with Triona's king because of our librarian's shared interest in ancient legends."

She shook her head. "No, nothing like that. I picked up two things, one following the other. The first one was the casting from Najora. The people of the hexisle just on the other side of these mountains, Provender township, are reporting earthquakes . . . and signs of cracks along its edges. Signs of an uplift beginning. We have maybe a year before the Vull is sundered in the turnover as hexisles everywhere start to rise and fall."

Kiers absorbed that as she bent and unbuttoned her boots. "That's . . . That is going to create a *great* deal of upheaval everywhere. The records from a century ago spoke of hysteria, of people rushing to try and claim land on the hexisles starting to lift, of the townships going to war to fight off the influx of too many refugees . . . Which makes me think of the guards after us. Did you hear anything from them? You said you heard two things."

Vee nodded. Handing him the backpack, she mounted the steps into the cabin proper, slipping her stocking-clad feet into the wool-lined boots as she spoke. "The sending from Najora's aetherometer operators was an ongoing report, one being cast far and wide since this is news that'll affect the whole world. But I found news on the other frequency, the ones the guards had last used. I didn't get the original message they sent down the line, but I did over-hear the return message from Jade Mountain, a response to their query as to what to do about the coming uplifts. They're being recalled."

"*Recalled?*" Kiers repeated, astonished. He followed her as she headed for the kitchen and the promised hot bath. "But . . . after all the time and resources they've poured into finding us . . . I don't get it."

"Did your family ever speak of a 'Project Skyloft'?" she asked, trying to unbutton her blouse with cold fingers. She tried three times before giving up. "Bother. My hands need to warm up, first. Ironic, as I'm trying to get warm in a bath."

"Here, let me," Kiers offered, nudging her hands out of the way. He unbuttoned her clothes as he had last night, adding little caressing touches as he helped her remove each layer. "As for the project . . . I vaguely remember a Project Skyloft from when I was young. Something about an experiment in mathematics to see how many airship lofts filled with thonite it would take to keep a hexisle afloat.

"If I remember correctly, my brother had discerned that it would be impossible because the number of lofts needed to lift an entire diamond of stone one hundred miles wide would require more airship lofts than could be safely tethered in place. The surface of the island would get no sunlight whatsoever from the sheer coverage of the balloons."

He removed her knickers, the last impediment. Vee blushed, but the heat radiating from the fire and the thought of soaking in hot water overrode modesty. "Do you remember anything else?"

Helping her into the tub, he thought about it for a few moments. "My other sister said that since we know thonite gas, which permeates the black rock of the hexisle, is what causes it to float, then it had to be some sort of alchemical interaction between that specific type of rock and the thonite itself. In order to make the hexisle float, you'd have to pump the gas back into the hexisle at great pressure to force it through the matrix and cause the enhanced lofting effects. She's always been interested in chemistry. In fact, there have already been some experiments conducted on the underside to try just that, though I've been told they were eventually abandoned because of costs."

Vee nodded. She was a little embarrassed to be completely naked before him, but was too cold not to appreciate the assistance. Sinking into the water, she frowned a little. "It's not very hot in here."

Kneeling beside the tub, Kiers smirked. Rolling up his sleeves, he tensed his toes and dangled his fingers in the water. "I realized while I was waiting if I made it too hot to start off, your chilled tender bits might get hurt. So . . . let me know when things get too hot, hmm?"

The way he dropped his gaze to her breasts, barely covered by the water filling the short but deep tub, let her know he meant it in other ways, too. She blushed again, thinking of his promise regarding tonight, and forced herself to finish her news before she forgot.

"Anyway, the soldiers have all been recalled from our trail and sent off on 'Project Skyloft' instead. I couldn't be sure, but it sounded like they were being told to go and buy up all the reserves of thonite cubes they could find and afford. The signal was never very clear, compared to the one I was receiving from Najora. We know their aetherometer is much bigger and stronger than ours, since they have it mounted on that airship of theirs," she added, "and they can send a signal all the way to the south—and the water is quite warm now, thank you."

"I'd like to think they really are being called off our trail," Kiers said. "But I don't think it would be wise to leave our little hideaway just yet, based on that assumption. If they ran across us while they're still in the area, they'd continue trying to capture us as a literal attack of opportunity."

Smiling, she ducked her head a moment, then looked up at him. "I don't think staying here will be a hardship, Mister Kiereseth. As soon as I've finished my bath, would you care to show me the rest of those pleasures you promised?"

"I am always at your disposal for such things, Miss Vielle," he promised. "But first, I promised you a hot bath, so you could relax and get clean." At the sight of her pout, slight but unmistakable, he grinned. "Of course, I suppose there's no harm in combining the two."

She lifted her brows as he stood . . . and sank deeper in the water with a blush, watching him strip off his clothing. Neatly folding and setting each garment in a stack next to hers on the cluttered table, he finally stepped carefully into the tub. Some of the water sloshed over when he settled between her feet, running across the floorboards before draining through the cracks between them.

"We should clean that up," Vee murmured, distracted by the mess they were making.

Kiers shrugged. The movement slopped a little more over the sides of the tub. "We will. Eventually. But I think we'll end up splashing quite a bit more before we're done, so why not wait until it's all over, yes? In the meantime, be prepared to be stroked from head to toe, my lovely Vielle. Because I am going to touch you everywhere until you beg for more."

"Beg for more?" she asked, somewhat skeptical. "Aren't I supposed to beg you to stop?"

He reached for the plate holding the bar of soap on the edge of the broad kitchen table, and flashed her a smirk. "Not if I do it right."

He definitely did it right. She couldn't walk.

She couldn't have flown a straight path if her life depended on it, either. But Vee could—and did—cling to him as he carried her up the stairs. None too steadily himself, of course, given the way she kept trying to kiss his throat, his shoulder, his chin, anything within reach. She clung firmly, keeping her arms and legs wrapped around him like a spider trying to wrap up a juicy, delicious fly. Certainly, she wanted to devour him somehow.

Despite being peppered with kisses and thrown off balance by clinging legs and groping hands, Kiers made it to the bed. She had shown him how to refluff it that morning with careful shaking, turning, and prodding, and the fluffed-up mound looked like the perfect landing pad for her backside. Except she wouldn't let go.

Dropping her onto the bed left him doubled over at the hips, his manhood sliding against the very wet folds he had stroked and fondled to a fever pitch during their bath. Her hands shifted from clutching to stroking, even scraping a little. Head swimming with pleasure, Kiers captured her mouth in slow, devouring kisses.

From the way she nipped and tugged at his bottom lip, the hungry lift of her hips, rubbing herself against his shaft, slow wasn't what she wanted. She growled it, too.

"More!" Vee demanded, tugging on his hair. The ache he had stirred wasn't going away. She needed relief even as she needed more pleasure. She just didn't know how to *say* it. "Give me more— I *need*, Kiers! Give me more!"

"J-just a moment!" he panted, trying to focus through his own need.

Concentrating, he carefully tightened the right set of muscles in his groin, invoking his Earth affinities. Earth-based thon, on the Water side, could be used to affect living flesh. He wasn't a fully trained healer by any means, but certain skills were important for a prince to know. With a grunt, he felt his thon activate, shutting off his fertility, then relaxed a little as he braced himself over her, panting.

"There . . . now you won't get in trouble," he promised her, breathing heavily. The effects dulled his pleasure somewhat, but not nearly enough to make him stop. Rocking against her, he continued to stroke his shaft against the folds of her femininity, until she tugged once more on his hair.

"Need! In!" she demanded breathlessly, bucking up into him.

Shifting his fingers between them, Kiers tested her with one, two, three fingers, pumping them slowly in and out. He had done this before, down in the bathtub. The moan his rubbing evoked pleased him, though he could have done without the hair-tugging.

"More! Put your thing in me!" Vee demanded, too hungry to blush very much.

He grinned, keeping to his task. "My *thing*? Come now, Vielle," he purred, enjoying her high desire. "Surely you can name it better than that?" He curled his fingers up inside of her until she gasped, arching against him. "What is it called, hm? You won't get it until you acknowledge it properly."

"Gah! Either you put your prick in me, Kiers, or I'll find someone who can!" she snapped, feisty even in her passion.

"Oh, you will, will you?" he challenged her, none too pleased with that thought. She was *his* companion, after all. She had chosen *him* for her first taste in partners. First and best.

"Yes, I will," Vee repeated, though the more she thought about it, the less she liked the idea.

"No, you won't," Kiers decided, wiggling his fingers a little. "You've already picked me, and that's that. You're stuck with me through pain and pleasure, thick and thin. Lucky for you, I'm very good at the pleasure part."

"Ohhh . . . you arrogant—! Put your damned manhood in already," she mock-groused.

Chuckling, he gripped and positioned himself. Pressing the tip into her, he pushed slowly, taking his time. Each little advance forward parted more of her hot, slick flesh, making his head spin. "Ohhhh, Vielle . . . you have no idea how good you feel to me."

She blushed, hearing her name sighed from his lips like that. The stretching hurt a bit, but no more than it had down in the bath with just his fingers. The look on his face, however, made her discard the ache as negligible. Rapt, that was the word for it. Caught in rapture, he strained over her with his eyes closed, brows slightly furrowed, and his mouth open not just to pant but to release a silent moan.

It was as if he couldn't spare the attention or the energy to actually moan aloud, though part of him wanted to try. Vee found that look captivating, enough that she barely winced when he finally pushed fully inside. It hurt, of course, but she was too busy being distracted by the impassioned faces he made to care. Lifting her hand, she caressed his brow, his cheek. "You are so handsome . . ."

At her words, Kiers turned his head, pressing his lips to her palm. A nuzzle allowed him to capture one of her fingers. Sucking on it, he looked at her. Vee found herself captivated by the intensity in his stare. When he finally moved in slow, firm thrusts, that intensity shot straight into her groin. The ache was still there, but the passion was back in full force, curling low in her belly and reaching up into her arms, into her breasts.

It was her turn to part her lips in silent, breathless ecstasy. Head tipping back, Vee arched her spine. That put his slow thrusts at a slightly different angle, increasing that lightning-like pleasure.

"That's it," Kiers whispered in encouragement, rocking a little faster. "Feel that? Do you like that?"

She managed a nod. It was such an intimate, intense feeling she almost feared she would fly apart. Clinging to his shoulders, she kissed his sweat-dampened skin. He nuzzled her cheek, increasing his pace, rubbing her in all the right ways.

"Come for me, my sweet Vielle," he whispered, lips nipping at the side of her throat. "Fly for me. I *need* to feel you flying beneath me . . . come!"

With a whimper, she tensed and shattered in pleasure. Kiers thrust harder, faster, pursuing his own moment of bliss. Coming down from the crux of it, Vielle found herself cooing soft endearments, stroking his skin in gentle caresses.

An accidental scrape of one nail made him shudder. Curious,

she scratched again. He swore and thrust hard and deep. That felt surprisingly good, so she did it again, dragging her nails down his back. Choking, he pressed in hard and bucked. A strange, warm tickling deep inside her body accompanied the flushing of his cheeks. Vee realized belatedly he had reached his own crux. She blushed as well.

Pressed deep inside her, he caught her face in his hands and kissed her deeply over and over. Gradually, those kisses eased, until he was merely brushing his lips lightly against hers. "Beautiful, beautiful Vielle," he finally sighed. Forehead resting against hers, he smiled slowly. "Beautiful, passionate Vee. I trust you liked all of that?"

"Most of it," she agreed. "I'll be happy to do without the achy bits when we get around to this again."

"Mm, yes," Kiers murmured, kissing her brow. He pushed up a little giving her more room to breathe. "Speaking of which, would you like to go again? Or wait until after luncheon?"

"Hmm . . . I *am* a bit peckish," Vee admitted—and pulled him back down, peppering his cheeks and chin with kisses. Her attack provoked a laugh from him, which made her giggle in turn.

Pecking her back, Kiers grinned. "Naughty, you."

A contented sigh escaped him. His feet were awkwardly braced on the floor and her legs dangled off the edge, now that they weren't clasped around his hips, and he was feeling a bit hungry for food . . . but he also felt incredibly good.

"So. We stay here for the full week, just in case the broadcasted retreat of my father's guards was a ruse, yes?" he asked.

"Yes," Vee agreed, looping her arms around his neck. "To give them time to go away—for one reason or another—and give ourselves time to relax. Nobody but Mister Horgen knows that we're here, after all."

"Well, to relax, and experiment with that gun-gizmo thingy, and make love, and figure out the puzzling powers of the ancients, and . . . and get ready for the whole world to change," Kiers murmured as one of their stomachs grumbled. He blushed, unsure if it was his or not, and met her smirk with a sheepish smile. "I think we've been overruled by fate itself on what comes next. But while we wait, care to teach me more of that mysterious, exotic skill known as cooking?"

She chuckled. "I think that could be arranged, yes. And after we've cleaned up ourselves and all that bathwater you made us spill, you could also teach me more of the mysterious skill known as lovemaking," Vee added. "But we really should clean up first. It wouldn't be polite to leave behind a set of warped floorboards in our kindly hunter's cabin."

"That, it would not," he agreed. Rising, he offered her his hand, and kissed her fingers when she clasped it. "I sincerely hope this week will not be the sole extent of our liaisons, Miss Vielle."

She considered that as he assisted her to her feet. "I think they could definitely continue. *If* you could bring yourself to call me Vee, instead of Miss Vielle."

"Of course, Miss Vee," he teased—and laughed as she mock-whapped him. "Vee! Vee! Just Vee!"

"Good man," she praised, embracing him. "Thank you, Kiers."

"You're most welcome, Vee," he murmured, hugging her back. Then he scooped her off her feet, making her squeak with surprise. "One more shared, hot bath, coming up!"

"Kiers!" she protested.

"Well, if we're going to clean up a mess made from lovemaking, we might as well make it a thorough one, right?" he offered mischievously. "Those poor, wet floorboards won't know what hit them, will they?"

"No, they won't, the poor things," she agreed, blushing. Looping her arms around his neck, she let him carry her downstairs. It made for a very nice change from her carrying *him* everywhere, whenever they flew.

NO SURPRISE
MORE MAGICAL

Hanna Martine

To my real high school creative writing teacher,
Mr. Harris, whose wonderful assignments
first showed my imagination what it could create.
I wish you'd been given the chance to affect more students.

ACKNOWLEDGEMENTS

Full credit for Dante Jenga must go to Dawn and Brian Chatham. I hope I honored the fat cat's memory.

I must thank the Chicago-North chapter of the Romance Writers of America for giving honest, helpful critiques that helped me shape the opening pages.

I also had seven wonderful beta readers: Erica O'Rourke, Eliza Evans, Clara Kensie, Lynne Hartzer, Sarah Shulman, Sonali Dev, and Ann-Marie Bauer. My love and thanks to you all.

CHAPTER ONE

David had returned to the land of the living. Sort of.

He bled from a throbbing knot on his temple. The laceration across his chest burned and wept red. The paper on the exam table crinkled as he shifted, the pain in his body just slightly eclipsing the nerve-racking anticipation over seeing the woman he'd successfully avoided for two months.

After a week spent tracking the Ofarians' most-wanted fugitive through the wilds of the Sierras, the activity of the clinic jarred. The lights glared too brightly. The buzz and hum of water elemental magic, emanating from his fellow Ofarians scurrying about their work, played havoc with his already woozy brain.

And then there was Dr. Kelsey Evans, opening the door.

She looked far more relaxed than the last time they'd spoken. Less burdened. He'd done the right thing by ending their engagement, even though seeing her now reminded him of what he'd almost had. That loss thrust hard and jagged into his chest.

Still, he smiled, because when it came to her, even with pain spiking through his body, he couldn't help it. "Hey, Doc. Mind telling me why I'm here and not at your mom's ER?"

"You're not an emergency." She entered but left the door wide open. "And I want to try a new treatment on you."

"Always wanted to be a guinea pig. Do I get to run around in one of those huge plastic balls?"

Great stars, he lived to make her smile. So rare. Always beautiful.

In sophomore year health class, he'd dressed up the two room skeletons in awful 1970s clothing and posed them doing it in front of the blackboard. He'd amassed a long detention schedule for that stunt, but when he'd first seen Kelsey's small smile shining out from the front row—on the face of the bookish girl who'd always been the most reluctant to lighten up—he'd been instantly hooked. Now, more than a decade later, he craved it like water.

Kelsey smoothed her bright hair, the color of a brand-new penny, into her trademark ponytail. Not sparing him a glance, she went right to the sink to wash up.

In his dreams, he got to see her without her ever-present white coat. In his dreams, he slid out the rubber band at her nape and let that hair brush her shoulders. In his dreams, they kissed and touched, and not because a bunch of old people had told them to marry and breed.

He'd never known why the former Ofarian Board had matched them in marriage in the first place. Him from the working class, she from the ruling. Kelsey hadn't wanted it—she'd never loved anything more than her career—so when the Board had been deposed three months ago and the old systems crumbled, David couldn't bear to hold her to a promise she hadn't willfully given.

So he'd ended it. For her sake.

Kelsey opened cabinets and removed rolls of gauze, scissors, and a clear pouch of water that sparkled like the sun setting over a lake.

"Did you get Wes?" she asked, turning to him.

The reminder of his most recent failure hurt almost as bad as his injuries. "No. He got away." David touched his sticky forehead and groaned. "A steep ravine and a sharp boulder got me instead."

Wes Pritchart, the last former Ofarian executive remaining to be tried and imprisoned, had been on the lam since the Board fell. He'd been chief operating officer of the Plant, which had secretly manufactured *Mendacia*, the magic product that had kept the Ofarians steeped in wealth and privilege for generations. Then the shocking secret behind *Mendacia* had come to light, setting their society on a path to destruction. David was proud to say he'd been among the treasonous few to have taken down the Ofarian Board. Its members and anyone knowingly involved in the Plant had been imprisoned. Everyone except Wes, who'd managed to escape.

Kelsey came to the edge of the exam table and peered at his temple, her expression assessing and professional. "Can you lean back for me? Yeah, thanks. Just relax."

When her latex-covered fingers touched his face, he inadvertently sighed. Their first touch in nearly six months, since the night of their matching ceremony. They'd held hands then, as a ribbon of glistening, enchanted water had bound them together.

The sting of the antiseptic wash didn't faze him. Over the sharp tang of the medicine, he could smell her. Feel her.

"This'll need some stitches," she said in that low, careful way of doctors, "but I've been working on something new. Secondary water magic combined with Primary medicine. If I'm right, it could be . . . monumental. Do I have your permission?"

She was bending over him, her voice a caress to match the lightness of her touch. Her sky blue eyes shone like stars, and he knew it had to come from the excitement of her work, not from his proximity.

"Do it, Doc. Whatever you want." He wasn't entirely sure of the innocence of his command.

Kelsey lifted the glimmering pouch over his head wound and

slit a corner. Words in the language of their birth poured out in time with the liquid. The sparkling water defied gravity to undulate in a cool bubble the size of a golf ball over his split skin. She whispered more Ofarian words, tapping into the magic swirling inside the bubble, and sent it surging into his body. Her words, her power, drifted inside him. Slipped into his bloodstream, his very being.

There was something else, too—the numbness of Primary medicine doing its thing alongside the Secondary magic. *Monumental*, she'd said.

"How does it feel?" she asked.

"Good."

Holy hell, it did. The quiet pulse of magic traveled down his arms and torso. Lower even, stirring him. He shifted on the table, trying to hide the neon sign that would tell her his body was lighting up. He'd successfully hidden his desire for twelve years. He wasn't about to show her now, here on her table, when he knew he wasn't wanted.

"That should do it. The combo should accelerate healing."

In Ofarian, she commanded the bubble to roll off his temple and into her palm. No longer sparkling—the magic and medicine transferred into him—she carried it, whole and wobbly, to the sink, where it splashed into the stainless steel basin. As she came back to him, she murmured clinical approval, numbed his temple, and started to stitch.

He relaxed into her touch, feeling the tug of the needle but not the pain, and let his eyes trail out the door to the flurry of nurses and lab technicians outside. "This is great, Doc, what you've built here."

"Thank you." Pride swelled her voice.

"So this is what you've been doing lately? Experimenting with mixed treatments?"

"Yes." Her hands left him and he gazed up at her. Damn, she was like the sun, her pale skin and coppery hair dazzling.

"Can I tell you something?" she asked, sitting back.

Anything. Please let it be what he wanted to hear. "Sure," he said.

"I was thinking that maybe, if my combined treatments work on Ofarians, they might work on Primaries, too."

Such an amazing thought. Such a *dangerous* thought. Right now, the Primary and Secondary human worlds—the former ignorant of magic, the latter dependent on it—didn't overlap. For Ofarians to reveal themselves as magic-users could be devastating. It had been one of the key issues behind the Board's destruction. But if Kelsey could actually *help* the Primaries, if her work could heal them . . . that could be quite the game changer. Or the *world* changer.

"Gwen and Griffin do want to better integrate into the Primary society," he said carefully. "Who knows? Maybe it'll happen."

"Thank you. For saying that. I worry about not being able to keep this place open, now that . . ."

The Ofarians don't have Mendacia, David mentally finished for her. Millions and millions of dollars had once poured in from that product, now all gone.

"Did you know," she said, returning to her work, "that the Board used to have access to all medical records? They had no concept of sanctity, of doctor-patient privilege. But here, all my work is confidential. I love that."

The Board had destroyed so much—and invaded even more—under the banner of "success." Griffin Aames, the first elected Ofarian leader, and Gwen Carroway, the woman who'd taken down the Board, wanted to build back up in the name of *progress*. David wanted whatever his new leader wanted because Griffin was fair and strong. Even though David was a soldier by birth, he remained in service by choice, and because Griffin was his best friend.

Kelsey cleared her throat, snipped off the thread. "Okay. On to the next. I want your shirt off."

If she weren't so professional, so frustratingly poised, he might have taken that statement another way. He *wanted* to take it another way. Instead, he reached for the buttons on his Ofarian-issued black shirt but couldn't disguise his wince. Pain streaked from his chest to his fingertips and his arms flopped back to the table.

"It's okay, you know." She held up the scissors. "You can say it hurts."

David looked into her impossibly clear eyes, surrounded by feathers of copper lashes, and laughed. "Then it hurts. Like a bitch."

But not as much as having to let her go.

She stretched for where the bloodied and shredded shirt was tucked into his black pants. He tortured himself by dreaming she reached for something else.

Though her hands were smooth with latex gloves, he imagined how she might trail her gentle fingers down his ribs, over his belly, and slide beneath the gap of his pants between his hipbones. Only the pain rippling across his chest kept him from getting hard.

She snipped the shirt up one side of the buttons. Tilting him on his side, she cut up the back of the shirt and pulled the two halves down his arms. Habit and his favorite defense mechanism longed to make a joke about his near nakedness, but she looked so serious, and there was only so much forced levity he could stand before it threatened to crush him.

As she patched his chest with another water-magicked pouch of liquid, he returned his attention to the open door, looking for someone in particular. There she was, right in his line of sight. A woman in her mid-forties, long hair pulled back at the sides, her body softened with age, sat at the central computer terminal. Her head in her hand, she stared unseeing at the monitor.

"Emily Pritchart," he muttered. Wes's sister.

Kelsey finished her quiet chanting. The healing magic coursed through the wound.

"Yes," she replied. "That's her."

"She's one of your nurses?"

"Not exactly. She's in charge of maintaining regular contact with our patients taking part in my test treatments. She interviews them, documents progress or problems, that sort of thing."

Weeks of frustrating chases ate at him. Wes eluded him far too easily, considering Wes had been a suit his whole life. It was like he had help or something.

David shifted his head on the thin, papery pillow and asked Kelsey, "Has her brother tried to contact her here at the clinic?"

Kelsey's eyebrows drew together. "Not that I know of. Why?"

"Has she mentioned him to you at all? Has she called him from here? E-mailed him? You guys are friends, right?"

Only when Kelsey's hand slid from his pectoral muscle did he realize she'd been holding it there. She adopted that opinionated, determined look he remembered from her spirited class debates back in high school. "What exactly are you getting at? That Emily is somehow helping Wes evade you? She's as devastated as the rest of us over what he was involved with."

David struggled up onto his elbows. "And Wes is also her brother. Blood is a powerful thing, Doc."

"She's *distraught*, David. Look at her."

As if Emily had heard them, the other woman glanced up and looked right at David—the man hunting down her brother. Emily jumped up from her chair, ducked her head, and hurried out of sight.

"Ouch!" His head whipped back to Kelsey, who'd slapped a huge bandage over his chest with none of her trademark gentleness.

"Can you sit up for me?"

He tried to do it himself, but in the end had to accept her help. Her cheeks flushed slightly as she wrapped gauze around his chest, passing the roll from hand to hand around his back. She had to move closer to do it, her body inserted between his knees, the short, sharp bursts of her breath on his neck. Her warmth coated his bare skin. He swallowed, willing away any pleasure his desperate body wanted to feel.

"I'm not trying to get at anything," he said. "I'm just asking. It's my job. Griffin wants Pritchart in custody. A lot—maybe everything—is riding on this capture."

Bottom line, ousting the old Board hadn't been a cure to what ailed their race. It had shattered Ofarian society into chunks and now it was Griffin's job to pick them all up and somehow glue them back together.

"I know." Kelsey backed toward the door, a steel veneer pulled down over her expression. "You're done. Come back after the Ice Rites for evaluation."

She left. And he'd been the one, again, to drive her away.

CHAPTER TWO

Kelsey measured her steps exiting David's exam room. Running would draw the wrong kind of attention. Not to mention crying.

Research first. Always first.

She sat at the central computer Emily had just left and logged in the specific spell and human medicine she'd used on her former fiancé. She'd told David the truth. Her new research could alter how the Ofarians viewed their position in the world. Now that they knew they were not alone—that other Secondary races existed on Earth—they had to carve out their space within that.

Medicine could help.

She'd always wanted to test Primary and Secondary combinations, but the Board had forbidden it for fear of the knowledge leaking out. She'd become a doctor under orders, groomed to take over her mother's position as head Ofarian physician when the older Dr. Evans retired, but now Kelsey's designated career had become her calling.

David had been so amenable to her tests, so genial despite his ordeal. That was David for you.

Finally finished with the report, she headed for the empty

break room and closed the door. Doing so, she shut out the doctor and responsibility, and for once, just let herself *feel*.

Sagging heavily against the door, she let loose a ragged sob of frustration and torment. Here, with no one watching, her lungs caught up with all the breaths she'd skipped ever since the call came through that David Capshaw had been injured in the hunt for the Ofarians' most-wanted fugitive.

Two months, three days, and nine hours since David had unknowingly broken her heart. Two months, three days, and nine hours since he'd told her, "You know, with the Board gone, there's no reason for us to get married now."

She'd just stared at him, determined not to show him how he'd taken a hammer to her glass heart. Determined not to reveal how she'd essentially trapped him into the marriage in the first place.

"Right?" he'd added with a raised eyebrow and that trademark off-center smile.

So she'd given him a casual wave, and replied, "Oh. Right. Absolutely."

Then he'd done the strangest thing. Instead of exhaling in relief or making a joke as he usually did, he'd simply nodded and said, "Okay, then."

He'd vanished after that, consumed by the hunt for Wes Pritchart, until reappearing today on her exam table.

Away from her patient, her professional manner dissolved. Its absence left her flayed to the bone. She looked down at her hands, now stripped of latex, and willed herself to forget how his skin had glided beneath them. How cutting away his shirt had revealed him inch by lovely golden inch. How the blood seeping into his thick blond curls had made her chest ache with worry. How she'd wanted to snap off those gloves and slide her hands over the ridges of his lean soldier's muscles, and under the gap of his waistband. It was too late; the memory had dug in deep and now she'd certainly lie awake that night, burning with regret and the dirty fantasies of him she'd entertained since high school.

The thing was, *everyone* loved David. Hell, when he'd been rolled into the clinic with blood streaming down his face, she'd watched from behind a curtain as he'd traded good-natured barbs with the EMTs and flirted with the nurses. It was no wonder he'd never wanted her, the girl who'd married her career before she ever even had one. The girl who'd always been way too serious to have any kind of life other than the one picked for her.

The Board had been wrong to match them. But by the time the betrothal had been announced, it was too late to correct what she'd started. At the matching ceremony, David had looked so overwhelmed, so scared. How could she ever admit to being the one to make him feel like that?

In self-disgust, she pushed away from the door and went for the sink. Tap water didn't call to Ofarians the way a clear mountain stream or a wave in the ocean did, but it was still water. It was still her element. Turning on the faucet, she rolled her hands underneath it, commanding the liquid with a whisper to follow the prescribed pattern she'd adopted in her youth to calm her nerves. The narrow stream wove around each finger. Trickled into her palm in a lovely spiral. Dripped off her fingertips in even measurements.

The ritual over, her mind automatically straightened. She went into the locker room to throw her soiled white coat in the laundry. From her locker she removed a new coat with her name stitched in blue over the left breast.

Her slim green wallet sat on the top shelf. Because she was a glutton for punishment, she removed the wallet and opened it. There, sandwiched between her driver's license and her sole credit card, she thumbed out the all-too-familiar rectangular piece of plastic. The tiny slip of paper encased inside, no bigger than a cookie fortune, had nibbled edges and numerous creases, all of which she knew by heart.

The faded letters read: There is no surprise more magical than the surprise of being loved: It is God's finger on man's shoulder.

With a snarl she threw the wallet back into the locker and slammed it. She'd had the damn thing *laminated* for stars' sake. If that wasn't pathetic, she didn't know what was.

She heard the scrape of a chair on the floor. Around the lockers, Emily Pritchart sat slumped at the tiny table in the back corner, her eyes rimmed with red, the bags beneath them puffy and purple. Severe silver roots showed at the scalp of her dyed brown hair. She clutched a pen in one hand and absently scribbled on the pink, rumpled take-out bag from El Tamale Loco.

Kelsey turned to go, to give Emily privacy, but her employee said in a flat voice, "They found him. Didn't they. That's why David Capshaw was in here, hurt."

Kelsey leaned against a locker. "David found him, then lost him."

Emily sagged and threw the pen across the table. "I wish he'd turn himself in. He's just delaying the inevitable."

Kelsey looked at the shiny white tile beneath her sneakers. The whole race felt slashed open, their wounds open to infection. Thanks to generations of selfish leaders—who had in turn created a race of entitled, selfish Ofarians—they were all bleeding out, the treachery and despicable acts of a precious few polluting them all.

One of the first things Griffin Aames had done was outlaw the old class system. Every Ofarian child would start on even ground. No more preordained tracks of service or soldiering or ruling.

Not every Ofarian, even if they'd opposed the old Board, was happy about these changes. Least of all Wes Pritchart. He'd grown into somewhat of an idol for the dissidents.

"Sorry, Dr. Evans. I'll get back to work."

"At times like this, Emily, you can call me Kelsey."

Emily threw her an unreadable look and stood. She crumpled up the pink tamale bag, and tossed it in the trash.

"Why don't you go on home . . ." Kelsey began, but Emily had already shuffled out of hearing range, and Kelsey was again left alone with her screaming thoughts.

CHAPTER THREE

David sprawled on his well-worn blue couch, legs kicked out, shirt unbuttoned so the fabric wouldn't scrape against the gauze wrapped over his still-tender wound. The plate that had once held a mound of baked manicotti balanced on the edge of the side table. The TV flickered but he wasn't watching it. Instead, he squiggled in the corner of the last page of his *Gigantic Book of Brain Puzzles*, the final mind-bender just completed. Flipping the cover closed, he tossed the brick of a book onto the pile of the others that needed to go out to the recycling bin.

Didn't matter that he'd always placed at the top of every class with Kelsey Evans; he'd been born into the soldier class of Ofarians, and that's who his parents had raised. It felt strange to be the one in charge of all the soldiers now. Strange . . . but good. It was that goodness that fed his fear of letting down both Griffin and his people.

David absentmindedly rubbed the stitches on his temple beneath the butterfly bandage, still feeling the flutter of Kelsey's touch. The wound on his chest twinged and burned, remembering how she hadn't been so nice tending to it. Because he'd brought up Emily Pritchart.

Despite Kelsey's insistence of Emily's innocence, Griffin's soldiers had been monitoring Emily Pritchart for months. Her phone, her mail, her house—all were under surveillance. And true, Wes hadn't attempted any contact through those means, but that didn't mean he wouldn't. The chase through the Sierras had been brutal, and David had almost caught the bastard, but he could tell Wes was weakening. Getting sloppy. Usually that's when people gave up . . . or reached out for help.

The only place Emily was open and vulnerable was at the clinic, behind Kelsey's veil of privacy. David understood the good doctor's vehemence over protecting the clinic's confidentiality—he really did—but there were huge issues riding piggyback on Wes's evasion. He had to get Kelsey to see that. It wasn't just Griffin's leadership at stake, it was the structure of the entire race.

His phone rang, and he had to dig it out from under the half-devoured bag of M&Ms on the coffee table.

"I got the report." Griffin rarely said hello anymore. Moments like this, David didn't know if he talked to his friend or his leader.

David scratched at his jaw. "He got away. Again."

Goddamn Ofarian senses that could pick out magic at fifty paces. Wes could always tell when he'd closed in.

"It's the closest you've gotten yet," Griffin said, his voice gruff. "He's running out of steam."

"Was just thinking the same thing."

Griffin sighed, deep and resigned, and David knew it was his friend now on the other end of the line. "Shit, man. You okay? Heard that fall was pretty spectacular."

David snorted and shifted higher on the couch, tugging the flaps of his shirt closed. "I will be."

"You see the doc?"

"Yep. You know she's experimenting with combinations of magic and Primary medicine?"

"Yeah." It was the first real spark of hope David had heard

from Griffin in weeks. Maybe months. "Pretty amazing stuff. Should've been done decades ago."

That's as far as they took that discussion. None of Kelsey's findings would matter if the race splintered apart, if they couldn't move forward into the future as one.

"How is she otherwise?" Griffin asked.

"Just told you."

"That's not what I meant."

David closed his eyes, pinched the bridge of his nose. "The same."

Griffin exhaled. "Sorry, man."

David had never voiced his feelings for Kelsey. He hadn't had to. Griffin was a smart son of a bitch who knew David's emotions, just as David was well aware of Griffin's heartache over his broken engagement to Gwen, who'd chosen another man, and a Primary at that. They were two sorry, unwanted assholes. Should have been funny, except that it wasn't.

"It is what it is. Or was. Or never will be." David struggled off the couch. "You calling on official business or just to remind me of my failures?"

"Both, apparently. I need your help."

"Whatever you need. You know that."

"I'm getting the Fragment out of the vault tomorrow before the Star Gala. I'd like you to come with me."

The Ofarians' most sacred artifact, used during their most revered holiday. A big deal, to say the least.

"Our fearless leader needs help turning the key in the lock?"

Griffin chuckled. "Fuck you."

"I'm not good for much else. My chest is black and blue and hurts like a mother. Not sure I can carry a hunk of rock very well."

"I'll carry it. I just . . . need you there."

The heaviness in Griffin's tone gave David pause. Many times over the past few months they'd been in the same room when important issues had barreled down on the race, but Griffin excelled in portraying confidence. Diligence. Intelligence. As an Ofarian, David didn't want to hear such fear and doubt in his leader's voice. As a friend, it hurt even more.

"Absolutely," he said. "Anything you need."

Griffin cleared his throat, the leader back in full force. "I'll send a car at three sharp."

And because David was David, he groaned like a raging orgasm was about to plow through him. "Ahh, God. I love it when you order me around."

Griffin laughed, even though it sounded strained. "See you tomorrow."

The line went dead and David's smile quickly died. Because when he thought about orgasms, he sure as hell wasn't thinking about his best friend. He adjusted his pants as the image of a heart-shaped face with ivory skin assaulted him all over again. As if he hadn't been tortured enough that day. He willed himself to be monkish; after all, he'd been doing it for years. But as usual, Kelsey's presence wedged itself nice and tight into his mind, ignoring all reason or truth. She burned brightly behind his eyelids. The image of her face, the memory of her hands slowly pulling out his shirt, didn't do anything to soften his body.

He buttoned his shirt, then slid on his shoes. Griffin didn't say it, but he was scared shitless that Wes was planning something that would destroy the Ofarian future. Griffin needed Wes in custody, and that was David's job. Emily was the strongest lead he had.

Which meant Kelsey was about to get some good, old-fashioned David Capshaw begging.

The San Francisco night was colder than usual, and David hadn't bothered to wear a coat. The deep breath he drew shot sharp and icy into his lungs. He lifted his hand and knocked.

Kelsey opened the door to her town house with the same expression she'd worn during their matching ceremony. Eyes round as marbles, mouth slightly agape. A deer in headlights.

David clenched a fist. If she was the deer, then he was the car. He fucking hated being the car.

Brush it off. Put her at ease. He dipped his chin and grinned up at her. "Hi?"

She startled out of her shock. "Oh. Hi. What are you doing here?"

It took all his effort to cement his smile in place. "I, um . . ." He rubbed the edge of the gauze through his shirt.

She stretched out a hand. "Are you in pain? Is there something wrong with the spell?"

So easily he could take that freebie and run with it. He could pretend to have complications or discomfort, let her peel off his shirt again.

"I'm not here for me," he said, while his brain screamed, *LIAR!* "I just got off the phone with Griffin and I need to talk to you."

"Oh. You couldn't have called?"

Ouch.

He deflected, as usual, widening his smile and jutting a thumb over his shoulder. "You want me to go sit in the park across the street and call you instead? It's colder than ass out here, but I'll do it."

Her cheeks pinked and her gaze fell to the floor. Suddenly she looked twelve years younger. He loved how her loose, shiny hair swished across her cheeks. He hadn't seen her wear it down since, hell, their matching ceremony six months ago.

When she lifted her face to him again, any hint of blush had disappeared. She gave him a companionable, controlled nod and stepped aside. "Sorry. Come in."

A set of steep, narrow stairs rose to the main floor and he followed her up. She wore jeans, of all things, that hung low on her hips and curved tightly around her ass. A huge hole in the denim gaped over her right knee and a small hole had just begun to fray under her left ass cheek. She wore a bra under her white tank top, the double sets of straps a weird attraction for him. The way her skin pebbled in the cold air, the slight push of her nipples against her clothing, challenged him to think straight.

Even though he'd always known where she lived, he'd never been here. Had never built up the courage to stop by. In truth, it was a miracle she was home now, given that her work was her life. But everything usually slowed down for the gala and rites, and he'd taken a chance that had paid off.

Her townhome's furnishings reflected the in-and-out nature of her domestic life—sparse but tidy, very little design. A few random prints of flowers and trees were slapped up on the wall. The granite kitchen counters were bare except for an open bottle of wine and a single, half-empty glass. Sort of lonesome, actually.

It reminded him of his place.

She clutched the back of one of only two kitchen table chairs. Her eyes darted around, like he'd burst in just as she was hiding her lover in a closet. Oh, he *hated* that thought.

"You're right," he said. "I should've called. Didn't mean to make you nervous by just showing up."

She looked coolly offended that he'd called out her agitation, as though she never allowed herself to be nervous. Come to think of it, he'd never seen her this way.

"Not at all," she said. "It's just . . ."

He smiled and leaned against the banister that zigzagged upstairs. "That whole 'We were supposed to get married' thing?"

What the hell was he saying? The question just spilled out. And it was too late to mop it up.

She choked a little, like she'd swallowed something too hot. Then, in classic Kelsey fashion—the Kelsey he recognized—she rolled back her shoulders and stared him right in the eye. His turn to be unsettled, because all he could think was, *God, you're beautiful.*

"Since you mentioned it," she said. "Yes."

"Oh." He ran a hand around the back of his neck, thrown by the fact he had no idea how to decipher her direct statement. "I didn't mean to bring it up." Not really.

"Okay." Her shoulders sagged. Just a tad. "So what's up?"

He pulled away from the banister, the action nudging him closer to her. Her divine chest lifted beneath the thin cotton of her tank top. Why had he come here again? Oh, yeah. Emily Pritchart . . .

"I was just talking with Griffin, and I, uh, I wanted to ask— holy *shit*, that's a fat cat."

A black basketball of fur waddled down the stairs. At least twenty pounds, probably more. The thing was downright *glaring* at David.

Kelsey covered her mouth with a hand, but behind her fingers he glimpsed his favorite smile. "He's not *that* big," she said.

"No, seriously. That's the fattest cat I've ever seen. What the hell do you feed that thing?"

She dropped her hand and there it was, the most perfect bow of a mouth, two shallow dimples set into her smooth cheeks. She made a cooing noise and scooped up the cat with a grunt.

He said, "Don't throw your back out."

"Aw, leave poor Dante alone."

"Dante?" David reached out to scratch the feline behind its ears. A paw that looked too small to support all that bulk batted him away. Dante's ears shot back, his teeth bared in a hiss. "Perfect name," David mumbled.

"Sorry." Kelsey dropped the cat and David swore the house shook. "Nobody can touch his head but me."

Dante tottered into the living room and plopped down in the middle of the braided rug.

She cleared her throat. "I opened a bottle of Zinfandel. Would you like a glass?"

"I probably shouldn't. One turns to two, two turns to four, and then I'm streaking and TP'ing Griffin's house."

Or kissing you and telling you exactly how I feel, no matter the damage to my heart.

She flashed him her smile. The opposite of nervous, the very definition of joy.

"So . . . was that a yes or no? It's always so hard to tell with you."

He held up a hand. "No, that's okay. I'm on duty early tomorrow and Griffin wants me with him when he gets the Fragment from the vault. I can just see my hungover ass dropping the thing."

"Wow, he asked you to do that?"

"It's more personal than anything. I'll be the guy who stands next to a piece of rock all day, growling at anyone who gets too close."

"A piece of Ofaria, you mean," she corrected with all seriousness. "It's still an honor."

He slid his hands into his pockets, wishing he could tell when people didn't want to hear wisecracks. "Absolutely. It is."

At length, she asked, "Mind if I finish my glass?"

"Not at all."

She didn't immediately take up her glass. First, oddly, she went to the sink and turned on the water. She ran her hands under the stream, her wrists graceful, her fingers relaxed. She whispered Ofarian and the water obeyed, trickling in thin rivulets around her knuckles and palms in a discernible pattern. Seemed like he wasn't the only one with strange habits.

When she was done, she ignored a towel and spoke the words to evaporate the liquid. She reached for the Zinfandel.

"Why don't you have a seat in the living room?"

David nodded, even though her back was to him. A palpable excitement ballooned inside him, as though all their previous interactions had led up to this moment—to the day they'd be given a chance to start again on their own terms.

A year after the skeleton prank in high school, he still hadn't gotten up the nerve to talk to her directly. So he'd done what he did best, and devised another stunt specifically to give him an excuse to approach her and be rewarded by her attention.

Junior year Creative Writing, and Mrs. Harris had assigned an awesome first semester final. She'd given the class a single word—*love*—and told them to present something—anything—creative associated with that word. It didn't even have to be writing.

David had found a quote by Charles Morgan, a novelist he'd never heard of, that read: "There is no surprise more magical than the surprise of being loved: It is God's finger on man's shoulder."

Perfect, he'd thought.

He had it printed on a thousand tiny slips of paper, crumpled them up, then stuffed them all into a bed sheet. Between second and third periods, he'd hung that sheet above the Creative Writing classroom door. As he worked, he'd turned to the gorgeous, studious, copper-haired girl whose desk was conveniently closest to the door.

"Hold this," he'd said, and handed her the string attached to the draped sheet. "And don't let go, or you'll ruin the surprise."

When he'd winked, she'd positively *bloomed*. But as he slid that string from her fingers, deliberately touching her, she'd swallowed that brilliant smile. The birth of the deer-in-headlights look.

When Mrs. Harris had sauntered into the classroom, clipboard at her hip, David had released the string, showering the teacher in tiny slips of paper. He went to one knee and shouted, "There is no surprise more magical than the surprise of being loved, Mrs. Harris! It is God's finger on man's shoulder!"

He'd gotten an *A*.

The sound of wine splashing into a glass brought him back to the present. Twelve years gone, and just now he and Kelsey were moving forward. At least, he hoped they were.

He turned toward her living room and stopped. "I can't get to the couch," he called over his shoulder. "There's a giant, black road block."

"Just step over him." She came to David's side. "He won't move."

"I don't know if my leg goes that high."

She giggled. Actually giggled. And he was a goner.

David raised a dubious eyebrow. "Will he go after me again?"

"He's lying down. You could seriously do anything to him right now and he won't move."

"Anything, you say?" David lowered himself to the floor, right next to Dante, who blinked slowly at him. David snatched the TV remote from where it balanced on the corner of the coffee table. "What if I put this on him?"

Kelsey edged around them to take a seat on the sofa. "Yep."

"I don't believe you."

She smiled into her wineglass. "Try it."

So he balanced the long, flat remote on Dante's wide, round belly. The stupid cat just pressed his head to the carpet as if to say, "More. Bring it."

"Here." Kelsey tossed him another remote, this one to the receiver. He laid it next to the other. Dante didn't even twitch.

She slid off the couch, her eyes mischievous, her hand stretching for a small, circular candle. "Now this."

David looked at the candle, then back into her glittering eyes, and shook his head. "You do it. But let's make it interesting."

"Yeah?" Her fingers tightened on her wineglass, little ovals of heat surrounding the tips.

"Yeah. Winner gets to ask a question. Any question. Loser has to answer. Truthfully."

She sucked in a breath, held it, and he realized he'd been holding his, too. Somewhere between the front door and her living room rug, this had turned personal. Right at that moment, he had no desire to ask her about the Pritcharts.

She licked her lips, and though it wasn't the first time the sight of her had gotten his dick hard, it was the most intense, because it was just the two of them, alone for the very first time in a quiet room.

"Okay." She exhaled, looking alternately excited and scared.

They settled on opposite sides of the black, furry monstrosity, whose side moved up and down under the two remotes. Kelsey set her wineglass aside and placed the little green candle near Dante's tail. She sat back, satisfied, a dare quirking her lips.

This was how he'd always wanted to be with her. A man and a woman with nothing in between—not books or school or work or duty. Or social classes or edicts from their elders.

Nothing except . . . the World's Largest Cat.

"So," he said, looking around and finding a blue crayon wedged next to the TV. He'd forgotten about her small nieces and nephews. He laid the crayon between the remotes. "Are you at the clinic tomorrow night? Or can you go to the Star Gala?"

The crayon wobbled, but eventually steadied.

She pressed her lips together in disappointment. "Thought for sure that would roll off."

He considered throwing the game, just to find out what she was so desperate to ask.

"The gala," he prompted. "Are you going?"

She pulled out a little statue of a cat carved from stone, and eyed him sideways. "You haven't won."

"That's not what I want to ask you."

She matched his stare for a long second, then leaned forward and balanced the statue on a fold of fat near Dante's back leg. "I'm closing the clinic for the gala. I'll be there."

"Good." He looked down at the game board. "All you left me was the neck and head!"

The sly grin she threw him was wonderfully evil. Deliciously seductive. It made him want to push the cat aside, snag the straps of her tank top and bra, and pull her to him. She'd kiss like she'd grinned just now, full of secrets and heat.

"It's your turn," she prodded.

Dante's tail thwapped against the rug. David looked around for a playing piece. There, on the end table, sat her anemic wallet—because Kelsey Evans would never carry along extraneous items. He'd bet she had her license in there, maybe one credit card, maybe a picture of her brother and his kids. When David stretched for the wallet, she quietly gasped.

"This okay?" he asked.

"Sure." Her voice had gone thready.

He bent over the cat. "Dante, sorry. She's making me do it."

Though the tail slapped harder, Dante didn't move as David nudged the wallet edgewise into the narrow space left on his neck, not quite on his forbidden head.

Kelsey chewed her lip. David couldn't tell if she feared losing or winning more. To be fair, neither did he.

She took down a tiny picture frame showing her nieces and nephews and held it over the two remotes. "You love me, Big D. I know you do. Don't fail me now."

She set down the frame. With a high chirp that didn't seem like it could come out of his massive body, Dante struggled to his feet, shaking the objects off his girth. He sauntered away, his belly swinging like a cow's udder.

Kelsey's shoulders sank in defeat. In any other situation David would be rubbing his hands together and gloating, making a joke out of it. Except that suddenly all the fun had been sucked from the room. The pile of discarded objects scattered between them, as real and divisive as all the questions he longed to ask.

Have you ever thought of me as anything other than the class clown?

How can I prove myself to you?

Can we start over?

She blinked at him, those plump, berry lips falling open. She looked expectant. Fearful. Hopeful?

Her breathing turned shallow, but in truth, he could have been confusing that with his own. The heat rumbling through the town house vents sounded like a tornado bearing down. She was the eye of the storm—his calm, his center.

They'd kissed once before. Well, not really—just on the cheek during their matching ceremony. He remembered the silk of her skin on his, the rigid inhalation of her breath as he'd pulled away. He didn't want tension from her. He longed for acceptance. He craved desire.

Turned out, he didn't need wine courage after all.

Quickly, before he could doubt himself, he leaned over and kissed her. Fingertips bracing his weight on the rug, only his mouth touched her. A swift, gentle brush of lips, worthy of new beginnings. It was impulsive. Sweet. Wonderful.

She just sat there at first, but then, *oh fuck*, she softened with an angelic sigh. Her lips parted, letting him in. He touched his tongue to hers so slowly it felt like twelve years passed. Because they had.

Her head tilted, and if he'd thought her mouth had perfectly fit his before, this new angle redefined sin. His sigh wasn't so angelic. He couldn't believe she was into this. *Don't scare her. Don't be self-indulgent*, he told himself, and skimmed his fingers down her cheek.

His lungs shuddered from the strain of wanting to take more, of wanting to give her more. Yet he pulled away, because suddenly this moment had grown too large, even for him.

Her eyes opened, revealing their brilliant pools of blue. She gazed at him, his beautiful doe, one hand rising to touch her lips. "That wasn't a question."

His heart thudded. His throat dried up. He sat back, stunned and expressionless. "I know."

And then he remembered why he'd come here in the first place.

CHAPTER FOUR

He'd *kissed* her.

Not even now, with the heat and tingle of David's mouth lingering on her lips, and a glass of wine erasing the edges of her nerves, could she bring herself to tell him she wanted him.

He always did this to her, managed to freeze her in place. All he had to do was look at her, and her doubts and desire clashed and turned her rigid. Moronic. She could run a medical research clinic with five employees. She could treat hysterical, dying patients. She could admit when she made mistakes and had never balked at asking for help . . . and yet David Capshaw's kiss had blanked out her speech and halted all muscle movement.

Even if she found the strength to speak now, it was already too late. She watched the conclusion cross his face. He'd tried her out and found her lacking.

He sat back—no smile, no jokes—looking terribly pale. And here she was, so full of heat and longing that she feared setting the rug on fire.

He gave a little shake of his head as if to clear it. Had she imagined the romantic way he'd kissed her? The gentle way he'd touched her face? He grazed the butterfly bandage on his temple, his arm muscles flexing under his shirt. Her body started to shake from the restraint of keeping herself in place, when all she wanted to do was crawl to him, straddle his lap, and wrap herself around him. Show him that she wasn't frigid or boring. That she loved him.

She swallowed. "Were you going to ask to kiss me?"

A troubled cloud settled over his eyes. "No." The hand feathering over the bandage now dropped to his stomach, as though he might be sick.

"Kelse," he began. He'd never sounded weak or unsure in his whole life.

Great stars, what was it? "Just ask me."

When his eyes found hers, there was far more than trouble behind them. There was mystifying pain. And regret. Over kissing her?

"I don't know if I can ask now, after . . ." he said. "But I have to."

"Ask me."

She prayed the question was about her feelings or their betrothal. Something personal. Because she was so shredded she knew she would tell him anything now, and it wouldn't hurt coming out.

"Okay." He drew a deep, shaking breath. Briefly closed his eyes. "Will you . . . spy on Emily Pritchart?"

Though she was sitting, she felt like she'd been pushed backward off a steep cliff. *"What?"*

He scrubbed his face with his hands, his "Aw, fuck," muffled behind his palms. His arms dropped and he looked her hard in the eye. "We're running out of time. I believe Emily is the key to finding Wes, and I came here tonight to ask for your help."

"That's why?" She scrambled to her feet, towering over him. The ghost of their kiss cackled and turned the air between them noxious. "Who told you?" she demanded.

There were no tears, just humiliation.

He pushed to his feet, and suddenly she wanted to hate his grace. "Huh?"

"Between this morning and now, how did you find out how I feel about you? And when did you decide to use it against me?"

He just stared. "How you . . . feel about me? Oh, shit," he whispered. He jammed fingers into his hair, the thick blond curls barely moving. "Look. Kelse. I'm sorry. I shouldn't have kissed you—"

"Damn straight you shouldn't have."

"I meant I . . . oh, man, I fucked this up."

Long ago, her heart had written a script detailing how it would go down should they ever kiss. Should he ever want her. Even though it was her own stupid fault for creating one in the first place, he hadn't just not followed it, he'd ripped it to pieces and lit the scraps on fire. All she could see in him now was a manipulator.

"You know, I always wondered if the charm was just an act, if all the flirting and witty banter was just to get you what you want. Now I know."

He thrust out his hands, his eyebrows drawing indignantly together. "Whoa. Just hold on a sec. That's not true."

"It's not?" she scoffed.

"You want to help your people, don't you? That's why you became a doctor, right? Because if we don't get Wes, if we don't bring the Ofarians back together soon, I don't think you'll have a clinic *at all*. It will be civil war, and if Wes's side wins, you won't be given access to *anything* Primary, let alone the medicine you want."

That was nonsense. "You want to know about Emily Pritchart? Fine. Her husband was an accountant who reconciled Secondary income with Primary taxes before he died two years ago. She took back her maiden name. She has two kids in high school. She gets takeout from El Tamale Loco every week. She chain-reads biographies. Oh, and she told me just this morning that she wants Wes caught as badly as you do. There. I spied. Now get out."

David consumed her living room. He'd invaded this space that had always been so carefully, purposely blank.

He backed away slowly, nodding as he slipped his hands into

his pockets. "Right," he murmured distantly. "Sorry to have bothered you. Enjoy your wine."

He turned, but not before she saw something terrifying on his face: heartbreak.

He bounded down the stairs faster than an injured man should have been capable of. She, however, couldn't move. He'd frozen her. Again.

He opened the front door but said over his shoulder, "What I was trying to say earlier was, I shouldn't have kissed you *here*. Tonight. I should have done it years ago."

And with that, she melted. Ice to water.

Kelsey opened her mouth to respond, to call him back, but he spoke again, this time the language of their ancestors.

Ofarian magic rippled over him, transforming his body into a glittering, undulating liquid statue, defying the rules of the Primary human world. Then, peeling off from the top of his head, his water body started to swirl into vapor—a thin coil of elegant, blue-white steam twining upward.

"David. Wait."

The wind caught his mist form and whisked him away.

CHAPTER FIVE

The two men's footsteps echoed loudly in the hallway leading to the vault. David felt the sounds bounce around in his hollow heart.

The Fragment of Ofaria—the chunk of their homeworld brought to Earth during the First Immigration over a hundred and fifty years ago—sat locked in the white Pacific Heights manor that had once housed Ofarian Chairmen. Griffin refused to live there, but had yet to find an equally suitable storage place for the Ofarians' most sacred relic.

The whole place was empty and hushed, like it hung its head in shame over the leaders who'd once lived here. The lone guard outside the vault jumped from his chair and interlaced his fingers in the position of deference, bowing low to Griffin.

Griffin bristled, though David might have been the only person to recognize it. "I'm not a Chairman," Griffin told the guard. "The gesture is no longer required."

Straightening, the guard nodded awkwardly, and Griffin gave the red-haired man a tight-lipped smile and a clap to the shoulder.

Once inside the vault and away from the guard's ears, David said to Griffin, "We need a leader. Don't diminish that role."

Griffin was already a dark man, with Greek-like skin, black hair, and thick, straight eyebrows, but the weight of his new leadership made him seem like he'd been cast in shadow. He didn't respond, but instead went to the pedestal in the center of the vault that cradled the shimmering Fragment. The rock—a delicate silver color streaked with sparkling blue—was about the size of a bag of sugar.

"Such a small thing," Griffin murmured, "to hold such power."

The Fragment had no magic in and of itself, but David understood.

"The Ofarians are broken." Griffin's obsidian eyes fixed on the rock's gleam. "The only things holding us together are our traditions. If the Rites don't go off without a hitch, my new order will die. It's already crumbling. Do you know how hard it is to keep something together when the pieces keep flying apart?"

Of course he did. Hadn't he managed to pull Kelsey close, then shatter their connection into tiny bits, all in one night? But Griffin wasn't talking about David's pathetic love life.

A new wave of guilt over having let Wes slip away again rolled through him. "Gwen destroyed the old ways and the people still chose her to lead the Ice Rites. That should tell you Ofarians want change. They support what she did and they support you."

"Not everyone."

David swallowed, remembering with a pang how Kelsey had refused to help him. "I'll get Pritchart. I promise you."

Griffin lifted the Fragment off its cushion and pillowed it in the crook of his arm. He gazed down at it like it was a newborn with all the reverence it was afforded as evidence of another world. Then he pinned David with an austere look. "Good."

David thrust back his shoulders, a soldier facing his commander in chief. "Just wait until tonight when the people see Gwen walk in with that thing. And tomorrow during the rite when she calls down the starlight? It'll be impossible not to be moved. The two of you will rally everyone behind you."

Griffin's lips flattened. "I hope you're right."

After they exited the vault and came out of the manor's maze of inner hallways, David's cell phone signal kicked back on. The voice mail alarm chimed. It was from Kelsey. The beat of his heart tripped out of rhythm.

Truthfully, he hadn't expected to hear from her again. With shaking fingers, he pressed PLAY.

"David, it's me." She sounded out of breath, the border of her voice tinged with panic. "Wes just sent Emily a letter. You need to see it."

It wasn't a letter. It was a fucking manifesto.

David hunched over the lone table in the clinic's break room, reading aloud to Griffin, who leaned against the counter near the soda vending machine. The Ofarian leader rubbed fingers over his bottom lip, his eyes gone black and focused far away.

Twenty pages long, the letter was the repetitious, circuitous ramblings of a madman, written longhand in one never-ending paragraph.

Water is ever powerful. It is the singular element, raised above all. We once commanded the universe, ruled from an invisible peak among the stars . . . yada yada yada.

David rolled his head on his neck. He'd been reading for ten minutes. "When is this going to get good?"

"Keep going."

We are privileged. Special. The Ofarians of the First Immigration fought for their lives, and everyone who seeks to erase the power and legacy they built is an enemy of the race. We do not belong among Primaries. We are superior. Anyone who wants to partner with them is my enemy.

"This isn't anything we haven't heard before," David commented. "He isn't even original in his hate speech."

Griffin motioned him to go on. "There has to be a purpose to this. Three months on the run and he picks now to contact his sister?"

David skimmed ahead. "Speaking of his sister . . ."

> *You, too, Emily, are my enemy. I should've known you'd turn your back. You always did like to squeal. Like the time you told Mom and Dad I scratched the car fender. Or when I hid in the hollow of the great redwood tree during the Ice Rites of 1977. I'm sure you will tell our false leader about this letter as well.*

"Is he twelve or fifty-seven?" David grumbled.
Then:

> *Gwen Carroway started the problem. But Griffin Aames is the wind on the brushfire. He wants to extend a hand to other Secondary races. This is wrong. We are singular and we are meant to rule. When Griffin tries to meet with these "others," he will die.*

Griffin pushed away from the counter.

"Is he fucking stupid?" David slapped the pages to the plastic table.

"He's outrun us for three months. He has strong, vocal supporters. No, I don't think he's stupid."

"He's talking assassination."

Griffin ground his teeth. "And now we have his target. Me."

David thought fast. "He won't go for it here. Too many people. Too many Primaries."

Griffin snapped his fingers. "In two weeks I head to Canada to try to find the air elementals. I bet that's when he'll attempt it."

David jumped from his chair. "So we cancel the trip."

"No." Griffin shook his head. "That'll tip him off. We want him. So we set a trap."

"And risk your life? No. Absolutely not. You're the glue, Griffin. All those pieces you were talking about a little while ago? You're what's holding everybody together. If anything happens to you, you can kiss it all good-bye. Everything Gwen sacrificed, every- thing you've built so far, everything you want to create in the future—it will all disappear."

Griffin stared at him for a long time, then his head dropped on his neck. "I don't want you to be right."

"And yet I am. So we'll set the trap. Only I'll be your decoy."

"You look nothing like me."

David snorted. "You're not that much bigger. I can stuff some styrofoam pads in my shoulders, pull on a black wig and gel it all up like a pretty boy. Maybe slap some fuzzy black caterpillars over my eyebrows—"

"Fuck you." But Griffin was grinning. He reached out to clamp a hand on David's shoulder and gave it a good squeeze. The grin faded. "Thank you."

"I'm not doing it because you're my friend. I'm doing it because I believe in you and what you stand for. You've done away with the classes, but I'll always be a soldier. I'll always protect you."

A muscle in Griffin's jaw jumped. "I know."

David pulled Griffin in for a shoulder bump and a hearty clap on the back. "Shit, I'll have to increase your guards tonight at the gala. My people'll be pissed they won't be able to drink."

"Tell you what," Griffin said, pulling away, "you keep me alive and bring in Wes Pritchart, and I'll buy them their own fucking vineyard."

"Will do."

David left Griffin with the manifesto.

Out in the hall, Emily broke away from the two soldiers flanking her and came up to him, her eyes red but expectant. "I have to keep the letter," he told her, and she nodded with a grimace. "Thank you for telling us about it."

"It was Kelsey. She said you deserved to know."

That was surprising.

"Just get him." Emily looked beyond fatigued, beyond heart-broken.

On the other side of the clinic, opposite the computers, Kelsey emerged from one of the exam rooms, her brow furrowed in concentration, a tablet computer tucked under her arm. Though she was busy and distracted, she stopped as though his stare owned a physical force. Maybe it did, because he felt something reciprocal and awful stab into his heart.

How did you find out how I feel about you? And when did you decide to use it against me?

He kept waiting for her scorn, for a piercing glare that told him what a shit he'd been. Instead she gave him a slight nod, which lessened the pressure some but didn't cure it, and then disappeared into the lab.

CHAPTER SIX

K elsey watched the Star Gala's procession—the official open-ing of the two-day holiday—from a place tucked far back in the crowd.

The doors to the hotel ballroom flew open, framing the queenly vision of the costumed woman absorbing the spotlight. Over a thousand pairs of Ofarian eyes swept to Gwen Carroway. Gorgeous and composed as ever, her pale blond hair piled high atop her head, wearing a glittering gown that turned her body into starlight, Gwen cradled the Fragment of Ofaria in her elegant hands. As she began the slow march down the center of the ballroom, part-ing the sea of Ofarians dressed in black tie, two small children fell in behind her, taking up the ends of the impossibly long train of the sparkling, high-necked costume.

She looked like a bride dressed in the night sky, about to marry the universe.

The whole ballroom had been decorated in billowing midnight blue fabric, and a lone beam of light illuminated the circular dais in the center. Gwen walked toward it with her chin high, her face solemn but commanding. Kelsey thought she looked like hope.

Not everyone agreed.

A woman to her left whispered bitterly to another, "She'll ruin us all, bringing a Primary in. Who does she think she is?"

Another woman made an ugly scoffing sound. "Selfish whore."

Kelsey edged away, knowing the gossip and conjecture they spouted weren't true. Gwen had destroyed the old corrupt Board because she was self*less*. Her reward had been finding love. Kelsey would never begrudge her that.

As she slid through the crowd and took a place along the wall with more air and fewer dissidents, Gwen reached the dais and placed the Fragment on a decorative pedestal. She intoned a short blessing on all Ofarians and declared the Ice Rites open.

In the past, these words had been met with cheers and the clinking of glasses. Now, only subdued applause followed.

"Feels different this year, doesn't it?"

Though the ballroom was warm, Kelsey's skin turned to goose bumps at the sound of David's voice. So close. When she turned, she was almost blinded by the sight of him in his tux. It fit him to perfection, and the clean wave of his dark blond hair, coaxed into a rare style, made him look like a god. She'd seen him dressed like this before, but never after she'd known what his lips felt like. That kiss had changed everything. Started something else. Ended more.

She drew a breath. "It does. Hardly anyone is drinking."

He grinned and it was almost her undoing. She had to look away.

"I know," he said. "Usually right about now I'm either walking in on couples making out in the bathroom or stuffing wasted Ofarians into taxis."

Across the room, Gwen descended from the dais. This was her first appearance back in San Francisco after the Board had fallen, and she was mobbed. Griffin stood close by, his eyes always on her. A ring of watchful Ofarian soldiers kept them both protected.

"It was smart of Gwen not to bring her Primary," Kelsey said.

"From what I understand, it's to prove that we can live amongst Primaries—even with them—and not compromise ourselves."

She thought of her clinic and where she wanted to take its purpose. It depended on Primary interaction.

"It must have been hard for Griffin," she said, "to lose his betrothed."

David shifted beside her. "Must have been," he murmured. Then, "Thank you. For telling us about the letter."

He always said "us" and "we," never "me" or "I," as though he never thought he'd make an individual difference.

She faced him. "I did it because it was out in the open, not sneaking around behind Emily's back. Betraying her trust."

He didn't flinch, his stance resolute. "You helped us. Can you keep a secret?" She nodded. "In the letter, Wes made a direct threat against Griffin. When he makes good on that threat, I'll be waiting for him."

"You?" she gasped.

He nodded once. "Me."

Foreboding knotted in her gut at the thought of David putting himself in that kind of danger, even though it was his job and he'd done it countless times before.

"Will you be careful?"

One side of his mouth quirked. "Worried about me?"

"Yes." *Always.*

"Never fear. You can't get rid of me that easily." That little smile died. His gaze caressed her face, lingered on her hair. When he swallowed, his Adam's apple made a slow undulation just above his bow tie.

I should have kissed you years ago.

He was beyond beautiful, beyond anything she could ever wish for, and suddenly she wanted to tell him. She wanted to start from the beginning and tell him . . . everything.

"David, I—"

His eyes suddenly shuttered, his focus dropping to the patterned carpet. He pressed a finger to his ear, where the curled cord of his radio device ended. Across the ballroom, tense, raised voices broke above the otherwise gentle susurrus of conversation. The sea of bodies shifted violently. A fight had broken out. Ofarian soldiers jogged from their positions around the ballroom and headed for the disturbance.

David threw Kelsey an apologetic glance and joined his uniformed men and women.

Over a hundred years of joyful, peaceful Star Galas, gone.

Nearly half an hour later, the mood in the ballroom had shifted so much that Kelsey's skin itched with discomfort. She paid her respects to Gwen, who was shielded behind a wall of soldiers, and decided to go home.

Out in the hallway, soldiers detained the young Ofarians who had started the fight. Established ways against the impending new, an ages-old argument. She'd lost sight of David in the melee, but that was just as well. The way he'd looked at her just before taking off had tantalized and disturbed and confused her. She was no longer angry with him for asking her to spy on Emily or for doing so after he'd kissed her. Sexual attraction did funny things to you, messed around with your priorities. Plus, he'd gotten pertinent information about Wes through the letter and no harm had been done to Emily.

A long, quiet hall led from the ballroom to the bank of elevators, dotted with doors branching off into deserted conference rooms. She made it halfway to the elevators.

"Kelsey."

Not "Doc." Not "Kelse."

Amazing how her name on David's lips could stop everything, not just her legs, from walking. Her lungs ceased to pump; her heart skidded to a stop. She turned to watch him approach. He moved with such elegant purpose after training his whole life to be that strong and agile.

He stopped three paces away. "You're not leaving, are you?"

"Yes." She glanced at the trouble in the ballroom lobby. "Is everything okay?"

He nodded, staring down at her with frightening, exhilarating intent. "It's under control."

She wasn't sure if he was talking about the fight or the powerful energy that sparked and sizzled between them. Hands in his pockets, he looked carefully rigid. Like he was holding himself back. She knew how that felt.

She thought about their kiss, the mismatched way his mouth had been so sweet and gentle, and how hot and desperate it had made her feel. What she needed to do was suck up her doubt and her pride, and just go for it.

She licked her lips, trying to find the moisture and courage to say what she wanted. Was he staring at her mouth? Her tongue darted out again, and his lips parted in response.

It was easy to get caught up in the magic of the Star Gala, she told herself. It was made for daring, drunken liaisons.

Except that neither of them had been drinking, and this had been the most solemn Star Gala in memory.

They both drew short, sharp breaths at the same moment, preparing to speak. Their eyes widened in a mirror image.

"What were you going to say?" His whisper echoed up and down the quiet hall.

"You first."

"No. You." He smiled in his charmer's way, and she hated that she continued to fall for it.

"I . . ." she began, but so many years of stashing her desire behind impenetrable walls didn't loosen so easily.

He inched closer, enough that the bottom of his tux coat touched the skirt of her black gown. "How about on the count of three? Just blurt it out. So will I."

Though his heat rippled over her like a warm breeze, she shivered. And nodded.

"One."

The sound of his voice drove her eyes shut.

"Two."

He touched her, his fingers sliding against her palms.

"Three."

They both inhaled.

He said, "I want to kiss you."

She said, "I want to sleep with you."

"What?" He released her hands.

Crap. She'd crossed a line. She'd embarrassed them both. But . . . wait. Slowly she opened her eyes. "What did you say?"

He barked out a laugh, his blue eyes holding a glitter that rivaled Gwen's costume. "What did *you* say?"

She just stood there, driven to speechlessness by his potent expression and the way he prowled so close his thighs brushed hers. Without warning or even tenderness, he grabbed her hand and yanked her toward the closest meeting room. Pulling open the door, he pressed her into the dark. She got a vague sense of an oblong conference table surrounded by chairs before he pushed her against the wall.

Sensation rocketed through her body. David, everywhere. His arms slid around her back. His mouth dropped to her neck, the hot cloud of his breath puffing over the collarbone and shoulder bared by her gown. He shoved one thigh between hers, sinking against her body. His scent—the tint of shaving cream mixed with the fabric of his fine tux—overpowered her. If he weren't holding her upright, she wouldn't have been able to tell up from down.

His signature—that invisible aura proclaiming his magic—enveloped her.

"Say that again, Kelse."

With trembling hands, she touched his face and chest in a most unclinical way. "I don't think I can."

"Yes, you can. To me and only me. I want to hear it again. I've been *dying* to hear you say it." Nudging aside her hair with his nose, he lightly ran his tongue along her neck. "Use the dark." His voice shook. "Say into it what you can't in the light."

He spoke the truth. There was anonymity in the darkness. Courage, too. Here, in a blackened room with the man she'd always wanted holding her, she could be the person she'd never been before. Not the careful doctor, but the uninhibited *woman*.

She slid her fingers into his hair and turned his head, whispering into his ear, "I want to sleep with you."

His whole body shuddered. A sound somewhere between a sob and a shout of triumph erupted from his throat. He released her, only to cradle her face in his warm palms. Even in the dark, she felt the magnitude of his stare.

"My God," he whispered. "Is this real?"

"Please tell me it is."

He answered with a kiss. One fierce and powerful, his breath sucking in through his nose. He abandoned chastity, and she opened her lips to him, letting his tongue dive in. Giving him hers. Her deep moan of pleasure, the instant, borderless reaction to his taste and his touch and his presence, vibrated through her. He sank hard against her, his weight crushing. In her mind, she begged for more. Begged for his erection that she felt thickening and growing against the top of her thigh.

This was David Capshaw, and he was more than she'd ever

imagined, in all her nights of lying awake, wondering what his passion might feel like.

"You really want me, Kelse?" His words came out staccato, hard bursts of breath rubbing across her lips.

His hands left her face, lowering to cover her breasts, to graze her nipples through the thin jersey of her gown. They both made some sort of inarticulate sound of pleasure. The back of her head ground into the wall. He yanked down her strapless dress, shoving the folds beneath her breasts. With a low groan, he lowered his mouth to her skin.

Worship. That's all she could call how he licked her nipples, and sucked them, and dragged the scratch of his chin and cheek around her curves. She flattened her palms against the wall and just let him *take*, because his pleasure had become hers.

"You really want me?" he repeated. The infuriating charmer; he already knew her answer.

She reached down and parted the long slit of her gown's skirt, separating the fabric all the way above her hips. He looked down at her unspoken invitation. One of his hands made a slow path down her belly and dove under the black jersey. Past the lacy string of her thong. Gliding easily into where she'd gone wet for him.

David collapsed, the wall now supporting them both. A cadence of Ofarian praises and oaths leaked from his lips, only half of which she understood. The other half were full of fiery promise.

He kissed her again, owning her mouth as well as the slick place where his fingers moved in achingly slow circles. He touched her, sliding in and out and over her with practiced care. Suddenly all her restraint dissipated like smoke.

"Yes," she said against his mouth. "I want you."

He smiled; she could feel the curve of his mouth as hotly and severely as the rising pressure on her clit. She sensed him reach for his magic. A little droplet of water formed around his finger, vibrating, intensifying his strokes as though they were electricity.

"Prove it." A little laugh colored his voice. "Come for me."

The wicked order streaked through her, shooting from her ears, to her brain, to the combination of his hand and his water magic. The words triggered her, shutting off every thought but those of him and what he was doing to her. All those years of fantasizing and masturbation, and her imagination had failed spectacularly. It had never even drifted close to this.

And then she came, bursting into orgasm like she dove into a pool from a hundred feet up.

"Yes. That's it," he said in her ear. "Oh, God, that's good. Keep coming, beautiful."

He'd always been so good at getting people to do what he wanted, so she was bound to comply. She shook around him. His hand became the center of her universe, and moved easily over her increasingly slippery flesh. She let him extract every last quiver of pleasure she knew was inside her, and several more she didn't.

She couldn't speak, so she jabbed her fingers into his thick hair and gave it a pull, telling him to stop. His hand left her, the dress swishing back over her sensitized skin. Strength started to seep from her legs, making her wobbly. With a gentle laugh, he wrapped an arm around her waist and pivoted them both. Kicking aside a leather conference chair, he planted her ass on the edge of the table. They watched each other, breathing heavily, the red light from the exit sign over the door casting a sexy aura over the room.

He'd called her beautiful.

Because she'd already been brave, she stretched for his bow tie. Pulled it loose, loving how it dangled, ribbonlike, down his chest. Beneath the collar of his shirt, his neck had gone damp with sweat. His earpiece was still coiled around his head, and she looked at it questioningly.

"I can hear them," he said, unwinding it from around his ear.

"They can't hear me unless I want them to. And believe me, after all this time, I want it to be just you and me."

Her breath hitched. Could he be saying what she thought he'd said? What she *wanted* him to say? She started to undo his shirt buttons, one by one. Taking the fabric in her fists, she slowly pulled the shirt out of his pants, a deliberate, sexual echo of how she'd undressed him in her clinic not two days ago. He met her eyes with a heated look.

Parting the halves of his shirt revealed the long white bandage across his chest. She laid her palm over it.

"It's practically healed," he said. "What you did, the mix of water magic and medicine . . . Stars, Kelsey, you're brilliant."

He leaned down, kissing her, and she pushed the tux coat and shirt from his shoulders in one move. She flashed back to high school, to that day when he'd first entered the halls after growing up and out practically overnight. She remembered not believing that the skinny, funny kid in baggy clothes had transformed into this leanly muscled young *man*. She recalled wondering what his new body might feel like, whether he would have been firm or if he'd have deflated like a cartoon.

Now she knew. And he was hot and hard and oh so real.

Her fingers started on his pants zipper.

"Here?" he growled, even as he pressed in closer. "Are you sure?"

"After all this time," she said, stealing his words, "*yes*."

His pants fell to the floor.

"We have so much to talk about"—he touched her wrist and pulled her to stand—"*after*."

"We do."

He slowly pulled down her stretchy, clingy dress and caught it near her knees, letting her step out of it.

He ran his tongue along the inside of his bottom lip as he took her in, whispering more praise in Ofarian. "I should have told you how gorgeous you looked before I took it off." He straightened. "I should have told you that the night of our betrothal, and pretty much every day before or since. You always wear scrubs and that white coat, and I really don't care, but I love the way you look dressed up. Your hair down—"

"David." His words were too much. Her body thrummed in anticipation.

He blinked up from where he'd been staring at her chest. "Yeah?"

"Shut up," she said. "Unless you want to tell me to come again."

Even in the darkness she could see his Cheshire grin. He scooped her closer, pressing her aching nipples into the gauze over his chest. She tried to pry herself away, afraid of further injury, but he wouldn't let her, and she gave up her half-assed fight rather quickly. Gave up thinking like a doctor.

Their kiss turned frantic and fast, teetering on the edge of pain. Little lights zoomed at her periphery and she had no idea if it was from oxygen deprivation or just . . . him. There were too many things she wanted to do to him. Too many things she wanted him to do to her.

She slid her fingers beneath the elastic of his underwear, taking them down. He kicked them aside. And then David Capshaw, the thick, hard length of him, was in her hands.

Twelve years of dreaming could never conjure the real thing. Twelve years of self-torture and pining, and he was finally hers. Maybe just for tonight, but that was okay. Two months ago he'd made it clear he hadn't wanted her forever. Maybe forever was overrated. Maybe tonight was the peak. If that was the case, she wasn't going to waste time thinking about the descent. She'd stand on the very top of the world and enjoy the ever-loving hell out of it.

"Kelse?" David slid his hand under her hair. She still had him in her grip, and his breath labored. "Where'd you go?"

She blinked, disconcerted to find her vision a little blurry with wetness. She kissed him to disguise it. "Nowhere. I'm right here."

And then she gave him a nice, slow, smooth pull that made him groan. He stroked her face with his thumbs as she stroked his erection. Finally, with a grimace, he peeled her fingers off him and gave her shoulders a gentle push back onto the table. She lay down, the faux wood cool against her hot skin. He crawled over her, the feeble exit sign light casting his muscles in crimson.

As he lowered himself to his elbows, she hooked a knee around his hip, loving the feel of his skin against hers. When he took his cock in his hand and rubbed it over her wetness, she whispered, "Is this really happening?"

And then he pushed inside her with a sigh as deep as the ocean.

"It is." He stared into her eyes. "Oh, my beautiful Kelsey, it is."

Of all the stars in the sky, in this universe and the next, nothing burned as brightly or as fevered as the feel of David moving inside her. His hips carried the movement of the waves, pushing her higher and higher away from herself. Great stars, she was full of him—where he stretched her and stroked her down below, and where his wordless whispers filled her mind.

She clung to him, digging in, scoring him. Loving him.

"I want you to come again." The demand timed with his thrusts. "I want to feel you. Around me. Come on, beautiful."

Because she'd always been powerless against him, she obeyed again.

"Oh, *yes*." He pumped faster now, driving into her with such determination and power that her body skidded backward on the table. She felt him pulse inside her—long, rippling waves of pleasure that he vocalized with deep, plaintive sounds.

He came down on top of her, pressing a kiss to the swell over her breast.

"It really happened," she said, when her mind and body realigned.

He raised his head and looked at her with such grave intensity that, if she wasn't more careful or smart, she might mistake for love. "It did."

From the pile of clothes on the floor, his earpiece crackled, and she knew he'd been called away.

CHAPTER SEVEN

The next day, Kelsey was still riding high on last night's adrenaline and rapture. She'd barely slept, the bedsheets too tantalizing on her skin. Her body craved more, her mind bursting with the memory of David over her. Inside her.

She always did her best work with this much positive energy pumping through her system. Over the years, she'd trained herself to harness it, aim it at her patients and research, and just *work*. Right then, she felt like she could cure cancer.

Even though she'd closed the clinic in observance of the Ice Rites that night, she needed to be there. In the cab on the way to the clinic, she ran her fingers over her lips that still tingled with David's taste. *After all this time*, he'd told her, *I want it to be just you and me.* She caught the reflection of her secret smile in the window glass. The cabbie saw it, too, and told her to have a great day as she exited on the curb.

"I already have," she replied, and tipped him way too much.

At street level, the clinic was labeled Ball Food Labs to protect its true nature from the Primaries. As she typed in her access code for the third-floor entrance, she was still smiling.

In the elevator, she mentally triaged what she had to do. She wanted to take a look at the reports from an animal bite treatment and then input what she'd glimpsed on David's chest last night. She needed to examine him again. Thoroughly. Preferably with him inside her.

Great stars, where had her professionalism gone?

She shivered and had to force down a deep breath to control the wave of desire derailing her with thoughts of shoving her hand down her jeans. She should change. Putting on her scrubs and coat was like flipping on a switch—personal to professional. Entering the clinic, she headed straight for the locker room.

Someone was in there. Moving around. Yet she'd given everyone, even the janitors, the day off. A surge of protective anger burst inside her. No one was messing with her clinic. She grabbed the fire extinguisher off the wall—the only available weapon she could think of—and flung open the door.

A female Ofarian soldier, dressed in black, rose calmly from where she knelt by the garbage can. Each piece of trash had been removed and now lay neatly organized on a sheet of plastic on the floor.

"Who the hell are you?" Kelsey demanded.

The woman shifted uncomfortably, then glanced to her right, to the line of lockers.

David stood at Emily Pritchart's locker, the door open, its contents lined up on the bench.

Kelsey dropped the fire extinguisher, the giant *clank* giving her an instant headache. "What the *fuck* do you think you're doing?"

David actually had the gall to not look guilty or regretful. Instead, he closed the green metal door with a muted click and came toward her with the same graceful poise he had in the hotel hall last night. Minus the lust.

"Gathering evidence," he said.

She started to quiver with fury. "This is *my* clinic—"

"This is an *Ofarian* clinic." His voice was infuriatingly soft.

"I told you about Wes's letter. You already talked to Emily. What more do you want?"

He crossed his arms over his chest, a defensive gesture if she'd ever seen one. "I suspected that wasn't the only contact between Wes and Emily, but I needed further proof."

"Holy shit, David. You broke into my clinic and are destroying Emily's privacy because of a hunch? Since when did you turn into the Board? Did you go through my patient files, too?"

Deep red seeped up his neck.

"Oh, God. No. You didn't."

She spun and raced into the main room, going for the central computer. She heard David following.

"Kelse. Wait."

The main computer was on, the screen bright. It showed a table of patient names.

She whirled on him, rage coloring her vision. "How could you?"

He showed her his palms. "It's not what you think. Let me explain."

"What's there to explain? You *are* the Board."

He jabbed a finger at the floor. "This situation means Griffin's life. It means the safety and future of our people. Do you understand that? A little sacrifice—a little *understanding*—please."

She recoiled. "Was last night your way of trying to butter me up so I'd let you in here? Let you snoop around?" She'd dismissed him as a manipulator too soon.

"If you really think that"—his voice quieted so much it fought with the whir from the air ducts—"there's nothing I can do or say to change your mind."

She glanced into the locker room, taking in the neat lines of trash on the floor, and Emily's dog-eared biographies and candy stash on the bench. The list of patient names on the computer screen glared at her.

"Confidentiality was a joke to the Board. And now you're making my clinic into a joke, too," she said. "But then again, that's what you're good at."

He went so still she thought he'd somehow stopped time. That had been wrong to say—far-fetched and cutting and spoken out of heat. But an apology might have been misconstrued as permission to go ahead with what he was doing, and she couldn't do that.

"You're right," he said, and she heard his pain. "That's exactly what I'm good at."

No man was worth this, this desecration of her dreams. She was too angry to argue anymore, and too furious to stand there and watch people who weren't her employees rifle through what she'd created. She turned and fled, reaching the street in record time.

In the not-so-distant past, she could have contacted her mom, and the head Ofarian doctor with deep, powerful contacts within the Board would have made a single phone call and all would have been well. The thought actually made Kelsey sick. Which situation was better? Which was worse?

Only when she raised her arm to hail a cab did she notice how it shook from fingertip to shoulder.

"Doc."

So they were back to that name, were they? Wasn't that indicative?

She didn't want to turn, but it was like her body had been trained, tuned to his presence and the sound of his voice. David stalked across the sidewalk toward her.

He's going to apologize, she thought, heart in her throat.

"The day I came here injured, you told me Emily was in charge of routinely following up with patients. I was checking the lists of names to make sure all the Ofarians on record actually existed, that she wasn't passing information under the pretense of false names. I never opened a single patient file, just verified the names were real people."

Kelsey gaped. "Why on earth would you think she'd do that?"

"Because of what she's already done." He reached into his soldier's vest and pulled out something pink. She blinked at it, hardly believing what he held contained any matter of consequence. Slowly, never removing his eyes from her, he unfolded the greasy, crumpled El Tamale Loco bag.

The pink paper was covered in doodles—figures and silly characters Kelsey had seen Emily draw countless times over the years. In between them, just barely distinguishable, ran a line of random letters. Unreadable, a mess.

David dragged a finger across the gobbledygook. "See this?" His voice was painfully lifeless. "It's a rail fence cipher. Know what it says?"

She couldn't swallow. "No."

"It says, 'Delivery successful.' A direct threat has been made against Griffin, Kelsey. We've been monitoring Emily, and when she came to the clinic today when we knew it was closed, we followed her. Caught her going through the trash looking for this, to change it or remove it or something. You said she gets tamales from this place every week. Chances are she's been communicating this way with Wes for a while."

Kelsey's mouth dropped open, but she found no words.

"We have her in custody. She said she doesn't agree with the lack of social structure. And that she objects to your experiments with Primary medicine and Secondary magic. She's not your friend."

By the time Kelsey's brain fumbled back into motion, David had gone back inside.

David didn't answer his phone all afternoon, but then, Kelsey hadn't expected him to. He'd made his point.

She sat with her parents, as was tradition, at the top of the rapidly filling amphitheater concealed in the cold forest two hours north of San Francisco. Winter wind blew off the Pacific and swirled through the tall trees. The Ofarian population, wrapped in bulky coats and scarves and mittens, took their seats facing the stage. The drone of formal greetings and water blessings passed from person to person, but there was very little enthusiasm behind the words or actions.

A heavy, somber cloak of uncertainty hovered above the crowd. The Rites—as opposed to the Star Gala—had always been solemn, but now the sharpness of volatility gave the whole thing an edge that had Kelsey's knee bouncing in unease.

The elder Pritcharts hadn't come.

Dissidents two rows back whispered that the Pritchart parents had taken Emily and had splintered off to be with Wes. Other detractors speculated they themselves might join the Pritcharts, and that if enough Ofarians left San Francisco, Gwen and Griffin would be without power. They said that Gwen had already backed away from her own world, and that Griffin didn't have a handle on things.

Kelsey felt sick, believing none of it, but unable to say anything. David hadn't released news of Emily's arrest, so it wasn't up to Kelsey to reveal.

Where was David anyway?

Craning her neck around, she spotted him, standing with his arms crossed in a green tent serving as security central. He made measured assessments of his soldiers, who winged out along the edges of the amphitheater. Never before had there been such an ominous presence of them during the Rites.

She was sitting just seven rows below David, so when his jaw clenched and his brow furrowed, she couldn't help but feel that maybe he'd sensed her eyes on him. And that he was deliberately avoiding her.

The Rites began with chimes, the symbolic call to worship. The sound of low, serious bells reverberated off the great trees shielding the amphitheater and then shot into the open, starry sky directly above. The congregation hushed.

Atop the center steps appeared three Ofarians robed in black. They descended to the stage in rhythmic motion and took their places behind three bronze urns filled with water. The first Ofarian, an elderly woman, swept the water into the air and heated it into a swirling, stationary mass of steam. The second, a middle-aged man, used his voice to lift the water from his urn and churn it in a midair cyclone. The final Ofarian, another older woman, sent her water surging into the air, only to freeze it with a crackle.

A children's chorus shuffled into a balcony on the amphitheater's left side. Griffin ascended to the stage and took his place in front of the ancient, enormous redwood tree around which the stage had been built. He *looked* like a leader.

The high, sweet voices of the children began to sing a song their ancestors had brought from the old world. It celebrated the beauty of the stars and the glory and goodness of the Ofarian people. They'd sung this song by rote for well over a century, and it had become nearly meaningless across the generations. But now the audience shifted uncomfortably under the words, as though hearing them for the first time and finding them as hypocritical as Kelsey did.

She understood why Griffin had kept this location for the Ice Rites this year. Too much upheaval at once might have backfired; he was letting his people use this place as an anchor. Everyone held memories of this forest and amphitheater. Every time Kelsey came here she flashed back to her first Rites at age six, remembering her awe at what the Fragment could do.

She remembered seeing David, too. As soon as he'd been old enough, his parents—also soldiers—had positioned him along the perimeter, teaching him how to observe.

Even Wes and Emily Pritchart had formed memories here. Kelsey had read Wes's disturbing, rambling letter. In it, he mentioned this place, the redwood in particular. How he'd hid inside the open, rotted part of the trunk—as most Ofarian kids learned to do at a certain age—and Emily had tattled on him.

Strange that even though the letter had been addressed to Emily, the whole thing had been twenty pages of nasty preaching and vindictive speech aimed at no one in particular. Except for that short paragraph when he specifically mentioned her, and berated her for the redwood tree incident.

Delivery successful.

She's been communicating this way with Wes for a while, David had said.

If the two Pritchart siblings had been crafty enough to pass each other messages through the trash, maybe that letter was more than a manifesto. Maybe it meant something even more horrible than an assassination warning.

More chimes resonated through the amphitheater and everyone rose to their feet, singing yet another hymn whose significance had shifted. At the top of the center steps, Gwen appeared in a long black robe, bearing the Fragment of Ofaria in her hands. All eyes turned to her. All eyes, except for Kelsey's.

Hers found David.

As Gwen began her slow procession down the steps, Kelsey nudged her way past her parents, ignoring their questions, and into the far aisle. She took the steps by twos to the top, and ran around the back of the amphitheater.

She shoved aside the flap to the green tent. David swiveled around, hand on his weapon, eyes fierce.

"Kelse—"

"No time," she whispered urgently. "I think the Pritcharts might have hid something in the redwood."

CHAPTER EIGHT

David much preferred Kelsey's anger over her panic. He'd never known her capable of fear, but now terror streaked across her face.

"Sam," David said to the other man in the security tent. "Take command."

"Yes, sir."

David grabbed Kelsey's arm and steered her out of the tent and into the cold, black forest. In the residual light glowing from the amphitheater, her face looked ghostly pale. She began to babble about the communications between Wes and Emily, and the cryptic mention of the tree and the Rites in the letter. David gripped her arms, feeling her shake under the thick of her coat.

"We thought of that, too," he said when she took a breath. "We already checked the tree. It was empty—no hiding kids, no foreign objects."

"Check it again." Her voice rose. "I just have a feeling."

And as she said it, David did, too. It burned on the back of his neck.

"Wait here." He spun, boots churning in the dead leaves, and sprinted around the amphitheater. The land sloped sharply downward, reminding him of the last time he'd chased after Wes

Pritchart's mess. Only the wide, black shapes of the great trees, creating holes in the night, told him where not to run.

The children's chorus crescendoed into a familiar tune, meaning Gwen had reached the stage and now faced the audience. She would be lifting the Fragment above the people's heads, praying in Ofarian. She would be setting the Fragment on the pedestal before she called down the starlight.

The feeling of dread built up inside David with every pounding step.

His toe struck a tree root. He went flying. No time to get his hands out. Not enough light to know what lay below. He hit the ground. Hard. A tree trunk abraded his cheek. The wound on his chest, mostly healed but not entirely, screamed with a new pain, and he knew he'd ripped something open.

Then small hands were on him, pulling him up and rolling him over. Patting him down.

"Jesus, Kelse," he panted. "I told you to wait up there!"

She blinked rapidly, as though just realizing she'd chased after him, and replied in a shaky voice, "You might need me."

"That's what I have soldiers for."

She didn't move. Their quick, hard breaths came out white, mingling in the cold air. She touched his head, her fingers coming away red. No time for being doctored. He shoved to his feet, ignoring the wave of unsteadiness passing through him.

They'd found the bottom of the embankment, where the great, serrated trunk of the redwood thrust out of the ground, and the back of the stage jutted up against it. David reached into his vest and pulled out a small flashlight. Flicking it on, the beam of light struck the bottom of the redwood, where time had eaten away a hole big enough to fit at least a couple of kids.

He fell to his knees, stuck his head into the hollow. He sensed Kelsey next to him, crouching low, peering up. "See? Nothing."

"There," she said, pointing.

He followed her finger with the flashlight. The far side of the trunk that abutted the amphitheater structure had been chipped away. He saw it now: a fresh line running perpendicular to the ground, small enough to have been missed during a cursory check. He crawled inside and pressed against the chipped seam. A sizable chunk of the trunk fell away.

Access underneath the stage.

Holy fucking shit.

Pressing his ear radio, he murmured, "Capshaw under the stage. Possible security compromise. Prep but stand down until my word. Over."

He and Kelsey exchanged a long look. He knew she was wondering why he didn't ignite the soldiers into action right now, get everyone away from this place as fast as possible. But that's exactly what Wes wanted. Even if there wasn't anything under there, Wes wanted mass panic. An example of Griffin's ineptitude. He wanted a frightening Ice Rites to go with the awful Star Gala last night.

In a flurry, David whipped off his bulky coat. "Stay here this time."

He slipped the flashlight between his teeth and crawled inside the tree. Moist, earthy, and woody scents assaulted his nose. He squeezed through the hole on his stomach and pushed through into the dark under the stage. Coming to a squat, he swiped spiderwebs from his face.

Scratching sounds came behind him. Of course Kelsey wouldn't have listened. Absolutely no time to argue about it now.

Removing the flashlight from his mouth, he speared it into the black. The stage was sixty or seventy feet wide—lots of ground to cover. Just ten feet above their heads, the Rites went on. Though he couldn't hear Gwen's words, he could tell by the songs being sung where they were in the ceremony. In a few minutes, she would use the Fragment to call the starlight and bless the Earth's ice.

And that's when he saw it. Kelsey did, too, her gloved hand clamping onto his arm.

A bomb.

A small silver box, wired to cylinders. Tiny, blinking lights on a panel.

Delivery successful.

If he were Wes or Emily, he'd have the thing timed to explode right as Gwen called the starlight. Maximum impact. Which meant he had about ten minutes to shut the thing off.

"Bomb under the stage," he murmured into his radio. "Hold your positions. Repeat, hold your positions."

"You need to get everyone out of here," Kelsey begged.

"No. *You* need to get out of here. Go, Kelse. *Now*." He shoved her.

All he thought about was the potential chaos. It took five minutes to clear the amphitheater—his people had trained for that. If he didn't take care of the bomb in four, he'd have them clear the area and deal with the aftermath and backlash.

He whipped out his phone, found the number he needed, and pressed "dial."

Two rings. "Who is this?" came the woman's suspicious voice.

"Adine? Adine Jones?"

Gwen had given David this number a month ago, but he'd never used it. Never imagined he'd have to. Adine Jones was a genius, according to Gwen—a technological master whose knowledge transcended this world . . . because she wasn't *of* this world. She was Secondary, but not Ofarian.

"My name is David Capshaw. I'm friends with Gwen Carroway—"

"I remember you, David." There were crunching sounds, like she was eating potato chips.

"Gwen's in trouble. What do you know about bombs?"

She sputtered and dropped the droll attitude. "If it's got wires and circuits, I know it. Lay it on me."

"Here's what I've got." David passed the flashlight all around the bomb, describing corners and connections, wires and etched letters, the explosives themselves.

Adine whistled in a high arc. "That's a short-range explosive. Small blast but capable of eviscerating anything or anyone within ten to twenty feet."

And his beautiful, stubborn Kelsey still hovered right next to him.

David lifted his eyes to the stage directly above. To where Griffin Aames and Gwen Carroway stood together. With the Fragment.

Take out the leaders. Sacrifice the relic. Show the rest of the people how stupid and blind the new regime is for letting such a threat get this close. Assume control and build up the fractured society in your own way. Wes Pritchart's perfect plan.

"Can I move it?" he asked Adine.

"No! Just do what I tell you."

"*Fuck.*" David shook his head at the dirt, then said into his radio, "Prepare to get everyone off the stage on my word."

"This'll take a bit of finesse," Adine said. He could hear her fingers flying across a keyboard. "You have an extra set of hands available?"

David didn't want to, but he looked to Kelsey. He briefly closed his eyes. "Yes."

"What do you need?" Kelsey whispered, and at that moment he loved her so much he nearly cried.

Her panic was gone. Her lips were pressed together in determination. *This* was the Kelsey he knew. The one who saw the problem, turned it over and over in her mind, and charged toward the solution.

"Go on," he said into the phone, but firmly held Kelsey with his eyes. "Tell us what to do."

Kelsey settled back on her heels and gave him a short nod of confidence. Adine started talking, fast enough he had to tell her to slow down.

"You have wire cutters?" Adine asked.

David patted his vest. "I have a knife."

"That'll do. Here's where you make the first snip . . ."

They worked diligently, quietly. Kelsey held or turned or cut whatever object Adine told her to, all without breaking a sweat. The unflappable doctor, intensely working on an emergency patient.

Above, the song that pleaded for the stars' blessing began in earnest. They were inside that five-minute mark, if that. All the lights on the circuit board were still lit up. All the Ofarians still sat in their seats.

"Okay," Adine said, "when you dislodge the canister top from the fuse, you need to completely unfasten the smaller black wire within three seconds. Unfasten. Don't bend it. Don't cut it. You got that?"

David wiped perspiration from his forehead using his shoulder. "I got it."

Kelsey wrapped her hands around the canister top while David pressed his fingers to the end of the indicated wire.

The lights on the circuit board started to blink. Faster and faster.

In the amphitheater, the song rose and rose. Gwen's footsteps moved to center stage, and David knew she was taking her position behind the Fragment.

"Ready?" Kelsey whispered.

When he nodded, she unsnapped the canister top. Twisted. The blinking lights went nuts, bouncing all over the place. David's fingers shook.

One.

Two.

The wire dislodged from the circuit board, the little metal tooth falling away, taking his heart and his breath with it.

The lights died. The bomb now nothing but a pile of metal and liquid in the dirt.

Overhead, Gwen's voice rang out in Ofarian. Through the tight seams of the stage floorboards streamed thin beams of stunning blue and violet light. The stars had answered Gwen's prayers, and cast their power and light into the Fragment. The rock then refracted it toward the urns, the heavens descending to touch their element in all its forms. The crowd stirred with the spectacle.

"Bomb disabled," he breathed heavily into the radio. "Stand down. Await orders."

David looked to Kelsey. Now her tears came, making her eyes shimmer like ocean shallows. She smiled and started to laugh. He reached out and yanked her to him with all the strength he had. He fell onto his back, pulling her with him down to the dirt, not caring whether he bled again under his shirt.

He only knew the greediness of his mouth on hers, the strain of their breath as they tried to catch it, and the wonderful way her legs parted over his hips. Only when his lungs cried out did he push her away, his hand curling over her hair, her mouth pressed innocently to the hot, damp skin of his neck.

He could've stayed like that forever, just the two of them drowning in adrenaline and euphoria . . . but he heard Gwen's muffled voice starting a new chant to bless the Earth's ice. The Rites would be over soon.

He gently set Kelsey aside and sat up, touching a dirty finger to her shining face. "Come on."

Leaving the bomb, they crawled out into a forest that was bursting with light emanating from the Fragment on stage. High above, the bared branches of the trees reached into that light, as though they, too, wanted to be blessed.

A tingle on his senses brought his head around, his eyes peering into the pitch of the forest. He'd been chasing Wes long enough to know his signature, that he was near. The asshole wouldn't have missed this show for the world.

"Stay here," he told Kelsey. "I'll send someone to get you and the bomb. And for stars' sake, listen to me this time."

"Where are you going?"

"To get Pritchart." He slid the flashlight into his vest pocket but kept the knife at hand.

Now worry darkened Kelsey's eyes. Not when faced with a messy, explosive death herself, but when he was about to charge after the enemy. He didn't know whether to roll his eyes or kiss her.

He stepped close enough she had to lean back to look up at him. "You want to know what I really wanted to ask after I won that stupid game with your cat?"

She nodded. A piece of copper hair blew across her face, attaching itself to her lip, and he tugged it down.

"I was going to ask you why you didn't want to marry me," he said. "And then whatever you said was the reason, I was going to fix it. Fight for you. Make you mine. Because I'm in love with you."

Then he stepped back, basking in her surprise, delighting in the way his heart felt lighter in her presence now. Twelve years of hiding how he felt . . . gone. Like that first kiss, he should have done it much, much sooner.

With a smile of his own, one that showed her everything he felt, he turned and sprinted into the forest.

"Teams C, F, and M with me," he huffed into the radio. "Circle around the western forest."

Tonight, he would finally bring in his prey.

CHAPTER NINE

Three days later, David finally got some sleep. Noon on a Tuesday and he was stretched out on the couch, sun on his face, one arm thrown above his head. A new puzzle book lay split over his belly.

Griffin had given him the day off. Which was completely expected since David had chased Wes Pritchart through the forest for nearly thirteen hours before finally catching him as he tried to steal a car. After dragging Wes out of the woods, David had had to escort the criminal to the jail located in the old Plant in bumfuck Nevada. He'd spent another whole day making statements and giving testimony.

The capture had been huge news, quieting the dissidents—for now; he wasn't sure how long that would last—and rallying Griffin and Gwen's supporters.

Griffin had decided to keep the bomb a secret. No one needed to know, he'd said, how close Wes had come to succeeding. The soldiers knew, of course, but they were loyal. David was fine with Griffin's decision. He didn't need or want recognition. That wasn't why he'd done what he had. Protect Griffin and Gwen and the Fragment— that's all he'd been focused on. That's all he'd ever wanted.

Well, not all.

He hadn't seen or spoken to Kelsey since the Ice Rites. As soon as he got back to San Francisco he'd asked about her, but she'd been immersed in her lab. Still was, as far as he knew. There'd been trouble at her clinic, and he'd been reluctant to disturb her in the middle of it.

He'd wait for her. He'd been waiting for twelve years; what was a few days more?

A gentle knock sounded on his door, so quiet he was sure he'd imagined it. But no, there it came again. He sat up, the puzzle book sliding to the hardwood floor. The prickle of an Ofarian signature out in the hall buzzed in the back of his brain.

He opened the door and could not suppress his wide smile.

Kelsey looked like sunlight after a month spent underground. She wore those jeans again—the ones with the holes, as though she'd known they drove him crazy—and a fitted, white button-down shirt with the sleeves rolled up. She carried her winter coat in the crook of her arm, and he wondered how long she'd been standing out here before she'd knocked. Her hair was down, and he hoped it was because of what he'd told her in the hotel.

She gave him a quick once-over, skimming up his bare feet, plaid flannel pants and white undershirt. Her eyes landed on his face with a gasp that was very un-doctorlike. "Look at you. Why didn't you come to the clinic?"

He'd avoided the mirror since he got back. The black eye was probably still pretty purple, but the throbbing along his cheek where Wes had landed a fist or two had lessened.

He waved her off. "It was just a couple of punches. I'll live." The way she frowned at him was turning far too impersonal, so he steered her attention elsewhere. "How'd you know which apartment was mine? Not that I'm complaining."

At first she tried to look away, to hide her blush, but then she seemed to change her mind and looked him right in the eye. "I've always known where you live."

Today was just getting better and better.

He opened the door wide and stepped back. "Then maybe it's time you came in."

She wandered inside, and he tried not to stare at her ass in those jeans, but who was he kidding? He let her look around his small, bright apartment, just as he'd assessed hers days earlier.

"Sorry to drop in on you like this. I should've called."

He closed the door, excitement steadily pumping through his body. He gave her a lazy grin. "No. You should always come over unannounced. Look how I dress up for you in preparation."

Her bow lips quirked, but there was sadness and trouble behind her sky blue eyes. He could only guess it was because of the clinic. "I heard," he said seriously, "about what Emily had done to your records."

She ran a hand through her hair and he noticed her fingers quivering. "Yeah. She'd been altering results. Changing patient reports, tainting findings, and messing with samples. I can't re-create the tests. I'll have to start all over."

"I'm sorry."

"That's not why I came."

He raised an eyebrow. "Oh?"

She took a deep breath. "I came to tell you a story."

"A story?" The sun burned through the corner bay window, hotter than a day at the beach. He gestured to the big, comfy chair in shadow. "Have a seat then."

She lowered herself to the cushion and put her purse on the floor. "You like puzzles," she said with a bit of wonder, pointing to his book. "Emily's cipher."

He shrugged and sat on the couch opposite her, hands clasped between his thighs. "Just a hobby. The cipher they were using is one of the simpler ones." He didn't want to talk about that, now that she was here. "So, what's this story about?"

She matched his stare. Amazing how twelve years of protecting his feelings had always led to such agonizingly awkward and terrifying encounters with her. Now that she knew how he felt, it was so much easier to be around her. How did that work, exactly? Shouldn't it have been the opposite?

"It's about you and me," she started, "and why we were matched. Didn't you ever wonder about that?"

He sat up, resting his elbows on his knees. "All the time."

"It was me. I did it."

She was acting all bashful, like he'd actually be mad about that. He hid his smile, but it was trying its best to poke out.

"What do you mean?" he asked.

She licked her lips. He wanted to lick them, too.

"At last year's Star Gala, I got pretty drunk. Well, drunk for me. I was excited to be almost done with my residency and I just wanted to let loose. My mom, she must've had a bottle of champagne all by herself, and she found me and asked me about finally being matched in marriage. She'd been matched right after school, too, you see."

He leaned forward. "So what'd you tell her?"

"That I wanted you. No one else. It had always been you."

Wes's punches had never struck him this hard. They'd never been this thrilling either.

"I didn't tell her because of the alcohol—well, maybe that helped—but because it was the truth and I knew I wouldn't get you anyway. If I could never tell *you*, I could tell my mom, right? Then the next week she came to me and said that the Board had approved the match. You remember what kind of pull she used to have with the Board?" He nodded. "Well, it turned out she went to them and asked for the two of us to be matched as a favor to her, and for the daughter who would take her place as the head Ofarian doctor. They agreed."

David could only stare. "No one ever got to pick their mates."

She shook her head, her brow furrowing. "And I felt horrible about that. Why should I have gotten the person I wanted when so many others had to marry who the Board told them to? It didn't seem fair. I was sick with guilt."

"That was such a weird time," he said, his faraway gaze drifting out the windows to the tall buildings just outside.

"But the worst part was," she went on, "I'd wanted you for so long and I was ecstatic at finally being able to be with you. And then at our matching ceremony you looked like a ghost who'd been dipped in bleach. Like you were caught in a mass of gears and would never be able to get out. *I'd* done that to you, I realized. I started to panic, worrying that if you'd ever found out I was the one who'd asked for us to be matched, who'd essentially tricked you into marriage, you'd hate me."

David fell to his knees in front of her before she could say another word. His hands slid up her thighs, his fingers digging into the crease of her hips. "You want to know why I looked like that that night? Because I felt guilty, too, that I'd been given the woman I wanted. And because I was so happy, and you looked so trapped. I assumed you'd been roped into marrying someone below your class, and that you were upset about it."

"But that wasn't true at all!"

His cheeks hurt he smiled so big. "See? We both suck because we made bad assumptions. We both suck at showing how we feel."

She exhaled. "I'm done with sucking."

He laughed, leaned forward, and brushed his stubbly cheek with her smooth one. "God, I hope not."

To his delight, she shivered but didn't pull away. Instead her arms slid around his waist. He almost shouted in victory as she tugged him tighter into the cradle of her thighs.

"You want to know the day I fell for you?" she said against his neck.

"You know the actual day?"

"I know the actual moment." She drew a long, slow breath. The words trickled across her skin. " 'There is no surprise more magical than the surprise of being loved.' "

He took her shoulders and pushed her back to search her face. "Are you serious?"

She was smiling now, that smile he remembered from that day in class. She nodded and reached for her purse. She pulled out the most incredible thing he'd ever seen: one of those slips of paper from Creative Writing. Laminated.

"And it's the truth, isn't it," she murmured, her focus dropping to his mouth and awakening a pounding in his cock.

"Amen to that," he growled, and consumed her mouth with a hard, wet, driving kiss. Her tongue tasted even better than it had that night in the hotel. The emotion that fueled him burned even stronger than the moment right after they'd defused the bomb.

Because she loved him.

That knowledge made his dick hard as a spike, and he ground into her. When she wrapped her ankles around the backs of his thighs, pressed herself even harder against him, the sound that came up from his throat didn't even sound human.

At last he pulled away, stunned to realize he'd lain himself across her, his weight pressing her into the cushion, her penny-colored hair spraying out with static across the back of his favorite chair.

He struggled to breathe. "We're so pathetic. Why didn't you say anything?"

"The same reason you didn't."

He pushed her hair away from her face. "How could two smart people be so dumb and insecure?"

"It's one of the world's greatest mysteries." Her hands slipped beneath the waist of his pants, grabbing his ass, and he groaned again. "It should have been you to speak first."

"Me?" he said drowsily, because her hand had traveled to his front and now stroked him over his underwear.

"You're the motormouth. You gave me that string to hold. You kissed me first. You—"

"Kelsey, shut up," he murmured, his eyes closed against the slide of her hand. "Unless you want to tell me to come."

She froze. His eyes opened. They smiled at the same time. And suddenly they were teenagers, the twelve years between them vanishing. They were messy and fumbling and giggling, grappling awkwardly at each other's clothing, shivering in anticipation. He couldn't steady his fingers to undo her buttons, so he just ripped off her shirt. He'd been dying to see what she looked like in one of his anyway.

He pulled off her jeans, paused only half a second to appreciate the gold lace of her underwear, and then those were gone, too. The sun shifted, coming through the window to hit her body perfectly, all spread out before him.

As he draped himself over her, kissed her, then entered her body in one smooth thrust, she said, "I want to start over. With us. Only this time I know how it's going to end."

"How?" he asked, pulling out slowly, making her gasp.

"With you marrying me."

He kissed her again, pushing back into her heat. "I thought you'd never ask."